Dear Reader,

I'm excited to see two of my favorite books together! I recently completed *Rescue at Cardwell Ranch,* bringing together McKenzie Sheldon and Cardwell cousin Hayes.

But it had been a while since I'd read *Wanted Woman.* I couldn't help but open the book and begin to read. I'd forgotten how much I loved Maggie Randolph and Jesse Tanner.

After completing a book, there are always other characters waiting, demanding their stories be told. So I have to move on. But how fun it is to go back and spend time with characters I love. I hope you enjoy both books about strong women and the men who deserve them.

B.J.

ABOUT THE AUTHOR

New York Times bestselling author B.J. Daniels wrote her first book after a career as an award-winning newspaper journalist and author of thirty-seven published short stories. That first book, *Odd Man Out,* received a four-and-a-half-star review from *RT Book Reviews* and went on to be nominated for Best Intrigue that year. Since then, she has won numerous awards, including a career achievement award for romantic suspense and many nominations and awards for best book.

Daniels lives in Montana with her husband, Parker, and two springer spaniels, Spot and Jem. When she isn't writing, she snowboards, camps, boats and plays tennis. Daniels is a member of Mystery Writers of America, Sisters in Crime, International Thriller Writers, Kiss of Death and Romance Writers of America.

To contact her, write to B.J. Daniels, P.O. Box 1173, Malta, MT 59538, or email her at bjdaniels@mtintouch.net. Check out her website, www.bjdaniels.com.

Books by B.J. Daniels

HARLEQUIN INTRIGUE

RESCUE AT CARDWELL RANCH
& WANTED WOMAN

New York Times Bestselling Author

B.J. DANIELS

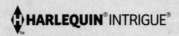

HARLEQUIN® INTRIGUE®

ISBN-13: 978-0-373-83799-1

RESCUE AT CARDWELL RANCH & WANTED WOMAN

Copyright © 2014 by Harlequin Books S.A.

The publisher acknowledges the copyright holder of the individual works as follows:

RESCUE AT CARDWELL RANCH
Copyright © 2014 by Barbara Heinlein

WANTED WOMAN
Copyright © 2004 by Barbara Heinlein

Recycling programs
for this product may
not exist in your area.

Printed in U.S.A.

HARLEQUIN®
www.Harlequin.com

CONTENTS

This one is for David Rummel, who makes me laugh with his stories and his wonderful joy for life. You definitely make our lives more fun.

RESCUE
AT CARDWELL
RANCH

CHAPTER ONE

FROM THE DARKNESS, he heard the sound of high heels tapping quickly along the pavement, heading in his direction, and smiled. This could be the one.

If not, he would have to give it up for the night, something he couldn't bear doing. For days his need had been growing. He'd come here tonight because he couldn't put it off any longer—no matter how dangerous it was to hunt this close to home.

Since it had gotten dark, he'd been looking. He hated to think of the women he'd let get away, women in their tight skirts and low-cut blouses, women who'd just been asking for it.

But waiting for the right woman, he'd learned, was the smart thing to do. It took patience. Tonight, though, he found himself running short of it. He'd picked his favorite spot, the favorite spot of men like himself: a grocery-store parking lot at night. Once he'd parked next to her car—he knew it was a woman's car because she'd left her sunglasses on the dash and there was one of those cute air fresheners hanging from the mirror—he'd broken the bright light she'd parked under.

Now the area was cast in dark shadow—just the way he loved it. He doubted she would notice the lack of light—or him with his head down, pretending to be packing his groceries into the trunk of his large, expensive vehicle. Women were less afraid of a man who appeared to have money, he'd discovered.

At the sound of her approaching footfalls, he found it hard not to sneak a peek at her. *Patience.* This would be the one, he told himself. He already felt as if he knew her and could easily guess her story. She would have worked late, which was why she was still dressed as she had been this morning, in high heels. She wasn't pushing a cart so she wasn't shopping for her large family.

Instead, he guessed she was single and lived alone, probably in a nice condo since she drove a newer, pricier car—the kind independent, successful single women drove. By the sound of her footfalls, she carried only one small bag of groceries. He could already imagine his hands around her throat.

The footfalls grew closer.

He'd learned a long time ago not to act on impulse. Snatch the first one he saw and bad things happened. He had a scar to prove it. That run-in had almost cost him dearly. Not that she'd gotten away. He'd made sure of that. But she'd wounded him in more ways than one. It was why he'd come up with a set of rigorous guidelines he now followed to the letter. It was the reason, he told himself, that he'd never been caught.

He closed his eyes for a moment, imagining the look in her eyes when she realized she was about to die. This woman *had* to be the right one because his need had grown to the point of urgency. He went over his guidelines, the memory of his only mistake still haunting him.

He wouldn't let himself be swayed by an alluring whiff of perfume. Nor would he risk a woman carrying anything that could be used as a weapon at a distance like an umbrella.

Then there was her hair and attire. It would surprise most women to know that what made her his target was her hairstyle. There was a reason women with short hair were not common prey of men like him. Give him a woman with a ponytail—a recent trend that filled him with joy—or a braid or even a bun—anything he could bury his fingers in and hold on for dear life.

Clothing was equally as important. She had to be wearing an outfit that would come off easily and quickly because he often didn't have a lot of time. Of course, he always carried a pair of sharp scissors, but a woman in a blouse and a skirt made his life so much easier, even with a blade handy.

Now as the sound of the high heels grew closer, he readied himself with growing anticipation. He was betting this one was wearing a nice short skirt and a button-up blouse. Tonight, he could even handle a matching jacket with the skirt. No blue jeans, though. They were such a pain to get off.

Her cell phone rang. She stopped walking. He groaned since if she'd been just a little closer, she would have already been in his trunk, her mouth duct taped as well as her wrists and ankles.

He cursed her cell phone even though it often made things easier for him. Women who were distracted—either digging in their purses for their keys or talking on their cell phones or unloading their groceries—were oblivious to the fact that he was already breathing down their necks.

He silently urged her phone call to end. Just a few more steps and he would grab her by the hair, overpower her and have her in the trunk of his car before she even knew what was happening. Once he got her to the place he had picked out down by the river...well, that was when the real fun would begin.

His next victim was still on the phone. She sounded upset, so upset that she'd stopped walking to take the call. She would be thinking about the call—not him right next to her car.

The call ended. She began to walk again, right toward him. He doubted she'd even noticed him bent over his car trunk, pretending to be taking care of his groceries.

He heard her vehicle beep as she unlocked it. Any moment she would walk within a few feet of him on his right. He would have only an instant to make his decision. An instant to see what she had in her hands, what she was wearing, how long her hair was. Even with his meticulous planning, there was always the chance that this could be the one woman who would surprise him. The one who would fight back. The one who would get away and ruin his perfect record.

His heart began to pound with excitement. He loved this part. None had ever gotten away—even the one who'd scarred him. He was too smart for them. They were like sheep coming down a chute to slaughter, he thought, as he looked up and saw her start past him.

CHAPTER TWO

MCKENZIE SHELDON CAME out of the grocery store thinking about work. Not work, exactly, but one of the men at her office.

She was going to have to do something about Gus Thompson. The warnings she'd given him had fallen on deaf ears. The man had reached the point where he was daring her to fire him.

Shifting the single bag of groceries to her other arm, she began to dig for her keys when her cell phone rang. She stopped and pulled out her phone, saw it was her receptionist and said, "What's up, Cynthia?"

"You told me to call you if I was having any more problems."

McKenzie let out an angry breath. "Let me guess. *Gus.* What has he done now?" she asked with a disgusted sigh.

"I'm sorry, Ms. Sheldon, but he won't leave me alone. If I work late, *he* works late. He always insists on walking me to my car. I've told him that I'm not interested, but it seems to make him even more determined. I make excuses to avoid him, but—"

"I know. Trust me. It isn't anything you're doing."

"He scares me," she said, her voice breaking. "Tonight I looked out and he was waiting by my car. I'm afraid to try to go home."

She started to tell Cynthia that she didn't think Gus was dangerous, but what did she know? "Is he still out there?"

"I don't know." Her receptionist sounded close to tears.

"Call the police. Or if you want to wait, I can swing by—"

"I don't want you to have to do that. I'll call the police. I wanted to talk to you first. I didn't want to make any trouble."

"Don't worry about that. Gus is the one making the trouble. I promise you I'll take care of this tomorrow." She heard her receptionist make a scared sound. "Don't worry. I won't mention your name." She thought of the night she'd looked out her window at her condo. Gus had been sitting in his car across the street. He'd seen her and sped off, but she'd wondered how many other nights he'd been out there watching her house. "I should have fired him a long time ago."

"But he's your best salesman."

McKenzie let out a humorless laugh. "Hard to believe, isn't it?"

"Still, I wouldn't want to be blamed for him losing his job."

"You won't. Trust me. I have my own issues with him." She snapped the phone shut, angry with herself for letting things go on this long.

She had talked to Gus after that incident outside her house. He'd shrugged it off, made an excuse and she hadn't seen him again near her place. But that didn't mean he hadn't been more careful the next time. There was just no reining Gus in, she thought as she found her keys and started toward her car.

She wasn't looking forward to tomorrow. Gus wouldn't take being fired well. There would be a scene. She really hated scenes. But this was her responsibility as the owner of the agency. Maybe she should call him tonight and hire security until she could get Gus Thompson's desk cleaned out and the locks changed on the doors at the agency.

With a sigh, she hit the door lock on her key fob. The door on her SUV beeped. Out of the corner of her eye, she barely noticed the man parked next to her, loading his groceries. His back to her, he bent over the bags of groceries he'd put in his trunk as she walked past him.

She was thinking about Gus Thompson when the man grabbed her ponytail and jerked her off her feet. Shocked, she didn't make a sound. She didn't even drop her groceries as his arm clamped around her throat. Her only thought was: *this isn't happening.*

HAYES CARDWELL FELT his stomach growl as he walked down the grocery-store aisle. The place was empty at this hour of the night with just one clerk at the front, who'd barely noticed him when he walked in. The grocery was out of the way and it was late enough that most people had done their shopping, cooking and eating by now.

His plane had been delayed in Denver, putting him down in the Gallatin Valley much later than he'd hoped—and without any food for hours. He still had the drive to Big Sky tonight, one he wasn't looking forward to since he didn't know the highway.

Being from Texas, he wasn't used to mountains— let alone mountain roads. He was debating calling his brother Tag and telling him he would just get a motel tonight down here in the valley and drive up tomorrow in the daylight.

He snagged a bottle of wine to take to his cousin Dana Savage tomorrow and debated what he could grab to eat. The thought of going to a restaurant at this hour—and eating alone—had no appeal.

In the back of the store, he found a deli with premade items, picked himself up a sandwich and headed for the checkout. His Western boot soles echoed through the empty store. He couldn't imagine a grocery being this empty any hour of the day where he lived in Houston.

The checker was an elderly woman who looked as tired as he felt. He gave her a smile and two twenties. Her return smile was weak as she handed him his change.

"Have a nice night," she said in a monotone.

"Is there a motel close around here?"

She pointed down the highway to the south. "There's several." She named off some familiar chains.

He smiled, thanked her and started for the door.

McKENZIE HAD TAKEN a self-defense class years ago. Living in Montana, she'd thought she would never need the training. A friend had talked her into it. The highlight of the course was that they'd always gone out afterward for hot-fudge sundaes.

That's all she remembered in the split second the man grabbed her.

He tightened his viselike grip on her, lifting her off her feet as he dragged her backward toward the trunk of his car. The man had one hand buried in her hair, his arm clamped around her throat. He was so much taller, she dangled like a rag doll from the hold he had on her.

She felt one shoe drop to the pavement as she tried to make sense of what was happening.

Her mind seemed to have gone numb with her thoughts ricocheting back and forth from sheer panic to disbelief. Everything was happening too fast. She opened her mouth and tried to scream, but little sound came out with his arm pressed against her throat. Who would hear, anyway? There was *no* one.

Realization hit her like a lightning bolt. The parking lot was empty with only one other car at the opposite end of the lot. With such an empty lot, the man who'd grabbed her had parked right next to her. Also the light she'd parked under was now out. Why hadn't she noticed? Because she'd been thinking about Gus Thompson.

She saw out of the corner of her eye that the man had moved his few bags of groceries to one side of the trunk, making room for her. The realization that he'd been planning this sent a rush of adrenaline through her.

If there was one thing she remembered from the defense class it was: *never let anyone take you to a second location.*

McKenzie drove an elbow into the man's side. She heard the air rush out of him. He bent forward, letting her feet touch the ground. She teetered on her one high heel for a moment then dropped to her bare foot to kick back and drive her shoe heel into his instep.

He let out a curse and, his hand still buried in her long hair, slammed her head into the side of his car. The blow nearly knocked her out. Tiny lights danced before her eyes. If she'd had any doubt before, she now knew that she was fighting for her life.

She swung the bag of groceries, glad she'd decided

to cook from scratch rather than buy something quick. Sweet-and-sour chicken, her favorite from her mother's recipe, called for a large can of pineapple. It struck him in the side of the head. She heard the impact and the man's cry of pain and surprise. His arm around her neck loosened just enough that she could turn partway around.

McKenzie swung again, but this time, he let go of her hair long enough to block the blow with his arm. She went for his fingers, blindly grabbing two and bending them back as hard as she could.

The man let out a howl behind her, both of them stumbling forward. As she fell against the side of his car, she tried to turn and go for his groin. She still hadn't seen his face. Maybe if she saw his face, he would take off. Or would he feel he had to kill her?

But as she turned all she saw was the top of his baseball cap before he punched her. His fist connected with her temple. She felt herself sway then the grocery-store parking lot was coming up fast. She heard the twenty-ounce pineapple can hit and roll an instant before she joined it on the pavement.

From the moment he'd grabbed her, it had all happened in only a matter of seconds.

HAYES STEPPED OUT into the cool night air and took a deep breath of Montana. The night was dark and yet he could still see the outline of the mountains that surrounded the valley.

Maybe he would drive on up the canyon tonight, after all, he thought. It was such a beautiful June night and he didn't feel as tired as he had earlier. He'd eat the sandwich on his way and—

As he started toward his rented SUV parked by itself

in the large lot, he saw a man toss what looked like a bright-colored shoe into his trunk before struggling to pick up a woman from the pavement between a large, dark car and a lighter-colored SUV. Both were parked some distance away from his vehicle in an unlit part of the lot.

Had the woman fallen? Was she hurt?

As the man lifted the woman, Hayes realized that the man was about to put her into the *trunk* of the car.

What the hell?

"Hey!" he yelled.

The man turned in surprise. Hayes only got a fleeting impression of the man since he was wearing a baseball cap pulled low and his face was in shadow in the dark part of the lot.

"Hey!" Hayes yelled again as he dropped his groceries. The wine hit the pavement and exploded, but Hayes paid no attention as he raced toward the man.

The man seemed to panic, stumbling over a bag of groceries on the ground under him. He fell to one knee and dropped the woman again to the pavement. Struggling to his feet, he left the woman where she was and rushed around to the driver's side of the car.

As Hayes sprinted toward the injured woman, the man leaped behind the wheel, started the car and sped off.

Hayes tried to get a license plate but it was too dark. He rushed to the woman on the ground. She hadn't moved. As he dropped to his knees next to her, the car roared out of the grocery parking lot and disappeared down the highway. He'd only gotten an impression of the make of the vehicle and even less of a description of the man.

As dark as it was, though, he could see that the woman was bleeding from a cut on the side of her face. He felt for a pulse, then dug out his cell phone and called for the police and an ambulance.

Waiting for 911 to answer, he noticed that the woman was missing one of her bright red high-heeled shoes. The operator answered and he quickly gave her the information. As he disconnected he looked down to see that the woman's eyes had opened. A sea of blue-green peered up at him. He felt a small chill ripple through him before he found his voice. "You're going to be all right. You're safe now."

The eyes blinked then closed.

CHAPTER THREE

MCKENZIE'S HEAD ACHED. She gingerly touched the bandage and closed her eyes. "I'm sorry I can't provide you with a description of the man. I never saw his face." She'd tried to remember, but everything felt fuzzy and out of focus. She'd never felt so shaken or so unsure.

"Is the light bothering you?" the policewoman asked.

She opened her eyes as the woman rose to adjust the blinds on the hospital-room window. The room darkened, but it did nothing to alleviate the pain in her head. "It all happened so fast." Her voice broke as she remembered the gaping open trunk and the man's arm at her throat as she was lifted off her feet.

"You said the man was big."

She nodded, remembering how her feet had dangled above the ground. She was five feet six so he must have been over six feet. "He was…strong, too, muscular." She shuddered at the memory.

"You said he was wearing a baseball cap. Do you remember what might have been printed on it?"

"It was too dark." She saw again in her memory the pitch-black parking lot. "He must have broken the light because I would have remembered parking in such a dark part of the lot."

"Did he say anything?"

McKenzie shook her head.

"What about cologne?"

"I didn't smell anything." Except her own terror.

"The car, you said it was large and dark. Have you remembered anything else about it?"

"No." She hadn't been paying any attention to the car or the man and now wondered how she could have been so foolish.

The policewoman studied her for a moment. "We received a call last night from your receptionist about a man named Gus Thompson."

McKenzie felt her heart begin to pound. "Gus works for me. You aren't suggesting—"

"Is it possible the man who grabbed you was Gus Thompson?"

McKenzie couldn't speak for a moment. Gus was big. He also had to know, after numerous warnings, that she was ready to fire him. Or at least, he should have known. Could it have been him? Was it possible he hated her enough to want to hurt her? "I don't know."

"We found a car registered to him, a large, dark-colored Cadillac. Did you know he had this car?"

"No. But his mother recently died. I think he mentioned she'd left him a car."

"He never drove it to work?"

"No, not that I know of." Again, she hadn't been paying attention. She knew little about Gus Thompson because she'd chosen not to know any more than she had to. "I saw him parked outside my house one night. I spoke to him about it and I never saw him again, but I can't be sure he didn't follow me sometimes." She thought of one instance when she'd noticed him driving a few cars behind her. But Bozeman was small enough that it hadn't seemed all that odd at the time.

The policewoman raised a brow. "You never reported this?"

McKenzie tried to explain it to herself and failed. "I guess I thought he was annoying but harmless."

"Did you ever date him?"

"Good heavens, no."

"But Gus Thompson probably knows your habits, where you go after work, where you shop?"

She nodded numbly. Gus could have followed her many times and she wouldn't even have noticed. She'd been so caught up in making her business a success....

The policewoman closed her notebook. "We'll have a chat with Mr. Thompson and see where he was last night at the time of your attack."

"He wasn't at the office last night when you sent a patrolman over there?" she asked.

The policewoman shook her head. "He'd already left. Your receptionist was unsure when."

McKenzie felt a shiver, her mind racing. Could it have been Gus who'd attacked her? She swallowed, her throat raw and bruised from last night. Gus was big and strong and she knew he resented her. To think she'd almost reassured Cynthia that Gus wasn't dangerous. He could be more dangerous than she would have imagined.

"I used to work with his mother when she owned the agency," she said. "I inherited Gus. He is my best salesman, but I know he felt his mother should have left him the business and not sold it to me."

The policewoman nodded. "This could have been building for some time. We'll see what he has to say."

She had a thought. "I hit the man last night several times, but I'm not sure I did enough damage that it would even show." She described the ways she'd hit him.

"Don't worry. We'll check it out. In the meantime, you'll be safe here."

As the policewoman started to leave the room, Mc-Kenzie said, "The man who saved me last night…" She had a sudden flash. *You're safe now.* She blinked. "I'd like to get his name so I can thank him."

"He asked that his name be kept out of it."

She blinked. "Why?"

"There actually are people who don't want the notoriety. I can contact him if you like and see if he might have changed his mind. What I can tell you is that he just happened to fly in last night and stop at that grocery store on his way to see family. Fortunately for you."

"Yes. Fortunate." She had another flash of memory. Warm brown eyes filled with concern. *You're safe now.*

"The doctor said they're releasing you this afternoon. We're going to be talking to Mr. Thompson as soon as we can find him. Maybe going to the office isn't the best idea."

"I *have* to go into work. I was planning to fire Gus Thompson today. Even if he wasn't the man in the parking lot last night, I can't have him working for me any longer."

"Why don't you let us handle Mr. Thompson. We have your cell phone number. I'll call you when he and his personal items are out of your business. In the meantime, I would suggest getting new locks for your office and a restraining order for both yourself and your business."

She must have looked worried because the officer added, "You might want to stay with friends or relatives for a while."

"I have a client I need to see tomorrow south of here. I could go down there tonight and stay in a motel."

"I think that is a good idea," the policewoman said.

"LOOK WHAT THE cat dragged in," Tag Cardwell said as Hayes walked into the kitchen on the Cardwell Ranch. "We were getting ready to send the hounds out to track you down."

"Hey, cuz," Dana said as she got up from the table to give him a hug and offer him coffee. It was his first time meeting his cousin. She was pretty and dark like the rest of the Cardwells. As Tag had predicted, he liked her immediately. "We thought you'd be in last night."

"Ran into a little trouble," Hayes said and gladly took the large mug of coffee Dana handed him.

"That's Texas-speak for he met a woman," his brother joked.

Hayes told them what had happened and how it was after daylight before he left the police station. He didn't mention the strange feeling he'd had when the woman had opened her eyes.

"Is she all right?" Dana asked, clearly shocked.

For months, Tag had been talking up Montana and its low crime rate among all of its other amazing wonders.

"She regained consciousness in the ambulance. Last I heard was going to be fine—at least physically. I'm not sure what a close call like that does to a person."

"Have the police found the man?" Dana asked, and hugged herself as if feeling a chill. Hayes thought about what his cousin had been through. She had personal experience with a psychopath who wanted to harm her.

"Unfortunately, the police don't have any leads. I wasn't able to get a license plate or even the model or make of the car the man was driving." He felt exhausted and stifled a yawn. He'd been going on nothing but adrenaline and caffeine since last night. "Hopefully, the woman will be able to give the cops a description so they can get the bastard."

"You look exhausted," Dana said. "I'll make you breakfast, then Tag will show you to your cabin. You two don't have anything planned until late afternoon, right?"

"Right," Tag said. "I'm taking my brother to see the restaurant space I found."

"Then get some rest, Hayes. We're having a steak fry tonight. Our fathers have said they are going to try to make it."

"That sounds great." He wasn't sure he was up to seeing his father. Harlan Cardwell had only been a passing figure in his life. Tag, who was the oldest, remembered him more than the other four of them. Harlan had come to Texas a few times, but his visits had been quick. Being the second to the youngest, Hayes didn't even remember his uncle Angus.

Hayes felt emotionally spent, sickened by what he'd witnessed last night and worried about the woman. He kept seeing her staring up at him with those eyes. He mentally shook himself as Dana put a plate of silver-dollar-sized pancakes with chokecherry syrup in front of him, along with a side of venison sausage and two sunny-side-up eggs.

He ate as if he hadn't eaten in days. As it was, he'd never gotten around to eating that sandwich he'd purchased at the grocery store last night. After he'd been plied with even more of Dana's amazing buttermilk pancakes, his brother walked him out to his rental SUV.

"So how are the wedding plans coming along?" he asked Tag as they got his gear and walked up a path behind the barn into the pines to his cabin.

He'd flown in a month early to talk his brother out of opening a Texas Boys Barbecue joint at Big Sky. The five brothers had started their first restaurant in a small old house in Houston. The business had grown by leaps and bounds and was now a multimillion-dollar corporation.

All five of them had agreed that they would keep the restaurants in Texas. But in December, Tag had come to Montana to spend Christmas with their father and had fallen in love with both Montana and Lily McCabe. Nothing like a woman and a little wilderness to mess with the best-laid plans.

It was now up to Hayes, as a spokesman for the other three brothers, to put Tag's feet firmly back on the ground and nip this problem in the bud.

"It's going to be an old-fashioned Western wedding," Tag was saying, his voice filled with excitement. "I can't wait for you to meet Lily. She's like no woman I have ever known."

Hayes didn't doubt it. He'd never seen his brother so happy. All of the brothers had the Cardwell dark good looks. Add to that their success, and women were often throwing themselves at one of them or another. Except for Jackson, none of them had found a woman they wanted to date more than a few times. They'd all become gun-shy after Jackson had bitten the bullet and gotten married—and quickly divorced after he found out his wife wanted nothing to do with their newborn son.

Hayes couldn't wait to meet this Lily McCabe to find

out what kind of spell she'd cast over his brother—and possibly try to break it before the wedding.

GUS THOMPSON HAD never been so angry. The bitch had called the cops on him. He glanced toward the empty receptionist's desk at the front of the real-estate office. It didn't surprise him that Cynthia hadn't come in today. Stupid woman. Did she really think he would blame *her?*

No, he knew Cynthia didn't do *anything* without checking with her boss.

So where the hell *was* McKenzie Sheldon? No matter what was going on, she was usually at work before him every morning. *She must have had a rough night,* he thought with a smirk.

Where was everyone else? he wondered as he checked his watch. Had they heard about the police coming by his house last night?

When the front door opened, he turned in his office chair, the smirk still on his face since he'd been expecting McKenzie. He felt it fall away as he saw the cops. Hadn't it been enough that an officer had shown up at his door last night, questioning him about stalking the receptionist at the office? Now what?

"Mr. Thompson?" the policewoman asked. Her name tag read P. Donovan.

"Yes?" he asked, getting to his feet. He saw them look around the empty office.

"Are you here alone?"

"Everyone seems to be running late this morning," he said, and wondered why that was. Because they'd all been given a heads-up? Gus noticed the way both cops were looking at him, scrutinizing him as if he had horns growing out of his head.

"We'd like to ask you a few questions," the woman cop said. "Ms. Sheldon has asked us to first see that you remove your belongings from the premises."

"What?" he demanded. "The bitch is *firing* me? Has she lost her mind?"

P. Donovan's eyes went hard and cold at the word *bitch.* The word had just slipped out. He'd known McKenzie had it in for him, but he'd never dreamed she'd fire him.

"I'm her biggest-earning salesman," he said as if there had been a mistake made and he hadn't made it. Neither responded. Instead, he saw the male cop looking around. "What?"

"Are there some boxes in the office you can put your belongings into?" the cop asked.

Hadn't either of them been listening? "She can't do this." Gus heard the hopelessness in his voice. He hated nothing worse than the feeling that came with it. He wanted to break something. Tear the place up. Then find McKenzie Sheldon and punch her in the face.

The male cop had gone into a storage room. He came back with two boxes. "Please take only those items belonging to you personally. We'll watch so we can tell Ms. Sheldon."

Gus gritted his teeth. McKenzie didn't even have the guts to face him. Well, this wasn't the last she'd see of him. He'd catch her in a dark alley. He started to shovel the top of the desk off into one of the boxes, but the male cop stopped him. T. Bradley, the name tag read.

"Leave any inventory you've been working on."

He grabbed up his coffee mug and threw it into the

box. The couple of tablespoons of coffee left in the cup made a dark stain across the bottom. The same way McKenzie's blood was going to stain the spot where they met up again, he told himself.

His personal belongings barely filled one box. That realization made him sad and even angrier. This business should have been his. When he was a boy, he used to sleep on the floor of the main office when his mother had to work late. This place had been more like home than home during those years when she'd been growing the business.

"Is that everything?" P. Donovan asked.

He didn't bother to answer as T. Bradley asked for his key to the building.

"Ms. Sheldon has taken out a restraining order against you," the cop said. "Are you familiar with the way they work?"

He looked at the cop. "Seriously? Do I look like someone who is familiar with restraining orders?"

"You are required to stay away from Ms. Sheldon and this building. If you harass her—"

"I get it," he snapped, and handed over his key. As he started toward the door, T. Bradley blocked his way.

"We're going to need you to come down to the police station with us to answer a few more questions."

"About what?" The receptionist, bloody hell. "Look, I haven't done anything that any red-blooded American male doesn't do. I like women." He realized they were staring at him. "Come on. She liked it or she wouldn't have led me on."

"Whom are you referring to?" P. Donovan asked.

He frowned. "Cynthia. The receptionist. She was threatening to call the cops last night, but I didn't really think she'd do it. Why would you ask me that? Who else called the cops on me?"

"Didn't she ask you to leave her alone?" the woman cop asked.

He shrugged. "I thought she was just playing hard to get."

"What about Ms. Sheldon? Did you also think she was just playing hard to get?" T. Bradley asked.

Gus closed his eyes and sighed. So she'd told them about that time she'd caught him in her neighborhood. "There's no law against sitting in your car on a public street. I didn't even realize she lived in the area. I was looking at the house down the block, okay?" Not even he could make the lie sound convincing.

"Let's go," P. Donovan said and led him out of the building as if he were a criminal. In the small parking lot, he saw his colleagues waiting in their vehicles for the police to take him away.

He wanted to kill McKenzie.

"Please open the trunk of your car, Mr. Thompson," T. Bradley said as Gus started to put the box in the backseat.

"Why?" he demanded.

"Just please open it," P. Donovan said.

He thought they probably needed a warrant or something, but he didn't feel like making things any worse. He cursed under his breath as he moved to the back of the vehicle and, using his key, opened the trunk. It was empty, so he put the box in it. "Satisfied?"

It wasn't until T. Bradley rode with him to the police station and they had him inside in an interrogation room that they demanded to know where he'd been last night after he'd left the office.

"We know you didn't go straight home," P. Donovan said. "Where did you go?"

So much for being Mr. Nice Guy. Through gritted teeth, Gus said, "I want to speak with my attorney. *Now.*"

CHAPTER FOUR

HE'D FAILED.

Failed.

The word knocked around in his mind, hammering at him until he could barely think.

You got too cocky last night, you and your perfect record.

It wasn't his fault. It was the woman's. The fool woman's and that cowboy with the Southern accent who'd rescued her.

That rationale didn't make him feel any better. He'd had one woman who'd fought back before, he thought, tracing a finger across the scar on his neck. But he hadn't let her get away and she'd definitely paid for what she'd done to him.

The possibility of not only failure, but getting caught was what made it so exciting. He loved the rush. But he also loved outsmarting everyone and getting away with it. Last night should have gone off without a hitch. The woman was the perfect choice. He'd done everything right. If he hadn't had to knock her out... Even so, a few more seconds and he would have had her in the trunk. Then it was a short drive to the isolated spot he'd found by the river.

His blood throbbed, running hot through his veins, at the thought of what he would have done to her before he dumped her body in the Gallatin River. He had to kill them for his own protection. If he were ever a suspect, there couldn't be any eyewitnesses.

Except last night he'd left behind *two* eyewitnesses— the woman and the cowboy. Had either of them gotten a good look at him or his vehicle? He didn't know.

A costly mistake. He mentally beat himself for not waiting until he could leave town before grabbing another one. The northwest was like a huge marketplace, every small town had perfect spots for the abduction and the dumping of the bodies. Small-town sheriff's offices were short on manpower. Women weren't careful because people felt safe in small towns.

Also, he had the perfect job. He traveled, putting a lot of miles on the road every year with different vehicles at his disposal. He saw a lot of towns, learned their secrets at the cafés and bars, felt almost at home in the places where he'd taken women.

But last night, after a few weeks unable to travel, he'd been restless. The ache in him had reached a pitch. His need had been too strong. He'd never taken a woman in his hometown. One wouldn't hurt, he'd thought. No, he hadn't been thinking at all. He'd taken a terrible chance and look what had happened.

He gingerly touched the side of his head where she'd hit him with whatever canned good had been in her grocery bag. Fortunately, other than being painful, the bruise didn't show through his thick hair. His shin was only slightly skinned from where she'd nailed him with her high heel and his fingers ached. No real visible signs of what she'd done to him. Not that he didn't feel it all and hate her for hurting him.

It could have been so much worse. He tried to console

himself with that, but it wasn't working. The woman had made a fool out of him. It didn't make any difference that he shouldn't have gone for so long since the last one. But it had begun to wear on him. Otherwise, he would never have taken one this close to home. He would never have taken the chance.

The television flickered. He glanced up as the news came on. This was why he couldn't let them live, he thought, as he watched the story about a botched abduction at the small, out-of-the-way grocery store the night before. He waited for the newsman to mention the woman's name and put her on camera to tell of her heroic rescue by the cowboy. He wanted to see the fear in her eyes—but more than anything, he needed her *name*.

The news station didn't put her on air. Nor did they give her name or the cowboy's who'd rescued her.

Furious, he tried several other stations. He'd gotten a good look at her last night after he'd punched her and had her on the ground.

But he foolishly hadn't bothered to take down her car license number or grab her purse. He hadn't cared who the woman was. She'd been nobody to him. But now he was desperate to know everything about her. All the others, he'd learned about them after their bodies were found. It had never mattered who they were. They'd already served their purpose. Now it was inconceivable that he didn't know the name of the only woman who'd ever gotten away.

Without her name, he wouldn't be able to find her and finish what he'd started.

STANDING IN THE hospital room half-dressed, McKenzie tried to still her trembling fingers. The morning sun was blinding. Her head still ached, but she'd kept that from the doctor. After the police had left, he'd made her spend the night in the hospital for observation. Today, though, she had to get back to work. It was the only thing that could keep her mind off what had happened. Worse, what could have happened if someone hadn't stopped the man.

"Let me," her sister said and stepped to her to button the blouse.

She stood still, letting her big sister dress her—just as she had as a child. "Thank you. I wouldn't have called but I needed a change of clothing before I could leave the hospital."

Shawna shook her head. She was the oldest of nine and had practically raised them all since her mother had been deathly ill with each pregnancy, especially with her last baby—McKenzie.

"Mac, I would expect you to call because I'm your *sister* and, after what you've been through, you need your family."

She didn't like needing anyone, especially her big sister. "I didn't want to be any trouble."

Her sister laughed. "You have always been like this." She straightened McKenzie's collar. "You've never wanted to be any trouble. So independent. And stubborn. There. You look fine."

She didn't feel fine. From an early age, just as her sister had said, she had been fiercely independent, determined to a fault, wanting to do everything herself and driven to succeed at whatever she did. She was still that way. Nothing had changed—and yet, after last night, everything felt as if it had.

It was as if the earth was no longer solid under her feet. She felt off-balance, unsure—worse, afraid.

"Are you sure you're ready to leave the hospital?" Shawna asked, studying her.

"The doctor says my head will hurt for a while, but that I should be fine. I need to get to the office and re-assure everyone. I had to fire one of my employees today." She swallowed, her sore throat again remind-ing her of the man's arm around her neck. Had it been Gus Thompson? The thought made her blood run cold. "I'm sure everyone is upset."

"You can't worry about them right now. You need to think about yourself. Just go home and rest. I can stop by your office—"

"No, this is something I need to do myself." She saw her sister's disappointment. Shawna lived to serve. "But thank you so much for bringing me a change of clothes."

"What do you want me to do with the clothes you were wearing?" she asked, picking up the bag. Her pretty new suit was blood-splattered from the now bandaged head wound. So was the blouse she'd been wearing.

"Throw them away. I don't want them."

She felt her older sister's gaze on her. "There doesn't seem to be anything wrong with the suit or the blouse. Once I get them clean… It seems a shame—"

"Then drop them off at Goodwill."

Her sister nodded. "Are the police giving you pro-tection?"

"They really can't do that. Anyway, there's no need. If it was someone I know, then they don't believe he'll try anything again with them involved. And if it was ran-dom…then the man could be miles from here by now."

Shawna didn't look any more convinced than Mc-Kenzie felt. "I guess they know best."

"I'm going to stay in Big Sky tonight. I have a client I need to see up there this afternoon so I'll spend the night and come back tomorrow."

"Do you want me to go home with you to your condo and wait while you pack?"

She thought of her empty condo. "No. That's not necessary." But even as she said it, she was already dreading facing it alone. "I know you need to get back to your job." She stepped to her sister and hugged her. Shawna had never married. But she kept busy with three jobs as if needing to fill every hour of her day doing for others.

"You've done enough," McKenzie said. Her big sister had always been there for her from as far back as she could remember. It made her feel guilty because she felt her sister had been robbed of her childhood. Shawna had been too busy raising their mother's babies.

"If you need anything…"

"I know." Sometimes she felt as if Shawna had made a life in Montana so she could watch over her. All the other siblings had left, stretching far and wide around the world. Only she and Shawna had stayed in the Gallatin Valley after their parents had passed.

But her big sister couldn't always protect her. Before last night, McKenzie would have said she could protect herself. Last night had proved how wrong she was about that.

Gus Thompson would never forget the humiliation he'd been put through at the police department. "Don't you know who I am?" he'd finally demanded.

They had looked at him blankly.

"My photo is all over town on real-estate signs. I am number one in this valley. I sell more property than any of the hundreds of agents out there. I'm *somebody* and I don't have to put up with this ridiculous questioning."

"You still haven't told us where you were last night." The woman cop was starting to really tick him off.

He looked to his attorney, who leaned toward him and whispered that he should just tell them since it would be better than their finding out later. "I went for a drive. I do that sometimes to relax."

"Did you happen to drive by the River Street Market?"

"I don't remember. I was just driving."

"We searched your car… Actually, the car that is still registered to your mother, and we found a gas receipt." The woman cop again. "You were within a quarter mile of the grocery last night only forty-two minutes before the incident involving Ms. Sheldon."

"So what?" he snapped. "Aren't you required to tell me what I'm being accused of? Someone steal McKenzie's groceries?"

"Someone attacked and attempted to abduct Ms. Sheldon."

"Trust me. The guy would have brought her back quick enough." Neither cop smiled, let alone laughed. He raked a hand through his hair. "Why would I try something like that in a grocery-store parking lot when I could have abducted McKenzie Sheldon any night right at the office?"

His attorney groaned and the two cops exchanged a look.

"Come on," Gus said. "I didn't do anything to her. I swear." But he sure wanted to *now.* Wasn't it enough that she'd fired him? Apparently not. She wanted to *destroy* him. Something like this could hang over his head for years—unless they caught the guy who really attacked her. What was the chance of that happening? Next to none when they weren't even out looking for him.

He pointed this out to the cops. "Get out there and find this guy. It's the only way I can prove to you that I'm innocent."

They both looked at him as if they suspected he was far from innocent. But they finally let him go.

Once outside the police station, Gus realized he didn't know what he was going to do now. Of course, another Realtor would hire him. The top salesman in Gallatin Valley? Who wouldn't?

Unless word got around about Sheldon's attack—and his firing. Everyone would think it was because he was the one who'd attacked McKenzie. How long would it take before everyone knew? He groaned. Gossip moved faster than an underpriced house, especially among Realtors.

McKenzie Sheldon better hope she hadn't just destroyed his reputation—*and* his career.

"I'm ANXIOUS FOR you to see the building I found for the very first Big Sky Texas Boys Barbecue," Tag said later that afternoon. "The Realtor is going to meet us there in a few minutes."

Hayes had taken a long nap after the breakfast Dana had made for him. He'd awakened to the dinner bell. Dana was one heck of a cook. Lunch included chicken-fried elk steaks, hash browns, carrots from the garden and biscuits with sausage gravy.

"This is the woman who should be opening a restaurant," Hayes said to his cousin.

"Thanks, but no, thanks," Dana said. "I have plenty to do with four small children." As if summoning them, the four came racing into the kitchen along with their father, Hud, the local marshal. The kids climbed all over their father as Dana got him a plate. It amazed him how much noise kids seven to two could make.

Tag's fiancée, Lily McCabe, came in looking as if she was already family. She declined lunch, saying she'd already eaten, but she pulled up a chair. Introductions were made and five minutes later, Hayes could see why his brother had fallen in love with the beautiful and smart brunette.

"We'd better get going," Tag said, checking his watch. He gave Lily a kiss then rumpled each child's hair as he headed for the door. Hayes followed, even though there was no purpose in seeing this building his brother had found for the restaurant.

They weren't opening a barbecue place in Big Sky. He wasn't sure how he was going to break it to his brother, though.

The road from the ranch crossed a bridge over the Gallatin River. This morning it ran crystal clear, colorful rocks gleaming invitingly from the bottom. Hayes watched the river sweep past, the banks dotted with pines and cottonwoods, and wished they were going fishing, instead.

At Highway 191, Tag turned toward Big Sky and Hayes got his first good look at Lone Mountain. The spectacular peak glistened in the sun. A patch of snow was still visible toward the top where it hadn't yet melted. This morning, when he'd driven to the ranch, the top of the peak had been shrouded in clouds.

"Isn't it beautiful?" Tag said.

"It is." All of the Montana he'd seen so far was beautiful. He could understand why his brother had fallen in love with the place. And with Lily McCabe.

"Lily was nervous about meeting you earlier," Tag said now, as if reading his mind. He turned toward Lone Mountain and what made up the incorporated town of Big Sky.

Hayes could see buildings scattered across a large meadow, broken only by pines and a golf course. "Why would she be nervous?"

"She was afraid my brothers wouldn't like her."

"What is the chance of that?" Hayes said. He had to admit that Lily hadn't been what he'd expected. She was clearly smart, confident and nice. He hadn't found any fault with her. In fact, it was blatantly clear why Tag was head over heels in love with the woman.

But Lily had reason to be nervous. She was backing Tag on the restaurant idea. A math professor at Montana State University in Bozeman, she didn't want to move to Texas with her future husband. A lot was riding on what Tag's brothers decided. Their not wanting a Montana barbecue place had nothing to do with liking or disliking Lily.

"Is she going to meet us at the restaurant building site?" Hayes asked, wondering how involved the bride-to-be was planning to be in the barbecue business. After the fiasco with Jackson's wife, the brothers had decided no wives would ever own interest in the corporation. They couldn't chance another ugly divorce that could destroy Texas Boys Barbecue. Or a *marriage* that would threaten the business, for that matter.

"No, she's doing wedding planning stuff," Tag said. "Who knew all the things that are involved in getting married?"

"Yes, who knew," Hayes agreed as his brother turned into a small, narrow complex. He saw the For Sale sign on a cute Western building stuck back in some pine trees and knew it must be the one his brother had picked out.

"Good, McKenzie is already here," Tag said just an instant before Hayes saw her.

He stared in shock at the woman he'd seen the night before. Only last night McKenzie had been lying at his feet outside a grocery store as her would-be abductor sped away.

CHAPTER FIVE

"Hayes, meet McKenzie Sheldon, Realtor extraordinaire," Tag said. "McKenzie, this is my brother Hayes."

McKenzie smiled, but she wasn't sure how convincing it was. Her sister had tried to talk her into moving this meeting to another day. Maybe she should have listened. She hadn't felt like herself all day.

While she'd tried to put what had happened last night out of her mind, she kept reliving it. Now she felt jumpy and realized it had been a mistake to take the attitude "business as usual" today.

But she couldn't bear the thought of hanging out at the condo all day when she knew nothing could take her mind off last night in that case. Her first stop had been the office where she'd assured everyone that Gus Thompson would no longer be a problem. While she was there, the locksmith came and changed all the locks, which seemed to reassure some and make others at the office even more nervous since Gus hadn't gotten along with any of his coworkers.

Then she'd gone to her condo, packed quickly for overnight and driven to Big Sky to meet her client. She'd worn a plain suit with a scarf to cover the bruises on her neck, but the gash on her temple where the man had slugged her still required a bandage if she hoped to hide the stitches.

As she caught her reflection in the empty building window, she saw with a start that she looked worse than she'd thought. How else could she explain Hayes Cardwell's reaction to her? His eyes had widened in alarm as he put out his hand.

He looked like a man who'd just seen a ghost. He'd *recognized* her. How was that possible when he'd only flown in yesterday?

"Pleased to meet you, Ms. Sheldon."

Tag had told her that his brothers shared more than a love of barbecue. The resemblance was amazing. Like Tag, Hayes Cardwell had the dark hair and eyes, had the wonderful Southern accent and was handsome as sin.

She thought of Ted Bundy as she took Hayes Cardwell's large hand, hers disappearing inside it, and saw his dark gaze go to the bandage on her head. "I had a little accident last night."

"You're all right, though?" He still held her hand. She could feel herself trembling and feared he could, too.

She put on her best smile. "Fine." Then she finally met his gaze.

His eyes were a deep brown and so familiar that it sent a shudder through her. Even though she'd told her sister that there was nothing to worry about, she was well aware that the man who'd attacked her last night could be closer than she thought.

HE'D STAYED HOME from work saying he didn't feel well, even though he knew that might look suspicious if he was ever a suspect. But he was too anxious and upset over last night to go to work today.

There'd been nothing of use in the morning paper, only a short few paragraphs.

Police say a man tried to abduct a 28-year-old woman about 10:35 p.m. last night in the River Street Market parking lot.

The man attacked the woman as she came out of the market and attempted to put her into the trunk of his vehicle. He is described as over six feet with a muscular build. He was wearing a dark-colored baseball cap and driving a newer-model large car, also dark in color.

If anyone has information, they should contact the local police department.

He knew he should be glad that the information was just as useless to the police. She hadn't gotten a good look at him, which was great unless they had some reason to withhold that information. That aside, nothing in the news was helping him find the woman.

Too restless to stay in the house, he decided to go for a walk in his northside neighborhood to clear his head. The houses were smaller on this side of town, many of them having been remodeled when the boom in housing came through years before.

House prices had dropped with the mortgage fiasco, but so many people wanted to live in his valley that prices had never reached the lows they had elsewhere. He was glad he hadn't been tricked into selling his house for top dollar. He could have found himself in a house he couldn't afford. Instead, his small, comfortable home was paid for since he lived conservatively.

Everything about his lifestyle looked normal on paper. He'd attended Montana State University right there in Bozeman. He'd bought a house after he graduated with a degree in marketing and had gone to work for a local company. He was an exemplary employee, a good neighbor, a man who flew under the radar. If caught, everyone who knew him would be shocked and say they never would have suspected him of all people.

As he walked around his neighborhood, he saw that more houses were for sale. It made him upset to think that his older neighbors were dying off because more college students would be moving in. Constant temptation, he thought with a groan.

He promised himself the next time he took a woman it would be in another town. Even better, another state. He couldn't take the chance so close to home ever again. If there *was* another time. Last night's botched abduction had left him shaken. She'd jinxed things for him. If he didn't find the woman and fix this—

At a corner he hadn't walked past in some time, he saw that another house had gone on the market. But that wasn't what made him stumble to a stop next to the strip of freshly mown lawn.

There she was! He could never forget that face and now there she was. Right there on the real-estate sign in the yard, smiling up at him as if daring him to come after her.

McKenzie Sheldon of M.K. Sheldon Realty.

"ARE YOU ALL RIGHT?"

McKenzie nodded, even though she was far from all right. Did she really think she recognized this man? She hadn't seen the face of the man who'd tried to abduct her so she couldn't have seen his eyes. This man's eyes were…familiar and yet she'd never met him before, had she? Would she look at every man she met and think he was the one who'd attacked her?

Hayes Cardwell was staring at her with concern and something else in his expression. Compassion?

It was the very last thing she needed right now. Tears welled in her eyes. She felt lightheaded and groped for the wall behind her for support.

"If you'd prefer to do this some other time," Hayes said.

She shook her head. "No, I'm fine. It must have been something I ate." In truth, she hadn't eaten anything since the day before. No wonder she felt lightheaded. But she'd toughened it out through worse, she told herself, remembering when she'd taken on the agency.

Tag Cardwell hadn't seemed to notice her no doubt odd behavior. He was busy looking in the windows of the building, anxious to get inside and show his brother the space.

"I think you're going to like this location for your restaurant," she said, turning away from Hayes Cardwell's dark, intent gaze and what she saw there. "Let me show you. It's perfect for what you have in mind."

Her fingers shook so hard, she didn't think she was going to be able to put the key in the lock. A large, sun-tanned hand reached around her and gently took the keys from her.

"Let me do that," Hayes said. His voice was soft, his Southern accent comforting and almost familiar.

She was going mad. She could smell his male scent along with the soap he'd used to shower that morning. He was a big man—like the man last night who'd attacked her. She touched her bruised throat and closed her eyes against the terrifying memory.

He opened the door and she stumbled in and away

from him. Her cell phone rang and she was startled to see that it was the police department.

"I need to take this. Please have a look around." She scooted past Hayes and back outside, leaving the two men alone inside what had been a restaurant only months ago. Her phone rang again. She sucked in a deep breath of the June mountain air and, letting it out, took the call. As she did, she prayed the man had been caught. She couldn't keep living like this.

"Ms. Sheldon?" the policewoman asked.

"Yes?"

"I spoke to the man who intervened last night during your attack. He still would prefer to remain anonymous."

"You're sure he wasn't involved?"

"Involved? No. The clerk at the store was a witness. He was leaving the store when he saw the abductor trying to lift you into the trunk of his car. The man saved your life."

"So why is this so-called hero so determined to remain anonymous?"

"As I told you, he's in town visiting relatives. He doesn't want the notoriety. But I can assure you, we checked him out. He just happened to be in the right place at the right time last night."

McKenzie felt as if she could breathe a little easier. "I'm sorry he won't let me thank him, but I certainly appreciate what he did. Is there any word on...?"

"No, but we are looking at Gus Thompson. We brought him in. He doesn't have an alibi for last night."

"You really think it was him?" She shuddered, remembering. He was about the right size and he *had* acted more than a little creepy in the past.

Behind her, the door opened. She heard Tag and his brother come out.

"Thank you for letting me know," she said to the patrolwoman and disconnected. "So what do you think?" she asked, but one look at their faces and she knew Hayes hadn't liked the place.

Tag had been so excited about the building. She could get it for him at a good price since the owner was anxious to sell. But she could see that Hayes was far from sold.

"We can't really make a decision until all my brothers see the place," Tag said. Hayes said nothing.

She could feel the tension between the two men. "Well, let me know. This property won't stay on the market long. I'll lock up." She moved past Hayes to turn out the light and lock the door.

When she came back out, the brothers were leaving. She shivered as she felt someone watching her. Her gaze shot to Hayes, but he was looking off toward the mountains and his brother was busy driving.

I'm losing my mind. Hayes Cardwell wasn't her attacker. So why, when she thought of his brown eyes, did some memory try to fight to surface?

Gus Thompson was going to see McKenzie no matter what anyone said. When he'd come out of the police station and climbed into his vehicle, he hadn't known where to go or what to do. He had to save his career, and McKenzie was the only one who could do that.

Restraining order or not, he *would* see her.

He had racked his brain, trying to remember where she said she had a showing today. Something about a listing in Big Sky. A former restaurant. He'd quickly checked to see what commercial restaurant space was under the multiple listings at Big Sky and laughed out loud when he'd found the restaurant with ease.

It didn't take much to find out what time she was showing the place. He'd called the office, changed his voice and pretended to be the person she was showing the restaurant to. Within minutes, he'd found out that McKenzie would be at the restaurant this afternoon at two to meet the Cardwells.

For a few minutes after he'd hung up, he'd tried to talk himself out of driving up to Big Sky. The last thing he needed was for her to call the police before she heard him out. It appalled him that she thought she could just fire him and he'd go away. Well, she was dead wrong about that.

Unfortunately, the forty-mile drive had taken longer than he'd expected. Summer traffic. He'd forgotten about the damned tourists so he hadn't been able to beat McKenzie to the restaurant—which had been his intent.

Fifty minutes later, he'd parked next to a small grocery in a space where he had a good view of the restaurant with the M.K. Realty sign out front. He'd arrived in time to see two men pull up in an SUV only moments after McKenzie.

He'd been forced to wait, telling himself it might work out better. He would grab her after her showing. He could get a lay of the land before he did anything stupid. More stupid, he thought, thinking of Cynthia, the receptionist. She wasn't even that cute.

While he had no patience for waiting, he was surprised when the showing only took a matter of minutes. He had to laugh. Boy, had that not gone well. And now

McKenzie had just lost her best salesman. She would definitely regret firing him, probably already did.

He saw his chance when the two men McKenzie had shown the property to got into their SUV and drove away. The restaurant location was somewhat secluded, separated from the other businesses by pine trees.

Once he got her alone, she'd be forced to listen to what he had to say.

As he started his vehicle, planning to park behind her car so she couldn't get away, he saw her looking around. Was she worried he might show up? Or was she looking for the man who'd attacked her last night? Her gaze skimmed over him in his vehicle where he still sat, motor running. He looked away, glad he'd driven his silver SUV that looked like everyone else's around here.

When he'd dared take a peek again, she was headed for her car. He couldn't let her just drive away. His best chance of talking to her was here rather than back in Bozeman.

Gus shifted the SUV into gear. He told himself all he wanted to do was tell her what he thought of her firing him, of accusing him of attacking her, of treating him like an employee rather than appreciating what he did for M.K. Realty.

He just needed to have his say. He wasn't stupid enough to touch her. Or threaten her. He had the right to have the last word. She couldn't just get rid of him in such a humiliating way and think he was going to let it pass.

But as he'd started to drive up the road to the empty restaurant, another vehicle pulled in and parked next to her car. Annoyed, he saw that he would have to wait again. He hadn't come all this way to give up. He killed his engine with a curse. If he couldn't get to her now, then soon. She would hear him out, one way or another.

MCKENZIE HATED THE scared feeling she had as she hurried to her car. Her gaze took in the activity lower on the hillside. She told herself she'd just imagined someone watching her. Down the road, there were families in vans with laughing and screaming children, older people trying to park in front of one of the small businesses that dotted the meadow, a young couple heading into the grocery store.

Everywhere she looked there were people busy with their own lives. It was June in Montana, a time when in Big Sky, it seemed everyone was on vacation. No one had any reason to be watching her.

Still, she gripped her keys in her fist until her hand ached as she neared her car. She wanted to run but she was afraid that like a mad dog, the person watching her would give chase. She couldn't see anyone watching her and yet the hair rose on the back of her neck. The afternoon sun had sunk behind Lone Mountain. Shadows moved on the restless breeze through the pines next to the building.

Fear was making her paranoid, but she couldn't shake off the feeling that the man from last night hadn't left town. Nor had he forgotten about her.

She reached the car, opened the door and climbed in, fumbling in a panic to get the door locked. The moment she did, she realized she hadn't looked in the backseat. Her gaze shot to the rearview mirror. She swiveled around. The backseat was empty.

Hot tears burned down her cheeks. She began to shake uncontrollably.

At the sound of a vehicle approaching, she brushed at her tears and tried to pull herself together. She was trying to put the key into the ignition, when the tap on her side window made her jump.

Her head swung around and she found herself looking up at Hayes Cardwell. She cursed herself. He would see that she'd been crying. She felt a wave of embarrassment and anger at herself.

"Are you all right?" Hayes mouthed.

She lowered the window a few inches. "I—"

"I know. That's why I came back. There's something I need to tell you."

"If it's about the restaurant space—"

"The police called me and asked me again if I would mind if they told you that I was the man who found you last night at the grocery store."

She felt her eyes widen in alarm. "You—" The brown eyes. A flicker of memory. *You're safe now.*

"I can't imagine what you're going through, that's all I wanted to say. I was worried about you. But I didn't want you thinking…"

She nodded, unable to speak around the lump in her throat. He'd seen her reaction to him. It was the reason he'd decided to tell her. He didn't want her thinking he was the one who'd hurt her. Her eyes burned again with tears.

"Call the police. I understand why you would suspect me. I'll be over here when you finish if you want to talk or anything." He stepped away from her car.

She put the window up and dug out her phone. When the patrolwoman came on the line she asked, "The man who saved me last night? Was his name Hayes Cardwell?"

"So he *did* contact you."

"It's true?"

"Yes. He and his brothers own a chain of—"

"Barbecue restaurants in Texas."

"That's right. He also works as a private investigator in Houston. Like I said, we checked him out thoroughly. Plus, we have an eyewitness who saw him rescue you."

"Thank you." She disconnected and, pulling herself together, climbed out of the car.

Hayes was standing at the edge of the building, looking toward the Gallatin River. In the afternoon sun, the surface of the water shimmered like gold. The scent of pine wafted through the June air. There was nothing like Montana in the summer.

"I'm so sorry I suspected you." He'd never know how much. "The police told me that I owe my life to you. Thank you."

He turned to look at her, kindness in his dark eyes. "No, please, don't feel bad. I didn't tell you so you could—"

"Thank you?"

He shrugged, looking shy. "I just happened to be in the grocery store."

"I didn't mean to make you uncomfortable."

"I'm afraid I'm the one who made you uncomfortable. I apologize for staring earlier. I was just so surprised to see you again."

She nodded and touched her bruised neck, remembering the man's arm around her throat and fighting for breath.

"Are you sure you should be working this soon after what you've been through?" he asked.

"I needed to keep my mind off...everything."

"Is it working?"

She gave him a weary smile. "No," she said and looked away. "I've felt jumpy all day and I haven't been able to shake the feeling that someone is…watching me." She glanced around again, the feeling still strong. She shivered, even though the afternoon was warm.

What if the man from last night wasn't through with her? Wasn't that what had been in the back of her mind all day?

HAYES LOOKED PAST her. He saw people coming and going at a nearby small business complex. No one seemed to be looking in this direction, though.

"You say you feel as if someone's watching you?"

She nodded. "I know I'm just being paranoid—"

"Your best defense is your instincts. Don't discount them."

She stared at him and tried to swallow the lump in her throat. "You think he'll come after me again?"

"I don't know. Is there any way he knows who you are?"

"I… The police think it might be a man I worked with. I fired him today. I have a restraining order—"

Hayes scoffed at that. "Restraining orders can't protect you from a predator. Where are you staying?"

"I checked into a motel up here for the night—"

He shook his head. "My cousin Dana owns a ranch not far from here. She recently built several guest cabins. I'd feel better if you'd consider staying there—at least until the police have a chance to catch this man." Hayes knew from experience that there was little chance they would catch him—unless he did turn out to be this man she'd fired.

"I couldn't impose."

"You wouldn't be imposing, trust me. My cousin Dana loves a full house and you would be doing me a favor."

She cocked a brow. "How's that?"

"I wouldn't have to worry about you the whole time I'm in town."

McKenzie smiled. It was a nice smile, a real one, and he was suddenly aware of how attractive she was. She had long hair the color of caramel. Most of it was pulled up with a clip at the nape of her neck, but a few strands had escaped, framing a face that was all girl-next-door—from the sprinkling of freckles that dusted her cheeks and nose to the wide-set tropical-blue eyes. But it was her mouth that kept drawing his attention. It was full, her lips a pale pink. Right now she worried at her lower lip with her teeth.

She had the kind of mouth a man fantasized about kissing.

He roped in his thoughts, telling himself not to make a big deal out of this coincidence. But he couldn't shake the memory of the first time he'd looked into her eyes. And now here she was, Tag's real-estate agent. As a private detective, he'd never bought into coincidences. This was definitely one that had him thrown off-balance.

"You'll like my family and you'll be safe." After that, he didn't want to think about it. Maybe the police would get lucky and catch the man.

"Are you sure about this? I know you didn't want to be involved…"

"I *am* involved," he said and smiled. Maybe more involved than he should be, he thought. "Do you need to stop by your motel to cancel your reservation?"

"I hadn't checked in yet. I can call."

"Why don't you follow me to the ranch, then, and meet the Cardwells. Trust me. You're going to love them and feel at home there."

"WHAT?" TAG SAID as they stood in the ranch house living room later. "McKenzie is the woman you saved?"

Hayes nodded.

"Talk about a small world. So you decided to bring her back to the ranch?"

"Look, I know you're upset with me about the restaurant—"

"I'm just trying to understand what you're thinking. Since you're only going to be here a couple of days, how do you intend to keep this woman safe?"

"I don't know what I was thinking, okay? She was scared. When I went back and found her, she was losing it, all right? She thought someone was watching her."

Tag looked skeptical.

"I think she was probably imagining it, but she's terrified this predator will come for her again. Who wouldn't be?"

"You did the right thing," Dana said from the doorway. "I'm glad you brought her here. It isn't like we don't have plenty of room. I put her in the cabin next to yours, Hayes. She can stay as long as she wants."

"With the wedding coming up July Fourth—"

Dana cut Tag off. "Your brothers can always bunk together if they haven't caught the man who attacked her by the time Jackson, Austin and Laramie arrive. I told her she is welcome to stay as long as she wants to and that is that."

Tag didn't look happy about it. "It makes it pretty

awkward since, from what I can gather, we aren't going to buy the restaurant space."

Dana looked to Hayes. "Is that what you and your brothers have decided?"

"We're still discussing it." That wasn't quite true but he really didn't want to get into this right now. If he couldn't talk his brother out of this, then he'd contact the rest of the guys and let them deal with it. His job had been to come up here and check out the situation and if at all possible, put an end to it.

"Why don't you take McKenzie for a horseback ride?" Dana suggested to Hayes. "It's beautiful up in the mountains behind the ranch and it will take both of your minds off your problems."

He was glad for anything that let him escape more discussion about the restaurant, so he jumped at it. "Good idea."

He found McKenzie standing outside on the wide Western porch, leaning on the porch railing and looking toward the mountains beyond. At his approach, she turned to smile at him.

"Thank you," she said, turning to him. She'd changed out of the suit she'd been wearing earlier into jeans and blouse. "This place is beautiful. I feel…safe here and I adore your cousin Dana."

"Everyone does. I thought you'd like it here. That was the plan. Dana suggested a horseback ride up into the mountains. What do you say?"

"Really? I'd love to." She sounded so excited he couldn't help but smile. He was reminded again of that moment last night when he'd looked into her eyes and felt…something.

"Great. Dana said she has two gentle horses that should be perfect for us greenhorns."

"Speak for yourself," McKenzie said. "I grew up riding and I suspect you did, too," she said, eyeing him. "Or is that Stetson and those boots just for show?"

He laughed. "I've ridden a few horses in my day."

Dana came out of the house then with a pair of boots she thought would fit McKenzie. They all visited as she led them up to the corral and got them saddled up for their ride.

Hayes noticed that McKenzie's step was lighter. He felt uncomfortable playing hero protector, but he preferred that to worrying about her. He'd learned as a private investigator to follow his own instincts. If she felt she was being watched, he knew there was the chance she probably was.

CHAPTER SIX

HE COULDN'T BELIEVE his good luck at finding McKenzie Sheldon's face on that real-estate sign. He took this as an omen that things were going to work out, after all.

Whistling all the way back to his house, he planned his new strategy. From the description the newspaper had run of the attacker, he felt assured that McKenzie hadn't gotten a good look at him. Which meant she wouldn't know him if she saw him again. But he had to be sure before he moved forward.

He checked the real-estate listings and found an open house she was hosting on Sunday, day after tomorrow. But to his delight, he saw that she was going to be the featured speaker at a real-estate conference being held at the university right here in town tomorrow.

He imagined that she was scared after last night. He just hoped she didn't cancel her speech or her open house or have someone else host it. Given the fight she'd put up last night, he had a feeling she wouldn't. He liked that about her and couldn't wait to see her again.

Excited now and much relieved, he felt better than he had since his failure the night before. But he wouldn't be satisfied until he fixed this.

From as far back as he could remember, he couldn't bear failing. He supposed that was his parents' fault. They'd expected so much of him—too much. He would have given anything to make them happy, and he'd certainly tried for years. But he'd only disappointed them time and time again.

The thought left a bitter taste in his mouth.

His parents weren't the only ones. He'd also disappointed his girlfriends. The thought of them made his stomach roil. He'd never known what they wanted from him. It was this secret that women kept among themselves. They would get that self-satisfied smirk on their faces, mocking you for failing.

"I should have expected as much from you," his high school girlfriend used to say. And when he begged her to just tell him what she wanted, she would add, "If you don't know, then there is really nothing more I can say."

The bitches had played their games with him throughout high school and then college. He'd tried to understand them. Even with his longest relationship after college, four years, he'd continued to disappoint. Nothing was ever good enough. And the nagging...

That was really when things had started to change. After his breakup following four years of torture, he'd picked up a woman at the bar and taken her for a ride out into the country. All he'd wanted was sex and a little peace and quiet. But it had proven too much to ask. She'd started going off on him, about how she should have known at the bar that he was a loser. He'd told her to get out of his car.

"Out here? No, you take me back to the bar where I left my car right now," she'd said.

He remembered looking at her. How ugly women were when they scowled like that. "Get out of my car right now or I am going to kill you."

She'd started to argue, but something in his expression had stopped her. She got out and began to cry, yell-ing obscenities as he backed up to leave. "I'm going to tell on you! Everyone is going to know about you!"

He'd hit the brakes, then threw the car into first gear and hit the gas as she began to run. That had shut her up. He'd chased her down the road until she'd had the sense to run into the trees. He'd been so calm as he'd turned off the car and gone into the trees after her.

She'd been easy to catch.

That was when he'd officially quit trying to please other people. Now he only worried about making him-self happy. And what would make him happy was find-ing McKenzie Sheldon and finishing what he'd started.

McKenzie shifted in her saddle as she stared across rows of mountaintops to the sunset. The waning sun had left streaks of pink, orange and gold that fanned up into Montana's big sky.

"It's breathtaking." She turned to look at Hayes. "Thank you for bringing me up here. You were right, your family is so inviting, especially Dana. This was so kind of her."

"She is one in a million, no doubt about that."

"You all seem so close. My family is spread out all over the place. I only have one sister here in town and I don't see her much. My fault. I work all the time." She let out a sigh.

"I never met the Cardwell side of my family until this trip," Hayes said. "My mother left my father when us boys were very young and took us to Texas to live. We only saw our father on occasion, so this is my first time in Montana—and meeting my cousin Dana."

McKenzie couldn't help being surprised. "You seem so at home here."

He chuckled at that. "Montana does that to a person. Look at my brother. He intends to stay, restaurant or no restaurant."

"You're opposed to opening a Texas Boys Barbecue here?"

"It's complicated."

"I'm sorry, I shouldn't have asked." She looked toward the sunset and breathed in the sweet scent of the tall pines around her.

"No, it's fine. It's just that we started small, in an old house in Houston, and the business just…mushroomed. My brother Laramie has a head for that end of it and runs the corporation so the rest of us can pursue other careers."

"I understand you're a private investigator in Houston?"

He nodded. "Maybe it's just me, but our little barbecue joint has grown into something I never wanted it to be. Adding another one in Montana… Well, it was never in the plans. We swore we would at least keep them all in Texas."

She said nothing, hating that she had a dog in the fight. This was something the brothers would have to sort out among themselves. Meanwhile, she feared Tag would lose the restaurant space and clearly he had his heart set on his own business in Big Sky.

"It makes it all the more difficult because there are five of us," Hayes said. "Do you come from a large family?"

She laughed. "Nine children."

His eyes widened in surprise. "Imagine all of them having to agree on something."

"Impossible."

Hayes nodded, but he looked upset by the situation.

"Your brother is still going to marry the woman he loves and stay in Montana no matter what happens with the restaurant, right?"

"Seems so. I just hate to disappoint him, but it isn't as if he needs a job."

"Some people just enjoy working," she said, realizing how true that was. She couldn't imagine retiring, say, ten years from now even though she probably could. What would she do all day if she did?

"I suppose we should head back," Hayes said as the sky around them began to darken. The breeze stirred the thick pine boughs and McKenzie felt a chill, even though the day was still warm. "Sorry to dump my problems on you."

"Yes, I have more than enough of my own," she joked. "Seriously, it was nice to think about someone else's for a while."

"I'm glad you're staying here on the ranch. Dana has invited us for a cookout tonight. You'll get to meet the rest of the family."

"I don't know how I will ever be able to repay her," McKenzie said.

"Just being here makes her happy since I think she gets starved for female companionship with all these Cardwell men around."

As they rode back toward the ranch, she couldn't help but notice the pines shimmering in the waning light. In the distance, she could see Lone Mountain, now a deep purple.

She couldn't remember a time she'd enjoyed a man's company the way she did Hayes Cardwell's. He wasn't hard to look at, either, she thought with a hidden smile, surprising herself. No man had turned her head in a very long time. And he really had taken her mind off last night.

But as they rode into the darkening ranch yard, she felt another shiver and tried to shake off that feeling of being watching again.

HAYES NOTICED HOW quiet McKenzie was at supper. Fortunately, his father and uncle hadn't been able to make it to the ranch so she'd only had to meet a few of the family members. He could tell she was exhausted. The ride, though, had put some color back into her cheeks.

After dinner, the two of them headed for their respective cabins on the mountainside behind the house and he asked, "Would it be possible for you to take a few days off? I'm anxious to have a look around the area and thought you might want to come along."

He could see that she saw through his ruse right away.

She smiled politely, though, and said, "I am speaking at a real-estate convention tomorrow at the university before several hundred people."

That had been his fear. "You can't get someone else to do it for you?"

"Are you kidding?" She laughed. "This has been planned for months."

He nodded. "So it's been widely publicized."

She frowned. "You can't think that the man who attacked me would come to something like this, hoping to harm me."

He wasn't sure what to think. "I don't like it because it will be hard to protect you in a crowd like that."

"Hayes—"

"If you're going to tell me that you don't want my protection, save your breath. I'm going with you."

"You'll be bored to tears."

"I hope so. I'm sure your speech will knock 'em dead, but with any luck, it will be uneventful."

"This conference is important. It's about growth in Montana, especially in this Big Sky area," she said as they neared her cabin.

Moonlight filled the canyon, casting long shadows from the pines. A breeze stirred the boughs, sending the sweet scent of pine into the night air. Overhead stars glittered above the canyon walls.

McKenzie met his gaze and smiled. "Good for *both* of our businesses, actually. There's a lot of money that has moved into Montana. A Texas barbecue restaurant at Big Sky wouldn't have made it maybe even five years ago. Now, though?" She raised an eyebrow.

"I know you aren't just saying that to sell the building we looked at."

"That building would already be sold if your brother hadn't put down money on it," she said.

Hayes's brow shot up. "Tag put money down on it?"

She realized she'd let the cat out of the bag. "I'm sorry, I got the impression it was his own money and merely to hold it until you could all see it."

"I knew he had his heart set on this, but…" He shook his head as they reached her cabin.

A small lantern-shaped light cast a golden glow from the porch over them and the wooden lattice swing that moved restlessly in the light breeze. Dana and Hud had the half-dozen guest cabins built to look as if they'd been there for a hundred years. They were rustic on the outside but had all the conveniences of home inside.

"I hope you and you brothers can work this out," McKenzie said.

"Me, too."

"Thank you again for everything," she said as she looked past him toward the old two-story ranch house below. "I've loved getting to know some of your family and the horseback ride… Well, I can't tell you how much I needed it, needed all of this."

"You know, Dana said you are welcome to stay as long as you want."

She smiled at that. "That is very sweet of her, but with Tag's wedding just weeks away… No, I need to get back to work."

"I understand. What time is this conference tomorrow?"

McKenzie told him and reluctantly agreed to his following her to her condo and then to the university.

"I hope you didn't think I was trying to strong-arm you into the restaurant site," she said.

He shook his head. "I didn't. McKenzie, I was thinking we should have dinner some night before I return to Texas."

"I would enjoy that."

He waited for her to enter the cabin and turn on a light before he started through the pines to his own cabin. As he walked, he pulled out his cell phone and called his brother Laramie. It was such a beautiful June night and he wasn't tired at all. If anything, he didn't want the night to end. He couldn't remember being this…

For a moment, he didn't recognize the emotion. Happy. He laughed to himself. He felt...happy.

"Tag has his heart set on opening a restaurant here," he said without preamble when his brother Laramie answered.

"We already knew that. What did you think about the location he picked?"

"What is the point of discussing that if we don't want to open one in Montana?" he demanded. "Wait a minute. He called you, didn't he?"

Laramie sighed. "He wanted to make sure I was flying in for the wedding in a few weeks so I could see the site and we could talk. You didn't tell him what we decided, I take it? Is this just a case of you not wanting to play the bad guy?"

"No, I'm actually reconsidering." Hayes told himself it had nothing to do with McKenzie Sheldon and much more to do with Montana. He was falling for the state. He wouldn't be here long enough to fall for the woman, which was another reason not to stay too long. Fate might have thrown them together, but then again, he didn't believe in fate, did he? "Tag made some good points."

"So would the location work?"

"The location is fine. Actually better than fine. And maybe Big Sky is ready for Texas barbecue, but is this really something we want to do? What's next, Wyoming? Minnesota?"

"Tag said that people from all over the world visit Big Sky and a lot of the homeowners have sophisticated tastes."

Hayes laughed. "You aren't really implying that our barbecue requires a sophisticated taste."

"Maybe not, but our beans definitely do."

They both laughed.

"So tell me about his fiancée," Laramie said.

"She's pretty, supersmart, has a great job and owns her own home here in Big Sky. And she's definitely wild about our brother."

"Sounds like our Tag hit a home run."

Hayes sighed. "She's nice, too. I liked her."

"I heard you found a woman up there, as well."

"*Found* being the operative word." Hayes told his brother what had happened.

"Crazy. I thought there wasn't any crime up there."

"Low crime. Not *no* crime." He'd reached his cabin. As he climbed up the steps and sat down on the porch swing, he said, "I'm thinking I might stick around for a while." It surprised him that he'd voiced what had been in the back of his mind.

"So it's like that," Laramie said.

"It's...complicated."

"Be careful, Hayes," his brother warned. "You know what Jackson went through with his marriage."

He did. His wife had left him right after their son was born, only to come back three years later and try to take Ford away from Jackson. "Could you fly up now instead of before the wedding?"

"Not going to happen. Let's remember that I'm the brother who keeps Texas Boys Barbecue Corporation going."

"We never forget that," Hayes said. Laramie was the business major, the brother who'd gladly taken the reins when the business had begun to take off. True, it had grown more than any of them had anticipated since then, but Laramie was still the best brother to be in charge. And there was that added benefit that none of them forgot. Laramie allowed the rest of them to do whatever they wanted, never having to worry about money.

"You know how thankful we all are that you took it on," he said, not that Laramie needed reassurance. His brother loved what he did and continued to make the corporation more than profitable.

"What about Austin?" Hayes had to ask.

Silence, then Laramie said in a worried tone, "He's on a case down by the border. I haven't been able to reach him for several weeks now."

Hayes let out a curse. When Austin got on a case, it was all-consuming. They often went for weeks, even months, with no word from him. He only seemed to take on the most dangerous cases. They'd almost lost him more than once.

"I thought he was working fewer hours for the sheriff's department."

"You know him better than that," Laramie said. "I'm sure he will do everything possible to make the wedding, though."

Hayes sure hoped so, but of the five of them, Austin was the loner of the family and possibly the most stubborn. "When are Jackson and Ford flying in?" He knew Jackson and his five-year-old son wouldn't miss the wedding, even though weddings were the last thing Jackson was interested in attending after his marriage had gone so awry.

"A few days before the wedding. Ford is excited about riding horses at the ranch. Apparently, cousin Dana promised him his own horse while he's up there."

"So what do you want me to do about Tag and the restaurant site?" Hayes asked.

"If you've already weakened, I'd say it was a done deal."

As Hayes disconnected, he thought about walking back to McKenzie's cabin and telling her to get the paperwork for the restaurant site ready. It was pretty much a done deal if Laramie was getting behind it.

But he stayed on his cabin porch. He could tell her tomorrow or maybe even the next day. It would give him an excuse to see her again. Not that he needed one. What was that old Chinese proverb? *He who saves a life is responsible for it.*

The woman brought out his protective instincts. He knew it was because she was so strong, so determined, so capable of taking care of herself under normal circumstances. But the man who'd attacked her had shaken her world and left her afraid and vulnerable.

Hayes told himself that whoever had tried to abduct her in the grocery-store parking lot was probably long gone.

But what if he wasn't? What if it was this man she'd fired?

He swore softly under his breath. It seemed that tomorrow he was going to a huge real-estate conference where a predator could be anyone in the crowd. And to think he'd actually considered leaving his gun in Texas, asking himself, *what were the chances he would need it in Montana?*

CHAPTER SEVEN

THE MOMENT THEY reached what McKenzie called the "field house," a huge, circular, dome-shaped building on the Montana State University campus, Hayes saw the parking lot and knew this was going to be a security nightmare.

As they entered the building, they were surrounded by people, many of them coming up to McKenzie. There were pats on the back, handshakes, people brushing her arm in welcome as she made her way down to the exhibits.

"Are you all right?" McKenzie asked when they finally got to M.K. Realty's booth.

"It's not me I'm worried about."

"You've been scowling since we got here," she said. "Haven't you ever heard of safety in numbers?"

She seemed to be at ease, as if she'd forgotten the attack, but Hayes wasn't fooled. He could see past the bravado. She was putting on a show, determined that her attacker wasn't going to change anything about her life.

But he already had. She either was pretending otherwise or the reality of it hadn't hit home yet.

"Sorry," he said. "I'll try to lighten up. Or at least look as if I have."

She gave him a grateful smile and squeezed his arm. "I really do appreciate that you're here."

Let's see if you do when this day is over, he thought, wondering how he was going to keep her safe in a place this packed with people.

As she had a word with her employees at their booth, he watched the crowd. He had some idea of who he was looking for. A large man, over six feet, strongly built.

He'd had a few cases involving these types of men. While he knew the general type, there were always exceptions. He wasn't going to make the mistake of trying to pigeonhole this one.

The place was filled with men, most of them alone. Any one of these men could be here to hurt McKenzie. The thought rattled him so much that he didn't hear her saying his name. When she touched his arm, he jumped.

She gave him a pleading look. She was trying so hard to hold it together. She didn't need him wigging out on her.

"He could be miles from here," she whispered as she stepped close. He felt her breath on his ear and shivered inwardly. Just the light scent of her perfume had his pulse thrumming.

Today she'd worn a business suit with a white blouse under the jacket that accentuated her olive skin and the thin silver necklace around her neck. At the end of the chain, a small diamond rested between the swell of her breasts. She'd put makeup on the bruises at her neck, hiding them enough that no one would notice. Diamond studs glittered on each of her earlobes with her hair pulled up off her long, slim neck.

She'd chosen a shade of lipstick that called attention to her full mouth. No way could this woman possibly blend into this crowd.

"Are you listening to me?" she asked.

He nodded, although his thoughts had been on the way the suit skirt hugged her shapely behind, dropping below her knees to her long legs and the matching high heels on her feet. McKenzie was the whole package. Any man in his right mind would want this woman.

As it was, somewhere in this building could be a man completely out of his mind who, if he got the chance, would hurt her and bury her in a shallow grave somewhere.

"Why don't you stay here? You'll be able to see me from here." She pointed to a raised area where she would be giving her speech.

Before he could object, she took off through the crowd. He went after her, fighting his way through the throng of people. He caught a glimpse of her head as she neared the platform and knew he wouldn't be able to catch up to her before she was on stage.

McKenzie couldn't help being irritated with Hayes. She needed his strength right now. Seeing the worry in his eyes only made her more aware of what had happened to her two nights ago.

But she'd put it behind her, convinced the man had been traveling through town and was now miles from here.

She cut through the crowd, not stopping even to say hello to people she knew. She was in the people business. It really did matter who you knew when you sold real estate, she was thinking as she neared the side of the raised platform and the podium and microphone waiting for her.

Rows of chairs had been placed in front and were already full. She'd been honored when asked to speak.

Some of the older Realtors resented her because she'd climbed so fast.

She thought of Gus Thompson's mother. She'd been McKenzie's mentor and had taught her the ropes.

"Of course they don't like it," she'd said once when McKenzie had mentioned that some of the Realtors had given her the cold shoulder. "Just keep your chin up and don't lose sight of where it is you want to go."

It had been good advice. She hadn't made enemies along the way and was glad of that. Instead, she'd kept her nose to the grindstone, working hard and now knew she had the respect of her peers. Several of the older Realtors gave her a nod as she passed.

She made her way to the stairs at the back of the platform near the wall and had started up the stairs when her hair was grabbed from behind. Her head jerked back. She heard the sound of something sharp cutting through her hair an instant before the pressure on it was released.

Fighting to keep from falling back down the couple of stairs she'd climbed, she swung around, thinking she must have caught her hair on something.

There were people everywhere but none were paying any attention to her. Nor could she see anything that might have caught in her hair.

Her hand went to her long, blond mane. In the middle of the back of her head she felt a place where a huge chunk of her hair had been chopped off only inches from her scalp.

She looked down to see a few long strands on the stairs along with the clip she'd used to put her hair up this morning.

Her body began to shake. Someone had grabbed her

from behind and chopped off a huge chunk of her hair? It was inconceivable. But then so was what had happened to her the night in the grocery-store parking lot.

On the stage, one of the Realtors was checking the microphone as she got ready to announce the guest speaker.

McKenzie looked again at the people milling past. No one seemed to pay her any mind. No one had a hank of her hair in his hand. But she knew it could have been any one of them.

She quickly stepped back down the stairs to retrieve her clip. Her fingers trembled as she pulled her hair up as best she could and anchored it with the clip.

She could do this. She would do this. She wouldn't be scared off. She wouldn't let whoever had done this win.

SOMETHING WAS WRONG. Hayes watched McKenzie walk onto the stage smiling. But he knew her smile and that wasn't it.

His heart began to pound. He shouldn't have let her out of his sight. The darn woman. She was so stubborn, so sure she could handle this on her own. She hadn't been out of his sight for more than a few moments—not until she'd gone behind the raised platform.

Whatever had happened must have occurred there. But with so many people around…

He watched her walk up to the microphone. He could see her trying to pull herself together. She looked down at her notes. Even from a distance he thought he saw her hands trembling.

She laid her notes down on the podium and leaned toward the microphone. Her voice was clear and true as she looked up at the crowd gathered to hear her speak.

Hayes had admired her, but right now he was in awe of her courage and fortitude. He could practically see the determination in her shoulders, in her voice, in those amazing eyes of hers. She stood there and gave her speech with probably more spirit than she would have if something hadn't happened before she'd stepped up to that microphone.

She was beautiful, a woman to be reckoned with, and Hayes knew he wasn't the only man in the audience who thought so.

When she finished, she was met with applause and even a standing ovation.

She beamed, raising her chin into the air, her eyes bright. The look on her face filling him with fear.

If the man who'd attacked her was somewhere in that crowd watching her, McKenzie was letting him know she wasn't scared of him and that she was far from defeated.

It was the kind of challenge that would only antagonize her attacker—and get her killed.

HAYES WAS WAITING for her as she descended the stairs behind the platform. She saw his expression and had to look away to keep from breaking down. He knew. How, she had no idea.

He took her arm without a word and led her toward the closest exit. She kept a smile on her face, nodding to people she knew. Hayes didn't slow down until he had her out the door and almost to his rental car.

"What happened?" he asked the moment he had her safely in the passenger seat with him behind the wheel.

She reached up and unclipped her hair. It fell past her shoulders except for the part that had been whacked off. She put down the car's visor mirror and got her first look at the damage that had been done.

Hayes let out a curse.

The savagery of the act more than the loss of the hair brought tears to her eyes. "It will grow back. It's just hair."

He let out another oath. "He's telling you that he's not done with you. He's telling you—"

"I know what he's telling me," she snapped as she turned to face him. "It's just hair. He won't get that close to me again."

Hayes pulled off his Stetson and raked a hand through his own hair as if he was too angry to speak.

"You can't give him another chance at you," he said after a moment. "Today? It was too dangerous. You need to cancel your appointments until the police find this guy."

"What I need is a haircut."

His expression softened as he met her gaze. He must have seen how close she was to tears and how badly she was fighting not to cry. "Where do you want me to take you?"

"A friend of mine owns a salon. I'm sure under the circumstances she will be able to squeeze me in."

"After that, we need to talk," he said as he started the car and pulled out of the lot, wondering if her attacker was watching them drive away.

HE PUT THE fistful of McKenzie Sheldon's hair to his nose and smelled the sweet scent. She'd probably shampooed it this morning in the shower. He let himself imagine her standing under the warm spray for a moment. He would never see her like that, arms raised as she gently worked the shampoo into her long, blond hair.

Rubbing the hair between his fingers, he studied it in the light of the men's room. It was hard to know the exact color. Pale summer sun, he thought. Too bad he couldn't show the hair to someone who would know what to call it.

He would keep the hair. Maybe he would tie a ribbon around it. Not even an hour ago, it had been growing on her head. That thought stirred the need within. He ached with it and wasn't sure how much longer he could go without fulfilling it.

Someone came into the men's room. He put the hair into the pocket of his jacket, careful not to let any of it escape. He'd lost some of the strands on the stairs as it was. He didn't want to lose any more.

The idea of cutting her hair hadn't even crossed his mind until he'd grabbed hold of it as she'd started up those stairs. He'd wanted her to stumble. Maybe even fall. He had needed to know if she would recognize him when she saw him. The idea of her falling into his arms was just too mouthwatering to pass up.

He'd told himself that just touching her again would be enough. But then she'd gone behind that platform out of sight of the cowboy she'd come with, the same one, he suspected, who'd saved her at the grocery-store parking lot.

Seeing his chance, he'd grabbed her hair, felt its silky smoothness… He always had his scissors with him, sharpened to a lethal edge. When he'd grabbed her hair, felt it in the fingers of his right hand, his left had gone for the scissors.

At that moment, he'd wanted a piece of her—since

that was all he was going to get until he could catch her alone.

Now, feeling better than he had since the night he'd failed, he left the bathroom one hand deep in the pocket of his jacket where he kept the scissors, the other gently caressing her hair. It was enough for today, he thought, anxious to get out of the building so he could be alone.

Soon, McKenzie Sheldon. Very soon and it will be more than your hair that I have my hands on.

"ARE YOU SURE you don't want me to take your open house today?" Jennifer Robinson asked when McKenzie called the office.

"No, I can handle it, but thanks, Jennifer." She wasn't looking forward to the open house. Someone had tried to scare her yesterday.

Now she looked at her short curly hair in the mirror. Hayes had complimented her hairdo when she'd come out of the salon. "It looks good on you."

She'd always hated her natural curly hair, brushing it straight every morning after her shower. It felt odd, the loss of weight she'd become used to. She raked her hand through the curls and told herself she liked it better short—a lie, one she told herself every time she remembered the sudden feel of her head being pulled back, then the sound of something sharp cutting through her long hair before her head snapped forward again.

It had happened so fast.

And could again, Hayes had reminded her. She knew he was angry with her for taking off yesterday without him with her—and for not hiding out. He didn't want her hosting this open house today. He didn't understand.

She couldn't hide. She refused to let this man take away everything she'd worked so hard for.

"At least come back to the ranch tonight," Hayes had pleaded yesterday after the conference. "I can keep you safe there."

She'd been scared and shaken enough that she'd agreed to go back up the canyon to Cardwell Ranch rather than return to her condo. Her evening had been so relaxing and enjoyable she'd never wanted to leave. Dana's husband, Marshal Hud Savage, had cooked steaks outside on the grill and they'd all eaten on the wide porch to enjoy the beautiful night.

She'd been completely captivated by the Cardwells, especially Hayes. He had an easygoing way about him that appealed to her. It amazed her that she'd thought there was anything threatening about him. It was his eyes. She'd remembered them from the night of the attack. They had been comforting. Just like his words. *You're safe now.*

Only she wasn't.

She reminded herself of that as she drove from Big Sky into Bozeman, determined to get on with her life.

"At least let me take you to your open house," he'd argued.

"You can't be with me 24/7 and I refuse to hide under a rock. He's trying to scare me."

"Until he tries to abduct you again and kill you. McKenzie, he knows who you are."

His last words had sent an icy chill through her. *He knows who you are.*

But she didn't know who he was. He could have been anyone in that crowd yesterday.

Angry with herself for letting her thoughts take that

turn, she told herself she would put the attack behind her. Big words, she thought as she drove up in front of her condo and just sat there, engine running, surprised how hard it was to face going inside. She knew it was crazy. The attack hadn't even happened here. And yet she had the crazy fear that he would be inside, waiting for her....

Getting out of her SUV, she gripped her keys as she made her way to the front door. She noticed her neighbor had already gone to work. A quiet had settled over the four units. She'd picked this condo because of all the pine trees and the creek that meandered past it.

Now, though, the thick pines made her nervous and the babbling stream quickly put her nerves on edge. She got the key into the lock and pushed open the door.

She wasn't sure what she'd expected to find. Maybe the place ransacked. Everything looked exactly as she'd left it. She stepped in. An eerie silence settled around her. She'd always loved coming home. The condo had been decorated simply with light colors that made the rooms feel welcoming. She'd always felt at peace here.

Now, however, she opened her shoulder bag and took out the pepper spray she'd bought yesterday. Holding it, she moved quickly through the two-story condo, checking closets and bathrooms and even under beds until she was sure she was alone.

She was trembling more from fear than from the effort of searching the spacious condo. The fear made her angry with herself. She couldn't keep living like this.

When her cell phone rang, she jumped. Stilling her heart, she took the call. It was her sister.

"How are you doing?" Shawna asked.

"Fine." The lie seemed to catch in her throat. "Not as well as I'd hoped."

"If you need company—"

"No, I'm keeping busy. I have an open house today."

"Work as usual, huh? That's my little sis. Well, if you need anything, you know to call."

"I will. Thank you."

As she hung up, she saw that Gus Thompson had left a message. She braced herself and played it.

"We need to talk. Call me. "

Just the sound of his voice made her stomach ache. What did he think they needed to talk about? And why was he so insistent? She still couldn't believe he was the man who'd attacked her, but maybe she just didn't want to. She'd worked with him for years. Surely she would have known he was dangerous, wouldn't she?

McKenzie quickly showered and changed for her open house, determined not to let Gus or anyone else keep her from her work. She had a business to run. She had to go over everything she needed, afraid that as distracted as she was, she would forget something important. The open house needed to go off just right. This was a major sale for a contractor she liked working with, so she hoped to get an offer before the day was out.

Hurrying so she could get to the house early, she exited her front door and was just pulling the door closed after her when the man stepped out of the shadows.

HAYES SWUNG BY the restaurant site before heading to McKenzie's open house. He wanted to see the traffic flow in the area and take another look around. The other day, he'd been distracted and determined they weren't buying the space. But after talking to his brother Laramie, he'd tried to reach Austin. He'd been told that Austin was on a case and couldn't be reached. He couldn't help worrying about him.

He felt at loose ends. His attempt to talk McKenzie out of hosting the open house today had fallen on deaf ears. Did she really think that by pretending none of this was happening it would stop this bastard? All she had to do was look in the mirror to see just how close the man had gotten to her—again.

He'd been shocked last night after dinner when she'd told him about the open house, but he'd tried not to argue with her. He'd seen the way she could dig her heels in. Look at what had happened yesterday. Maybe his concern *had* put her in more danger. He was determined not to let that happen again.

"Can't someone else host it?" he'd suggested.

"I could get someone else to do it, but…I can't." She'd shrugged as if it was hard to explain.

"I get it," he'd said. "You're like my brother Laramie. We've offered to help with the load, but…"

"He has it handled."

"Yep, and he does a fine job of it. I noticed that you own your realty company." She was young to have accomplished so much so quickly. He wondered if she'd had help and decided not. It was that tenacity about her that intrigued him. But also frustrated him because her determination not to let her attacker interfere with her life put her in danger.

"It was a lot of hard work, but when you want something badly enough…" Her voice had dropped off and he'd realized she was thinking about the man she'd fought off repeatedly the night of her attack. Neither would have given up. If Hayes hadn't come out of the store when he had…

"What kind of open house is it?" he'd asked to derail her thoughts—and his own.

"A brand-new, state-of-the-art, spacious, three-thousand-square-foot executive home overlooking Bozeman with beautiful views of the Spanish Peaks."

He'd laughed and she'd joined him. He was glad she could laugh at herself.

"I did sound like a Realtor, didn't I?" She sighed. "Bad habit."

"Let me guess. All restaurant-quality appliances and granite countertops in the massive kitchen. I had the flu recently and found myself watching some of those home shows on television. Talk about over the top."

She'd nodded in agreement. "You do see a lot of… extravagance in some of the homes in this area, too. Gold faucets, heated driveways, dual master suites."

"You love what you do," he'd said as if he'd just seen it.

She'd smiled, tears in her eyes. "That's why I can't let him stop me."

"Or me stop you," he'd said, and she'd nodded before she'd leaned over and gently placed a kiss on his cheek.

Their eyes met and locked and for one breath-stealing moment he'd almost taken her in his arms, even though he knew he wanted a lot more than a kiss. Fortunately, or unfortunately, they'd been interrupted by the kids running in to say good-night as they headed to bed.

The moment had been lost, filling him with regret and relief at the same time. His life was in Houston. He reminded himself of that now.

Determined to get at least the barbecue joint settled,

he called Jackson. Ford answered the phone. The five-year-old sounded so grown-up. Hayes tried to remember the last time he'd seen his nephew. It had been too long, that was for sure.

"Hey, kid," he said. "What have you been up to?"

Ford was a chatterbox on the phone. Hayes listened to stories about sports, the trouble his nephew had gotten into and how they would be flying to Montana for his uncle Tag's wedding to some girl before Ford launched into an excited story about the horse Dana had picked out for him to ride once he got to Montana.

Finally, Hayes had to ask if he could speak to the boy's father.

Jackson came on the line.

"How much of that can I believe?" Hayes joked.

His brother laughed. "Ford's into Texas tall tales I'm afraid, just like his uncles. What's this I hear about Laramie supporting the Montana restaurant?"

"I talked to him last night. Tag's convinced him. I have to admit, I've weakened, as well."

"What about this future bride?"

Hayes could hear the concern in Jackson's voice. He'd gotten burned badly. He didn't want to see his brother Tag go through a divorce.

"She's nice. I liked her. She's got plenty of her own money, a good job, a nice house up on the mountain behind Big Sky. Clearly, they are crazy about each other."

Jackson snorted. He knew crazy.

"I'm standing in front of the restaurant space right now. I think we should move ahead with this."

Jackson sounded surprised. "What changed your mind?"

"I actually think it's a good business decision. Also, I guess I want to do this for Tag."

"Is everyone else in agreement?"

"Can't reach Austin. Nothing new there." But he figured Austin would go along with whatever was decided. He had little interest in the business, too involved in being a sheriff's deputy and saving the world.

"As long as Tag's new wife isn't involved in the business in any way, I'm good with it," Jackson said. "I still have time to meet her and see what I think before he can get the place open."

No one was more cynical than Jackson.

"I think this is the right thing to do," Hayes said, checking his watch. "I'll tell the Realtor when I see her."

GUS WAS GLAD he'd scared her. He took enjoyment in McKenzie's shock and fear. How did she think he felt being interrogated by the police and suddenly out of a job?

"Gus." She said his name on a frightened breath, her hand going to her chest as she stumbled back against her closed condo door.

He'd seen her lock it so he knew she wasn't going to be able to get back inside away from him until he had his say. He closed the distance, forcing her up against the door, towering over her. She'd cut her hair. It surprised him. He'd always thought she liked it long. He wondered what had precipitated this? Out with the old, in with the new? Had she already replaced him at the agency?

"What do you want?" Her voice actually squeaked. Where was that ball-breaking woman he'd worked for the past six years?

"What do I *want?*" he repeated. "I want to know why you're ruining my life."

Some of her steel returned to her voice. "This isn't the place to talk about this."

He laughed. "Where would that place be, McKenzie? You've taken out a restraining order against me so I can't go near the office or you."

Some of the color came back into her face. "It should be obvious why I had to do that."

"Because you think I'm some kind of psycho? Do you really think I attacked you in a grocery parking lot?"

"I don't know. Were you at the conference yesterday?"

"Why? Were you attacked again?" He smirked. "Do you really think I can show my face at a real-estate conference right now?"

He could tell she didn't believe him. "I thought I saw you there."

"Well, you were wrong. The same way you were wrong to fire me."

"I'm sure I wasn't the first person you've stalked. You've been harassing my receptionist. I told you that if I had to warn you again…"

He looked at her in disbelief. "Maybe I was *interested* in you, did you ever consider that? I came by your house that day to ask you out, but about the time I finally got up my nerve, you saw me. Your expression… Well, let's just say I knew my answer."

The woman he'd known was back. Anger flared in her eyes. She moved away from the door, forcing him to take a step back. "It's too bad you didn't take no from Cynthia."

He felt off-balance, something she'd made him feel way too many times. "I don't expect you to believe this, but she led me on. She liked me flirting with her."

"Up to a point, I'm sure that was true."

"And yet you fired *me*."

"It was a combination of things, Gus, not just a couple of incidents and you know it. You've always resented working for me."

He nodded, finally seeing it. His own anger boiled to the surface. "You were just waiting for my mother to die so you could get rid of me. As long as she was alive, you wouldn't dare."

"That isn't true." McKenzie looked at her watch, dismissing him. The old McKenzie Sheldon, businesswoman, had come back. "You're going to make me late for an open house and there really is no point to this discussion. I'm not changing my mind. If you promise to leave me alone in the future, I will write you a recommendation, not that you need one. You're a great salesman. Just stop trying to sell yourself to women who aren't in the market."

"That's it?"

"You brought this on yourself, Gus." She slipped past him.

He had no choice but to let her go. As he watched her drive away, he felt as if she'd punched him in the gut. He knew the best thing he could do was leave her alone, take the recommendation and start looking for another job.

But this still felt unfinished to him.

HE STOOD OUTSIDE the open house for a moment, wondering who could afford such a home—and what the commission would net McKenzie Sheldon. Probably more money than he made in months. He would never admit that that alone made him want to hurt this woman. The woman was obviously very successful. It would seem small of him to want to destroy her simply out of jealousy.

But a part of him had to admit, he liked to target successful women. He liked bringing them down. He smiled to himself, thinking how many of them he had made beg for their lives. They weren't so arrogant and sure of themselves then.

People were coming in and out of the open house. Beautiful June days probably brought more people out than stormy, wintery ones, he thought. He waited and fell behind a group of five. Being a salesman at heart himself, he quickly sized them up. The elderly married couple looked serious about home buying. The two women behind them were just gawkers. The lone man who'd led the way looked like another Realtor.

Once inside, he cut away from the others. The elderly couple made a beeline for McKenzie and the flyer she was handing out. He only got a glimpse of her. The last thing he wanted to do was get caught staring at her.

His plan had worked beautifully. He would wait until there were a lot of other people going through the house so he blended in. But at some point, he would have to get close enough to McKenzie Sheldon so he could look into her eyes and find out whether or not she recognized him.

Even a hint of recognition and he would get out of there. The best plan was to park a few blocks away and walk. Not that he expected her to chase him out to his car. Or even scream.

The house was no surprise. Every room was large and over the top with expensive features and furnishings. He wandered around, saw the older couple inspecting the fixtures and heard the two women oohing and ahhing over the kitchen.

As spacious as the house was, he felt claustrophobic and knew he couldn't take much more of this. He was working up his nerve to return to the main entrance and get one of the brochures from Ms. Sheldon, when he came around a corner and almost collided with her.

She pretended the encounter hadn't startled her, but he'd seen the terror flash in her eyes. Nice eyes, more green than blue today. Those eyes widened and for just a moment, he feared she'd recognized him. She was blocking the hallway and his way out. A fissure of panic raced along his nerve endings. Perspiration dampened his shirt and hairline.

He told himself that if she opened her mouth, he'd hit her. There wasn't anyone else around. He'd punch her hard enough to knock her out and then he'd push her into one of the bedrooms and leave quickly. He balled up one fist and took a breath.

But she didn't scream. The flash of terror had only lasted an instant then she'd looked relieved and relaxed a little.

"Sorry," she said. "You startled me."

Not as much as I did a few nights ago. He looked right into those aquamarine waters. Not even a hint of recognition. He almost laughed since just an instant before he'd been planning to knock her senseless and make his escape.

"I'm sorry," he said. "We both must have been distracted."

"How do you like the house?" she asked, covering her initial reaction to him.

"It's beautiful." *Just like you.* She blew him away. She was much more striking than her photo on the real-estate signs. There was a sweetness about her. Strength? Oh, he knew her strength and her determination only too well. Sweet, strong and successful—his perfect woman.

"You might want one of these." She held out a flyer.

"Yes," he said and smiled. "Thank you. Oh, and do you have a business card?"

She brightened. "Of course. I usually have one stapled to the flyers. I forgot this morning. I have one in my purse if you'd like to follow me." She headed back toward the entrance. He followed her, admiring the part of her body he had some history with.

From under an entertainment counter, she pulled out her purse, removed a business card and handed it to him. The card was thick, nicely embossed. He rubbed it gently between his fingers. A business card told a lot about a person.

He carefully put it into his shirt pocket and folded the flyer she'd given him.

"Is there anything else I can help you with?" she asked.

"No, I think I have everything." He smiled. "But you'll be hearing from me."

McKenzie was just about to ask the man for his name when the front door opened and her attention was drawn away as she saw Hayes Cardwell come through the door.

A mixture of pleasure and relief filled her at the sight of the big cowboy. He wore jeans, a Western shirt and a gray Stetson over his longish dark hair. Unlike yesterday, he looked more relaxed.

Almost instinctively, she started to move toward him, but remembered the man who'd shown an interest in the house. She turned her attention back to him. "I look forward to hearing from you if you have any questions about the house or would like to see any others."

"Next time, I'd like to bring my wife along. I'll give you a call," the man said, glancing at Hayes before he quickly moved off.

McKenzie turned to Hayes. She always felt she had to be "on" at open houses. Even though she loved her job, sometimes it wasn't just her high-heeled shoes that made her hurt. Her face often ached from smiling so much.

"Decided you wanted a kitchen with all stainless-steel appliances and granite countertops?"

"Can't imagine living without them."

She chuckled at that. "You're saying you don't have them at your house in Houston?"

"I live in an unremodeled house in the older part of Houston."

She cocked an eyebrow at that.

"I have…humble tastes."

"Nothing wrong with that," she said. "Excuse me a moment." McKenzie saw a few more people she needed to talk to before they left. The elderly couple sounded interested. She gave them her business card. As she started to go look for Hayes, she saw the man she'd spoken to earlier before Hayes had come in.

The man was walking away when he suddenly stopped and turned to look back at her as if he'd known she'd be there framed in the front window, watching him. He gave a slow, vague kind of smile. She quickly stepped back out of sight, even though she feared he'd seen her. His smile had almost been mocking, as if he'd put one over on her.

She'd dealt with enough people at open houses that she had a pretty good sense of who was genuinely in the market for a house and who wasn't. The man had seemed interested and yet he hadn't asked any questions about the house—unlike the elderly couple. Maybe he *had* just been putting her on.

McKenzie went to find Hayes, annoyed with the man and herself. He might have fooled her once, but she would be watching for him at her next open house.

HAYES LOOKED AROUND the large residence, killing time until the open house was over. Several men came through. Any one of them could have been McKenzie's attacker.

At four o'clock, he found McKenzie finishing up with a couple and waited as she packed up to leave.

"Dinner. You name the restaurant," he said.

"I really should—"

"Work?" He saw her hesitate. "I figured since we both need to eat…"

She brushed a lock of hair back from her face. She'd dressed up for the open house, taking extra pains with her appearance. Probably to give herself more confidence. But under the surface, he would see that she was still running scared.

"Hayes, I appreciate what you're trying to do…."

"*Eat?* I like to do it three times a day, if possible."

"You know what I mean." She sighed. "You can't

protect me forever, especially since you will be leaving soon."

He nodded. "So that must mean I'm just hungry, don't you think?"

She laughed. "Are you always so determined?"

"Always." He led the way out of the house and waited while she locked up. "By the way, how long do we have on that restaurant space at Big Sky?"

"Changed your mind?" she asked as they walked toward their vehicles.

"Tag isn't changing *his* mind." They'd reached his rented SUV. "Why don't you leave your car," he suggested. "I'll be happy to bring you back after dinner."

"Okay. Just let me put my things away."

He watched her put the flyers in the passenger seat and helped her place the Open House signs in the trunk. But as they finished, he noticed her look past him and frown. He turned but didn't see anything out of the ordinary.

"Is everything all right?" he asked.

"Hmm," she said distractedly. "Just someone I saw earlier at the open house. He must live in the neighborhood. It's nothing."

They ate a nice dinner, talked about everything but her attacker. Not that it kept the man from being present. Hayes doubted the attack was ever far from either of their minds.

He'd hoped McKenzie would be staying in the cabin at Cardwell Ranch, but she couldn't hide out, given her career. Not that a woman like her would let herself hide out forever, anyway, and the man might never be caught. Still, he didn't like the idea of McKenzie staying in her condo alone.

He'd told his brother he was staying until the wedding. It was only a few weeks away and if they were going ahead with the restaurant, he could help out. At least that was his excuse. In truth, he couldn't leave McKenzie. Not yet, even though she was right. He couldn't stay forever. Maybe it was best for her to start adjusting to living with never knowing when the man might reappear in her life.

"Dinner was wonderful," she said as they left the restaurant. "And a great idea."

"Thanks. I'm just full of great ideas," he said with a chuckle. "Like this one. I wish you would come back up to the ranch tonight."

She shook her head as he pulled up behind her car where they'd left it earlier for the open house. With the houses so far apart, the neighborhood was dark in the huge spaces between streetlamps. No lights burned in the house she'd shown earlier. With the houses bordered by tall, dense trees or high hedges, there were lots of places for a man to hide, he thought.

How many houses just like this did she show alone? He hated to think. In other places, he'd heard that real-estate agents now worked in twos to be safer. But this was Montana. People felt safe here.

"Thank you for the offer," she said. "I appreciate it, but I have a lot to do tomorrow."

He nodded, not surprised.

She opened her car door. "Have your brother give me a call about the restaurant space."

So that was how it was going to be? Business as usual? The woman was stubborn as a mule. She refused to take some time off, leave the state or at least town for a while. There was no way he could keep her safe and he couldn't just walk away.

He got out and caught up to her, catching her hand to turn her toward him. "I have a favor." She raised a brow. "I need a date for the wedding."

"Your brother's wedding?"

"Yes."

She shook her head. "I'm not your responsibility. I told you, you can't keep me safe."

"It's more complicated than that," he said as he touched her cheek. "From the moment I first looked in your eyes..." His words died off. She was staring at him. He shook his head. "Maybe I can't get you out of my mind—"

"I know what you're up to."

"I doubt that," he said, and leaned toward her, his hand looping around the back of her neck as he gently drew her to him. "Because if you could see what I was up to, then you'd know I was about to kiss you."

He brushed his lips over hers, then pulled back to gaze into her eyes. He'd been captivated by those eyes two nights ago. That hadn't changed. "Sorry, I couldn't resist."

"You don't have to treat me as if I'm made out of glass and might break," she said. "I'm a little battered right now, but I'm resilient and strong, a lot stronger than I look."

"Is that right?" He looped an arm around her waist and pulled her to him right there in the street between their vehicles. He kissed her like he meant it this time. Her full lips parted in surprise. Her sweet, warm breath comingled with his own. She let out a soft moan as he tasted her. Drawing her even closer, he deepened the kiss, demanding more.

McKenzie came to him, fitting into his arms as she answered his kiss with passion. He felt desire race in a hot streak through his veins. He didn't want to ever stop kissing her.

But when she pulled back, he let out a shaky breath. "Wow," he said and laughed.

She sounded just as breathless. She met his gaze in the moonlight. "Hayes, what is this?"

"*This?* This is crazy. Worst possible timing ever."

McKenzie nodded agreement.

"And yet, from the first moment I looked into your eyes…"

She shook her head. "I…I really can't…. Hayes, I'm not sure of anything right now and quite frankly, I'm suspicious of your motives."

"My motives for kissing you? It was just a kiss, right?"

She studied him openly in the dim light.

"Quite the kiss, though, wouldn't you say?" he asked, grinning.

She smiled at that. "Quite the kiss."

"Glad you agree. I'm still going to follow you home and make sure you're all right."

She looked as if she wanted to put up a fight, but no longer had the energy to. "Thank you," she said as she turned and started for her car. He watched her. She seemed a little wobbly on her high heels, strange for a woman who lived in them. He hoped the kiss had smacked her silly the way it had him. He'd kissed his share of women, but none had lit a fire in him the way McKenzie's kiss had.

As she reached the car, she hesitated. He saw her glance back at him, then reach for something on her windshield. His pulse leaped. Something was wrong. He was running toward her as she took what looked like a folded sheet of paper from under the wiper blade.

CHAPTER EIGHT

MCKENZIE HAD BEEN shaken even before she found the note. The kiss had her whirling. It had been a while since a man had kissed her. She couldn't recall anyone who'd made her surrender so completely to a kiss before, though. She'd felt...*wanton,* and that wasn't a word she would have used about herself. She'd also felt out of control and that scared her.

Hayes had her blood running hot. He'd sparked something in her that made her ache for more. That alone was enough to turn her already crazy world upside down. She'd been content with her career, with her life, with an occasional date. Hayes had changed all that in just one kiss. Now she wanted...Hayes Cardwell. Bad timing or not.

But she questioned whether he was interested in her as a woman. Or if he was just hardwired to protect the woman whose life he'd saved because he was a Texas cowboy and a gentleman.

When she'd found the note under her windshield wiper, at first she'd thought it was an advertisement.

Instead, scrawled words had been written on the sheet of paper.

I'm watching you.
This time you won't get away.
I am going to miss your long hair.

The paper began to shake in her fingers. She had *felt* him watching her. It hadn't been her imagination. He was out there and he wasn't through with her.

She read the words again, all easily visible in the diffused light from the closest streetlamp. All her bravado fell away. The man wasn't giving up. He was out there. Maybe even watching her right now, wanting to see her fall apart.

McKenzie slumped against her car as she looked out into the darkness, unable to pretend any longer that she wasn't terrified. She'd thought she could go on as if nothing had happened. As if nothing kept happening.

Suddenly, Hayes was at her side, his arms coming around her. "What is it?" His gaze took in the sheet of paper trembling in her fingers. Using his sleeve, he took it from her. "Get in my car. I'll call the police."

She nodded and started for his rental SUV. Earlier, she'd told him how strong and resilient she was. She didn't feel either right now. She wanted to lose herself in his strong arms. For so long she'd made her way alone, determined not to lean on anyone, not to need anyone. Right now, she needed Hayes—and more than just to protect her.

Behind her, she heard him on the phone. Her gaze swept through the dark neighborhood. A breeze stirred the tree boughs, throwing shadows everywhere. Was he out there watching her? Enjoying tormenting her?

McKenzie quickened her step, grabbed the passenger-side door handle and flung it open. She practically threw herself into the car, slamming the door behind her. Heart pounding, she tried to catch her breath. Anger mixed with fear, a deadly combination that had her wiping furiously at her tears.

She'd never felt helpless before. It was a horrible feeling, one she couldn't bear. Somehow, she had to make it end, and falling into bed with Hayes wasn't the answer as much as she would have liked to.

As Hayes finished his call and climbed into the SUV behind the wheel, she turned to him. "I have to find this man."

"I've called the police. They're on their way. They'll see if they can get a print off—"

"He won't have left fingerprints on the note he left for me. He's too smart for that." She shook her head. "Nor do I believe the police will find him. That's why I have to."

Hayes stared across the seat at her. "What are you saying?"

"I need to set a trap for him."

He held up a hand. "Hold on."

"No, I can't let him continue to torment me. I have to find him and put an end to this, one way or another."

HAYES DIDN'T KNOW how to tell her, but decided honesty might be the best approach. "I would imagine he will find you before you find him." He saw her reaction to his words. "He's fooling with you because you made a fool of him the other night. He has only one option. He needs to right this. Which means there's a really good chance that he isn't some psycho passing through town who just happened to see you the other night. He's a hometown psycho who isn't finished with you."

Her lower lip quivered for a moment before she bit down on it. "You sound as if you've dealt with this kind of...person before."

He nodded. "I've crossed paths with several. They're

calculating, cunning and unpredictable—and extremely dangerous."

She leaned toward him and he was reminded of their kiss. He could smell her clean scent and remembered the feel of her in his arms. "Help me set a trap for him. I don't want to wait until it's on his terms."

"It's not that easy—"

McKenzie drew back. "I'm sorry. I shouldn't have asked. You have your brother's wedding and you're leaving town—"

"Do you really think I can leave you now?" He thought of that strange feeling the moment he'd looked into her eyes three nights ago—not to mention the kiss just moments before. He took her hands in his, reveling at the touch of her skin against his. This woman made him feel things he'd never felt before, never dreamed he would ever feel.

"I can't let you go after this man alone. I'm staying until I know you're safe." He wasn't sure he could leave even then and that scared him more than he wanted to admit.

He thought of his brother Tag coming to Montana for Christmas and falling for Lily. Now Tag was getting married and talking about settling in Big Sky. Hayes had thought his brother was nuts to leave behind everything like that.

Hayes felt as if his head were spinning. All he knew for sure was that he had to protect this woman—whatever it took. He couldn't think beyond that, didn't dare.

"I won't be safe as long as he's out there. You said so yourself. I don't see that I have a choice."

A car turned onto the street. The headlights washed

over them. Hayes glanced in his rearview mirror as the cop car pulled up behind them.

Hayes didn't have a choice, either. He leaned over and kissed her quickly before climbing out with the note that had been left on her windshield. Like her, he doubted there would be fingerprints on it. Just as he doubted the police would be able to find this man, given how little they had to go on.

The only thing Hayes didn't doubt was that the psycho would be coming for McKenzie.

THE POLICE OFFICER bagged the note her attacker had left and promised to let her know if they found any prints. McKenzie could see that Hayes wasn't holding out any more hope than she was.

The cop walked around the neighborhood, shone his flashlight into the bushes and trees, but to no one's surprise, found nothing.

"He's right," Hayes said after the officer left and he walked her back to her car. "The best thing you can do right now would be to take a long vacation somewhere far away from here."

They stood under Montana's big sky. Millions of stars glittered over their heads and a cool, white moon now buoyed along among them. The June night had turned crisp and cool. This far north even summer nights could chill you. Especially if there was a killer on the loose.

"Do you really think the man would forget about me?" She didn't give him a chance to answer because they both knew that answer. "I can't run away. I would always be looking over my shoulder. No, I have to end this here and soon."

Hayes groaned. "How did I know you were going to say that?"

She shrugged and met his gaze, losing herself in his dark eyes. It would have been easy to get on a plane with him and go to Texas and pretend none of this had happened.

But it *had* happened. Not to mention, she had a business here, people who were counting on her. She wasn't going anywhere—not that Hayes had given her the Texas option to begin with.

She felt strangely calmer as she leaned against the side of her car and looked at the Texas cowboy standing by her. Once she'd settled down enough so she could actually think clearly, she'd made the decision quickly— just as she'd done with her business.

She couldn't wait around for this horrible man to try to abduct her again and do nothing. If Hayes wouldn't help her, then she would figure out something on her own. She'd been on her own and done all right. She wasn't going to let one crazy psycho change that.

"I have another open house tomorrow." She held up her hand before Hayes could argue. "As you said, he knows who I am. He also knows where I am going to be. For all I know he was one of the people who came through the house earlier. I could have talked to him." She shuddered at the thought and hugged herself.

"I wouldn't be at all surprised that he was one of the men who came through today," Hayes said. "Seeing you feeds whatever it is that drives him. He likes seeing you scared. He'll play with you until he's ready to make his move, until an opportunity presents itself."

She was no fool. She was still scared, but knowing that the man wanted her scared made her determined not to let her fear hold her back. "So you're saying it could be a while before he makes his move?"

"Possibly. Unless you give him the opportunity he needs—like at an open house. You do realize this is speculation based on what I know about men like this. As I said earlier, they're unpredictable. I could be completely off base. There is no way to know what he will do next."

She nodded, considering this. "He feels safe because I didn't see his face the night he attacked me. If you're right about what drives him, he won't be able to stay away."

Hayes took off his Stetson and raked a hand through his thick, dark hair. She recalled the feel of those fingers when he'd taken the nape of her neck in his hand during their kiss.

"If you're determined to do this, then I'm staying down here in the valley tonight. I'm also going to the open house tomorrow," Hayes said.

She shook her head. "He won't make his move as long as you're around."

He stuffed his hat back down on his head and stepped to her to take her shoulders in his hands. "He's just waiting for the chance to get you alone again. He will make that happen with or without me around because he knows I can't watch you all the time. I'll be there tomorrow, like it or not."

McKenzie knew she didn't have the strength to tackle this tonight. "All right," she agreed. She had mixed feelings about having Hayes around. On one hand she would definitely feel safer, but he was a distraction she couldn't afford right now. She had to think clearly.

"He'll come to the open house tomorrow."

Hayes nodded in agreement. "That would be my guess. He's trying to build up his confidence. Being around you and you not knowing how close he is…well, that will make him feel more in control."

"Is there any way to get photos of everyone who comes through the open house?"

"Consider it done. I'll also talk to the police about running the license plates of those who show up."

She smiled at him. "I do appreciate what you're trying to do to keep me safe." She sobered as she looked into his handsome face. "I don't like involving you in this. If this man is as dangerous as we both suspect—"

"Don't worry about me. I'll follow you to your condo. But first let me check your car."

McKenzie watched him look under and around her car before popping the hood and checking the engine. "You can't think he'd put a bomb under my hood."

"Not really. But I do think he might disable your car so it stalls on the way to your condo and while you're trying to figure out what is wrong…"

She got the idea. Distraction. That's how she'd fallen into the man's snare the first time. A memory of the dark night at the grocery-store parking lot flashed before her. She'd been fiddling with her keys, her mind on the phone call and Gus. Gus, she thought with a silent curse. Maybe she should have called the police after she found him on her doorstep at the condo. Was this note merely him trying to scare her? Or was it from the man who'd tried to abduct her?

As she looked out into the darkness, McKenzie wasn't sure who would be caught in the trap she hoped to set for her would-be abductor. Whoever he was, she didn't feel him out there watching her. But he had been there. A psycho who, for whatever reason, had set his sights on her.

AT HER CONDO, McKenzie unlocked the door while Hayes surveyed the neighborhood. He hated that there were too many places for a man to hide. Also, because Bozeman was so small, he had to assume that the man knew where she lived.

He had McKenzie remain by the door until he could check to make sure they were alone in the condo. The place was neat and clean and sparsely furnished. He got the feeling that she didn't spend much time here other than to sleep.

The lower floor consisted of a kitchen, dining room, living room and half bath. Upstairs he found a full bath and two bedrooms. Just the right size for a single woman who worked all the time.

"Can you tell if anyone has been here?" he asked her when he returned to where he'd left her downstairs just inside the door.

She glanced around, clearly startled by the question. "I don't think so. How would he have gotten in?"

"I didn't see any forced entry, but if the man is someone you know and has access to your keys..."

"You mean like an old boyfriend?" She shook her head. "No one has a key to my condo. Nor can I recall anyone having access to my keys."

"Good." He met her gaze. "Do you own a weapon?"

She swallowed and looked uncomfortable. "I have pepper spray, Hayes." His name seemed to come of its own volition. She appeared surprised as if she, too, had just realized that she'd never said it before. "I also have a spare bedroom, if you want to..." She looked away.

"Thanks," he said without hesitation. He was planning to stay, whether she liked it or not.

"The spare bedroom—"

"I know where it is," he said.

She nodded. "I can't take being afraid all the time."

"We'll find him." Even as he said it, Hayes hoped he wasn't promising something he couldn't deliver. He *would* find him, but before the man got to McKenzie? That was what worried him.

She glanced at her watch. "Would you like a drink? I could use one." She headed for the kitchen.

He followed. As she pulled out a bottle of wine from the refrigerator, he said, "I'm going to need to know about everyone who came through the open house today—at least all of them you can remember. Do you have something I can write on?"

She poured them each a glass of wine before removing a notebook and pen from the small desk in the corner of the kitchen. They sat down in the living room on furniture that felt and smelled new. He doubted she had many—if any—guests over, including men. No time to date, he suspected.

That also explained why the man who had attacked her had chosen her. A businesswoman with a lot on her mind. She was a classic case of the perfect female victim. Had the man been following her? Or had he picked her at random? Hayes wished he knew. It would help find the bastard.

"Okay, from when the first person came in after you got to the open house…"

She nodded, took a sip of her wine and began to go through them. He quickly weeded out the women and most of the couples.

"There was that one man near the end..." She stared thoughtfully into space for a moment. "You might have seen him. I was talking to him when you arrived."

Hayes recalled a tall man with a head of thick, brown hair and light-colored eyes. He looked like a former football player. In fact, Hayes recalled wondering if the man had played for the Bobcats while attending Montana State University. He'd been wearing a Bobcat jacket.

"Early forties, big, not bad-looking?"

She nodded. "He seemed interested in the house—until I saw him later when he was leaving."

Hayes frowned. "What changed your mind?"

"You're going to think I'm silly, but he hadn't driven to the open house. I realized he must live in the neighborhood."

"He could have parked some distance away."

She nodded. "I suppose, but as I was watching him walk away, he seemed to sense me watching him and turned. It was his expression... This is where you're going to think I'm nuts, but he turned to look back, right at me as if he knew I would be there watching him, and the look on his face..." She took a drink of her wine. "It was as if he'd put something over on me."

Hayes felt a fissure of unease move through him. "You think it could have been the man who attacked you?"

"He was big enough." She shook her head. "I don't know. He mentioned that he had a wife."

"Probably to put you at ease."

"Maybe. It's just that he seemed...nice, gentle even, almost shy."

"Ted Bundy seemed the same way to *his* victims."

MCKENZIE FINISHED HER wine and poured them both another glass. "Why would he take a chance like that, not just coming to the open house, but actually talking to me?"

"Maybe he wanted to see if you recognized him."

She cupped the wineglass in her hand as she felt a shudder move through her. "Is it possible I was that close to him again and I didn't know it?" That alone terrified her. Could she really not sense the danger?

"It's why the cops take video of people at crime scenes and funerals. Criminals like to return to the scene of the crime. In your case, be close to one of their victims."

"He is safe—until he tries to abduct me again." She shivered. "If he doesn't try again, he'll have gotten away with it." She felt her eyes suddenly widened in alarm. "There have been others, haven't there?"

"More than likely. But that can help. If we find out who this man is, maybe we can place him wherever those other abductions took place."

"You think he *killed* them."

Hayes didn't answer. He didn't have to. "I'm sure the police are looking into other abductions or missing persons around the area.... I'll check with them tomorrow. Tell me about tomorrow's open house."

"It's out in the country. It's fairly...isolated."

"Then I'm definitely going to be there. Don't worry, I'll be discreet. You won't even know I'm around. I'll want to go out earlier than you. Will you be going to your office in the morning even though it's a Sunday?"

"Yes. My job isn't eight to five. Nor five days a week."

"Neither is mine, so I get it," he said, and finished

his wine. His gaze met hers and she felt that bubble of excitement rise inside her, along with a longing that she knew only this man could fill. She wanted him, but not like this. Maybe once this was over...

As if sensing her thoughts, he said, "It's late. We should get some rest." He got to his feet.

"The bed is made up in the spare room. There are towels in the bathroom cabinet...."

"Thank you. I'm sure I have everything I need."

Wasn't that what the man at the open house had said?

Hayes met her gaze. "I'll be right down the hall if you need me."

She nodded. She *did* need him. It was that need that kept her silent as she watched him head upstairs. She heard him go into the bathroom and turn on the shower. She could hear water running and closed her eyes at the thought of Hayes naked in her shower. The Texas cowboy had done something no other man had. He'd reminded her she was a woman, a woman with needs other than her career.

McKenzie poured herself another glass of wine, finishing off the bottle. Normally, she had only one glass before bedtime. Tonight, she didn't mind indulging. Better to indulge in wine than in what she would have liked to indulge in. Her life was complicated enough without getting any more involved with Hayes Cardwell than she already was.

The wine made her feel lightheaded. Or was that her fantasies? Upstairs, Hayes came out of the bathroom. She heard him walk down the hall to the spare bedroom. She waited for him to close the door, but he didn't.

Shutting her eyes, she tried not to think about him lying in bed just down the hall from her own bedroom.

A wild yearning raced through her as out of control as a wildfire. Her need quickly became a burning desire as it mixed with the wine already coursing through her veins.

McKenzie had always prided herself on thinking logically. She assessed every situation, looked at it from every angle then made a decision based on the facts—not emotion.

With Hayes, she knew she wasn't thinking rationally. She wanted him, needed him, like no man she'd ever met.

But she wouldn't act on it. Couldn't. At least until the crazy after her was caught. Even then, she wasn't sure she could let herself go. She'd been so wrapped up in her business that she hadn't given much thought to men. Now she couldn't stop thinking about Hayes Cardwell, but she would force herself to. She needed her wits about her and if she gave in to whatever this was between them... The thought made her ache.

She wouldn't let herself go there.

Feeling on moral high ground, she took the empty bottle and the glasses into the kitchen. She tossed the bottle in the trash and hand-washed the glasses, dried them and put them away before she went up to bed. Alone.

Hayes woke to the sound of a phone ringing. He'd had a devil of a time getting to sleep, knowing McKenzie was just down the hall—and that there was a psychopath out there after her. If the man who'd come to the open house was her attacker, then he was definitely brazen. He was practically daring them to catch him.

The phone rang again. He heard McKenzie fumbling to answer it.

"Hello?"

Silence.

"Hello, who is this?"

Hayes was out of bed and down the hall to her room in a matter of a few strides. He reached for the phone. She handed it to him, those amazing eyes of hers wide and terrified. All the color had drained from her face and the hand that relinquished the phone had trembled.

He could hear heavy breathing as he put the phone to his ear. The man on the other end of the line chuckled softly. To his surprise, McKenzie jumped out of bed and ran to the window.

"Who is this?" Hayes demanded.

The chuckle died off. He could almost hear the anger in the breathing just before the call was disconnected. He checked caller ID. Blocked.

"It was him," McKenzie said, turning from the window. She wore a short cotton nightgown that left little to the imagination—not that Hayes's imagination needed any help.

He'd always thought of himself as a strong man. But right now he felt helpless against emotions that threatened to overpower him when he looked at this woman. "McKenzie." He said her name as if that alone could put distance between them and keep him from taking her in his arms.

She turned to him, her voice breaking as she said, "I heard something else besides his breathing." Her gaze locked with his. "I heard my neighbor's wind chimes. He called from those pines below my bedroom window."

CHAPTER NINE

Gus Thompson was lost. He'd driven around town to-night feeling as if his life were over. The last place he'd wanted to go was home to an empty house. He still couldn't believe everything had changed in an instant.

He was thirty-eight years old. Not even in his prime. He would get another job. At least that's what he told himself. And yet just the thought of approaching other Realtors had turned his knees to jelly. He'd never had to actually ask for a job before. His mother had seen that he had jobs from the time he was sixteen. Nepotism wasn't something he'd ever thought about—until now.

If his mother were alive, she would have put in a call, got him on somewhere and he'd just show up for work. She'd had those kinds of connections. Even better, his mother would have made McKenzie pay. Her wrath would have rained down like a firestorm on M.K. Realty. She might even have put dear McKenzie out of business just for spite.

But his mother was gone and he was jobless and lost. And all because of McKenzie Sheldon.

He hadn't known where he was driving until he found himself in her neighborhood. Parking down the block, he'd cut the engine, having no idea what he was going to do when she returned. Their "talk" earlier had left him cold. He needed more from her than a lukewarm recommendation. He was a great salesman, but if there were even a whiff of gossip that he was difficult to work with or that he hit on women in the office, it would kill the deal.

McKenzie had to hire him back. It was the only way.

As that thought settled over him, he'd seen her come up the street and pull into her drive. He'd started to get out, afraid how far he would have to go to get her to agree to rehire him, when an SUV had pulled up in her drive next to her vehicle.

Gus had ducked back into his car as he watched the Texas cowboy get out. McKenzie and the man headed for her front door. "What the—" They'd disappeared inside. A few minutes later, the cowboy had come back out and driven his vehicle into her garage.

It was the same cowboy he'd seen her with at Big Sky. The same man he'd followed to the Cardwell Ranch only to have neither appear again even after Gus had waited an hour.

Determined to wait this time, though, he settled in. The cowboy would leave before daylight, he told himself. He must have fallen asleep because something awakened him. He sat up to find it was the middle of the night. All the lights were off inside the condo—just like the other condos on the block.

Angry and frustrated and feeling even worse, he was about to leave when he noticed something odd. A man had been sitting in an old panel van up the street. Gus watched him get out and head into the trees next to McKenzie's condo. A few moments later, Gus saw a light flash in the trees. Not like a flashlight. More like a small screen, making Gus suspect the man was making a call on his cell phone next to her condo.

How many men did McKenzie have on the string? he wondered. Definitely the cowboy.

So who was the man in the trees? His heart began to pound as he realized it could be the same guy who'd attacked her.

Before he could react, the man came out of the trees, walking fast. He jumped into the van. Gus hurriedly started his car, a plan crystallizing as he drove. If this guy was McKenzie's attacker and he could catch him, she would have to give him back his job.

HAYES, DRESSED ONLY in jeans, ran back to his room and grabbed his gun after the call and what McKenzie had heard on the other end of the line. He raced down the stairs and out the front door. If she was right, the man had been right outside her condo in the dense trees.

But as he reached the trees, he heard tires squeal and looked out on the street as a large car sped past. This time, though, the car passed under a streetlamp and he was able to get the license plate number.

Back in the condo, he found McKenzie wrapped in a fluffy white robe and matching slippers. She stood hugging herself at the front window.

"Did you…" Her words died off as she saw his expression. "He got away."

"I got his license plate number as he was speeding off." Hayes was already dialing the police. He asked for the same officer who they'd talked to earlier and told him about the phone call and the car.

"Give me a minute," the cop said as he ran the plate. "The car belongs to Ruth Thompson. Wait a minute. It's the same car Gus Thompson admitted to driving the night Ms. Sheldon was attacked."

"She has a restraining order on him."

"I see that. I'll make sure he gets picked up."

"Thank you." Hayes hung up and turned to look at McKenzie. "Did you actually see him in the trees?"

She shook her head. "He was just a shape. Large."

"The car that I saw racing away was Gus Thompson's mother's." She groaned. "Is it possible he also made the phone call?"

She seemed to think for a moment. "The man didn't say anything, he just…breathed." She closed her eyes and sighed. "It would be like Gus to try to torment me. He's furious that I fired him. So you think it wasn't the man who attacked me?"

"Not unless that man was Gus Thompson."

"WHAT THE DEVIL?" He looked in his rearview mirror, surprised that the car he'd seen earlier was still following him. He knew it couldn't be either McKenzie Sheldon or the cowboy he'd seen her with before. So who was it?

Not the police or they would have already pulled him over.

He had spotted the tail right away, but hadn't thought anything of it. He had too much on his mind to care. What was the cowboy doing at her house? He could only imagine. He gritted his teeth, remembering the male voice on the phone. The Texas accent had been a dead giveaway. It had to be the same cowboy, the one who'd rescued her at the grocery-store parking lot. The same one he'd seen her with before. And now the man was in her condo with her? Close enough he'd gotten on her *phone?*

A wave of disgust and fury washed over him like

acid on his skin. He'd never taken women out of any kind of anger. If anything, it was about control. So this scalding fury made him feel impotent. He had to do something about this situation and soon.

But how could he get control again—and quickly? If he acted out in anger, he would be more likely to make a mistake, one that could cost him dearly. No, he had to rein in his emotions. He couldn't let this woman and her hero cowboy get to him.

But even as he'd thought it, he felt his blood boiling. How dare the two of them! It was as if they were laughing behind his back. Mocking him. Now the cowboy had something that belonged to him. The woman was *his,* not some stupid bystander's who'd come to her rescue.

He had to think, plan. The woman had known he was outside her window. How? He remembered the way she'd stood at the window at the open house, watching him leave. He'd sensed her watching him. Had she also sensed how close he was to her tonight?

Or had it been something else? That's when he remembered the wind chimes. He'd noticed them when he'd been waiting in the trees. They had been tinkling lightly so he hadn't paid much attention. But right when she'd answered the phone, a gust had caught them... *She'd heard the wind chimes.* The woman was more astute than any of the others, a worthier prey. It should have filled him with pride since she was now his.

The only thing spoiling it was the cowboy.

He thought of how he'd planned it, borrowing the old van he sometimes used at work, waiting until she'd be asleep before he'd called. He'd wanted to wake her, to catch her off guard. He hadn't known she wouldn't be alone.

A curse on his lips, he glanced again in his rearview mirror. The car was still with him! The driver had been staying back, but clearly following him. It was one reason he hadn't gone home. Instead, he'd been driving around, trying to clear his head and ditch the tail. But the fool was still with him.

It couldn't be the cowboy, could it? No. Then who? He reached under the seat for the tire iron he kept there, and was about to throw on his brakes and see just who was following him when he caught the flash of cop lights behind them.

Fear turned his blood to slush—until he realized that the cop wasn't after him, but whoever had been following him. He kept driving up another block before he turned and circled back. He had to know who'd seen him at the condo. Who was stupid enough to put himself in jeopardy?

Fortunately, as he drove by, neither the cop nor the man bent over his car's hood being handcuffed paid any attention to him.

The man being arrested wasn't the Texas cowboy, but he did look familiar.

AFTER HAYES LEFT the condo this morning, McKenzie locked the door behind him as he'd ordered. She was still upset that the man who'd called last night had been right outside her condo. *He knew where she lived!*

But if the man was Gus... She still couldn't believe that even though the police had called to tell her that the car Hayes had seen speeding away belonged to Gus

Thompson and that Gus had been arrested, but was expected to be out on bail soon.

"I really don't like you doing this open house," Hayes had said this morning before he left. "This nutcase is going to strike when you least expect it."

"Then I will have to be on guard all the time."

Once ready for the open house, she called to remind him that she had to stop at her office.

"I'll meet you there," he said.

"That really isn't necessary."

"I'll be the judge of that."

Only Cynthia and another real-estate saleswoman were in the office this morning. The others either had open houses or had taken the day off. She'd always felt a sense of euphoria when she walked into her office. She'd worked hard for this agency and felt a sense of pride that she'd done it alone through hard work.

But today she felt edgy. She couldn't forget for a moment that she was being hunted like an animal. It set her nerves on end and made her start whenever the phone rang.

McKenzie knew she had to pull it together. Last night she'd been angry, filled with a determination to track down this bastard and stop him. But in the light of day, she was too aware of how ill-prepared she was. She'd gotten lucky the other night and had been able to fight the man off—at least long enough that Hayes had seen what was going on and had saved her.

She couldn't count on his saving her again. That's what he was trying to tell her earlier at the condo.

And yet when she saw him drive up, she'd never been so happy to see anyone. "I told you I was driving myself," she said, glancing at the clock. The open house wouldn't start for several hours.

"There's somewhere we need to go." He sounded mysterious, but she followed him out to his SUV and climbed in. He drove out into the country, down a narrow dirt road until they were back into the foothills away from town.

When he stopped, she glanced around. "What are we doing?"

"You really think you're ready for this?" he asked as he pulled out a gun.

She felt her eyes widen in alarm. He held the gun out to her. "You ever fired one before? I didn't think so. You think you can kill someone?"

"Is this really necessary? I have pepper spray that I carry—"

"Pepper spray isn't going to stop this guy. I've seen the way you grip your keys when you get out of the car. If he gets close enough to grab you, your keys aren't going to stop him, either. You're going to have to kill him or he is going to kill you."

She stared at the gun for a moment. Then she swallowed the lump in her throat as she reached for it. Her hand trembled. She stilled it as she got a good grip on the pistol.

"Will you show me how to fire it?"

He'd raised a brow. "You really think you can do this?"

"I don't think I have a choice, do you?"

He took the gun from her. "Come on, then." Climbing out he led the way to a gully where he set up a half-dozen rusted beer cans on rocks. "Familiarize yourself with the gun. Here is how you load it. Here is how you fire it."

Turning toward the cans, he showed her how to hold the gun and take aim. She did as he had done, looked down the barrel and pulled the trigger. The gun kicked in her hand, the shot going wild.

"Don't close your eyes when you pull the trigger," he said.

She tried again, holding the gun tighter. The next shot was closer. The third one pinged into a can, knocking it to the ground. She felt a surge of satisfaction, missed the next shot, but centered the cans on the next two.

Feeling cocky, she turned to look at him. "Well?"

"You killed a few old beer cans. You will have only a split second to make the decision whether to pull the trigger or not—and that's if you can pull the gun fast enough when the man surprises you," Hayes said. "He'll be counting on those few seconds when you hesitate."

"WHERE ARE YOU?" Tag asked, not long before noon. "I checked your cabin. It hasn't been slept in."

Hayes was driving north, leaving Bozeman and traveling out into the country past wheat fields broken by subdivisions. "I stayed at McKenzie's last night. Quit smirking. Nothing happened—at least not what you're thinking."

"Oh?"

He found the road he needed and turned down it. The sun had cleared the mountains to the east this morning and now splashed the valley in gold. "This guy who attacked her is still after her. She's determined to find him before he finds her. I'm helping her."

"Did you read something on a fortune cookie that says if you save someone's life, you're responsible for it?"

"I can't just leave her," Hayes said as he saw the house come into view.

"Really? That's all it is, just you needing to play hero?"

"I can't get into this right now. I'll call you as soon as I know something definite, but I might be staying until your wedding. Also, I told McKenzie we will take the restaurant building at Big Sky. I haven't talked to Austin but—"

"Was this McKenzie Sheldon's doing? Never mind. Whatever the reason you've changed your mind, I'm glad. You won't be sorry."

"I hope not."

"Now try not to get yourself killed before my wedding."

As Tag hung up, Hayes sped up the SUV, driving past the house and up the road for a half mile before he turned around and headed back, going slower this time.

The ranch-style house was huge, sprawled across twenty acres with a guesthouse, barn and stables behind it, along with an assortment of outbuildings. All kinds of places for a person to hide. He noticed there was also a dirt road that went up into the Bridger Mountains behind the house.

As he drove on by the house a second time, he called McKenzie. "Get someone to do the open house for you. It's too dangerous."

Gus had been arrested last night for violating the restraining order. But McKenzie had received a call earlier, warning her that he was already out on bail.

What had Hayes upset was what else the police-woman had told her. "He swears he saw a man beside your condo last night using a cell phone. He says he was chasing the man when he was arrested."

"Did he get a good look at the man?" McKenzie had asked.

"He says he didn't."

The policewoman hadn't believed Gus about any of it.

Hayes didn't know what to believe. Gus could be be-hind both the note on McKenzie's car and the call last night. Gus was angry, according to the police, which gave him reason to want to torment his former boss, even if he wasn't the man who'd attacked her.

"It wasn't Gus," she'd again said this morning on the drive back from shooting the gun.

"But Gus would know about the convention speech and the open house," Hayes had argued. "And he was definitely at your condo last night."

"You said he sped away. You didn't see another car?"

He hadn't been looking for another car once he'd seen Gus speeding away.

"I went by Gus Thompson's house," he said now. "He's not there. This open house is in the paper with your name on it, right?"

"It's not Gus."

"Okay, then if true, I would say you have two angry men after you now. Which is yet another reason you shouldn't do the open house."

"The police are going to have a car in the area of the open house."

"The area is too large and there are too many places a man could be hiding."

"*You'll* be there."

Her words hit him at heart level. "Why do you think I'm so worried?"

"I trust you."

Her first mistake. He opened his mouth to speak, but shook his head, instead. A part of him was touched by her words. Another part was afraid he would fail her.

"Hayes?"

"I'm still here."

"I know. I'm grateful."

He sighed. "Let me know when you leave the office for the open house. Keep your phone on. I won't stop worrying until I know you made the drive safely. Then, once you get here, I can really start worrying."

"So you agree with me that he'll show?"

"He'll be here. He couldn't possibly pass up such a perfect location with all these places to hide. The question is where."

GUS WAS NO longer angry at McKenzie. He was *furious*. She hadn't really had him *arrested?* Not when he was following the man who he assumed had attacked her.

When he'd first gotten released from jail he'd thought about just letting the crazy bastard get her. She deserved it, right?

After a while, though, he'd tamped down his fury, focusing instead on the look he'd see on her face when he caught her stalker. When he *saved* her.

He dug the handgun from the drawer beside his bed. He'd bought the pistol at a gun show years ago. The gun was loaded, but he grabbed another box of ammunition.

As he walked through the kitchen, he grabbed a sharp knife. He put the knife in the top of his boot.

Today he'd worn jeans, hiking boots, a long-sleeved shirt. He had some dirty business to get done today.

In the garage, he walked past his mother's car to his SUV. He felt like a commando going into battle. The man after McKenzie had been at her condo last night. That had been a gutsy move. So Gus figured, given where the open house was being held, that the man would show. All Gus had to do was get there early for a place to hide out and wait. It would be like shooting fish in a bucket—barrel, whatever.

He'd checked out the house and grounds when the ranchette had first come on the market, so he knew where to park the SUV so it wouldn't be noticed. There was literally a forest that backed up to the property. He knew the perfect spot where he would be able to see anyone coming.

McKenzie GREW MORE anxious as she neared the ranchette. She remembered what Hayes had said last night. But her car seemed to be running fine. However, she was relieved when she reached the turnoff to the house.

She didn't see Hayes anywhere around, but then again, she didn't expect to. He was here, though, she assured herself. The property was twenty acres, just as Hayes had said. While she'd seen the place before, she found herself looking at it from a totally different perspective than she had the first time.

Now she saw all the places a man could hide and wait for that moment when she was alone. And she would be alone some of the time because the asking price of this place was high enough that she didn't expect a lot of viewers.

Fear rippled over her, dimpling her skin and giving

her a chill as she got out at the turnoff to put up the
Open House sign. She couldn't help looking over her
shoulder, hurrying to get the sign up and back into her
vehicle as quickly as possible.

She was shaking by the time she climbed behind the
wheel again. Did she really think she could do this? To
catch this man she would eventually have to come face-
to-face with him. He had to be caught in action. Her
heart began to pound at the memory of his arm around
her throat, the way he'd picked her up off her feet—

Turning down the road, she heard another vehicle.
An SUV turned down the long drive behind her. She
glanced at the car's clock. Her first viewer was early.
As she pulled in, she saw that the car had slowed as if
to study the place at a distance. Hurrying, she climbed
out, taking everything with her as she moved toward the
empty house. Her heart hammered in her chest as she
opened the door and felt a blast of stale, cold air hit her.

She had to calm down. Taking a few breaths, she
reminded herself how far she'd come. She hadn't gotten her success by being a wimp. She straightened her
back as she put down the flyers and turned to watch
the SUV cruise slowly up the road toward her. The sun
glinted off the windshield so she couldn't see the driver.

This could be him.

Or he could already be in the house waiting for me.

CHAPTER TEN

LAST NIGHT HAD been a close call. Some fool had chased him. Fortunately, the police had pulled the man over. He'd gotten a good look at the man's familiar face but it wasn't until he got home that he placed him. He'd seen Gus Thompson's face enough times when he'd been perusing the real-estate ads looking for McKenzie Sheldon's smiling face.

Just the thought of her made him feel better. But he couldn't ignore the fact that the man had given him chase last night. Did McKenzie now have *two* men protecting her? That made his stomach roil. It was bad enough that the cowboy kept getting in his way. Now this other fool?

To settle himself down, he thought about the open house and Ms. Sheldon. He would see her again today. Unfortunately, just seeing her wasn't helping much anymore. He needed more. He smiled in memory of the terror he'd seen on McKenzie Sheldon's face last night when she'd found the note and what he'd heard in her voice when he'd called and woken her up.

But even that wasn't enough. He had to get his hands on her.

True, she had needed a reminder that he was still here, that he was still coming for her. It had been a dangerous thing to do, calling attention to himself that way. But he relished in the fear, both his own and, of course, hers.

He'd been curious to see, after the note and the phone call, whether or not she would go ahead with the open house today. The listing was out in the country, miles from town and enough acreage and buildings that not even her cowboy or Gus Thompson, real-estate salesman extraordinaire, could keep her safe.

She'd proven to be a worthy opponent. But today would tell if the woman was equal to the challenge.

He'd already decided that he had to show up at the open house. She might be suspicious of him after yesterday since he'd been one of only a handful of men who'd come alone to the open house.

Today he would assure her she had nothing to fear from him.

After all, the one thing he could do well was *act* normal. He'd spent his life fooling people—even those closest to him. He knew exactly how he would play it and couldn't wait.

HAYES FELT HIS stomach tighten as viewers began to arrive. When he'd spoken to the police earlier, they'd agreed to run the plates of those attending the open house. They'd asked the sheriff's department to send a car out to the area, as well.

Given the price of this so-called ranchette, he'd thought that number would be low. He'd been surprised by the turnout.

Most were just curious, he was betting. But some actually appeared to be interested, walking much of the grounds, looking in the many structures. He'd heard that expensive houses in the area had continued to sell, even during the recession. It was easy to understand why people fell in love with Bozeman's charm, along with the beautiful valley, the nearby mountains and inexhaustible outdoor entertainment.

He took down each license plate number and snapped a photo of the people attending. He had a half dozen written down when the man drove up. He recognized the man right away as the one he'd seen talking to McKenzie the day before at the open house. Was this her attacker? He was dressed in jeans, boots and a Western shirt and had a cocky way about him.

As the man climbed out of his SUV, he glanced around as if taking in the place for the first time, then he headed for the front door.

McKenzie had been talking to a middle-aged couple and turned to find the man directly behind her.

"I'm sorry. I didn't mean to startle you." He held out his hand. "Bob Garwood."

McKenzie battled back her initial surprise and took his hand. It was cool to the touch, the handshake firm. She even found her voice. "It's nice to meet you, Mr. Garwood."

"Please, call me Bob." He let go of her hand and glanced around the living area. "I like this much better than yesterday's listing. How many acres?"

"Twenty. Most of it is now leased for hay."

He nodded. "That's great." His gaze came back to hers. "Mind if I take one of those?"

She handed him a sales flyer. Her hand was hardly shaking.

"Sheldon, right? McKenzie Sheldon. I almost called

you last night. You gave me your card with your cell phone number, remember?"

She nodded numbly. If this was the man who'd attacked her, then he *had* called her last night. In fact, he'd been outside her condo. Her heart began to pound harder.

He smiled. "This might seem a little forward, but I wanted to ask you to dinner sometime."

"I don't date clients."

His smile broadened as he pulled out his card and handed it to her. "Good thing I'm not a client yet."

With that he walked away, his gaze going from the sales flyer in his hand to the house as if he seriously was looking for something to buy. She glanced down at the card. Robert Garwood. Apparently, he sold high-tech workout equipment for gyms.

"Are you all right?"

She jumped before she recognized the voice and turned to find Hayes behind her. "How long have you been here?"

"Long enough to hear him ask you for a date."

She let out a nervous laugh. "Maybe that's all he was doing, just hitting on me."

"Maybe. I'll run his name. Bob Garwood, right?"

She nodded as a few more cars pulled up out front. Two women climbed out of one vehicle, a couple out of another and one man, alone.

"You remember him from yesterday's open house?" Hayes asked.

The men's faces were all starting to blend together. "I think so."

"I'll be close by if you need me," he whispered and left.

McKenzie braced herself as the man who'd just arrived looked up at the house, then started up the walk. She recognized him as being one from yesterday's open house. As she took a closer look at the couple, she realized the husband also looked familiar.

"Holler if you need me," Hayes said and left out the back way.

McKenzie jumped as the front door opened. She plastered a smile on her face as the group entered. The lone man took a flyer, gave her a nod and moved off through the house behind the two women. The husband she recognized from the day before came up to her.

"You're a busy woman," he said. "Didn't I see you yesterday at an open house in town?"

She nodded, wondering if he really didn't remember. He was large and there was something about his light blue eyes that made her feel naked. He was the one who'd acted as if he was pulling something on her yesterday.

His gaze locked with hers and she felt a shiver move through her. She tried to repress it as she handed him a sales flyer.

He nodded, his gaze still on her as if he was trying to place her.

McKenzie tried to pull herself together. She'd been so determined last night, so sure she wanted to trap the man. But being this close to a possible suspect…

He was still looking at her.

"Jason?"

"Sorry," he said, turning to the woman with him. "I was just lost in thought for a minute there." He let out a self-deprecating laugh. "I'm Jason Mathews. This is my wife, Emily."

She shook the wife's hand, then Jason Mathews's.

He had a firm handshake and held her hand a little too long, making her even more nervous.

"I was surprised when Jason suggested we buy something larger," Emily said. She was a small woman with dark hair and eyes. Her handshake had been limp and cold. As she spoke, she kept looking at her husband. "We own a house in town that's paid for, but I would love a place in the country. This might be too much for us, though. I hate to even ask what it costs."

Jason Mathews smiled at his wife. "Well, let's have a look. You might be surprised what we can afford." He gave McKenzie a conspiratorial wink and handed her his card before leading his wife toward the kitchen.

McKenzie tried to catch her breath as she glanced down at the card in her hand. Jason Mathews. Under his name was: Antiquities Appraiser and his business number.

She groaned inwardly as she realized how foolish she had been. The man apparently really was interested in buying a house. With a sigh, she turned to welcome more people into the house.

But every man who came in alone to see the ranchette made her wonder if he was the one she had to fear.

THERE WERE TOO many people here. He finally found himself alone next to one of the outbuildings and took a breath. He couldn't believe how smooth he'd been when he'd seen McKenzie Sheldon again. It had taken some of the sting out of failing. He couldn't wait to get her alone.

Talking to McKenzie Sheldon had his blood running hot, though. He felt his need growing, worse this time because of his failure. Just the thought of his hands on her bare skin— The things he would make her do. The things he would do to her.

A flash of light caught his attention. He stepped back into the shade of the building and cupped his hands to look up the hillside toward the forest. There was someone up there in the barn loft. The flash must have been binoculars. A cop? Or that damned cowboy?

He'd known the cowboy would be here protecting McKenzie. It irritated him, but would give him such satisfaction when he stole the woman from the cowboy right in front of his eyes. He smiled just thinking about it.

In the shadow of the building, he waited and watched, hoping for a glimpse of whoever was hiding up in the barn loft. Finally, his patience paid off. He caught a glimpse of a face and swore.

It was that man who'd followed him last night from McKenzie's condo, the same man he'd witnessed getting arrested. Obviously, Gus Thompson had gotten out of jail.

He didn't need to speculate on who the man was looking for. Stupid fool.

A hot well of need rushed through his blood. The women he took fulfilled a variety of his needs on several levels. At first, killing them had been just a precaution, but over time he'd begun to enjoy that part, as well.

If he couldn't have McKenzie just yet, well, maybe he could satisfy at least one of his yearnings.

GUS CAUGHT MOVEMENT out of the corner of his eye. He had found the perfect spot in the barn loft. Through a small window, he had been able to watch the property as well as the comings and goings at the house. He'd picked the barn because he'd known that few people would come all the way up the hillside to the big barn, let alone climb up to the hayloft.

A few had made the hike but only given the barn a cursory look. The stables were much more interesting, and even some of the outbuildings. But since the place was immaculate, all the buildings painted white with dark green trim, it was easy to see that everything was well maintained.

He could sell this place in a heartbeat, he thought with aching regret. What did McKenzie know about selling this property? It should have been his listing.

He was thinking that when he saw movement off to his right in the pine trees. Gus turned, fear making his movement jerky. He'd forgotten why he was here for a moment and that kind of distraction was just when the man who had attacked McKenzie would take advantage.

But to his surprise, there was no one in the pines next to the barn. The breeze stirred the branches, casting shadows over the dry needles on the ground.

He reminded himself that he couldn't get caught here by anyone or he would be going back to jail.

He might have convinced himself that he'd imagined the movement if he hadn't heard a sound below him. As his heart began to pound, he pulled the pistol he'd brought and moved cautiously toward the hole in the floor where the ladder came up.

He'd lied to the cops about the man he'd seen at McKenzie's condo. Even though it had been dark and the man had been dressed in a hooded black sweatshirt, he'd gotten a pretty decent look at him in the streetlamp. Once he saw him again, he'd know him.

He heard nothing below him. He thought about going

down the ladder when he realized there was another way up into the loft—a second ladder on the other side of the large stack of hay.

Gun ready, he cautiously moved in that direction. The smell of the hay and dust filled his nostrils. As the floor beneath his feet creaked, he couldn't hold back the sneeze. He stopped and listened again. No sound other than the breeze in the pines nearby.

There was no one. He felt both relieved and disappointed. His only hope of getting his job back was saving McKenzie, he thought as he heard a slight rustle in the stack of hay next to him.

HAYES MENTALLY KICKED himself as he walked the perimeter of the property one last time. The open house had ended almost an hour ago but there were some visitors who were just now leaving. He'd texted McKenzie just moments ago. She'd texted back that she was fine. He tried to relax since the stragglers were either couples or several groups of women. No lone male. At least not one who he'd seen.

Earlier he'd found tracks coming from the road behind the house. But with the property bordering the forest, there were too many places to hide for him to search for a vehicle. He couldn't be sure that the tracks weren't from the owner or one of the people viewing the house and property.

He'd also found a place where someone had stood for a while on a rise with a view of the house. The boot tracks were men-sized, but they could belong to anyone. He felt as if he were looking for a needle in a haystack. He couldn't even be sure the man who'd attacked McKenzie was even here.

Since arming her with the gun, he'd had his misgivings. The gun had been more about making him feel better than any real protection for her. Now he hoped he hadn't made things worse and she shot some innocent fool who surprised her.

But he couldn't watch her all the time. Was it wrong to want her to have a fighting chance? Whether or not the gun would give her that…well, he couldn't say. It would all depend on when her attacker decided to strike again.

He was about to head for the house when something caught his eye. For a moment, he almost ignored it. He was anxious to get to McKenzie. The last of the viewers were leaving. That would mean she was alone.

Staring up at the barn, he saw what had drawn his attention. The barn had four small octagonal windows across one side on the loft level. He saw now that there was something in one of the barn windows that hadn't been there earlier.

Hayes glanced down the hillside toward the house, torn. Whatever was in the barn window probably was nothing. He needed to get to McKenzie. And yet… He quickly texted her.

Everyone gone?

Yes.

He could almost feel the relief in that one word.

Lock all the doors and wait for me.

Pocketing his phone, he walked quickly up the hillside toward the barn.

Earlier it had been hot, but now with the waning sun, the air felt cool. He could smell the pines, hear the breeze rustling the boughs. As he neared the barn, he slowed. A prickling at his neck made him pull his weapon before he stepped into the cool, hollow darkness.

The inside of the barn was empty. He glanced overhead to the loft, then at the ladder. There was fresh manure on several of the steps. Someone had been up there, someone who'd come in through the corral where the horses were kept.

At the foot of the ladder, he saw that there was another way up into the loft—a second set of stairs, these much easier to climb. Moving to them, he began to climb, the only sound inside the cavernous barn the pounding of his heart.

Hayes slowed near the top, weapon ready. The moment he peered over the top, he saw the man sprawled on the loft floor, the strewn hay around him discolored with the man's blood.

As he eased up through the opening to the loft floor, he saw that the man's throat had been sliced from ear to ear. From the color of the blood straining the hay, he hadn't been dead long.

Hayes hurriedly surveyed the area, then careful not to contaminate the scene, checked the man's wallet and identification.

Gus Thompson, the man McKenzie had fired.

CHAPTER ELEVEN

As HAYES CAME through the door, McKenzie turned, clearly startled. Hayes saw her hand go to the gun in her bag, but stop short when she recognized him. Relief washed over her features as she dropped the bag and stepped into his arms.

"You're shaking," he said as he hugged her to him.

"The deputies wouldn't tell me anything, just to stay in the house. I saw the ambulance. I was so afraid it was you. What happened?"

"It's Gus Thompson. I found him in the barn on the property."

"Gus?"

"He's dead. He was…murdered."

McKenzie shook her head in obvious disbelief as she stepped out of his embrace. *"Murdered?"*

"The sheriff's department is investigating. That's all I can tell you."

She looked as stunned as he'd been when he'd ID'd the dead man. "What was Gus…?"

"Your guess is as good as mine."

"If he was the one who attacked me…" Her voice trailed off. "He wasn't."

"It doesn't appear so, but he definitely seemed to be stalking you. It could be he crossed paths with your attacker."

"So my attacker was here! He was someone who came through the house."

"Maybe. As I told you, with a property this size, he may have sneaked onto the place without anyone seeing him."

"Except Gus." She shivered. "I can't believe he's dead."

"I'm sure the deputies will want to question you about who came through the open house."

"But I don't know *anything.* A half-dozen men came through alone, but that isn't unusual."

"What about that man who asked you out? Bob Garwood."

She shook her head. "He's not the first man who came to an open house hoping to get a date with the Realtor. There were other men who could have been the one who attacked me." She described several of the men who'd come through. "There was one, Jason Mathews. He gave me a funny feeling, but he came through with his wife, Emily, so...."

"I'll check him out along with the others but there is a good chance the man who killed Gus didn't come into the house."

"You took down all the license plate numbers?"

"I did. I've turned them over to the sheriff's department." He hated to get her hopes up. If he was right about this man, the killer had gone years learning how to not get caught. He was good at this and he knew it. "We might get lucky, though."

McKenzie had stopped trembling, but she was still shocked and shaken. After she'd talked to the deputies, Hayes had followed her back to her condo. She'd worked so hard, determined to be successful and independent. She hadn't wanted to need anyone. Now her carefully built world was coming apart at the seams, and it scared her more than she wanted to admit how dependent she'd become on Hayes Cardwell.

She had to get control of her life again. That meant she needed answers—even those she knew she didn't want to hear. "You said you were going to do some research to see if other women... There have been others, haven't there?"

"Maybe you should sit down," he suggested as they moved into the living room.

She shook her head, crossing her arms over her chest as if she could hold back the fear that filled her. "Just tell me."

"More than two dozen have disappeared over the last ten years. The more recent ones match your profile."

"*My* profile?"

"Successful, single businesswomen who work late, shop late, have a lot on their plates."

She tried to swallow the lump in her throat. "I'm his type, that's what you're saying. Did any of them...?"

"None got away. I believe you might be the first."

"Then they are all..."

"Still missing."

She tried not to imagine the other women. "In other words, they're probably dead." She waited, seeing that he knew more than he was telling her.

"Several have turned up in shallow graves. They all went missing mostly out West. I suspect this man travels with his job. Since you have been the only one who he attempted to abduct in this area, I think there is a good chance that he lives here." At her frown, he added, "Predators don't normally hunt in their back-yards. Too dangerous."

"But he *did*."

Hayes nodded. "With what I know about his type, he probably can go for a length of time and then something just snaps or builds to the point where he can't help himself."

"So I just happened to be in the wrong place at the wrong time."

"Probably."

"But now he knows who I am and if I'm the only one that ever got away…"

"That's why you can't stay here."

She shook her head. "How long do you think I can hide from him, Hayes? I have a business to run. I need to work."

He shook his head. "I don't have all the answers."

"I know." She looked into his kind, handsome face. He hadn't asked for any of this. All she wanted to do was bury her face in his strong chest. In his arms, she felt safe. But Hayes wouldn't always be there to hold her and protect her. It was one reason she had to know everything she could about the man after her.

"You talked to the police about Gus?" She saw the answer on his face. "Tell me."

"The coroner said Gus was hit with a piece of pipe. The blow wasn't enough to kill him, but probably knocked him down, at least stunned him long enough for the killer to…" Hayes met her gaze. "Are you sure you want to hear this?"

"I got the man killed."

"That's not true and you know it. You had a restraining order against him. If Gus had stayed away, he would still be alive today."

She stepped to the window, her back to him, her mind reeling. "What was Gus doing in that barn?"

"The police think he was spying on you. They found binoculars near the window and a bag with candy bars. It was the bag I saw in the window fluttering in the breeze that made me go up to the barn. He had hooked it on a nail next to him. When the breeze came up…"

She turned to look at him. "Why would he spy on me?"

"You said he wanted to talk to you. Maybe he thought he could get you alone and convince you to give him back his job." Hayes shook his head. "Who knows."

"The police think his killer was the man who tried to abduct me, don't they?" She didn't wait for him to confirm it. "Gus swore to the police that he followed him last night after the man called me from down in the pines by the wind chimes. If he was telling the truth, maybe he wasn't there spying on me but looking for the man. But why would Gus do something like that?"

"Maybe he wanted to play hero and it got him killed."

"If he was looking for my attacker, that means he could recognize him. *Gus lied to the police.*" That shouldn't have surprised her. It would be just like Gus. Tears filled her eyes. "This is all because I fired him."

Hayes stepped to her and took her in his arms. She didn't fight it. She rested her cheek against his chest, soaking in his warmth, hoping to chase away the chill that had settled in her, even for a little while.

"McKenzie, none of this is your fault. Gus made some very poor decisions. That's what got him killed."

"Playing hero, isn't that what you called it?" she

asked as she pulled back to look into his dark eyes. "So anyone who tries to protect me—"

"Don't," he said, as if seeing where she was headed with this.

She shook her head and stepped away from him. "He'll come after you next. I can't let that happen."

"I'm not Gus. He wasn't trained for this. I am."

"I want you to go back to Texas."

"Ain't happenin'," Hayes said. "I'm staying right here and there is nothing you can do to drive me away, so don't even try."

She looked up at him, her eyes brimming with tears. "I couldn't bear it if anything happened to you because of me."

He reached her in two long strides and took her shoulders in his hands. "Nothing is going to happen to me. Or to you. We are going to catch this guy." He could see that she didn't believe that. He wondered if he did himself.

"I thought if we set a trap for him... I thought today..." Tears spilled down her cheeks. She had a swipe at them. "It was a stupid idea and look what happened because of me."

He could see her fighting to be strong. He'd never met a more courageous woman. "It wasn't stupid. He was there, just as you'd thought he would be. Unfortunately, Gus was, too. Listen, I have a plan. It's dangerous—"

She laughed, but there was no humor in it. "More dangerous than waiting around for him to attack me again after what he did today?"

"If I am right about this man, he's had some experience at this. He'll *expect* a trap. He knows the police and now sheriff's department are involved. I'm sure he knows I'm involved, as well."

"What are you saying? That he'll lie low for a while?"

He nodded. He didn't want to tell her that killing Gus would have relieved some of the killer's...tension. The man would be satisfied for a while. "But whatever drives him will eventually reach the point where—"

"He'll try to grab some other woman!"

"No. He can't move on until he's finished with you."

"You don't know that."

"Not positively, but based on what I know about these types of predators..." He held her gaze. "But understand. The longer he goes, the more dangerous he will be."

"Then you need to go back to Texas. Like you said, he knows you're involved. If he killed Gus because he thought he was in the way..."

"Who knows what happened with Gus. The truth is, I believe you're the only one who will be able to satisfy his need."

McKenzie swallowed. "This plan you have..."

"Right now, you're too accessible. He can fill some of his need too easily by simply seeing you and seeing that you're afraid or cutting off part of your hair as a souvenir. You need to hide out for a while. The longer we let him dangle, the more his confidence will decline. He won't know where you've gone. Then when you surface again...he'll make mistakes."

She felt her eyes fill with tears. "At least that's what you're hoping for."

He nodded, not telling her what else he was hoping for.

"So I hide out until…until what?"

"Until he can't take it any longer." Hayes pulled her into his arms and stroked her back. He was hoping that he would find the bastard before that happened. "You have to trust me." He drew back to look into her eyes. "Do you trust me, McKenzie?"

She nodded.

"Then the two of us are going to Cardwell Ranch."

HE LICKED AT a spot of blood on his wrist that he'd missed and smiled. When he closed his eyes he could feel the warm flow of blood running over his fingers. But the best part was the look in Gus Thompson's eyes when the man realized he was going to die—and with his own knife.

The fool had gone for a knife in his boot after his gun had been taken away from him. It had been too easy to cut his throat. True, killing him had been a risky thing to do, especially killing him in the barn loft. But the dried hay would make it hard for forensics to find anything. Not to mention all the people who had tromped through that place.

He was reasonably sure he'd pulled it off without a hitch. He'd wiped off most of the blood on his hand in the hay, having cut the man's throat from behind him. Then he had slipped out of the barn to wash his hands in the hose on the back side of the barn.

He'd been careful not to leave any footprints next to the faucet. The police would suspect that he had to clean up. The creek would probably be their first choice, the hose behind the barn too obvious.

Either way, he'd managed to clean himself up and

leisurely walk back to the house without causing anyone to take note of him.

All in all, it had been an amazing day. He felt better about everything. Now all he had to do was finish McKenzie Sheldon and life would be back to normal. Well, as normal as his life could be, under the circumstances.

But he was in no hurry. Killing Gus Thompson had filled his growing need. Now he could just relax and watch McKenzie sweat. With her former salesman's death, she would be terrified. He chuckled. And her cowboy would realize he was no match for him.

Soon he would call and ask to see a house. He knew exactly which one he would want to see. When he'd gotten home from the open house, he'd searched the paper and internet for a listing in the area that would work to his advantage.

As he picked up her card and ran his fingers over the dark engraving, he had no doubt that Ms. McKenzie Sheldon would accommodate him in every way possible.

CHAPTER TWELVE

DANA MET THEM at the ranch house door. "I am so glad you decided to come back."

McKenzie couldn't help being touched by the warm welcome, but she still had misgivings about being here. It must have showed in her face because Dana hugged her and said, "I have something I want to show you in the kitchen," leaving the men in the living room. Because it was late, the children were already in bed. The large, two-story ranch house was quieter than McKenzie had ever heard it.

"I know that you didn't want to come here," Dana said, the moment the kitchen door closed behind them.

"Only because there is a killer after me. I couldn't bear it if I brought my troubles here and put your family in danger."

"We've had our share of trouble at this ranch, believe me, and I'm sure we will again," Dana said. "For me this place has always been a sanctuary. If it can be for others…" She smiled and took McKenzie's hands in her own. "Then I'm glad. My mother loved this ranch, fought for it. It's that Old West spirit that lives here in this canyon. Hayes did right bringing you back here."

McKenzie wasn't as sure of that. But she had to admit, she felt safer here and more at home than she did even in her condo as the two of them joined the men.

"We're going down to the Corral tonight," Dana said as if the idea had just come to her. "You dance, don't you, McKenzie?"

She started to shake her head.

"Not to worry," Hayes said. "I'll teach you Texas two-step."

"It's Saturday night in the canyon," Tag said. "You really do not want to miss this. Isn't that right, Lily?" His fiancée laughed and agreed.

McKenzie couldn't help but get caught up in their excitement. "Saturday night in the canyon. How can I say no?"

Hayes smiled at her. "It's going to be fun, I promise."

She didn't doubt it. The Cardwells were a family that had fun; she could see that. She found herself smiling as they all piled into a couple of rigs and drove up the canyon to the Corral Bar.

"I forgot to mention that my father and uncle are playing in the band," Dana said as they got out.

McKenzie could hear the music, old-time country, as they pushed through the door. The place was packed, but Hayes pulled her out onto a small space on the dance floor, anyway.

The song was slow, a mournful love song. He took her in his arms, drawing her close. She'd danced some in her younger days, mostly with her sisters, though.

Hayes was easy to follow and she found herself relaxing in his arms and moving with the music.

"You're a fast learner," he whispered next to her ear, making her smile.

They danced the next couple of songs, the beat picking up.

"Are you having fun?" Hayes asked.

She was. She laughed and nodded as he spun her, catching her by the waist to draw her back to him. She loved being in his arms and it wasn't just because she felt safe there. She was falling for Hayes Cardwell.

"Here, you need this after that last dance," Tag said, handing each of them a beer as they came off the dance floor. "Some nice moves out there, little brother." He winked at Hayes. "Who knew he could dance?"

"He is a man of many talents," McKenzie agreed as she tried to catch her breath. Just being around Hayes made her heart beat faster and her pulse sing. When he looked at her like he was doing now… "He just taught me the Texas swing."

"Come to Texas and I'll teach you all kinds of things," Hayes said, meeting her gaze and holding it.

She laughed that off but she could tell he was serious. Texas? She didn't think so. She hadn't spent years working her tail off to get her business where it was to pack up and move.

And yet when she looked into his dark eyes, she was tempted. She told herself it had only been an off-handed remark. They hardly knew each other. A woman would be crazy to pack up and move clear across country because of a man, wouldn't she?

HAYES COULD HAVE bitten his tongue. He'd seen his brother's surprised expression. He'd been joking. Or at least he thought he had when he'd started to suggest it. But by the time the words were out of his mouth…

He shook his head and took a long drink of his beer. From the moment he'd looked into McKenzie Sheldon's eyes he'd been spellbound. He couldn't explain it but the woman had cast a spell on him.

The band took a break and Dana and McKenzie headed off to the ladies' room together. He decided it was as good as any time to go over to say hello to his father and uncle.

"I heard you were in the canyon," his father said, giving him a slap on the back. Harlan Cardwell was still strong and handsome for a man in his sixties.

Tag had bonded with their father on his visit to Montana last Christmas. Hayes only had vague memories of occasional visits from his father while growing up.

"Good to see you," he said, then shook his uncle Angus's hand. The two had been playing in a band together, Tag had told him, since they were in high school. .

"I've gotten to know Dad better," Tag had said when their father's name had come up. "He's a loner, kind of like Austin. He and his brother are close, but Uncle Angus doesn't even see his own daughter Dana that much."

"So you're saying our uncle is just as lousy a father as our own?" he'd asked Tag. "That's reassuring."

"I'm saying there's more to them. Dad cares, but neither he nor his brother, it seems, were cut out to be family men."

Several locals came up to talk to Harlan and Angus. Hayes told his father he would catch him later and went to find McKenzie.

Hayes had always wondered about his father. What man let his wife raise five boys alone? Not that their mother wasn't one strong woman who'd done a great job.

"That's your father?" McKenzie asked, studying the elderly cowboy.

"That's him." Hayes had only recently learned that

his father and uncle had spent most of their lives working for various government agencies. Both were reportedly retired.

He didn't want to talk about his father. "About earlier when I suggested you come to Texas…"

"I might come down just to see what all the fuss is about sometime," she said and quickly added, "Just to visit."

Fortunately, the band broke into a song. McKenzie put down her beer and, taking her hand, he led her back out on the dance floor.

As he pulled her into his arms, though, he couldn't bear to think about the day he would have to go back to Texas without her.

"ARE YOU ALL RIGHT?" Hayes asked as they walked toward their cabins after they'd closed down the Corral. Tag had stayed behind to talk to Hud on the porch, while Dana had gone into the house to see how the kids were. Her sister Stacy had come up from Bozeman to watch all the kids for them.

The night was cool and dark in the pines. Only the starlight and a sliver of white moon overhead lit their way through the dense trees. In the distance, McKenzie thought she could hear the river as it wound through the canyon. It reminded her of the music back at the bar and being in Hayes's arms.

"I'm fine," she said and breathed in the sweet summer night's scents, wishing this night would never have to end.

He took her hand, his fingers closing around hers, and instinctively she moved closer, their shoulders brushing.

"I enjoyed visiting with your father tonight. He

seems sweet." She glanced over at Hayes. "He said he wants to get to know his sons. I can tell he's sorry he missed so many years with the five of you." She saw that it was a subject he didn't want to talk about. There was hurt there. She wondered what it would take to heal it. With Hayes in Houston and his father here, well, that was too many miles, too much distance between them in more ways than one.

"I had a great time tonight," she said, changing the subject. She didn't want anything to ruin this night. She felt still caught up in the summer night's festivities. If anything, she had fallen even harder for the Cardwell family tonight.

"Me, too. So you aren't sorry I brought you here?"

She laughed as she looked at him. He wore his gray Stetson, his face in shadow, but she knew that face so well now that she knew he was pleased she'd had fun. "I'd rather be here with you than anywhere else in the world tonight."

He squeezed her hand then drew her to a stop in the pines just yards from her cabin. A breeze swayed the boughs around them, whispering softly, as he pulled her to him. The kiss was warm and soft and sweeter than even the night.

"McKenzie, that isn't just the beer talking, is it?" he joked.

She cupped his face in her hands, drawing him down to her lips. All night she'd wanted his arms around her. All night she'd wanted him. As she put into the kiss the longing she had for him, he dragged her against him with a groan. Desire shot through her blood, hot and demanding.

When she finally drew back, she whispered on a

ragged breath, "I want you, too, Hayes Cardwell, and that isn't the beer talking."

They were so close she could see the shine of his dark eyes in the starlight. Without another word, he swept her up in his arms and carried her into the cabin.

As the cabin door closed behind them, Hayes lowered McKenzie slowly to her feet. His need for her was so strong that he would have taken her right there on the floor. But not their first time, he told himself as he looked into her eyes, losing himself in the clear blue sea.

"Last chance," he said quietly.

"Not a chance."

She started to unbutton her blouse, but he stopped her, moving her hands away to do it himself. He was determined to take it slow. As he slipped one button free, then another, he held her gaze. Her blouse fell open. He slowly lowered his eyes to her white-laced bra against the olive of her skin.

He brushed his fingertips over the rise of her breasts. She moaned softly as he dipped into the bra. Her nipple hardened under his thumb, making her arch against his hand. Her skin felt as hot as his desire for her. He released the front snap of her bra, exposing both breasts. Need burned through him, making him ache.

He'd wanted her for so long. When his gaze returned to her face, he saw her own need in her eyes. In one swift movement, she unsnapped his shirt, making the snaps sing. She pressed her palms to his chest.

He felt heat race along his nerve endings. He bent to kiss her then drew her against him, feeling her full breasts and hard nipples warm his skin and send his growing desire for her rocketing.

His mouth dropped to her breast, his tongue working the nipple. His hand slipped up under her skirt and her panties. She arched against him, rocking against his hand until she cried out and sagged against him.

He unhooked her skirt. It dropped to the floor. Her white lace panties followed it. Naked, she was more beautiful than he could have imagined. He swung her up in his arms again and carried her into the bedroom. As he started to lower her on the bed, she pulled him down into a hot, deep kiss and then her hand was on the buttons of his fly.

Lost in the feel of her, he made love to her slow and sweet, but it took all of his effort to hold back. The second time, he didn't hold back. They rolled around on the bed, caught up in a passion that left them both spent.

Later, as they lay on the bed staring up at the skylight overhead and trying to catch their breath, he looked over at McKenzie. She was smiling.

PATIENCE. HE KNEW things would be hot for a while with the cops, which meant there was no going near McKenzie's condo or office. Killing Gus came at a cost. Now he had to live with the consequences.

Tonight he sat on his porch considering his options. One would be to go back to work. It would look better should he find himself on the suspect list. Anyone who'd been to the open houses would be scrutinized. He wasn't worried. He looked great on paper.

Gus hadn't told the police anything—just as he'd sworn before he died. He'd had to make sure the police didn't have the license plate number of the van he'd been driving that night outside McKenzie's condo. Gus hadn't given the police even the make of the vehicle he'd been driving. He couldn't believe his luck—or Gus Thompson's stupidity. Gus was the only one who could have identified him and now he was dead.

Luck was with him. It buoyed him in this difficult time. He could last a couple of days without seeing McKenzie, without going near her. Unless there was another way.

The idea came to him slowly, teasing him in its simplicity. The only way he could get to McKenzie Sheldon sooner would be if her attacker were caught. He thought of the men he'd seen at the open house. A couple of them had looked familiar. In fact, there was one he knew. He was the right size. All it would take was a couple of pieces of incriminating evidence to be found at the man's house. The police would think they had their man.

So would McKenzie Sheldon.

There would be no reason for her not to go back to work as usual.

He felt good as he got up and went to bed. When he closed his eyes, he relived every moment from the time he hit Gus Thompson and knocked him to his knees until he saw the life drain out of the man. It had been a good day.

But he couldn't stop himself from dreaming about the day he would take McKenzie Sheldon for his own. Normally, he only spent a few hours with each one. Too much time increased the chance of being caught.

With McKenzie, though, he wanted to take his time. He would have to find some place where they could be alone for more than a few hours.

McKENZIE LAY IN the bed, the stars glittering like tiny white lights through the skylight overhead, Hayes Cardwell lying next to her.

"So I have to know," McKenzie said, rolling up on one elbow to look at him. "What makes good Texas barbecue?"

Hayes smiled over at her. "Are you serious?"

"Come on. You can tell me your secret. Isn't that how you and your brothers got your start? It has to be some kind of special barbecue."

He nodded as he rolled up on his side to face her. "You have to understand. We were raised on barbecue." He closed his eyes for a moment and sniffed as if he could smell it. "You've got to have the smoke," he said as he opened his eyes and grinned at her. "And that takes a pit and a lot of patience. Most people don't know this, but cooking whole animals over smoldering coals is thought to have originated in the Caribbean. The Spanish saw how it was done and called it barbacoa. It's been refined since then, of course, and every region does it differently. Texas is known for its brisket, cooked charred black and bursting with flavor."

She laughed. "What makes your brisket so special?"

"We cover them with special seasonings and then smoke them for twelve to eighteen hours in wood-burning pits."

"Secret seasonings, right?"

"You better believe it. But wait until you taste our barbecue sauce."

"I can't wait. Am I going to get a chance to taste it?"

"Count on it," Hayes said and kissed her. It was a slow, sexy kiss that sent a throbbing ache of desire through her. She knew it wouldn't take much to find herself making love with him again. He'd been so tender the first time. The second time he'd taken her in a way that still had her heart pounding.

Just the thought brought with it the remembered pleasure. But as intimate as their lovemaking had been, she needed to know more about this man. She'd put her life into his hands. She felt as if he had done the same.

"I heard you started with just one small restaurant," she said.

He nodded. "We opened the first place in an old house with the pit out back. It was just good ol' traditional barbecue like we grew up on. You can take a cheap piece of meat and, if you cook it properly and with the right wood, it becomes a delicacy. One whiff and I can tell whether hickory, post oak or mesquite was used. But in the end, give me a piece of marbled pork shoulder and I will make you a tender, succulent pulled pork sandwich like none you've ever had before. The secret is that you've got to have smoky pork fat."

She smiled at him, hearing the pride in his voice. "Coleslaw?"

"Of course. You have to slather some sweet slaw on the pulled pork along with our spicy barbecue sauce to cut the richness of the pork. We also do a mean Southern potato salad and you are not going to believe our beans."

She had to laugh. "You're making me hungry."

"Me, too." His gaze locked with hers, making it clear it wasn't just barbecue he was hungry for.

"So the business just took off."

He nodded, almost sheepishly, as if embarrassed by their success. "None of us saw that coming."

Just like they hadn't seen this coming, she thought

as Hayes kissed her. This time she let nature take its course. She couldn't bear the thought, though, that with a killer after her, this could be the last time they made love.

"WHAT'S GOING ON, HAYES?" Tag demanded.

Hayes started as his brother stepped out of the trees next to his cabin a few hours before daylight. He was surprised and more than a little irritated. "Have you been waiting for me this whole time?"

"Don't try to avoid the question. What's the deal with you and McKenzie Sheldon?"

Hayes thought about telling him it was none of his business. But since the five brothers had been little, they'd taken care of each other. He knew his brother was asking out of concern, not idle curiosity.

"I don't know."

"This is moving a little fast, don't you think?" his brother asked.

"Oh, you're a good one to talk, Tag. You come up here for Christmas and the next thing we know, you're engaged to be married and want us to open a barbecue joint up here."

"I fell in *love*. It happens and sometimes, it happens fast." Tag studied him for a moment. "Are you telling me that's what's happening to you?"

Hayes looked out at the mountains, now dark as the pines that covered them, then up at the amazing big sky twinkling with stars. Had he ever seen a clearer sky—even in Texas?

"What if I am falling in love with her?" he demanded.

Tag laughed and shook his head. "The Cardwells just

can't do anything the easy way, can they? Bro, there is a killer after her and probably after you, as well, now."

"Don't you think I know that? I have to find him before..." He pulled off his hat and raked his fingers through his hair. "I have to find him."

"Okay, and then what?"

Hayes met his brother's gaze. "I don't know. I think about Jackson and his marriage—"

"It doesn't have to end up that way," Tag said as he followed him into the cabin. "Jackson was blinded by first love. He didn't see that all she really wanted was his money. Does McKenzie Sheldon want your money?"

"No." He let out a chuckle. "I'm not even sure she wants me for the long haul."

It was Tag's turn to laugh. "I've seen the way she looks at you. You're her hero."

"Yeah. That's what bothers me. I'm no hero. What happens when she realizes that? Worse, what if I get her killed?"

CHAPTER THIRTEEN

HAYES LOOKED TOWARD the house where McKenzie and Dana had just disappeared inside.

"Sorry I came down on you like I did last night," Tag said. "It's none of my business."

In the clear light of day, Hayes now understood why his brother had been so upset with him the night before. "Last night shouldn't have happened. It's all my fault. I should never have let it go as far as it did. My life is in Texas."

"Shouldn't you be telling her this instead of me?" his brother asked.

Hayes barely heard him. "Her life is here. She's spent these years building up a business she is proud of. I couldn't ask her to give that up. Not that I would. Not that things have gone that far."

"Take it easy, bro. You made love to her. You didn't sign away your life in blood."

"I take making love seriously."

Tag laughed. "We all do."

"You know what I mean."

"Did you tell her you loved her?"

"Of course not."

"Because you don't?"

"No, because we barely know each other. I don't even know how she feels or how I do, for that matter."

Tag shook his head. "You're falling for this woman."

He could see Dana and McKenzie inside the house. They seemed to be having a heart-to-heart. He could almost feel his ears burn just thinking what McKenzie might be telling his cousin about last night.

"If you care about her, you should tell her," Tag said. "It sounds to me like you need to figure out how you feel about her."

"It's complicated."

"It always is," Tag said. "But God forbid if anything happens to her, you'll never forgive yourself if you don't tell her."

DANA HAD PACKED them a picnic lunch and offered to help saddle horses for the ride up the mountain to the lake. "It's beautiful up there. Crystal clear and surrounded by large boulders. There is one wonderful rock that is huge and flat on top. Have your picnic up there. Or there is a lovely spot in the pines at the edge of the water. I think that is my favorite."

McKenzie gave Dana a hug. "Thank you."

"My pleasure." She smiled as she looked out the window to where her two Cardwell cousins were standing by the corral after a huge Montana breakfast of chicken-fried venison steaks, hash browns, biscuits with milk gravy and eggs peppered with fresh jalapeños from Dana's garden.

Tag was handsome as sin, but nothing like Hayes, McKenzie was thinking.

"He's special, isn't he?"

She gave a start, but didn't have to ask who she was referring to.

"Hayes reminds me of Hud." Dana met her gaze. "He's a keeper."

"His life is in Houston."

"So was Tag's," she pointed out with a grin. "It wouldn't hurt to have two Cardwell cousins up here, making sure this barbecue restaurant is a success. Wouldn't hurt to have a private-investigative business here, either."

"You're a shameless matchmaker," McKenzie joked.

"Just like my mother. Did I tell you that she made a new will before she died, leaving me the ranch? Unfortunately, she was killed in a horseback-riding accident and no one could find the will. I almost lost the ranch. If Hud and I hadn't gotten together again I would have never found the will and been able to keep this place."

"Where was the will?"

"In my mother's old recipe book marking the page with Hud's favorite cookie recipe," Dana said and laughed. "Love saved this ranch."

McKenzie had to laugh, as well. The more she was around Dana Cardwell Savage, the more she found herself wanting to be a part of this amazing family. For a few moments, she could even forget that there was a killer after her.

THE HIGH MOUNTAIN lake was just as beautiful as Dana had said it would be, Hayes thought as he swung down off his horse.

"It's breathtaking," McKenzie said as she dismounted and walked to the edge of the deep green pool.

"*You're* breathtaking," Hayes said behind her.

She smiled at him over her shoulder, then bent down and scooped up the icy water to toss back at him. He'd told himself that last night had been a mistake, that he wouldn't let it happen again. But right now all he could think about was McKenzie being in his arms again.

The droplets felt good, even though he jumped back, laughing. He loved seeing her like this, relaxed and carefree as if she didn't have a care in the world. He doubted she'd ever been like this—even before the attack. The woman had been driven in a single-minded determination to succeed. He couldn't help but wonder if any of that mattered now. Was it the attack that had changed her? Or could it possibly be that she had feelings for him? Long-lasting feelings?

He'd spent the morning on the phone with the police and doing some investigating online. The police had run the license plates of those who had attended, but with Gus Thompson's murder, they weren't giving out any information. All they'd told him was that they were checking into everyone who'd been there both for the attack on McKenzie *and* Gus Thompson's murder.

Hayes had run checks on the two men who had provided McKenzie with their names.

Would her attacker be so brazen as to give her his real name, though?

The first name he ran was Bob Garwood. The man had a military background, special ops, and had received a variety of medals before being honorably discharged.

If anything, it showed that he had special training, something that could be an advantage for a man who abducted women and killed them.

Bob Garwood had no record, not even a speeding ticket. He looked clean. Maybe McKenzie was right and he *had* been merely looking for a date the two times he'd come to her open houses.

Or maybe not, Hayes thought, as he saw that Bob Garwood owned a gym-equipment business. Did that mean he traveled? Hayes bet it did. The company he owned was called Futuristic Fitness, promising to sell the most up-to-the-moment, technologically advanced equipment on the market. That could explain why the man was in such good shape.

The next name he ran was Jason Mathews. He was an antiquities appraiser, another job where he no doubt traveled. Like Bob Garwood, Jason Mathews looked clean. He was married, owned his house and volunteered for several charitable organizations— not that any of that cleared him, Hayes thought, reminded of Gacy who dressed as a clown at charitable functions.

The police hadn't found anything suspicious about any of the other viewers who'd attended the open house from what he'd been told. They were still investigating.

Hayes had finally given up in frustration. He couldn't even be sure that McKenzie's attacker had driven to the open house. He could have come by foot; in fact, that seemed more likely since when he stumbled upon Gus Thompson, he hadn't hesitated to kill him, even though it was a dangerous thing to do.

"I guess swimming is out," McKenzie said wistfully.

"Not necessarily," Hayes answered as he began to pull off his boots. He could use a cold dip in the lake. Not that he thought it would help. "Dana packed towels as well as a blanket." He raised a brow and McKenzie laughed as she hurriedly began to undress.

"Last one in has to unpack the lunch."

THE CALL CAME forty-eight hours later. The police had received an anonymous tip from a neighbor. When they'd gone to a man by the name of Eric Winters's house to talk to him, they'd spotted incriminating evidence in his car and gotten a search warrant. Inside the house, they'd found the knife believed used to kill Gus Thompson along with items believed to have belonged to female victims that he'd kept as souvenirs—including McKenzie's red, high-heeled shoe.

McKenzie began to cry when she got the news as she thought of his other victims. The name Eric Winters meant nothing to her. Even when the police described the man to her, she couldn't place him, but apparently he'd come through the open house for the ranchette. He'd just been one of a dozen men who could have been her attacker.

"So it's definitely him?" she asked, weak with relief.

"Given the evidence we found at his house, we have the man who attacked you. Your shoe will have to be kept as evidence."

"It's all right. I won't be wearing those heels again, anyway. Thank you so much for letting me know." For so long she'd thought they would never find him, that she would always be looking over her shoulder. She hung up and turned to look at Hayes. Her eyes welled again with tears as she said, "They got him," and stepped into Hayes's arms.

Dana threw a celebratory dinner complete with champagne that night. "Stay," she pleaded when McKenzie thanked her for everything and told her she would be moving out of the cabin in the morning.

"I wish I could stay. I love it up here, but I have a business to run. I've been away from it for too long as it is." The business had been her world just a week ago. It had taken all of her time and energy as well as her every waking thought. Until Hayes, she hadn't realized what she was missing.

But now he had no reason to stay and she had no reason not to return to her life, even if it did suddenly feel empty.

"And Hayes?" Dana asked, as if sensing her mood.

McKenzie looked across the room where the men were gathered. "I guess there is nothing keeping him in Montana now," she said.

Dana lifted an eyebrow in response. "You could ask him to stay... Otherwise, he'll be back next month for Tag's wedding...."

McKenzie smiled at her new friend. "He *has* asked me to be his date."

Dana grinned knowingly. "That's if he can stay away from you until the wedding. I guess we'll see."

"I guess we will," she agreed. The thought of the wedding buoyed her spirits a little, but there was no denying it. Things had changed. *She* had changed. While she had to get back to work, it wasn't with the same excited expectation that she usually felt at the prospect. True, she would never feel as safe as she had, not in Bozeman, not in her condo. But it was more than that.

She'd fallen for the man, for his family, for even this ranch lifestyle. Not that she was about to admit that to him or his cousin, for that matter. As she'd told Dana, Hayes had a life in Houston. She had a life here. He hadn't asked to get involved. He hadn't even wanted her to know he was the one who'd saved her that night, she reminded herself.

As Hayes turned to look at her, he smiled and she felt her heart rise up like a bubble. She smiled back, fighting tears.

WHERE WAS SHE?

The words had been rattling around in his brain for four days now. It had taken the police several days to arrest Eric Winters. But now two more days had passed. Hadn't the police told her that her attacker had been caught? What was she waiting for? She should be back at work—and so should he. He couldn't afford to take much more time off. As it was, people were starting to notice. He couldn't keep saying he was taking off time to look for another house.

Unfortunately, his Realtor had disappeared. He'd expected her to hide out for a while after poor Gus Thompson's death. But that was almost a week ago. She hadn't been staying at her condo. Nor had she been going to her office. When he'd called the office, he'd been told that she couldn't be reached. He'd declined another real-estate agent, saying he had talked to Ms. Sheldon and only she could answer his questions.

From the exasperated tone of the receptionist's voice, he gathered that he wasn't the only one trying to reach her. Like him, surely she couldn't be away from work too long. Not a woman like her. She must be champing at the bit to return. These days away must be driving her insane.

Her absence was certainly pushing him over the edge. He didn't know how much longer he could stand it. He had to find her and finish this.

His instincts told him that she was with the cowboy. Before he'd killed Gus Thompson, he'd found out that

the cowboy's name was Hayes Cardwell and that he
was from Houston, Texas. He was considering opening a restaurant at Big Sky.

Cardwell. Wasn't there a ranch up there by that
name? That had to be where McKenzie Sheldon was
hiding. It would be too dangerous to go to the ranch.
No, he had to find another way to flush her out.

He picked up the phone and called her office. He'd
been careful not to come on too strong with the receptionist. He hadn't wanted to call too much attention to
himself. But this time— "M.K. Realty, may I help you?"

"I sure hope so. I've been hoping to reach Ms. Sheldon, but now another house with another Realtor has
come up—"

"I would be happy to put you through to her—"

"I've already left messages for her."

"Ms. Sheldon is at her desk this morning. I'll put you
right through. May I say who's calling?"

HAYES LOOKED OUT the office window at the Houston
skyscape. Just hours ago he'd been in the Gallatin Valley looking out at the mountains as his plane banked
and headed south. Now here, he couldn't believe there
had ever been a time that this had felt like home.

"What's bothering you?" Laramie demanded behind
him from his desk. "If you still have doubts about opening a restaurant in Montana—"

"It's not that," he said, turning away from the view.
The offices for Texas Boys Barbecue had started out
in a corner of an old house not all that long ago. Now,
though, it resided in a high-rise downtown with other
corporations that pulled in millions of dollars a year.

"What is it, then?" Laramie demanded. "You've been acting oddly since you walked into my office."

"It's nothing." He didn't want to talk about McKenzie. It only made it harder. Better to put her and Montana behind him. "Have you talked to Austin?"

"You really want to talk about Austin?" his brother asked as Hayes took a seat across from him. "I've never seen you mope around over a woman before."

"I'm not—"

"Have you talked to her?"

Hayes gave up denying his mood had nothing to do with McKenzie. "She sounds like she is back at work and doing fine."

"And you probably told her you are back at work, too, and doing fine, right?"

He made a face at his brother. "She's happy with her life."

"Is that what she told you? Hayes, do you know anything about women?"

He had to laugh. "Not really. But I'm not sure you're the man to give me advice. Have you dated a woman more than once?"

"Very funny. One of you has to say it."

"Say what?"

Laramie groaned. "That you're in love. That is the problem, you know. You've fallen for the woman." He raised a hand. "Don't even bother to deny it. The question now is what are you going to do about it? Mope around and feel sorry for yourself or go get your woman?"

Hayes started to tell him how off base he was, but he saved his breath. "Just fly up there and go riding in

on my white horse? Then what? I have a house, an office and a job here in Houston."

"Are you serious? You would let a simple stumbling
block like those things keep you from what you really
want? What did you do with my brother Hayes who has
always gone after what he wants?"

"I've just never wanted anything this badly and I
don't even know if I can have her," he admitted and
not easily.

"Only one way to find out. Better saddle up and
get yourself back to Montana." Laramie picked up the
phone. "Take the corporate jet. I'll have the pilot standing by."

"Ms. SHELDON?" He couldn't believe she was actually
in her office, actually on the other end of the line. "I'm
so glad to catch you in your office."

He'd been following the story about Eric Winters
in the newspaper and on the evening television news.
The man hadn't even been able to get out on bail. And
now they were saying he could be a serial killer, having abducted and killed women all across the West.
McKenzie must feel so safe, believing her attacker was
finally behind bars.

"My wife and I are interested in seeing one of your
houses. I was hoping you would be able to show us the
residence as soon as possible. My wife was very impressed by you when we met you a while back. I told
her I would see if you were free to show the house yourself. I know you own M.K. Realty." He'd learned that
acknowledging that he knew who he was dealing with
often worked.

"When were you thinking of seeing the house?" she

asked, even though he could tell she had been ready to give him to someone else at the agency.

"My wife is very anxious. She doesn't want this house to get snatched up by someone else. I would imagine that now is too soon?" He heard her surprise. Before she could draw a breath, he said, "It's the one you have listed as executive, high-end home with a million-dollar view."

"I'm familiar with the house."

"I believe it also has a several-million-dollar price tag. I can't tell you what I would have to contend with if we lost it before my wife even got a chance to see it."

"We can't have that," she said and he knew he had her. "I suppose I could show the house in, say, an hour?"

"I really appreciate this. My wife and I will meet you out there, if that is all right." This was working out even better than he'd hoped.

"I look forward to it. I'm sorry. I didn't catch your name."

"It's Jason. Jason and Emily Mathews."

"Yes, I remember we met at several of my showings." She sounded uneasy and he knew he had to mention the murder.

"I was so sorry to hear about your colleague being killed. That was such a shock. I'm glad the murderer has been caught. You just don't expect that kind of thing in Montana."

"It's rare, fortunately," she said and quickly changed the subject. "I'll see you soon, then, Mr. Mathews."

"Please call me Jason."

CHAPTER FOURTEEN

THE MOMENT MCKENZIE got off the phone she walked over to one of the cubicles.

"Jennifer, would you be able to take one of my showings this afternoon?"

The real-estate agent looked up in surprise. McKenzie had never asked any of them to take her showings until this moment.

The woman blinked then said, "I'd be happy to. Are you not feeling well?"

McKenzie almost laughed. "It's just that I have one before it that could take a while. Also I don't want you going alone. See if Rafe can go with you. I've decided from now on, we won't be showing houses alone if at all possible, but definitely any that could run over after dark."

"But aren't you showing one now alone?" Jennifer asked tentatively.

"It will be all right this one time. I'm meeting a man and his wife at the Warner place."

"I'm sure Rafe can go with me."

"Great. Thanks for doing this." As she walked back to her office, McKenzie felt relieved. She had the other showing covered and after today, she would start relying more on her staff. If being gone had taught her anything, it was that she was not indispensible. For so long, she'd thought she had to do everything herself and yet when she'd returned after being gone for a week, she found that the agency was doing just fine.

There'd been numerous calls for follow-ups on houses she'd shown, but her staff had taken care of all but a couple of them. One of those was probably Mr. and Mrs. Mathews. Jason Mathews came across as the kind of man who only dealt with the boss or owner. Well, she was taking care of that one now.

McKenzie felt as if a weight had been lifted off her shoulders and at the same time, she couldn't help feeling a little sad. She hadn't heard from Hayes other than a quick phone call from the airport after he'd landed in Houston.

She'd gotten an agency call she'd had to take so she'd been forced to cut the call with Hayes short. When she'd tried to call him back, she'd gotten his voice mail. She hadn't left a message. What was there to say?

He'd asked how it felt to be back at work. She'd lied and said, "Great."

She'd asked him if he was glad to be home. He'd said he was.

That pretty much covered anything they had to say to each other, didn't it?

Outside her office, dark clouds had moved in. Thunder rumbled in the distance. The weatherman had warned that they might get some summer storms over the next few days.

Packing up her things, she headed for the door, also surprising her staff. She was always the first one in the office and the last to leave. As she walked out to her car in daylight, she couldn't help thinking of Hayes and Cardwell Ranch.

Was Hayes missing it and her as much as she was him? She pushed the thought away. She'd see him next month for Tag's wedding. The thought lightened her step even when it began to rain.

HE WAS WAITING for her. Anticipation had his heart racing. He'd failed once. He couldn't let that happen again.

Arriving early, he'd waited and gone over all the things that could go wrong. She might see that he hadn't brought his wife and panic, taking off before he could stop her. Or she might send someone else. Maybe even more possible, she might bring an associate.

He just couldn't let anything happen that would allow her to get away. Again.

He'd taken even more precautions since his failure with her the first time. He'd secured a place for them nearby. He couldn't chance transporting her any distance. Knowing Ms. Sheldon the way he did, she would be one of those women who got loose in the trunk, broke out a taillight and signaled for help.

Another precaution he was taking was knocking her out quickly. He'd opted to use a drug. He couldn't take the chance he might hit her too hard and kill her before all the fun began. It felt like cheating, drugging her, but he'd lost her once. That wasn't going to happen again. That's why he'd carefully chosen this huge monster of a house in the middle of the valley—and the abandoned house through the trees, only a short walk away.

Normally, he just dragged them out into the woods. But McKenzie Sheldon wasn't getting his quick and dirty usual fare. No, she was going to get the full treatment and that meant he would need a room inside a house.

He'd found one near the house he'd told her he wanted to view. He was counting on her not telling anyone where she was going. He was counting on it, based on the fact that she was the boss and that she would no longer be afraid since as far as she knew, her attacker was still behind bars.

The hard part would be getting her away from this house quickly and to their private spot. He would have to act fast, taking her in her car then coming back for his own car.

At the sound of a vehicle approaching, he tensed. McKenzie Sheldon was right on time. He checked the syringe in his pocket. Now, if she was alone, then nothing could stop him. He carefully adjusted the large straw hat balanced on the back of the passenger seat. From a distance it would appear his wife was sitting in the car waiting.

He glanced in his rearview mirror. It was McKenzie and she was alone. He smiled excitedly as he opened his car door and stepped out. All he needed was a few precious seconds and she'd be his.

HAYES THOUGHT ABOUT what his brother had said on the flight to Montana in the corporate jet. He also thought about McKenzie Sheldon's well-ordered life.

Like him, his career had taken up the greater part of his life. But that, he realized now, was because there hadn't been anything else that had interested him.

Now, his career, as important as it was, wasn't the first thing he thought of when he awakened in the morning. But was that true of McKenzie?

He'd seen her checking the messages on her phone, especially after a few days at the ranch. She'd been worried about her business. Not that he could blame her. She'd been such a major part of the agency he doubted she thought it could survive without her.

Hayes called McKenzie's office the moment the jet touched down outside of Bozeman, but was told she'd left work early.

"Have you tried her home?" the receptionist asked when he gave her his name. Word must have gone around the office that she'd spent almost a week with him up the canyon at Cardwell Ranch.

"She's already gone home?"

The receptionist laughed at his surprise. "I know it isn't like her. She even asked one of the associates to show a house for her this afternoon. We all thought she might have a date or something."

A date? He heard the woman try to swallow back her words.

"I mean we thought she was going out with you." Another gulp. "Is there a message I can give her if I hear from her?"

"No." He'd disconnected, wondering what he was doing flying to Montana. A *date?*

Well, what do you expect? he asked himself. *It wasn't as if you asked her to wait for you or even told her how you felt.*

Still, he hadn't been gone *that* long.

He tried her cell but it went to voice mail. On impulse, he called the office back and asked to speak to the sales associate who McKenzie had gotten to cover for her.

"This is Jennifer Robinson."

Hayes introduced himself and asked if she knew whether or not McKenzie was showing a house.

"She is, the Warner place."

That was the McKenzie Sheldon he knew, he thought with a sigh of relief. "Can you tell me how to find the Warner place? If she just left, I might be able to catch her."

McKENZIE SAW THE large, newer-model expensive car parked by the house as she came up the drive.

Jason Mathews got out as she approached. She remembered him from the open house where Gus was killed. For a moment, she almost drove on through the circular drive and left.

You have nothing to fear. Your attacker was caught. Not only that, he brought his wife, right? As she glanced to the passenger seat, she saw a large summer straw hat and remembered that Emily Mathews was a tiny woman. Relief washed over her.

For a moment, though, she was sorry she hadn't brought another agent with her. Her heart just wasn't in this, even though the sale would mean a very large commission. This was one of a number of houses in this area that the bank was anxious to get sold after a rash of foreclosures.

Having two agents go on every showing wasn't the best use of manpower. Also, she knew the nonlist agent would complain about losing money. Still, she wanted her agents to be safe and she would have gladly shared the commission.

Shutting off the car, she turned toward the passenger seat to dig the house keys out of her purse. To her surprise, her car door opened. She turned, startled to find Jason Mathews standing next to her car.

"I appreciate you taking the time to do this today," he said.

She tried to find her voice as she told herself he was just being polite, opening her door like that. "Just let me get the keys."

As she picked them up, she gripped them like a knife. Hayes's words came back to her that keys weren't much of a weapon because by then the attacker would be too close. Women lost their advantage up close because they were often the weaker sex.

At that moment, she was sorry she'd given Hayes back the pistol she used to have in her purse. She still had the can of pepper spray, but it would be in the bottom of her purse, not easily accessible.

All these thoughts hit her in a matter of seconds before Jason Mathews said, "I'll get Emily. She is anxious to see this house. Great location since she likes the idea of no neighbors within view."

He stepped away from the car and McKenzie felt herself breathe again. She chastised herself as she climbed out, dragging her purse out after her.

As she headed toward the house, she saw that Mr. Mathews was leaning into the car talking to his wife. For a woman who was anxious to see the house, she certainly was taking her time getting out of the car.

McKenzie headed for the front door of the house, just assuming the two would follow. Whatever discussion was going on between them, she didn't want to eavesdrop.

When her cell phone rang, she stopped partway up the wide front steps to dig the phone out of her purse. Busy thinking about Mrs. Mathews and hoping this hadn't been a wild goose chase, she didn't bother to check to see who was calling. "Hello?"

"McKenzie Sheldon? This is Officer Pamela Donovan with the Bozeman Police Department. I don't want to alarm you."

Alarm her? Surprised, she didn't hear Jason Mathews come up behind her until she felt the needle he plunged into her neck.

HAYES'S RENTAL CAR was waiting for him with the map inside just as he had requested. The Warner place, as Jennifer had called it, was about five miles outside of town to the south.

That meant it was at least fifteen miles from the airport. The worst part was the traffic. While nothing like Houston's, he'd managed to hit the valley during the afternoon rush hour. Just his luck.

He'd left a message with both Jennifer and the receptionist to have McKenzie call him if they heard from her. That's why when his phone rang he thought it would be her.

He was thrown for a moment when he realized the female voice on the other end of the line was the policewoman who'd worked with McKenzie after her attack.

"Yes, I remember you, Ms. Donovan."

"I just tried to reach Ms. Sheldon."

It was the worry he heard in her voice. "Is there a problem?"

"I didn't want to alarm her, but there is some news about the man we arrested in her attack. It might not mean anything—"

"What is it?" he asked as he drove toward the Gallatin Range of mountains to the south.

"McKenzie Sheldon isn't with you, by any chance, is she?" the policewoman asked.

"No. I was just on my way to the house she's showing. Why?"

He heard her hesitate before she said, "I just tried to reach her. We were cut off."

Unconsciously, he found himself driving a little faster. "Why were you trying to reach her?" Again the pause. "Officer—"

"There is some question whether or not the man we have in jail for her attack is guilty," the deputy finally said. "I can't get into it, but the dates of the other abductions aren't adding up for him and there is some question about the evidence we found in his house."

His heart pounded. "The dates. They don't add up for him, but they do for someone else, someone who was at the open house where Gus Thompson was killed, right?"

"When we went to bring Jason Mathews in for questioning, his wife told us that he'd had to leave town for a few days."

Hayes swore under his breath. "I was told at McKenzie's office that she was showing a house to a husband and wife." He prayed that was true and that the man sans the wife wasn't Jason Mathews. "I'm on my way there now." He gave her the directions he'd been given.

"We'll have a patrol car there as soon as possible."

Disconnecting, he drove as if his life depended on it, all the time mentally kicking himself for ever leaving. Worse, for never telling McKenzie how he felt about her.

MCKENZIE WOKE TO darkness. She tried to open her eyes but her lids felt too heavy. For a moment she couldn't remember anything. She cracked an eyelid open as she attempted to move. Her hands were bound with duct tape at the wrists in front of her, her feet were bound at the ankles and she was strapped to a wheelchair.

A shot of adrenaline rocketed through her as memory came back in a wave of nausea. The prick of the needle, the horror of what was happening as she slumped against Jason Mathews, the fleeting glimpse of the empty car except for the carefully positioned summer straw hat on the back of the passenger seat.

She looked around, terrified to see where he'd brought her.

"Well, hello," Jason Mathews said from where he stood nearby. "Nice to have you back."

With relief she saw that she was still dressed, but that several of the buttons on her blouse were open. She shuddered at the thought of this man's hands on her as she lifted her gaze. The room was small. A walk-in closet or maybe a pantry. Were they still at the Warner house? She didn't think so, but all of these high-end houses had similar features.

Drugged, it took her a moment to realize he hadn't gagged her. She opened her mouth and tried to scream. The sound that came out was weak. She tried again, stopping only when he erupted into a fit of laughing.

"No one can hear you. There's no one around for miles. Not that I mind hearing you scream. I plan to make you scream a whole lot more before this day is over."

His smile curdled her stomach. She tried to fight down the terror that weakened her as much as the drug he'd given her. Her mind raced. Had she told anyone at the office where she'd gone? Yes, Jennifer. She'd told

her she was meeting a husband and wife at the Warner
place. Not that there would be reason for anyone to start
looking for her for hours. More like days.

Her heart dropped at the thought as the man stepped
in front of her, forcing her to raise her gaze to his.

"Finally, we are alone," he said, smiling. "I was worried it wasn't ever going to happen. We are going to have
so much fun. Well, I am," he added with a laugh. "First
I want to show you the house. It is only polite, since you
showed me several houses." He stepped behind her and,
kicking off the wheelchair brake, propelled her out of
the small room into a larger one.

She saw that she'd been right about the space he'd
had her in being a walk-in closet, even though there
were no shelves or rods on the walls yet.

"The master bedroom!" he announced with a flour-
ish. "I haven't had time to decorate, or even get a bed,
so we'll have to make due."

Dust coated the floor. She frowned, trying to make
sense of where they were. Not in the Warner place.
She'd shown it before and it had been clean, although
empty for some time like a lot of other houses in the
neighborhood this far out of town. Were they in one of
those houses? Some had been abandoned by the contractors when they'd gone broke and the banks had been
slow to move on selling them.

Her gaze stopped on a pile of items in the corner of
the room. Terror turned her bones to mush at the sight
of the duct tape, handcuffs, gag ball and an array of sex
toys, including a whip.

She closed her eyes, dropping her head, unable to
look. She couldn't let herself give in to this. She had
to find a way to escape. This wasn't the way she was

going to die, not in this dirty, abandoned house with this madman.

"You need to wake up," he said next to her ear.

She didn't open her eyes. She needed to get away from him. She needed a weapon. She needed even half a chance. She could still feel the drug in her bloodstream. It made her limbs feel lifeless, her reflexes slow.

While driven, she'd still always been a realist. No one was going to save her and she didn't see any way to save herself, bound the way she was. He'd done this before. He knew what he was doing. And since she'd gotten away from him once, he had made sure she wouldn't this time, she thought as she tested the tape on her wrists and ankles.

He was going to kill her.

But not until he hurt her. She had seen the cruel glimmer in his eyes as soon as she'd looked at him moments before. For whatever reason, he liked hurting women. It must make him feel superior, not that his reasons mattered.

"I must have given you too much of the drug," he said, sounding disappointed, even angry. "I don't want you to miss a minute of the fun so you are going to have to wake up."

She kept her eyes closed. Let him think it was the drug.

The slap made her eyes fly open and slammed her head back against the webbing on the wheelchair seat. His face was inches from her own now, his breath rank as he laughed.

"I thought that might bring you out of it," he said with another laugh, and stepped behind the chair again.

"Pay attention or the next time, I'll have to do something much more painful to get your attention."

He wheeled her through a door and into the large master bath. Her heart stopped at the sight of a roll of plastic in the bathtub and several new blue tarps spread over the floor. "That's for later. I want to put that part off as long as possible this time. You deserve my best after what you've put me through."

She heard the underlying anger in his voice. It made her blood run cold. He planned to hurt her for as long as he could keep her alive. A sob caught in her chest. "Why?" she cried, hating to let him see how terrified she was.

He laughed as he shoved her into the bedroom again then whirled the wheelchair around to face him. The blade of a pair of scissors caught the light, shimmering in his hand. She gasped and tried to draw back as he moved in closer.

"Why?" he asked mockingly. "Because I can."

The knife blade cut through the tape holding her to the chair an instant before he stepped behind the wheelchair and unceremoniously dumped her into the middle of the master bedroom floor. The sound of the blade cutting through the tape reminded her of it cutting through her hair.

"Tour over," he said. "It's time for the fun to begin."

She looked up at him from the floor where she lay on her side, bound and helpless. If she couldn't get away, then there was only one thing to do. She had to make him so furious that he killed her quickly.

CHAPTER FIFTEEN

HAYES HIT A rain shower near the mountains. It was still spitting rain as the Warner place came into view. The massive house sat on a small rise with a stand of aspens and pines behind it. From the third floor, he would guess there was a three-hundred-and-sixty-degree view of the valley. The house was just as Jennifer at the agency had described it. Massive, tan with matching stone and a circular driveway. The driveway was empty.

"No!" he yelled and slammed his fist against the steering wheel as he slowed. She couldn't have already come here, shown the house and left, unless... Once off the narrow paved road, the circular drive was an intricate pattern of cobblestones. Unfortunately, Montana winters had done their worst, breaking some and dislodging others. His tires rumbled over them as he neared the elaborate front door.

Unless the couple she was supposed to show the house to had called and canceled. He tried her number again. Again, it went straight to voice mail. Still, he was about to grasp onto that theory like a life raft when he saw the muddy footprints.

Hayes threw on the brakes. The rain had stopped. His windshield wipers scraped loudly across the dry glass. He shut them off, then leaving the rental running, got out.

The prints appeared to be muddy boot tracks. What had caught his eye was how they had trailed onto the cobblestones from the side of the house.

So she had shown the house to someone? He started to follow the tracks along the side of the house. The landscaping had never been finished except for a little out front. Peering in a window, he found the house was empty. It had that never-lived-in look and he was reminded of something McKenzie had told him about overbuilding back in the early two thousands. Building contractors had gone broke, leaving grandiose spec houses for the banks to deal with. This appeared to be one of them.

As he neared the back of the house, he expected the tracks to head for the rear entrance, assuming they must be from whomever McKenzie had shown the house to.

But the tracks veered off into the trees. Strange. The hair rose on the back of his neck as he realized the tracks had been heading out of the woods behind the house—and ended on the cobblestones out front.

What the hell? He'd put on his gun and shoulder holster after the call from the policewoman. He checked his gun now as he realized what he was seeing. Whoever had recently come to the Warner place from the trees hadn't walked back. They'd driven.

"DOES YOUR WIFE KNOW?"

He'd never let the others talk. He'd kept their mouths duct taped. He hadn't needed to hear their screams. The eyes were more than windows into the soul. He had been able to see their terror as their eyes widened in disbelief. None of them had been able to believe it was happening to them. When the realization that they were about to die finally hit them, it, too, was in their eyes. He hadn't needed to even hear more than their muffled screams.

"If Emily really is your wife, then she *must* know," McKenzie said. "No woman could be that stupid."

"Don't talk about my wife. She doesn't know anything," he snapped.

"She probably turns a blind eye, just thankful it isn't her."

"Emily isn't like that. She's sweet and kind and… If she knew…" His voice trailed off, the thought too horrifying. Emily loved him. She trusted him. She looked up to him. She wasn't like these successful bitches who looked down their noses at him. If only she had come along years ago before…the others.

"I bet she can smell it on you when you come home. Does she make you shower? Or does she like it, the smell of another woman's pain on you?"

"Enough!" he bellowed, his voice echoing in the cavernous empty room. "You don't know anything about it."

"Don't I? You know she can see it building up inside you, then you leave and when you come back…" She met his gaze, hers hard as stone. "Believe me, she knows."

He kicked her, catching her in the stomach and flipping her over. A painful cry came out of her so he kicked her again, shutting her up except for the second groan of pain. He flipped her back over to face him as he dropped down beside her and cupped her face in his hands, pulling her a breath's distance from his own face.

"You want to know why I do this? Because of women like you. You think you're so smart. Bitches, all of you.

But once you realize that you're mine to do with whatever I want, then you change your tune. Like the others, you will cry and whine and plead with me."

She spit in his face.

He screamed in fury, releasing her to slap her as hard as he could. Her head snapped back, smacking the floor. He hurriedly wiped her saliva from his face with his sleeve, cringing at the horrible feel of it on his skin. "I am going to kill you!" he yelled. "I'm going to—"

"Big man, killing a woman who is bound and helpless. This is what makes you feel better? If you were a real man—"

He snatched up the whip from the corner of the room and swung it at her. She tried to roll away from him, only managing to flip over once before the cattails sliced the back of her blouse open along with her skin. She screamed.

As HAYES ENTERED the dark stand of trees, he pulled his weapon. Droplets from the rain still shone in the bright green leaves of the aspens and dripped down occasionally as he followed the tracks.

He hadn't gone far when the trees opened a little. He glimpsed the backyard of another house. Around him, everything was deathly quiet. He didn't even hear a birdsong, just the drip of the trees.

Hayes moved along the edge of the trees until he could see the front of the house. No vehicles and yet the tracks were fresh. Two sets. Both disappearing into the garage. His heart began to pound faster as he worked his way toward the back of the house, keeping out of sight of the rear windows.

He passed an old greenhouse, the door dangling

open. Inside he would see where the vegetation had taken over, but rather than being green, everything appeared crusted with a thick layer of dust. It was the kind of thing that had creeped him out when he was a kid exploring old houses with his brothers.

He moved past the greenhouse and through an old garden spot, the dried cornstalks giving him cover until he was within a dozen yards of the back entrance to the house.

The muddy tracks ended on the back step. He drew out his phone and called 911. He was headed for the door when a scream pierced the silence.

The back door wasn't locked. That was because the man inside hadn't been expecting company? Or had set a trap for him? Hayes took a chance, slipping through and moving fast through the big, empty house.

He couldn't tell where the scream had come from, but there were tracks in the dust on the floor. One set of man-sized footprints and two narrow wheel tracks. What the hell?

"Not so mouthy now, are you?" Jason said as he crouched down next to her.

The initial pain had been incredible. She'd never felt anything like it and could no more have held back the scream as she could have quit breathing.

Worse, she knew this was just the beginning. She could feel blood soaking into her blouse, running down her back.

He was kneeling next to her, his face close, so close she could feel his breath on her again. It took all her courage to look up into his face, knowing what she would find there. Satisfaction. He knew now that he could break her. There had probably never been a doubt in his mind. She was the fool for thinking she could trick this man into killing her.

He smiled. "I'm sorry. Did you have something else you wanted to say?"

As he started to move back from her, she swung her arms up, looping her bound wrists around his neck. She brought him down hard, pulling him off-balance and slamming his face into the floor next to her.

McKenzie knew it had been a stupid thing to do. She knew it wouldn't knock him out. If anything, it would only make him more furious and more determined to make her pay. She'd acted out of pain and fear and desperation.

He let out a bellow of pain and fury. She tried to slam his face down again, but he broke free of her hold, swinging wildly at her. She managed to roll away after only one blow, quickly rolling a second time so her back wasn't turned to him when he stumbled to his feet.

Dazed, his nose appearing broken and bleeding, he stared at her for a moment. He was breathing hard and looked unsteady on his feet. As he started toward her, she swung around on her butt and kicked him, knocking his feet out from under him.

He went down hard, hitting the wood floor with an *uhftt*. This time, he got up much faster and even as she tried to push herself back into the wall, he was on her, grabbing a handful of her short hair to drag her out into the center of the floor again.

"You have no idea what you've done!" he screeched at her as he held one hand to his bleeding nose and groped in his pocket with the other hand. Something silver flashed in his free hand an instant later.

McKenzie saw the scissors blade gleam in the late-afternoon light an instant before he lunged at her.

HAYES HADN'T GONE far into the house when he heard what sounded like a battle going on overhead. Of course, McKenzie would put up a fight just as she had the night she was attacked in the grocery-store parking lot, fighting for her life.

Rushing through the massive house, he finally found the stairs. What he saw brought him up short. There were no footprints in the dust on the steps and for an instant he stood confused, fighting to make sense of what he was seeing. He could hear sounds of a fight going on upstairs and yet—

That's when he spotted the elevator and the tracks leading into it—the same ones he'd found just inside the back door—a man's muddy boot prints and the two narrow wheel tracks.

He took off up the stairs at a dead run, weapon drawn. McKenzie's scream filled the air as he topped the stairs. He followed the sound, still running, breathing hard, knowing he would kill the man. Blinded with rage, he wanted to tear the man limb from limb. Hayes had never felt that kind of anger. It scared him and yet it also fueled him as he ran toward the heartbreaking sounds. He just prayed he would reach McKenzie before the madman killed *her*.

As JASON MATHEWS lunged at her with scissors, he let out a roar. She caught a glimpse of the insanity burning in his eyes. He came at her like a wounded animal, only this animal didn't just want to fight back. This animal yearned for retribution as only a human animal can.

He came at her so fast, she didn't get a chance to swing around with her feet. He came at her face, slashing the blades wildly. Had he simply tried to stab her, she might not have raised her hands to protect herself. But then again, she might have instinctively. She would never know.

She felt the blades slash across the backside of one wrist where she was bound by the thick tape. Because of that, she didn't feel the pain at first. She'd drawn her feet up as he'd struck her and managed to kick out at him, catching him in one knee. She heard screaming and thought at first it was her.

His leg buckled and he came down on top of her. She tried to roll out from under him, but he was too heavy. He had her pinned to the floor as he tried to struggle to his feet.

He rose just enough that he could get the scissors between them. He was going to kill her. Not the way he had wanted. But he could no longer hold back. She saw it in his expression as he struggled to rise.

Defeat, it was in his eyes, as well as disgust and pain. His nose was still bleeding and there was a bruised spot on his forehead from where it must have connected to the floor. The bright red blood had run down onto his white shirt.

How would he explain that to his wife?

That crazed, terrified thought came out of nowhere. The random thought of a woman about to die.

Hayes. The thought of him came with such regret she felt tears well in her eyes. She didn't want to die without at least telling him that she'd fallen in love with him.

Jason steadied himself as he timed his next thrust, this one aimed at her heart. They were both breathing hard, his breath making a loud almost snoring sound because of his broken nose. Neither of them heard the pounding of footfalls in the hallway.

Jason raised the scissors, meeting her gaze with one of rage and pain. He looked as if he was about to cry. McKenzie wanted to look away, but she couldn't. Her eyes locked with his. He almost looked afraid of her. He just wanted it to be over, she thought and realized that killing her this way wouldn't give him what he needed so there would be other women—and soon. That thought filled her with more sorrow than the thought of her own imminent death.

With the look of a man about to drive a stake into a vampire's heart, he grabbed the scissors in both hands and brought the blades down.

The sound of the gunshot was like an explosion, even in the large master suite. Another shot filled the air. Then another and another.

McKenzie had accepted that she would die. She'd told herself not to fight it as Jason drove the scissor blades down at her heart. But the gunshots into his back threw off his aim and gave her a few seconds to shift her body to the side. The blades came down into her side in a searing pain. Her cry was lost in the echo of the gunshots.

HAYES THOUGHT OF the first time he'd laid eyes on McKenzie Sheldon. She'd been lying on the ground bleeding and then her eyes had opened....

He shoved the madman's body off her and dropped to his knees next to her.

"McKenzie!" There was blood everywhere. He couldn't tell how much of it was hers as he felt for a pulse, praying with every second that he would feel one. "McKenzie?"

He found a pulse and tried to breathe a little easier as McKenzie's eyes blinked open. What was it about those eyes? "McKenzie. Sweetheart. How badly are you hurt?"

She shook her head and tried to smile through the pain. "The bastard cut me. His name is Jason Mathews. He—"

"Don't try to talk," he told her. He could hear sirens in the distance. "You're going to be all right. You're safe now."

She closed her eyes as he took her hand. He thought about the first time he'd told her that. It had been a lie. She hadn't been safe. But she would be now, he thought as he looked over at the dead man.

Outside police cars and an ambulance had pulled up. He didn't want to let go of her hand, but he did only long enough to go to the window and direct the EMTs up on the elevator.

As he dropped down onto the bloody floor next to McKenzie again, he realized he was shaking. He thought about what he'd seen the moment he'd cleared the bedroom doorway. McKenzie bound up like that on the floor and that man standing over her, a pair of long-bladed scissors clamped in his hands, the man's beaten face twisted in a grimace—

That was all he remembered until he was on his knees next to McKenzie. He didn't remember pulling the trigger, couldn't even say how many times he'd shot the man.

That thought scared him. He'd been in the P.I. business for ten years. He considered himself a professional. He'd never lost control before.

Suddenly the room was filled with cops and EMTs and a stretcher. He let go of McKenzie's hand and moved back out of the way.

"Is she going to be okay?" he asked as two EMTs went to work on her.

"She's stable. We'll know more once we get her to the hospital."

Hayes wanted desperately to ride in the ambulance with her but one look at the cops and he knew he wasn't going anywhere. "Mind if I call my brother so he can go to the hospital to be with McKenzie until I can get there?"

CHAPTER SIXTEEN

McKENZIE WOKE WITH a start. As her eyes flew open, she saw the woman standing next to her hospital bed. Had she been able to forget yesterday's horror, she might not have recognized the woman at first.

But she hadn't been able to escape Jason Mathews, even filled with anesthesia in the operating room or later in a sedated sleep. He'd followed her into her nightmares.

"Emily Mathews?" She tried to sit up but the woman placed a hand on her shoulder, holding her down on the bed. McKenzie looked up into Jason's wife's face. A pair of dark brown eyes stared back at her.

"I had to see you," the woman said in that small, timid voice McKenzie remembered from the day at the ranchette showing. "Jason's dead, you know."

Dead, but far from forgotten. She tried to sit up again, but she was weak from whatever she'd been given after the surgery. Her side hurt like the devil from where she'd been stabbed. She saw that one of her wrists was bandaged and there was something plastered to her back under her nightgown that burned.

She felt foggy, as if caught between a nightmare and reality. Was this woman even really in her room or was this yet another nightmare?

As she felt the pain and recalled what the madman had done to her, she knew she wasn't dreaming.

"Here, let me do that," Emily said as McKenzie reached for the nurse call button. The woman didn't press it to call a nurse. Instead, she moved it out of her reach.

Fear spiraled through her, making her feel as if she might throw up. Jason was dead but this woman… She tried to sit up again. "What are you—"

The door burst open. McKenzie fell back with such relief that she could no longer hold back the tears. "Hayes." There'd been only one other time she'd been so happy to see him and that had been yesterday. She reminded herself that he'd also saved her the first time they'd met, as he rushed to her bed and took her hand.

"Are you all right?" he asked.

She couldn't speak. Tears rolled down her cheeks as she tried to swallow down the fear that had settled like a dull ache in her chest.

Behind him was a male police officer. "Mrs. Mathews, you shouldn't be in here."

"I had to come," Emily said in her tiniest voice.

"Well, you need to leave now. You're upsetting Ms. Sheldon," the cop said.

"Of course," the woman said, and turned to look at McKenzie. "I'm sorry."

McKenzie thought for a moment that she had misunderstood the woman's intentions. Maybe Emily had only come here to tell her how sorry she was for what her husband had done. But then she looked again in the woman's eyes. There was no compassion. The only emotion burning there was fury.

The woman was sorry, but not for the reasons anyone else in the room thought.

As the policeman led Emily out of the room, she turned to Hayes. "She *knew.* She knew the whole time. Her only regret was that I lived and he died."

EPILOGUE

"You're going to get sunburned."

McKenzie opened her eyes to look over at Hayes and smiled. "The sun feels so good."

Hayes sat up and reached for the suntan lotion. Since they'd been in Texas, the color had come back into McKenzie's cheeks and she'd gotten a nice tan. She looked healthy, even happy. But he knew she hadn't forgotten her ordeal. Never would. Neither would he.

The scars weren't just on her body, he thought as he rubbed the cool lotion on her back. He'd been surprised when she hadn't wanted to see a plastic surgeon about having the scar on her back removed or the others.

"What would be the point?" she'd said. "For me, it will always be there. Anyway," she'd said, tracing one along his shoulder, "we all have scars."

He remembered each of his scars that he'd gotten growing up with four brothers as well as the ones he'd gotten working as a P.I. Life was dangerous. Sometimes you got lucky and survived it.

"I'm going to be all right, you know," she said when he'd finished applying the lotion.

"I never doubted it."

She sat up to look out at the Gulf of Mexico, her back to him.

"You are the strongest, most determined woman I know."

She smiled at him over her shoulder. She had the most amazing smile. Her hair was even shorter than it had been in Montana. He liked it, but wondered if she missed her long hair. She hadn't known that men like Jason Mathews targeted women with long hair. Women exactly like her. She hadn't known a lot about killers, but she did now.

"I like Texas," she said as she took a deep breath of the gulf air.

He waited, anticipating a "but" before he said, "That's good. You haven't seen much of it yet. It's a big state."

She was watching the waves as she had other days, lying in the sun, wading in the water, seemingly content to spend her days on the beach. The hot sun beat down on the white sand while the surf rolled up only yards from their feet, just as it had all the other days.

Only today, Hayes felt the change in her.

"I've had an offer on the agency," she said after a long moment.

He held his breath, not sure what he wanted her to say. He'd known she couldn't be content spending the rest of her life as a beach bum. That wasn't her. It wasn't him, either. Their lives had been in limbo for weeks now. He'd known she needed time and had been determined to give it to her.

She turned around to face him, sitting cross-legged on the towel. Her skin was tanned, her high cheekbones pink from the sun, her amazing eyes bright. She looked beautiful. She also looked more confident than he'd seen her in a long time.

"I spoke with your cousin Dana. She wanted to know what our plans are for the wedding."

The sudden shift in subjects threw him off for a moment. "You still want to go to Tag and Lily's wedding?"

"Of course. He's your brother and I adore Lily." She frowned. "You do realize this—" she waved an arm, a motion that encompassed the Galveston beach "—this has been wonderful but only temporary, don't you?"

He nodded. "I've just been waiting for you to get your strength back."

She smiled and placed a cool palm on his bare leg. "What about you?"

"What about me?"

"I know you can afford to spend the rest of your life on this beach if you wanted to, but I don't think that is what you want to do, is it?"

"No, I need to work. Not for the money so much as for the work itself."

She licked her lips, catching her lower lip between her teeth for a moment. He felt a stirring in him, his desire for this woman a constant reminder of how much he loved her and that he hadn't yet told her.

The timing had felt all wrong. He wanted her strong. He wanted that unsinkable McKenzie Sheldon back before he laid that on her.

Now as he looked into her eyes, he saw that she was back.

"There is something I have to tell you," he said as he took both of her hands in his and got his courage up. His parents' marriage had failed. His brother Jackson's, as well. He wasn't sure he ever believed in love ever after, but he damned sure wanted to now.

McKenzie smiled, amusement in her eyes. "Is it that hard to admit?"

He chuckled. "I've been wanting to say it for weeks. I just had to wait until I was sure you were going to be all right."

"I'm all right, Hayes."

"I can see that." He gripped her hands, his gaze locking with hers.

McKENZIE LOOKED INTO his dark eyes, afraid of what he was going to say. They hadn't talked about the future. She knew he'd made a point of not pushing her. He'd given her time to heal and she loved him for it.

"I love you."

She laughed. "And I love you. I have for a long time."

He let out a relieved breath and pulled her into his arms for a moment. "I want to spend the rest of my life with you. I don't care where it is as long as we're together."

"Are you saying you would go back to Montana with me?"

"If that is what you want. I could open a private-investigation business in Bozeman or even in the canyon. Dana was telling me about a ranch near hers that was going on the market. I would need a good real-estate agent to handle things."

She couldn't believe what he was saying. "After staying at the Cardwell Ranch, I'm spoiled to live anywhere but the canyon. Could we really do this?"

"Only if you agree to marry me." He looked into her eyes again. "But be sure. This is a no-holds-barred offer till death do us part with kids and dogs and horses and barbecues behind the house."

She laughed as she threw herself back into his arms, knocking them to the sand. "Yes," she said as she looked down into his handsome face. "Yes to all of it."

"And I haven't even made you any Texas Boys Barbecue yet." He flipped her over so he was on top. "Woman, you are in for a treat."

She sobered as she looked up at him. "You've saved my life in so many ways," she said as she touched his cheek. "Do you think it was fate that night that we met?"

"I don't know. But I think I knew the moment I first looked into your eyes that you were the only woman who could get this Texas boy out of Texas."

He kissed her with a promise of good things to come as the surf rolled up to their feet and Montana called.

* * * * *

WANTED WOMAN

This book is gratefully dedicated to the Bozeman Writers' Group for all their wonderful support and encouragement. Thank you, Randle, Wenda, Kitty, Bob, LuAnn and Mark. You're the best!

CHAPTER ONE

Puget Sound, Seattle

THE SMELL OF fish and sea rolled up off the dark water on the late-night air. Restless waves from the earlier storm crashed into pilings under the pier and in the distance a horn groaned through the thick fog.

Maggie shut off the motorcycle and coasted through the shadows and damp fog. She couldn't see a thing. But she figured that was good since he wouldn't be able to see her. Nor hear her coming.

She'd dressed in her black leathers and boots. Even the bulging bike saddlebag was black as the night. She told herself she was being paranoid as she hid the bike and walked several blocks through the dark old warehouses and fish plants before she started down the long pier.

He would be waiting for her somewhere on the pier. With the dense fog and the crashing surf, she wouldn't know where until she was practically on top of him. She assured herself that she had taken every precaution— short of bringing a weapon.

But she was no fool. He had the advantage. He'd picked the meeting place. He was expecting her. And because of the fog, she wouldn't know what was waiting for her at the end of the deserted pier until she reached it.

Fortunately, she was a woman used to taking chances. Except tonight, the stakes were higher than they'd ever been.

The sound of the sea breaking against the pilings grew louder and louder, the wet fog thicker and blinding white. She knew she had to be nearing the end of the pier.

And suddenly Norman Drake materialized out of the fog.

He looked like hell. Like a man who'd been on the run from the police for three days. He looked scared and dangerous—right down to the gun he had clutched in his right hand.

He waved it at her, his pale blue eyes wide with alarm. And she wondered where he'd gotten the gun and if he knew how to use it. He was young and smart and completely out of his league—a tall, thin bookworm-turned-law-student-turned-law-assistant. She could smell the nervous sweat coming off him, the fear.

"You alone?" he whispered hoarsely.

She nodded.

"You sure you weren't followed?"

"Positive."

He exhaled loudly and wiped his free hand over his mouth. "You bring the money?"

She nodded. The ten thousand dollars he'd demanded weighted down the saddlebag. She reached in slowly and held up one bundle. Unmarked, all old, small denomination bills, dozens of bundles making the bag bulge.

It took him a minute to lower the weapon. His hands shook as he shoved it into the front waistband of his wrinkled, soiled slacks. Not a good idea under any circumstances. As nervous as he was, he'd shoot his nuts off.

"I didn't know who else to call but you," he said, his gaze jumping back and forth between her and the fogged-in pier behind her. "They killed Iverson and they'll kill me, too, if I don't get out of town."

Clark Iverson, her father's longtime attorney, had been murdered three days ago. The police had determined that his temporary student legal assistant was in the building at the time. There was no sign of forced entry. No sign of a struggle. Visitors had to be buzzed in. That's why the cops were actively looking for Norman.

"You told me on the phone you had important information for me about my father's plane crash," she said, keeping her hand clamped on the saddlebag, keeping her tone neutral.

He nodded, a jittery nod that set her teeth on edge. "It wasn't an accident. The same person who murdered Iverson killed your father."

She felt shock ricochet through her. Then disbelief. "It was determined an accident. Pilot failure."

Norman shook his head. "A week before the crash, your father came into the office. He seemed upset. Later, after he left, I overheard Iverson on the phone telling someone he couldn't talk your dad out of it."

"That's not enough evidence—"

"I was there three nights ago. I heard them talking about the plane crash. Iverson had figured out that the

plane had gone down to keep your father from talking. He threatened to go to the Feds. I heard them kill
him—" Emotion choked off the last of his words.

"You actually heard someone admit to murdering
my father?"

He nodded, his Adam's apple going up and down,
up and down. She watched him, shock and pain and
anger mixing with the grief of the past two months
since the single passenger plane had gone down on a
routine business flight. She fought to keep her voice
calm. "You said *they?*"

He seemed surprised by the question. "Did I? I only
heard one man talk but—" He frowned and looked
away. "I remember thinking I heard two people coming down the hall after the elevator opened." He was
lying and doing a poor job of it. Why lie about how
many killers there were? "You believe me, don't you?"

She didn't know what to believe now. But her father
had liked Norman, thought he was going to make a good
lawyer someday. Good lawyer, an oxymoron if there
ever was one, her father would have joked. "Norman,
how did they get in? The building was locked, right?"

He nodded, looking confused. "I guess Iverson
buzzed them up. All I know is that I heard the elevator and—" He looked behind her again as if he'd heard
something. "I somehow knew not to let them know I
was there."

A foghorn let out a mournful moan from out beyond the city.

"You're telling me Clark didn't *know* you were still
in the office?"

Norman fidgeted. "I'd fallen asleep in the library

doing some research for him. The door to his office was closed. Earlier, he'd told me to leave, to do the rest in the morning. I guess he thought I'd left by the door to the hallway. The elevator woke me, then I heard voices arguing."

Just seconds before he'd said he'd heard two sets of footsteps coming down the hall after the elevator opened. No wonder Norman hadn't gone to the police. His story had so many holes it wouldn't even make good Swiss cheese.

"You heard them arguing?" she asked.

He nodded. "Then I heard this like…grunt and glass breaking—" He closed his eyes as if imagining Clark Iverson's body, the lamp he'd grabbed as he went down shattered on the floor next to him, his eyes open staring blindly upward, a knife sticking out of his chest at heart level, just as he'd looked when his secretary and Maggie had found him the next morning. Just as he must have looked when Norman saw him.

"You didn't see the killer."

"No, I told you, I just ran."

"Why didn't you call the police?" It was the same question the cops wanted to ask him.

Norman closed his eyes tightly as if in pain. "After they killed him, they rummaged around in his desk drawers, in his file cabinets. I could hear them. I was afraid that at any minute they'd come into the library and find me." Another look away, another lie. "I just ran. I took the stairs, let myself out the back way and I've been running ever since. If they find me, they'll kill me."

"Did you recognize the one voice you heard?"

He shook his head.

"But you heard what they were arguing about."

"Iverson said the secret wasn't worth killing people over."

"What secret?"

Norman squirmed, his gaze flicking past her. "An illegal adoption."

She felt a chill come off the ocean as if she already knew what his next words would be.

"You were the baby," Norman said, the words tumbling over themselves in their struggle to get out. "Iverson wanted to tell you the truth. That's why they killed him. He said your father had found out and was going to tell you."

"Found out what?" So her parents hadn't gone through the proper channels. So what? "I'm twenty-seven years old. Why would anyone kill over my adoption no matter how it went down?"

"It was the way you were…acquired," Norman said. "Your father had found out that you were kidnapped."

Kidnapped? She'd always known she was adopted and that was the reason she looked nothing like her parents. Nor was anything like them.

Mildred and Paul Randolph had always seemed a little surprised by their only child, a little leery. Maggie had come into their life after they'd tried numerous adoption agencies, they'd told her. She'd been a miracle, they'd said. A gift from God.

Maybe not quite.

Although well-off financially, her parents weren't the ideal adoptive candidates. Her mother had been confined to a wheelchair since childhood polio and her father was considered too old. He'd been fifty when Maggie had come along. But, according to both Mildred and Paul, they'd finally found an agency that understood how desperately they wanted a child and had given Maggie to them to love.

No child could have asked for more loving parents. But they'd been horribly overprotective, so afraid something would happen to her, that Maggie had become fearless in self-defense. By the age of twenty-seven, she'd tried everything from skydiving and bungee jumping to motorcross, heli-skiing and speedboat racing.

Her parents had been terrified. Now she realized they'd been afraid long before their only child had become a thrill-seeker. Now she knew why she'd seen fear in her father's eyes all of her life. He'd been waiting all these years for the other shoe to drop.

It had finally dropped. He'd found out she was kidnapped and couldn't live with the knowledge.

She heard a board creak behind her, heavy with a tentative step. "Norman, you have to tell the police what you told me. They'll protect you."

"Are you *nuts?* You can't trust anyone. These people have already killed twice to keep their secret. Who knows how influential they are or what connections they might have."

He'd seen the killer and knew something he wasn't telling her. That's why he was so afraid. Well, maybe the cops could get the truth out of him. "Norman, I called the detective on the case after I talked to you. Detective Blackmore."

"What?" He looked around wildly. "Don't you realize what you've done?" He grabbed for the saddlebag.

"Give me the money. I have to get out of here. Quick. He'll kill us both if—" Norman broke off, his gaze riveted on something just over her left shoulder, eyes widening in horror.

She heard the soft pop, didn't recognize the sound until she saw blood bloom across the shoulder of Norman's jacket. The second shot—right on the heels of the first—caught him in the chest, dead-on.

His grip on the saddlebag pulled her down with him as he fell to the weathered boards, dropping her to her knees beside him.

"Oh, Norman. Oh, God." Her mind reeled. The police wouldn't have shot him. Not without a warning first. But who else had known about their meeting?

The third shot sent a shaft of pain tearing through her left arm as she tried to free herself of the saddlebag strap and Norman's death grip.

"Timber Falls," he whispered, blood running from the corner of his mouth as his fingers released the bag of money and her. "That's where they got you." Adding on his last breath, "Run."

But there was no place to run. She was trapped. Behind her, she heard the groan of a board, caught the scent of the killer on the breeze, a nauseating mix of perspiration, cheap cologne and stale cigar smoke.

She had only one choice. She fell over Norman, rolling him with her, using his body as a shield as a fourth shot thudded into his dead body.

As she fell, she looked up, saw the man with the gun come out of the fog. Shock paralyzed her as her eyes met his and she realized she knew him.

She let out a cry as he raised the gun and pulled the

trigger. Two more shots thudded into Norman's riddled body as she rolled off the end of the pier, taking Norman and the saddlebag with her, dropping for what seemed an eternity before plunging into the cold, dark roiling water below.

CHAPTER TWO

Outside Timber Falls, Oregon

JESSE TANNER HAD been restless for days. He stood on his deck, looking down the steep timbered mountain into the darkness, wishing for sleep. It had been raining earlier. Wisps of clouds scooted by on a light breeze.

He sniffed the cedar-scented air as if he could smell trouble, sense danger, find something to explain the restlessness that haunted his nights and gave him no peace.

But whatever was bothering him remained as elusive as slumber.

A sound drew him from his thoughts. A recognizable throaty rumble. He looked toward the break in the trees below him on the steep mountain to the strip of pavement that was only visible in daylight. Or for those few moments when headlights could be seen at night on the isolated stretch of highway below him.

The single light came out of the trees headed in the direction of Timber Falls. A biker, moving fast, the throb of the big cycle echoing up to him.

Jesse watched the motorcycle glide like warm butter over the wet, dark pavement and wished that he was on it, headed wherever, destination unknown.

But that was the old Jesse Tanner. This Jesse was

through wandering. Through with the open road. This Jesse had settled down.

Not that he still couldn't envy the biker below him on the highway. Or remember that heady feeling of speed and darkness and freedom. There was nothing like it late at night when he had the road to himself. Just an endless ribbon of black pavement stretched in front of him and infinite possibilities just over the next rise.

He started to turn away but a set of headlights flickered in the trees as a car came roaring out of a side road across the highway below him. He watched, frozen in horror as the car tore out of Maple Creek Road and onto the highway—directly into the path of the motorcycle.

He caught a flash of bright red in the headlamp of the bike and saw the car, a convertible, the top down and the dark hair of the woman behind the wheel blowing back, in that instant before the bike collided with the side of the car, clipping it. The bike and rider went down.

Jesse gripped the railing as the bike slid on its side down the pavement, sparks flying as the car sped away into the darkness and trees, headed toward Timber Falls, five miles away.

He was already running for the old pickup he kept for getting firewood. Other than that, all he had was his Harley. Taking off down his jeep trail of a road in the truck, he dropped down the face of the mountain, fearing what he'd find when he reached the pavement.

At the highway, he turned north. It was darker down here with the forest towering on each side of the two-lane. In the slit of sky overhead, clouds scudded past, giving only brief glimpses of stars and a silver sliver of moon.

He hadn't gone far when he spotted the fallen bike in his headlights. It lay on its side in the ditch, the single headlamp casting a stationary beam of gold across the wet highway. Where was the biker?

Driving slowly up the road, he scanned the path with his headlights looking for the downed rider, bracing himself for what he'd find.

A dozen yards back up the highway from the bike, something gleamed in his headlights. The shiny top of a bike helmet. The biker lay on his side at the edge of the road, unmoving.

Jesse swore and stopped, turning on his emergency flashers to block any traffic that might come along. He didn't expect any given the time of the night—or the season. Early spring—the rainy season in this part of the country. People with any sense stayed clear of the Pacific side of the Cascades where, at this time of year, two hundred inches of rain fell pretty much steadily for seven months. The ones who lived here just tried not to go crazy during the rainy season. Some didn't succeed.

Following the beams of his headlights, he jumped out of the pickup and ran across the wet pavement toward the biker, unconsciously calculating the odds that the guy was still alive, already debating whether to get him into the back of the truck and run him to the hospital or not move him and go for help.

As he neared, he heard a soft moan and saw movement as the biker came around. Jesse figured he was witnessing a miracle given how fast the motorcycle had been traveling.

"Take it easy," he said as the figure in all black leathers coughed as if gasping for breath and tried to sit up. The biker was small, slim and a damned lucky dude.

As Jesse knelt down beside him in the glow of the pickup's headlights, he saw with shock that he'd been wrong and let out an oath as a hand with recently manicured nails pulled off the helmet. A full head of long dark curly hair tumbled out and a distinctly female voice said, "I'm okay."

"Holy…" he said, rocking back on his heels. This was one damned lucky…*chick.*

She had her head down as if a little groggy.

He watched her test each leg, then each arm. "Are you sure you're not hurt?" He couldn't believe everything was working right. "Nothing's broken?"

She shook her head, still bent over as if trying to catch her breath.

He waited, amazed as he took in the leather-clad body. Amazed by the bod and the bike. She was wheeling a forty-thousand-dollar ride that most men couldn't handle. A hell of a bike for a girl. It was too heavy for anyone but an expert rider. No wonder she'd been able to dump the bike and not get hurt.

She tried to get up again.

"Give it another minute. No hurry," he said, looking from her back up the highway to her bike. This gal had nine lives, a whole lot of luck and she knew how to ride that fancy bike. He wasn't sure what impressed him more.

"I'm all right." Her voice surprised him. It was all female, cultured and educated-sounding and in stark contrast to her getup and her chosen mode of transportation.

But the real shocker was when she lifted her head, flipping back her hair, and he saw her face.

All the air went out of him as if she'd sucker punched

him. "Sweet mother—" he muttered, rearing back again. She was breathtaking. Her skin was the color of warm honey, sprinkled with cinnamon-and-sugar freckles across high cheekbones. And her eyes… They were wide and the color of cedar, warm and rich. She was exquisite. A natural beauty.

And there was something almost familiar about her…

She tried to get to her feet, bringing him out of his dumbfounded inertia.

"Here, let me help you," he said and reached under her armpits to lift her to her feet. She was amazingly light and small next to him.

She accepted his help with grace and gratitude even though it was clear she liked doing things for herself.

She took a step. "Ouch," she said under her breath and swayed a little on her feet.

"What is it?"

"My left ankle. It's just sprained."

Maybe. Maybe not. "I'll take you to the hospital emergency room to see a doctor."

She shook her head. "Just get me to my bike."

"It's not rideable." He'd seen enough twisted metal on it even in passing to know that. "I'll load it into my pickup. There's not a bike shop for a hundred miles but I've worked on a few of my own. I might be able to fix it."

She looked up at him then as if seeing him for the first time. Her eyes narrowed as she took in the boots, jeans, bike rally T-shirt and his long dark ponytail. Her gaze settled on the single gold ring in his earlobe. "You live around here?"

"Right up that mountain," he said, pointing to the

light he'd left on. It glowed faintly high up the mountainside.

She studied it. Then him.

It was three in the morning but he had to ask. "Is anyone expecting you up the road, anyone who'll be worried about you? Because I don't have a phone yet."

She didn't seem to hear him. "You have ice for my ankle at your place?"

He nodded.

"Good. That's all I need."

"I have a clean bed you're welcome to for what's left of the night," he offered.

She flashed him an in-your-dreams look.

He smiled and shook his head. "All I'm offering is a bed. Maybe something to eat or drink. Some ice. Nothing more."

She cocked her head at him, looking more curious than anything else. He wondered what she saw. Whatever it was, he must have looked harmless enough before she started to limp toward her bike. "I need my saddlebag."

"I'll get it," he said, catching up to her and offering a hand. "No reason to walk on that ankle any more than you have to." She quirked an eyebrow at him but said nothing as she slipped one arm around his shoulder and let him take her weight as she hobbled to the pickup.

As he opened the passenger-side door and slid her into his old truck, he felt way too damned chivalrous. Also a little embarrassed by his old truck.

She glanced around the cab, then settled back into the seat and closed her eyes. He slammed the door and went to load her bike.

He'd only seen a couple of these bikes. Too expensive

for most riders. It definitely made him wonder about the woman in his pickup. The bike didn't look as if it was hurt bad. He figured he should be able to fix it. He liked the idea of working on it. The bike intrigued him almost as much as the woman who'd been riding it.

He rolled the bike up the plank he kept in the back of his pickup, retrieved her saddlebag and, slamming the tailgate, went around to climb into the cab of the truck beside her. He set the heavy, bulging saddlebag on the seat beside them.

She cracked an eyelid to see that the bag was there, then closed her eyes again.

"The name's Jesse. Jesse Tanner."

She didn't move, didn't open her eyes. "Maggie," she said, but offered no more.

He started the engine, shifted into first gear and headed back up the mountain to his new place. The road was steep and rough, but he liked being a little inaccessible. He saw her grimace a couple of times as he took the bumps, but she didn't open her eyes until he parked in front of the cabin.

She looked up at the structure on the hillside, only the living-room light glowing in the darkness.

"This is where you live?" she said and, opening her door, got out, slipping the saddlebag over her shoulder protectively.

Something in her tone made him wonder if she meant the cabin or the isolated location. The only visitors he'd had so far were his younger brother, Mitch, and his dad. He figured if he wanted to be social, he knew the way to town and it was only five miles. Not nearly far enough some days.

He looked at the cabin, trying to see it through her

eyes. It was tall and narrow, a crude place, built of logs and recycled cedar, but he was proud of it since he'd designed and built it over the winter with the help of his dad and brother. It had gone up fast.

Three stories, the first the living room and kitchen, the second a bedroom and bath with a screened-in deck where he planned to sleep come summer, the third his studio, a floor flanked with windows, the view incredible.

Unfortunately, it was pretty much a shell. He hadn't furnished the inside yet. Hadn't had time. So all he had was the minimal furniture he'd picked up.

Lately, he'd been busy getting some paintings ready for an exhibit in June, his first, and— He started to tell her all of that, but stopped himself. It wasn't like she would be here more than a few hours and then she'd be gone. She didn't want his life history, he could see that from her expression.

He'd been there himself. No roots. No desire to grow any. Especially no desire to be weighed down even with someone's life story.

She was standing beside the pickup staring up at his cabin as he climbed out of the truck.

"It's still under construction," he said, irritated with himself for wanting her to like it. But hell, she *was* the first woman he'd had up here since it was built.

"It's perfect," she said. "Neoclassical, right?"

He smiled, surprised at her knowledge of architecture. But then again, she was riding a forty-thousand-dollar bike and had another couple grand in leather on her back, spoke like she'd been to finishing school and carried herself as if she knew her way around the streets. All of that came from either education, money

or experience. In her case, he wondered if it wasn't all
three.

She caught him admiring the way her leathers fit her.

"Let's get you inside," he said quickly. "You hungry?"

She shook her head and grabbed the railing, limping up the steps to the first floor, making it clear she
didn't need his help.

"You sure you don't want to see a doctor? I could
run you into town—"

"No." Her tone didn't leave any doubt.

"Okay." He'd had to try.

They'd reached the front door. She seemed surprised it wasn't locked. "I haven't much to steal and
most thieves are too lazy to make the trek up here." He
swung the door open and she stepped inside, her gaze
going at once to his paintings he'd done of his years
in Mexico.

He had a half dozen leaning against the bare living-
room wall waiting to go to the framer for the exhibit.
She limped over to them, staring at one and then another.

"How about coffee?" he offered, uncomfortable with
the way she continued to study his work as if she were
seeing something in the paintings he didn't want exposed.

He couldn't decide if she liked them or not. He wasn't
about to ask. He had a feeling she might tell him.

While she'd been studying the paintings he'd been
studying her. As she shrugged out of her jacket, he saw
that she wore a short-sleeved white T-shirt that molded
her breasts and the muscles of her back. She was in

good shape and her body was just as exquisite as he'd thought it would be beneath the leather.

But what stole his attention was the hole he'd seen in the jacket just below her left shoulder—and the corresponding fresh wound on her left biceps. He'd seen enough gunshot wounds in his day to recognize one even without the telltale hole in the leather jacket.

The bullet had grazed her flesh and would leave a scar. It wasn't her first scar, though. There was another one on her right forearm, an older one that had required stitches.

Who the hell was this woman and what was it about her?

"These are all yours," she said, studying the paintings again. It was a statement of fact as if there was no doubt in her mind that he'd painted them.

"I have tea if you don't like coffee."

"Do you have anything stronger?" she asked without turning around.

He lifted a brow behind her back and went to the cupboard. "I have some whiskey." He turned to find her glancing around the cabin. Her gaze had settled on an old rocker he'd picked up at a flea market in Portland.

"That chair is pretty comfortable if you'd like to sit down," he said, as he watched her run her fingers over the oak arm of the antique rocker.

She looked at him as she turned and lowered herself into the rocker, obviously trying hard not to let him see that her ankle was hurting her if not the rest of her body. Maybe nothing was broken but she'd been beat up. Wait until tomorrow. She was going to be hurtin' for certain.

He handed her half a glass of whiskey. He poured himself a tall glass of lemonade. The whiskey had been a housewarming gift from a well-meaning friend in town. He'd given up alcohol when he'd decided it was time to settle down. He'd seen what alcohol had done for his old man and he'd never *needed* the stuff, especially now that he was painting again.

He watched Maggie over the rim of his glass as he took a drink. He'd made the lemonade from real lemons. It wasn't half-bad. Could use a little more sugar, though.

She sniffed the whiskey, then drained the glass and grimaced, nose wrinkling, as if she'd just downed paint thinner. Then she pushed herself to her feet, limped over to him and handed him the glass. "Thank you."

"Feeling better?" he asked, worried about her and not just because of her bike wreck.

"Fine."

He nodded, doubting it. He wanted to ask her how she'd gotten the bullet wound, what she'd been doing on the highway below his place at three in the morning, where she was headed and what kind of trouble she was in. But he knew better. He'd been there and he wasn't so far from that life that he didn't know how she would react to even well-meaning questions.

"I promised you ice," he said, and finished his lemonade, then put their glasses in the sink and filled a plastic bag with ice cubes for her ankle. "And a place to lie down while I take a look at your bike." He met her gaze. She still wasn't sure about him.

He realized just how badly he wanted her to trust him as he gazed into those brown eyes. Like her face, there was something startlingly familiar about them.

She took the bag of ice cubes and he led her up the stairs, stopping at his bedroom door.

"You can have this room. The sheets are clean." He hadn't slept on them since he'd changed them.

"No, that one's yours," she said and turned toward the open doorway to the screened-in deck. There was an old futon out there and a pine dresser he planned to refinish when he had time. "I'll sleep in here."

He started to argue, but without turning on the light, she took the bag of ice and limped over to the screened windows, her back to him as she looked out into the darkness beyond.

Fetching a towel from the bathroom, he returned to find her still standing at the window. She didn't turn when he put the towel on the futon, just said, "Thank you."

"De nada." He was struck with the thought that if he had been able to sleep he would never have seen her accident, would never have met her. For some reason that seemed important as if cosmically it had all been planned. He was starting to think like his future sister-in-law, Charity, and her crazy aunt Florie, the self-proclaimed psychic.

He really needed to get some decent sleep, he concluded wryly, if he was going to start thinking crap like that. "There are sheets and blankets in the dresser and more towels in the bathroom." He would have gladly made a bed for her but he knew instinctively that she needed to be alone.

"About my bike—"

"I think I can fix it," he said. "Otherwise, I can give you and the bike a lift into Eugene."

She turned then to frown at him. "You'd do that?"

He nodded. "I used to travel a lot on my bike and

people helped me. Payback. I need the karma." He smiled.

Her expression softened with her smile. She really was exquisite. For some reason, he thought of Desiree Dennison, the woman he'd seen driving the red sports car that had hit Maggie. "I can also take you in to see the sheriff in the morning. I know him pretty well."

"Why would I want to see him?" she asked, frowning and looking leery again.

"You'll want to press charges against the driver of the car that hit you."

She said nothing, but he saw the answer in her eyes. No chance in hell was she sticking around to press charges against anyone.

"Just give a holler if you need anything," he said.

Her gaze softened again and for an instant he thought he glimpsed vulnerability. The instant passed. "Thank you again for everything."

My pleasure. He left the bathroom door open and a light on so she could find it if she needed it, then went downstairs, smiling as he recalled the face she'd made after chugging the whiskey. Who the hell was she? Ruefully, he realized the chances were good that he would never know.

MAGGIE HURT ALL OVER. She put the ice down on the futon and limped closer to the screened window. The night air was damp and cool, but not cold.

She stared out, still shaken by what had happened on the dock, what she'd learned, what she'd witnessed. She'd gotten Norman killed because she'd called Detective Rupert Blackmore.

Below, a door opened and closed. She watched Jesse

Tanner cross the mountainside to a garage, open the door and turn on the light. An older classic Harley was parked inside, the garage neat and clean.

She watched from the darkness as he went to the truck, dropped the tailgate, pulled out the plank then climbed up and carefully rolled her bike down and over to the garage.

For a long moment he stood back as if admiring the cycle, then slowly he approached it. She caught her breath as he ran his big hands over it, gentle hands, caressing the bike the way a man caressed a woman he cherished.

She moved away from the window, letting the night air slow her throbbing pulse and cool the heat that burned across her bare skin. She told herself it was the effects of the whiskey not the man below her window as she tried to close her mind to the feelings he evoked in her. How could she feel desire when her life was in danger?

She'd been running on adrenaline for almost thirty-six hours now, too keyed up to sleep or eat. Her stomach growled but she knew she needed rest more than food at this point. She could hear the soft clink of tools in the garage, almost feel the warm glow of the light drifting up to her.

She took a couple of blankets from the chest of drawers. Wrapping the towel he'd left her around the bag of ice, she curled up on the futon bed, put the ice on her ankle and pulled the blankets up over her.

The bed smelled of the forest and the night and possibly the man who lived here. She breathed it in finding a strange kind of comfort in the smell and sound of him below her.

She closed her eyes tighter, just planning to rest until he was through with her bike, knowing she would never be able to sleep. Not when she was this close to Timber Falls. This close to learning the truth. Just a few more miles. A few more hours.

Tonight on the highway when the car had pulled out in front of her, she'd thought at first it was Detective Rupert Blackmore trying to kill her again.

But then she'd caught a glimpse of the female driver in that instant before she'd hit the bright red sports car.

She'd seen the young woman's startled face in the bike's headlight, seen the long dark hair and wide eyes, and as Maggie had laid the bike on its side, she'd heard the car speed off into the night all the time knowing that the cop would have never left. He would have finished her off.

She feared that Norman's body had washed up by now. And it was only a matter of time before Blackmore realized her body wouldn't be washing up because she hadn't drowned.

How soon would he figure out where she'd gone and what she was up to and come here to stop her?

But what was it he didn't want her finding out? That she was kidnapped? Or was there something more, something he feared even worse that she would uncover?

Right now, all she knew was that people were dying because of *her.* Because her parents had wanted a baby so desperately that they'd bought one, not knowing that she'd been kidnapped from a family in Timber Falls, Oregon.

Her ankle ached. She tried not to think. Detective

Rupert Blackmore was bound to follow her to Timber Falls. Unless he was already in town waiting for her.

Sleep came like a dark black cloak that enveloped her. She didn't see the fog or Norman lying dead at her feet or the cop on the pier with the gun coming after her. And for a while, she felt safe.

CHAPTER THREE

MAGGIE WOKE WITH a start, her heart pounding. Her eyes flew open but she stayed perfectly still, listening for the thing she feared most.

The creak of a floorboard nearby. The soft rustle of clothing. The sound of a furtive breath taken and held.

She heard nothing but the cry of a blue jay and the soft whisper of the breeze in the swaying dark pines beyond her bed.

She opened her eyes, surprised to see that the soft pale hues of dawn had lightened the screened-in room. She'd slept. That surprised her. Obviously she'd been tired, but to sleep in a perfect stranger's house knowing there was someone out there who wanted her dead? She must have been more exhausted than she'd thought.

She listened for a moment, wondering what sound had awakened her and if it was one she needed to worry about. Silence emanated from within the house and there was no longer the soft clink of tools.

Sitting up, she retrieved the bag and towel, and swung her legs over the side of the bed. The ice she'd had on her ankle had melted. Some of the water had leaked onto the futon. The towel was soaked and cold to the touch.

She scooped up both towel and bag and pushed to her feet to test her ankle. Last night she'd been scared that her ankle was hurt badly. Anything that slowed her down would be deadly.

Her ankle was stiff and painful, but she could walk well enough. And ride. She stood on the worn wood-plank flooring and took a few tentative steps toward the screened windows. That is, she could ride if her bike was fixed.

She glanced out. The garage door was shut, the light out. The back of the pickup was empty. Her bike sat in front of the house, resting on its kickstand, her helmet sitting on top, waiting for her. He'd fixed it.

The swell of relief and gratitude that washed over her made her sway a little on her weak ankle. Tears burned her eyes. His kindness felt like too much right now. She turned toward the open doorway. She'd left her door open and so it seemed had he. As she neared the short hallway between the rooms, she could see him sleeping in his double bed, the covers thrown back, only the sheet over him.

He was curled around his pillow on his side facing her, his masculine features soft in sleep. A lock of his long, straight black hair fell over one cheek, shiny and dark as a raven's wing. She caught the glint of his earring beneath the silken strands, the shadow of his strong stubbled jaw, the dark silken fringe of his eyelashes against his skin.

Even asleep the man still held her attention, still exuded a wild sensuality, a rare sexuality. This man would be dangerous to a woman. And she didn't doubt he'd known his share. Intimately. Or that he was a good lover. She'd seen the way he'd touched her bike. She'd seen his artwork. Both had made her ache. Fear for her life hadn't stolen her most primitive desires last night. Nor this morning.

But what surprised her wasn't her attraction to the man, but that she felt safe with him. Too safe.

She moved silently down the hallway. He'd left a small light burning in the bathroom for her. That gesture even more than the others touched her deeply. She closed the door behind her and poured what water was left in the plastic bag down the drain, then hung up the towel.

She washed her face, avoiding looking at the stranger in the mirror. She'd spent too many years questioning who she was. Now she was about to find out and she didn't want to face it or what her adoptive parents might have done in their desperation for a child.

She knew money had exchanged hands. Most adoptions involved an exchange of money, although she hated to think what her parents had paid for her. What frightened her was how the purchase had been made. And why someone was now trying to kill her to keep her from finding out.

No one committed multiple murders to cover up an illegal adoption or even a kidnapping. Especially after twenty-seven years. There had to be more to it. What was someone afraid would come to light?

According to Norman, the answer was in Timber Falls—just a few miles away now. She had raced here, running for her life, rocketing through the darkness toward the truth. But now that she was so close, she feared what she would find.

When she was younger, she'd often thought about finding her biological parents. Of course, her adoptive parents had discouraged her. Now she knew it wasn't just because they didn't want to share her.

Unfortunately, now she had no choice but to find out who she really was. And hopefully the answer would save her life. But what would her life be worth once she knew the truth?

As she turned to leave the bathroom, she froze. A sheriff deputy's uniform hung on the hook of the closed door.

THE CALL CAME before daylight. Detective Rupert Blackmore was lying on his bed, fully clothed, flat on his back, staring up at the ceiling. Certainly not asleep. He'd been waiting for the phone to ring, willing it to ring with the news he needed.

Praying for it. Although praying might not have been exactly what he'd been doing. Right now he would have sold his soul to the devil if he hadn't already traded it to Satan a long time ago.

He let the phone ring three times, then picked up the receiver. "Detective Blackmore."

"Just fished a body out of the sea near the old pier," said his subordinate, a young new detective by the name of Williams. "Six gunshot wounds. Dead before the body hit the water. Definitely a homicide."

Rupert Blackmore held his breath as he got to his feet beside the bed. "Has the body been IDed?"

"Affirmative. Norman Drake. Wallet was in his pocket. The guy we've been looking for in connection with the murder of his boss, attorney Clark Iverson."

As if Rupert didn't know that. He tried not to let Williams hear his disappointment that Norman's body was the only one found so far. "Close off the entire area.

I want it searched thoroughly. Drake didn't act alone and now it appears there's been a falling out among murderers."

He hung up and cursed, then in a fit of rage and frustration, knocked the phone off the nightstand, sending it crashing to the floor.

He sat down on the edge of the bed and lowered his head to his hands. Her body would wash up. Then all of this would be over. He took a deep breath, rose and picked up the phone. Carefully he put it back on the nightstand, thanking God that his wife, Teresa, was at her mother's and wouldn't be back for a few more days. Plenty of time to get this taken care of before she returned.

As he headed for the door, he tried not to worry. Once Margaret Randolph was dead, no one would ever find out the truth. And it would never get back that he hadn't taken care of this problem twenty-seven years ago as he'd been paid to do.

One moment of kindness… He scoffed at his own worn lie. He'd done it for the money. Plain and simple. He'd sold the baby instead of disposing of it. And he'd never regretted it—until Paul Randolph found out the truth. Now Rupert had to take care of things quickly and efficiently before everything blew up in his face. No more mistakes like the one he'd made the other night at the pier. There was no way he should have missed her. He'd been too close and was too good of a shot.

He tried to put the mistakes behind him. Look to the future. And the future was simple. If Margaret Randolph wasn't floating in Puget Sound with the fish, she soon would be.

Maggie stared at the sheriff's deputy uniform and tried to breathe. Jesse Tanner was a cop? Last night he'd said he knew the sheriff. She'd just assumed because it was a small town, everyone knew everyone else.

She stifled a groan. Not only had she stayed in the house of the local deputy, but now he might have the plate number on her bike. If he'd had reason to take it down.

Fear turned her blood to ice. He could find out her last name—if he didn't already know. Worse, he could tell Blackmore that not only was she alive but that she was in Timber Falls.

But why would Jesse Tanner run the plate number on her bike? She hadn't given him any reason to. Cops didn't need a reason, though. And everyone knew they stuck together.

Except Jesse was different. He didn't act like a cop. Didn't insist she go to the doctor last night or the sheriff this morning. Didn't ask a lot of questions.

She tried to calm her pounding heart. Her hands were shaking as she wiped down the faucets and anything else she might have touched. Were her fingerprints on a file somewhere? She didn't know.

She thought she remembered being fingerprinted as a child. She knew her parents had worried about her being kidnapped. How ironic. And she'd always thought it was because of their wealth.

As she opened the bathroom door, she half expected the deputy to be waiting for her just outside. The hallway was empty. She stood listening.

Silence. Tiptoeing down the hall, she passed his open doorway again. He had rolled over, his back to her now.

She prayed he would stay asleep as she eased into the screened-in deck where she'd slept.

She picked up her boots, her jacket and the saddlebag stuffed with most of the ten grand from the pier. Then she looked around to make sure she hadn't left anything behind before she limped quietly down the stairs.

At the bottom, she glanced at his paintings as she pulled on her boots, the left going on painfully because of her ankle. What she now knew about the man upstairs seemed at odds with his art. Jesse Tanner and his chisel-cut features, the deep set of matching dimples, the obsidian black eyes and hair, the ponytail and the gold earring didn't go with the deputy sheriff's uniform.

There was a wildness about the man, something he seemed to be trying to keep contained, but couldn't hide in his artwork. The large, bold strokes, the use of color, the way he portrayed his subjects.

Her favorite of the six paintings propped against the wall was a scene from a Mexican cantina. A series of men were watching a Latin woman dance. The sexual tension was like a coiled spring. In both the work and the painter.

He was talented, too talented not to be painting full-time. So why was he working as a sheriff's deputy? He didn't seem like the type who liked busting people for a living. Quite the opposite.

She glanced around the cabin. She liked it. Liked him. Wished he wasn't a cop. She told herself she shouldn't feel guilty for just running out on him.

Last night she'd been shaken from her accident, hurt and exhausted. She had needed a refuge and he'd provided it, asking nothing in return. He would never know how much that meant to her.

Under other circumstances, she would never have left without thanking him. But these were far from normal circumstances, she reminded herself and remembered the glass of whiskey she'd drunk last night.

Going to the sink, she turned on the faucet and washed both glasses thoroughly, then dried them. Being careful not to leave her prints anywhere, she set the glasses back on the cabinet shelf with the others and wiped down the faucet and handles just as she had in the bathroom upstairs.

She knew she was being overly cautious. But maybe that was why she was still alive.

Her bike was sitting outside, her helmet on the seat as if he'd put it there to let her know it was ready to go. He'd fixed the kickstand and straightened the twisted metal, as well as the handlebars. The bike was scraped up but didn't look too bad considering how close a call she'd had. Now if it would just run as well as it had.

She strapped on the saddlebag, then climbed on the bike, rolled it off the kickstand and turned the key.

The powerful motor rumbled to life and she felt a swell of relief—and appreciation for the man who'd fixed it. As she popped it into gear, she couldn't help herself. She glanced up at the house, then quickly looked away. He was a cop. She had learned the hard way not to trust them. Not to trust anyone. If she hoped to stay alive, she had to keep it that way.

JESSE TANNER STOOD at the screened window watching her leave. He'd been awakened by the sound of running water downstairs and had half hoped she was making coffee. He should have known better.

But he couldn't help worrying as he watched her

ride off into the dawn. Last night after he'd finished with the bike, he'd looked in on her. He felt guilty for snooping but he'd looked into the heavy saddlebag and seen the bundles of money. Maybe she didn't believe in traveler's checks. Maybe she'd withdrawn all of her savings from the bank for a long bike trip. Or maybe she'd robbed a savings and loan.

Either way, she was gone and not his problem.

Nor should he be surprised she would leave like this without a word. Last night he'd gotten the impression she wasn't one for long goodbyes.

Still, he would have made her pancakes for breakfast if she'd hung around. Hell, he hadn't had pancakes in months, but he would have made them for her.

He went downstairs, foolishly hoping she'd left him a note. He knew better. Her kind didn't leave notes. No happy faces on Post-its on the fridge, no little heart dotting the *i* in her name. She was not that kind of girl.

He made a pot of coffee and saw that she'd washed their glasses and put them away. He stood for a long time just staring at the clean glasses as the coffee brewed, then he poured himself a cup and took it back upstairs while he showered and dressed in his uniform hanging on the back of the bathroom door, all the time dreading the day ahead.

It wasn't just the biker chick with the bag of money and worry over what she might be running from that had him bummed. She was miles away by now.

His problem was Desiree Dennison. He'd recognized the little red sports car that had sideswiped the biker last night. He couldn't turn a blind eye to what he'd seen: Desiree leaving the scene of an accident.

But the last thing he wanted to do was go out to the Dennisons and with good reason.

CHAPTER FOUR

MAGGIE CRUISED THROUGH Timber Falls in the early morning, surprised to find the town even smaller than the map had led her to believe. The main drag was only a few blocks long. Ho Hum Motel, Betty's Café, the Busy Bee antique shop, the Spit Curl, Harry's Hardware, a small post office, bank and auto body shop.

Past the *Cascade Courier* newspaper office she spotted the cop shop. She turned down a side street, avoiding driving by the sheriff's department even though she knew Jesse Tanner couldn't have beat her to town. But she had no way of knowing how many officers there were in this little burg, or who might be looking for her.

When she'd rolled off the pier, she'd taken Norman's body with her into the water. The surf was rough that night. As far as she knew Norman's body hadn't turned up yet, but then, she hadn't had a chance to check a newspaper. Until Norman's body was found, Blackmore might not be aware that she was still alive.

Last night she hadn't gone home. Fortunately, she'd been smart enough to hide her motorcycle before going down to the pier to meet Norman. When she'd crawled out of the water after being shot, she'd come up a hundred yards down the beach near a small seafood shack.

Keeping to the shadows, she'd broken in, stripped off her leathers down to the shorts and tank top she wore underneath and bandaged her arm as best she could with the first-aid kit she found behind the counter.

Then she'd set off the fire alarm, hiding until the fire trucks arrived. In the commotion, she'd worked her way back to her bike, carrying her leathers in a garbage bag she'd taken from the café's kitchen.

She'd feared the cop would have found her bike and have it staked out but she didn't see anyone. Nor had she found any tracking devices on it when she'd checked later.

Running scared, she'd gone the only direction she could. Toward Timber Falls, Oregon, a tiny dot she'd found on a service station map. With luck, she'd bought herself a little time. Once Norman's body washed up and hers didn't, they were bound to get suspicious. Whoever they were.

Norman. Oh, Norman. She still felt sick and still blamed herself for his death. If she hadn't called Blackmore…

She'd called Rupert Blackmore because he was the detective investigating Clark Iverson's murder and she'd read in the paper that he was actively looking for the attorney's legal assistant, Norman Drake, for questioning. She knew nothing about the cop, let alone if he had a tie in with Timber Falls. Or her.

But she understood now why Norman was so freaked out. He had seen Detective Blackmore kill Iverson and, like Maggie, he had probably seen the recent photograph of Blackmore in the paper getting some award from the mayor for bravery and years of distinguished service in the Seattle Police Department.

Who would believe that a cop who'd been on the force for thirty years and received so many commendations was a killer? No one. That's why Norman hadn't gone to the cops. That's why Maggie knew she couldn't until she knew why Blackmore had murdered the others—and tried to kill her, as well.

Now she passed through a small residential area of town, coming out next to the Duck-In bar and Harper's Grocery. Her stomach growled and she tried to remember the last time she'd eaten and couldn't.

Parking beside the market in the empty lot, she went in and bought herself a bag of doughnuts and a carton of milk, downing most of the milk as she gathered supplies. She purchased some fruit and lunch meat for later and a bottle of water. She wouldn't be back to town for hours.

As she started to check out she saw a rack of newspapers and braced herself. But before she could look for a story in one of the larger West Coast papers about a body floating up on a beach, she spotted a headline in the *Cascade Courier* that stopped her heart cold.

"HERE, YOU FORGOT this," Sheriff Mitch Tanner said from his recliner as Jesse walked through the door. Jesse's first stop in town was to see how his brother was doing—and talk to him about the accident last night on the highway.

Mitch had always been the good one. College right after high school, then he'd taken the job as sheriff and bought a house. Mr. Law-Abiding.

Jesse on the other hand had been the wild older brother. Always in trouble. When he'd left Timber Falls it had been in handcuffs. After that little misunderstanding was cleared up, he'd headed for Mexico and had spent years down there, half-afraid to come home and yet missing his brother and dad.

"It's required that you have it with you at all times—and keep it turned *on,*" Mitch said, tossing him a cell phone.

Jesse groaned as he caught the damned thing. It was bad enough being a cop, let alone having to carry a cell phone. He stuffed it into his pants pocket, telling himself it was only for a couple of months tops. "It's one of those that vibrates, right?" he asked with a wink. "Maybe it won't be so bad."

Mitch rolled his eyes and lay back in the recliner, his left leg in a huge cast and a pair of crutches leaning against the wall next to him. He'd taken two bullets: one had broken the tibia of his left leg. The other had just passed through his side. Both had laid him low, though.

Worse, Mitch hadn't taken it well that his first bullet wound in uniform would be from someone he knew—the most famous man in Timber Falls, Wade Dennison. Wade had shot Mitch while struggling over a .38 with his estranged wife, Daisy. Mitch had just been in the wrong place at the wrong time.

Or at least that was Wade's story.

Jesse thought being behind bars was the perfect place for Wade. The man owned Dennison Ducks, the wooden decoy carving plant and pretty much the reason for the town's existence, and because of that Wade Dennison had thrown his weight around for years.

Well, after being patched up at the hospital he was now behind bars facing all kinds of charges, including assault with a deadly weapon, resisting arrest and domestic abuse. His wife, Daisy, was fighting for no bail, saying she feared for her life should Wade be released.

Needless to say, it made great headlines in the *Cascade Courier,* the weekly local paper run by Mitch's fiancée, Charity Jenkins. In fact, Charity seemed to be doing everything she could to keep the story page one.

And, as always, the news kept the gossips going at Betty's Café.

Jesse knew a lot of people in town resented Wade because of his money and his overbearing attitude and were hoping when the trial rolled around that Wade got the book thrown at him. Jesse just hoped Wade never went gunning for Mitch again. He would definitely take it personally next time.

Meanwhile, since Mitch was off his feet, he'd asked Jesse to stand in as acting deputy until he was completely recovered. Jesse had helped him out before since his return to Timber Falls. Because the town was in a remote part of Oregon, the sheriff had the authority to deputize whatever help he needed.

Jesse suspected Mitch thought putting him in a uniform would help straighten him up. He smiled at the thought because the job was a mixed blessing. He had only started this morning and already hated it. Still, he figured he was doing Mitch a favor and he could use the money, but he'd never been wild about cops since his wild youth and now he was one. The only one in Timber Falls.

The good news was that Timber Falls seldom had any real crime. Although this rainy season had had more than its share. But Jesse was hoping that with Wade Dennison locked up in jail and no more Bigfoot sightings, things would quiet down.

"You look like you're doing all right," he said to his brother as Charity came into the room with a tray of coffee, freshly squeezed orange juice, scrambled eggs, bacon and toast. She put it down on Mitch's lap.

Jesse raised a brow. "Damn, the woman can even cook?"

"Very funny," Charity quipped. "It's genetic. All women are born to cook and clean. Men are born to be asses."

Jesse faked a hurt expression.

"Except for Mitch," she added with a smile as she touched his shoulder. Charity had been crazy about Jesse's younger brother since she was a kid and he couldn't be more excited that the two of them were finally getting married. Mitch, while lying in a pool of his own blood, finally got smart and proposed to her after she'd helped save his life. The man was slow, but not stupid.

"I need to talk to my little brother for a moment," Jesse said. Mitch was two years younger, but several inches taller than Jesse. "Sheriff's department business."

Mitch groaned. "That's like waving a red flag in front of a bull to talk sheriff's department business in front of Charity, ace reporter."

"It's nothing you'd find interesting for the newspaper," Jesse assured Charity as he sat down next to Mitch and stole a piece of his bacon. Charity stuck around just in case. She was the owner, editor and reporter of the *Cascade Courier* and she was a bloodhound when it came to a good story.

"You know those forms you said I have to file every week?" Jesse said, chewing the bacon. "Where again do you keep them?"

Charity picked up her purse and headed for the front

door. "Jesse, if you're going to be here for a few minutes, I need to run by the paper."

"I *can* be left alone, you know," Mitch called to her. "I'm not a complete invalid."

Charity paid him no mind.

"I'll stay here until you come back," Jesse proposed so she would finally leave.

"Forms?" Mitch said after she'd gone.

Jesse shrugged. "Couldn't think of anything else off the top of my head. The real reason I wanted to talk to you is that I witnessed an accident last night. Desiree Dennison ran a biker off the road."

Mitch swore. "Anyone hurt?"

Jesse shook his head. "It was a hit-and-run, though. She didn't even stop to see if the biker was okay."

"You're sure it was Desiree?"

"Saw the car with my own eyes. She had the top down. No one has a head of hair like her." Desiree took great pride in that wild mane of hers.

He was trying to put his finger on just what color it was when he was reminded of the biker's hair. It was long and fell in soft curls down her back and was a dark mahogany color that only nature could create. Desiree's was darker than he remembered and he realized she must have put something on it.

"Any other witnesses?" Mitch asked.

"Not at 3:00 a.m."

"What about the biker?"

"Wasn't interested in pressing charges. You know bikers."

Mitch grunted. He knew Jesse and that was enough.

"There's going to be damage to the car. The biker hit the passenger-door side. I'd say pretty extensive damage and I took a sample of the paint from the bike."

Mitch was nodding. "You have to write Desiree up. The judge is going to take her license, has to after all her speeding tickets."

Jesse nodded. "I just wanted to tell you before I go up there. I'm sure there will be repercussions."

Mitch snorted. "With a Dennison?"

"I heard Wade might make bail."

"No way. Daisy's fighting it. So am I. He's too much of a risk."

"I hope the judge sees it that way," Jesse said as he took a piece of Mitch's toast. He'd never had much faith in the system. And Charity had been writing some pretty inflammatory news articles about Wade and the rest of the Dennisons, dragging up a lot of old dirt.

If Wade got out, who knew what he would do. He'd threatened to kill Charity at least once that Jesse knew of.

"Have you considered cutting your hair?" Mitch asked, eyeing him as Jesse wiped his bacon-greasy hands on his brother's napkin.

"Nope." That was the good part about being deputized in this part of Oregon. A lot of the rules in the big city just didn't apply. How else could someone like Jesse become an officer of the law?

He heard Charity's VW pull up. "Your woman's back. Better eat your breakfast."

"What's left of it," Mitch grumbled. "Be careful up there at the Dennisons'. I swear they're all crazy."

Jesse wouldn't argue that.

Maggie stared at the newspaper headline. After Twenty-Seven Years in Hiding Following Daughter's Kidnapping, Daisy Dennison Ready for New Life.

"Is that all?" the grocery clerk asked.

Maggie dragged her gaze away from the newspaper to look at the older woman behind the counter. Twenty-seven years. Kidnapping. "What?"

"Is there anything else?"

"I'll take a few papers," Maggie said, feeling light-headed and nauseous as she grabbed the two larger West Coast papers and one of the tiny *Cascade Courier.* She shoved them into the grocery bag with her other purchases, her hands shaking.

The clerk eyed her for a moment, then rang up the newspapers. Maggie gave her a twenty and accepted the change the woman insisted on counting out into her trembling palm. Stuffing the change into the bag with the groceries, Maggie left, trying not to run.

Outside she gulped the damp morning air as she scanned the streets, not sure if she was looking for the face of a killer, that of a handsome dimpled sheriff's deputy or maybe a face that resembled her own.

The streets were empty at this early hour. She looked back to find the clerk still watching her.

Climbing onto her bike, Maggie backtracked a few blocks to make sure no one was following her, then rode south out of town to one of the dozens of state campgrounds she'd seen on the map. She picked a closed one, wound her way around the barrier until she found a campsite farthest from the highway, deep in the woods and near the river.

It wasn't until she was pretty sure she was safe that

she dragged out the newspapers, starting with the article in the *Cascade Courier*.

She read it in its entirety twice. There was little about the original kidnapping. Mostly it was a story about a woman named Daisy Dennison who had been a recluse for twenty-seven years after her baby daughter had been stolen from her crib.

Her husband, Wade, the founder of Dennison Ducks, a local decoy carving plant, was behind bars for a variety of things including shooting the sheriff during a recent domestic dispute with Daisy.

Wade Dennison's attempts to make bail had been thwarted by his wife. Daisy, it was alleged, had filed for divorce and had started a new life.

What a great family, Maggie thought sarcastically.

But what Maggie did get from the story was that the couple's youngest daughter, Angela, had been kidnapped twenty-seven years ago. No ransom had ever been demanded. Angela was never seen again.

Angela Dennison. Was it possible Maggie was this person? If what Norman had told her was correct, she had to be. How many other babies had been kidnapped from this tiny town twenty-seven years ago?

She quickly set up her two-man tent and finished off the milk and a couple more doughnuts before going through the larger newspapers. Nothing about Norman. She breathed a sigh of relief.

She knew she should try to get some sleep but the river pooled just through the trees near her campsite, clear and welcoming. She left the tent and walked over to the small pool, stripped down and took a bath. The icy-cold water did more than clean and refresh her. It assured her she was alive. At least for the time being.

Full and feeling better, she still felt restless—anxious for the cloak of darkness so she could return to town—and worried about the deputy she'd stayed with part of the night. He had no reason to come looking for her. Unless he'd been warned she might be headed to Timber Falls. But then, that would mean Jesse Tanner had been in contact with Detective Rupert Blackmore and Blackmore knew she was alive.

Would the deputy help Blackmore find her? Why wouldn't he? It would be her word against a respected detective. No contest.

She hid her bike in the trees, then brought the saddlebag full of money and her meager toiletries and clothing into the tent to wait until dark.

CHAPTER FIVE

JESSE HAD MADE a point of steering clear of the Dennisons since the time he was a boy. The last thing he wanted to do was ruin the morning by confronting Desiree, let alone her mother, Daisy.

But he stopped by the sheriff's department just long enough to leave his Harley and pick up the patrol car Mitch insisted he use along with that damned cell phone.

The Dennisons lived a few miles outside of town not far from Dennison Ducks.

Jesse hadn't seen Wade and Daisy's daughter Desiree since the shooting at the Dennison house when his brother had been wounded.

But he'd heard Desiree had been frequenting the Duck-In bar more than usual and driving like a bat out of hell in that cute little sports car Daddy had bought her before he went to jail.

The last time he was at the house he'd found them all in the pool house, Mitch lying on the floor bleeding and Daisy with the gun trying to kill Wade. Fun family. Charity had saved the day—and Mitch—and all Jesse had needed to do was handcuff Wade and haul him off to the hospital then jail, adding to the scandal that had been a part of that family from as far back as Jesse could remember. Long before their youngest daughter had been kidnapped twenty-seven years before.

Needless to say, neither Daisy nor Desiree was going to be anxious to see him again. The feeling was mutual.

He parked his patrol car near the four-car garage and climbed out, the Dennison mansion looming out of the forest in front of him.

The place had been built with one thing in mind, letting everyone know just how much money Wade had and how much more could be made through duck decoys. It was an overdone plantation house straight out of *Gone with the Wind*. Antebellum style with huge pillars, a massive veranda complete with white wicker and inside, a Timber Falls' version of Southern belles. Except Daisy, like her daughter Desiree, was no Southerner. Nor was either a belle.

He checked the garage first, peeking in the windows. There was Wade's SUV. Daisy's SUV. And Desiree's little red sports car, the passenger side caved in. He opened the garage door and stepped in, taking the chip of paint he'd scraped from the bike out of his pocket and holding it up against the car door panel. Perfect match. As if there had ever been any doubt. Then he headed for the main house.

"Would you please get Miss Desiree up, ma'am," he said in his best Rhett Butler imitation when the housekeeper answered the front door of the house a few minutes later. "It's the law come a calling." He flashed his credentials.

The German housekeeper didn't get the accent or the humor, what little there was. Nor did she look the least bit concerned. It wasn't as if this was the first time a uniformed officer had come to the door looking for Desiree.

"She is indisposed."

Jesse laughed. "She's still in bed. If I have to come back it will be with a warrant for her arrest."

"I'll take care of this," said a female voice from the cool darkness of the house. Daisy stepped from the shadows. She was close to fifty and still a very attractive woman. It seemed as if the years she'd spent in seclusion after Angela's kidnapping had made her more reserved, less haughty. Her dark hair had been recently highlighted with blond streaks and cut to the nape of her neck so that it floated nicely around her pretty face.

But Jesse would always see her as he had at the age of nine, a goddess with long dark hair and a lush body, riding bareback through the tall grass behind his house, smelling of fancy flowers and what he later realized was sex.

"Hello, Jesse. Can I offer you some coffee? Or perhaps a glass of iced tea? Zinnia just made some."

"No, thank you, Mrs. Dennison." He supposed it was natural he was disposed not to like the woman even if he had never spoken more than two words to her before. "I need to see Desiree."

"I'm sure she's still in bed. Please. Call me Daisy."

"I'm going to have to insist you get her up, Mrs. Dennison."

Daisy's back stiffened. So did her features. "It's that important?"

"Yes, ma'am, it is."

She sighed. "Very well. If you'd care to wait in there." She pointed toward a small sitting room, the walls lined with books. "I'll go get her." Her look said Desiree would not be happy about this.

Too bad. He was a hell of a lot less happy about this than the princess of the house.

It was a good forty-five minutes later before Desiree made an appearance. Jesse had reacquainted himself with several classics in the small library by the time she burst into the room.

Her scent preceded her. She smelled of jasmine, her hair still wet from her shower, her face perfectly made-up. She was wearing all white, a blouse that floated over her curves and white Capri pants that set off her sun-bed tanned legs. She gave him her come-hither look, but being seductive came as easily as breathing for Desiree.

"Jesse," she cooed. "You really should call a girl before you drop by so she can be presentable."

He was struck by the color of her eyes. But it wasn't just the eyes, he realized.

She moved past him, darting to plant a kiss on his cheek and brushing one of her full breasts against his arm as she did.

He found his voice. "This is not a social occasion and you know it."

She turned to smile at him. Desiree Dennison had found that she possessed a power over men and she loved it.

"I'm here on sheriff's department business," he said. "I witnessed an accident last night on the highway by my place. I saw you hit a motorcyclist when you pulled out from Maple Creek Road."

She drew back, gave him a get-real look, then lied right to his face. "I don't know what you're talking about."

"Where were you at three in the morning, after the bars closed?"

A brow shot up. "In bed."

"Anyone's bed I know who can give you an alibi?"

She pouted. "In my own bed, alone."

He shook his head. "Give me your car keys."

"What?"

"Your car keys. Now."

"I'll have to go upstairs and get them." Her cheeks flamed with obvious anger as if the walk was more than she was up to this morning. Or maybe it was being caught.

"I'll wait."

She turned her back on him to buzz the housekeeper on the intercom. "Get me some juice," she snapped. "Orange juice. A large glass." Then she left the room.

He half expected to hear the sports car engine roar to life, but Desiree was too used to getting out of scrapes to make a run for it. Daddy always bailed her out. Only Daddy couldn't even make bail himself right now. And maybe Mommy was over Desiree's shenanigans.

But it was Daisy who returned with the car keys. "If you had told me why you were here, I could have saved you the trouble of waking Desiree. I was driving my daughter's car last night."

He stared at her, not bothering to take the keys she

held out to him. "You were the one up Maple Creek Road? You realize that's the local make-out spot?"

She smiled. "Is it? I'm afraid I was only turning around. I took Desiree's car because I felt like having the top down. I pulled into the turnoff at Maple Creek Road. I didn't see the biker. I know I should have reported it at once."

"Or maybe stopped to see if the biker wasn't killed."

Daisy blanched. "Is he all right?"

Jesse didn't correct her on the rider's gender. "Yeah."

Her expression said she expected charges to be filed, probably a lawsuit by the biker, maybe even her own arrest, but she was ready. Like her daughter, she'd always come away from scrapes unscathed. Except for the loss of her youngest daughter, Angela, when Desiree was two.

"Are you sure you want to take the rap for your daughter?" Jesse asked, holding her gaze. "I know Desiree was driving the car. I saw her."

"Really? You were making out on Maple Creek Road last night, deputy?" Daisy asked.

He smiled. "No, I was standing on the deck of my cabin. I can see the highway from there."

"From your house?" Daisy repeated. "From that distance and in the dark you are absolutely sure it was Desiree behind the wheel?"

"Yes."

"How is that possible when I was the one driving her car?" Daisy asked.

He knew exactly what she was saying. He could call her a liar and press this. It would be his word against hers. He might be wearing a deputy's uniform but she would be more credible—even after the shoot-out in her pool house. Maybe more so because she had come off as the victim. Plus she would hire the best attorney money could buy.

"Look, the worst that will happen is Desiree will lose her driver's license," he said patiently. "And you know that's probably the best thing that could happen, getting her off the streets for a while. Next time she might kill someone. Or herself. And there *will* be a next time."

"I told you I was the one—"

"I know what you told me," Jesse interrupted. "You also told me that Wade was the one who shot my brother but it was your gun and your hand over Wade's when the shots were fired."

Daisy's gaze turned to granite. "I'm sorry about Mitch. I was only trying to defend myself."

Or make sure Wade was out of her life—and without the money, the house, the business. Jesse fought to hold his temper in check. "Isn't that the same thing Wade said when he killed Bud Farnsworth?"

She flinched imperceptibly. The former production manager at Dennison Ducks had pretty much confessed to kidnapping baby Angela from her crib twenty-seven years ago. Unfortunately, Bud never had the chance to implicate the person believed to have masterminded the kidnapping—or tell anyone what he'd done with Angela.

According to Charity, who'd been there, Bud had been trying to say something when Wade shot and killed him. Wade's defense was that he was protecting Charity and Daisy.

"In two months' time, you've been involved in two shootings," Jesse pointed out.

"I was shot myself by Mr. Farnsworth, you might recall," Daisy said. "And almost killed by my estranged husband. In my emotional state is it any wonder I didn't see that motorcycle last night let alone that I panicked and foolishly didn't stop?"

He had to laugh. She would play whatever card it took to get herself out of this—and damned if she wouldn't walk.

"Are you going to arrest me?" she asked. "If so, I'd like to call my lawyer."

"You can call your lawyer from the sheriff's office," Jesse said. "Sure you don't want to rethink what you're doing, Mrs. Dennison?"

She hesitated but only for a moment, then held out her wrists to be handcuffed.

It was a temptation. "I don't think that will be necessary as long as you promise to come along without any trouble."

She smiled and walked to the intercom. "I'll be back shortly, Desiree."

Desiree didn't come back downstairs. Not even when Zinnia showed up with a large glass of freshly squeezed orange juice.

CHARITY CHECKED TO make sure Mitch had fallen asleep before she let Aunt Florie in the front door and took her aside.

"Don't try to force anything with tofu in it on him, all right?" Charity whispered so as to not disturb Mitch who was snoring softly in his recliner. "Or zucchini."

"He likes my zucchini bread," Florie said.

Sure Mitch did. If Charity hadn't been desperate, she would never have even considered leaving Florie with Mitch, but Wade Dennison's sister, Lydia Abernathy, had asked her to stop by the antique shop. Charity was dying to know what that was about. Wade and his recent arrest probably. Charity had always suspected Lydia knew a lot more about what went on at her brother's house than she was telling.

"And no reading his palm or his tea leaves, got it?" Mitch wouldn't be happy to wake up to Florie. But Charity's aunt and all her other screwball relatives came with the marriage package. No wonder Mitch had taken so long to pop the question.

"Whatever." Florie smiled. She'd been doing that a lot lately. Ever since Liam Sawyer had become single again. "Just a minute. I don't know what to wear to the party this weekend." She whipped two caftans out of her bag, one in swirls of bright colors, the other in splashes of bright colors. "Which do you like best?"

That was a tough one. They were both garish at best. "I have an idea," Charity said, looking at her aunt. "I think it's time for a makeover."

Florie, now hugging seventy, was the local psychic and ran her business, Madam Florie's, via email from an old motel on the south end of town. The motel units were now bungalow rentals and Florie did readings out of the office-slash-apartment, as well as on the internet.

Whether or not Florie was clairvoyant was debatable. But she definitely played the part. She wore her long dyed red hair wound around her head like a turban, and dressed in bright caftans that mirrored the turquoise eye shadow she wore to highlight her blue eyes. Her fingers were adorned with dozens of rings and her slim wrists jangled with an array of colorful bracelets. She looked like an exotic bird, blinding in its plumage.

"What's wrong with the way I look?" Florie asked.

Charity didn't have enough time to get into that. "I just think maybe Roz and I could give you a new look for the party." Roz was Liam Sawyer's daughter. The party was to celebrate the fact that her best friend Rozalyn was back in town to stay. Also, Charity suspected, to announce Roz's engagement to Ford Lancaster.

"A new look?" Florie repeated.

Charity nodded enthusiastically. "A surprise for Liam."

The older woman's eyes brightened and Charity knew she had her. Florie had been in love with Liam for years.

"I'll talk to Roz. Don't you worry. It's going to be great," Charity whispered, backing toward the door. "I'll be back as soon as I can. Don't forget, nothing funny on Mitch."

Florie had that dreamy look on her face, obviously lost in thought about Liam, as she waved from the front porch.

Charity had to smile as she climbed into her VW Bug. It was nice to know that falling in love had no age limit. She hoped things worked out for her aunt and Liam. Meanwhile, she couldn't wait to find out what Lydia Abernathy wanted. Lydia only called when something was up.

AFTER LOCKING UP Daisy Dennison, Jesse drove through town, fighting a bad mood, hoping to see that fancy motorbike he'd rolled into the back of his pickup last night.

He couldn't get Maggie—if that was her real name—off his mind. Or the money he'd seen in her saddlebag. But there was no sign of her.

Back at the office, he whizzed past Sissy, taking the handful of messages she waved at him as he went by. Sissy, a thirtysomething large woman with an attitude, managed to get in one of her your-name-is-mud looks before he closed the door.

He sat down behind his brother's desk, glaring at the computer. After a moment, he looked through the messages. Barking dog, missing trash can, abandoned car, noise complaint. He recognized the names of the people who had called. Constant complainers. All people his brother had to deal with on a daily basis—especially this time of year when the constant rain caused a bad case of cabin fever. Jesse wondered how Mitch did it.

Dropping the messages on his desk, he stared at the computer. He'd written down the license number from Maggie's bike last night when he'd hoped she would press charges. Now he hesitated.

"Sissy?" he said, buzzing the clerk.

"Yeesss?"

He cringed; only desperation would make him call

her in here, but he was about as wild about computers as he was cell phones. "I need help."

That soft knowing chuckle of hers. "Don't I know it."

A minute later she opened the office door and stepped in, hands on hips. "If you want coffee, you get it yourself. Doughnuts, I get 'em every morning, anyway, so I don't mind picking up a couple for the sheriff. He liked lemon-filled."

"Lemon-filled works for me," Jesse said.

"And it would help if you told me where you were going when you left. Better yet," she said, swinging her head to one side with obvious attitude, "if you bothered to show up in the morning at all. People call wanting to know there is someone in charge and what am I supposed to tell them?"

"I thought *you* were in charge," he said and smiled.

She mugged a face at him. "You better believe it."

He reminded himself that he only had to do this for a couple of months tops and if he could deal with Daisy and Desiree Dennison he could put up with Sissy Walker. As long as he didn't spend too much time in the office.

"You know how to run this damned thing?" he said, motioning to the computer.

She smiled that smug smile of hers. "The Pope wear boxers?"

He didn't have a clue. But she hadn't moved. "Can you *show* me how to use it?" She still didn't move. "Please? Pretty please and I buy the doughnuts?"

A smile burst across her ample face and she sashayed

over, shooed him up and planted her wide hips in his chair. "What you want?"

"Show me how to find out things. Like…how do I track down a name from a license plate number?"

"What state?"

"Washington. A motorcycle license."

She kicked up an eyebrow and gave him a look but began to tap the keys. He paid attention. He might not like computers, but he was a fast learner and he wasn't going to call in Sissy every time he needed to look up a plate number.

"What's the number?"

He told her, then watched the screen anxiously to see what she came up with.

Sissy let out an "uh-huh," as the name appeared on the screen. "I should have known it would be some broad."

"Biker chick," he corrected, reading the name Margaret Jane Randolph—Maggie—and the address, a better-known wealthy residential area in West Seattle. He hadn't expected anything less.

Sissy started to get up.

"Wait, one more thing. How would I see if there are any priors on her?"

Sissy gave him that eyebrow thing again but continued typing. "You know how to pick 'em," she said as an APB came up for the woman in question.

Margaret Jane Randolph was wanted for questioning in a murder investigation in West Seattle. Murder? The photo accompanying the APB looked as if it was her mug shot from her driver's license. Her hair was different but she was obviously the woman he'd picked up off the highway last night. No two women had a face like that even if some of her features might remind him of another woman.

He swore softly under his breath.

"Anything else?" Sissy asked, sounding disgusted as she pushed herself up and started toward the door.

"No. Thanks," he said as he lowered himself into the chair she'd vacated.

Sissy stopped in the doorway. He glanced up at her. She was shaking her head, giving him the once-over, her gaze halting on his ponytail for a moment.

"How do I make a printout?" he called after her.

"Press Print. Some deputy you make," she said under her breath as she left the room, closing the door behind her.

He turned back to the screen.

An instant message box had flashed up, advising any inquiries to be routed to Detective Rupert Blackmore of the West Seattle Police Department. The message was marked urgent and included the detective's phone number.

Jesse stared at the message and swore. What the hell? It seemed pretty clear Maggie wasn't just wanted for questioning. Was it possible she was a suspect in the murder investigation? And where did all the cash fit in? Or did it?

Jesse got up and walked to the window, telling himself there was no reason to call the detective. No reason to pursue this. She was long gone. Hell, she could be halfway to Mexico by now. Or at least California.

Outside, it had started to rain again, another gray day. Nothing new there.

The woman was wanted for questioning in a murder investigation? Damn.

He went back to the computer, jotted down the detective's name and number on a piece of scrap paper.

Then he hit the close key.

It took a long moment for the screen to clear and as he watched it, he wondered if Detective Rupert Blackmore was at this very moment wondering why someone at the sheriff's department in Timber Falls, Oregon, was interested in Maggie Randolph.

CHAPTER SIX

DETECTIVE RUPERT BLACKMORE left the crime scene trying not to panic. Margaret Randolph's body hadn't floated up and now he knew it wouldn't.

Williams had informed him that a fire alarm had been set off at a café a quarter mile downstream. A false alarm. Not just that, the owner of the café had told Williams that the place had been broken into, there were drops of blood on the floor and someone had used the first-aid kit kept behind the counter.

After Rupert had shot them both, he'd waited in the fog for the bodies to float ashore. Waited until he heard the fire trucks and saw the flashing lights a quarter mile down the water at some wharfside café. He hadn't put it together then because he'd been so sure they were dead.

Hell, she'd gone down with the geek and she'd been hit. Even if the bullets hadn't killed her, the fall and the cold churning water would have, his mind argued. But the fog had been too damned thick to tell if she'd surfaced.

He reminded himself that she'd had on all leather. It would have acted like a wetsuit. And the woman was an athlete.

Rupert knew it was time to quit lying to himself. Margaret Randolph's body wasn't going to float up.

Worse, he couldn't forget those last few moments on the pier when she'd looked up at him. *Recognized* him.

He sat down at his desk and began to fish around in the top drawer for some Tums. His stomach was killing him.

He'd made the mistake of keeping an eye on her over the years. It was crazy, but he felt as if she were his kid. Like he'd been the one to give her life. Hell, he had. If he'd done what he'd been paid to do, she would have died as a baby and been buried up in the mountains.

Was that why he'd blown it at the pier?

But if she was alive, then why hadn't she contacted his superiors? Or the Feds? If she was alive, wouldn't she tell someone what she knew?

Out of the corner of his eye he caught the flashing icon on his computer screen. His gaze jerked to it and he felt his heart take off like a thief.

He shot a quick glance behind him and saw that Williams was on the phone with someone and paying no attention. Hands shaking, he clicked on the icon and tried to catch his breath.

As the inquiry came up, his chest ached as if he'd been shot and for a moment he couldn't think, couldn't breathe. Funny, but he didn't even mind the thought of falling over dead at his desk. At least he didn't mind for those first few seconds. A heart attack seemed a better way out than any of the other alternatives right now.

But then he caught his breath, regained his senses, felt that primal survival instinct kick in. He wasn't ready to go out feetfirst. Hell, if he could weather this storm, he would retire like Teresa had been trying to get him to do. And he'd buy that damned RV she had her heart set on and the two of them would head south. No more rainy winters in the Northwest. They'd go to Arizona and he'd sit in the sun by the pool. Hell, yes. Maybe he'd take up shuffleboard or bingo. Why not?

He deleted the information on the screen, grabbed his coat and left the police station, driving around aimlessly, trying to think.

He'd tagged inquiries about Margaret Randolph only so he'd know firsthand when any evidence surfaced. He'd never dreamed he'd get a hit from some hick sheriff's department. And in Timber Falls, Oregon, of all places. Margaret Randolph's motorcycle tags had been run along with a check for any outstanding warrants on her. What the hell? Did that mean what he feared it did?

He tried to convince himself that someone else had her bike. Maybe had stolen it since he hadn't been able to find the bike after he'd seen her go off the end of the pier and into the icy, churning water below. She'd been wearing her biker outfit so he'd known she'd come by bike. He'd looked for it but was forced to leave for fear of being seen by emergency personnel. Her bike must have been hidden.

So where the hell was it now?

In Timber Falls, Oregon.

And how had it gotten there?

If Margaret Randolph had been riding it then… Hell, then she knew. Norman Drake must have overheard more than Rupert thought he did. Damn. If only he'd gotten to Norman Drake sooner. If only…

He pulled the car over, his hands still shaking, and waited for his heart rate to return to normal, knowing it wouldn't until he found her and finished the job.

Maybe her bike had been stolen, though. Maybe her body *would* wash up.

His cell phone rang as if on cue. He fumbled it open, his pulse a deafening pounding in his ears. "Blackmore."

"It's Williams. The boys are done. It's raining and they haven't found anything else. You want me to leave a man down there? I'm not sure what else you were hoping we would find."

Another damned body. But then he couldn't very well tell Williams that, could he? "Tell them to pack it in. Listen, I'm not feeling very well."

"Ulcers again?"

"Goes with the job," he said. "I'm thinking I might take a day or two of sick pay. If there's anything new on the Iverson and Drake homicides just call me on my cell."

"Hope you get to feeling better," Williams said, but Rupert could hear his relief. The fool thought he could solve both cases and make a name for himself with the guys upstairs in the next forty-eight hours.

Down the block Rupert spotted a phone booth. He didn't want to use the company cell for this call. He parked, got out and ran through the pouring rain. He was soaked to the skin and breathing hard from the exertion by the time he ducked inside the booth. He promised himself he'd get in shape once he got to Arizona.

He dug out a handful of coins from his pocket, dialed the long-distance number and listened to it ring twice as he lit a cigarette and tried to calm down.

"Hello."

Teresa's voice brought tears to his eyes. He wiped at them with the back of his hand. "Hey, baby," he said, his voice breaking. "I was hoping I'd catch you."

"Is everything all right?" He could hear the worry in

her tone. She knew him too well. But she didn't know the half of it. And he would die before he'd let her find out.

"I've got to go out of town for a couple of days on a case," he said. "I just wanted to let you know so you wouldn't worry about me if you called the house. How's your mom?"

"Better. She says to tell her favorite son-in-law hello."

It was an old joke between the three of them. "If I see him, I will."

Teresa laughed as she always did. "I miss you."

"Me, too." He could feel himself getting choked up again. He wished they'd had kids. Wished to hell he'd retired last year. Wished they were in Arizona right now.

But even as he thought it, he knew this wasn't something he could have avoided. Not even in Arizona.

"I'll call you when I finish this job," he said. "I've got to go."

"You take care of yourself, you hear?" It was what she always said.

"For you," he answered as he always did. He started to tell her he'd decided to retire. That they would buy that RV she liked as soon as she got back from her mother's so it would be all ready for them to go south at the first drop of rain next fall, but she'd already hung up.

As he put the receiver back and stood staring out through the soiled glass at the driving rain, Rupert realized what else had been bothering him.

The officer in Timber Falls who'd made the inquiry about Margaret Randolph hadn't called him. Why, when the hick cop had to have seen the message that he was to notify Detective Rupert Blackmore immediately?

He swore under his breath. He was sweating profusely even with the rain hammering the phone booth and a cold wet wind blowing up under the door.

He wasn't spending his golden years behind bars with criminals he'd put there. But he doubted that was even an option. If the person who'd hired him all those years ago found out who Margaret Randolph really was, then it would be clear that he hadn't killed her twenty-seven years ago. That he'd sold her instead and pocketed the cash. And then he'd be a dead man.

He watched the rain drum the glass of the phone booth without even hearing it or feeling the cold or the damp. After a few minutes, he started to breathe a little easier. He felt better. There was nothing like a plan.

He was going to Timber Falls. He'd put an end to this mess once and for all.

Pushing open the phone-booth door, he took a deep breath of the damp Seattle air and thought about Arizona.

Hell, by this time next year he could have a tan.

JESSE HAD JUST looked up from the computer when he caught a flash of color streak by on the street beyond his window. For just an instant, he thought it might be Maggie Randolph on that bike of hers.

But as he peered out the window, he saw it was Desiree's bright red sports car.

"I'll be a son of a—" He ran outside just as Desiree swung the car into Betty's Café and came to a dust-whirling stop.

He swore again and went after her.

Desiree was already sitting in a booth when Jesse walked in. She groaned when she saw him coming toward her. At least she knew she was in trouble. That was a start. He went straight to her booth and slid in across from her.

For a long moment, he just looked at her. She really was a pretty young woman, great bones, nice eyes. There was no denying that. But Desiree lacked something that the woman he'd met last night had in spades. Something beyond looks that had made her impossible to forget.

"What?" Desiree asked peevishly.

"I know your mother took the blame for you this morning," he said quietly. She started to argue but he held up his hand. "You don't learn. I just saw you speeding down Main Street. You're going to kill someone. Or yourself."

"Are you going to write me a ticket?" she asked, as if bored with this particular lecture.

"Desiree…"

She smiled and leaned toward him. "Yes?"

"Get a job. Do something with your life before it's too late." He couldn't believe those words had come out of his mouth.

Neither could she. "Jesse Tanner telling *me* to do something with *my* life?"

He smiled then and shook his head. "I know I'm the last person who should be giving career advice since I'm just starting to get my act together and you're six years younger than me."

"No kidding."

He tried another tack. "Is this about your father? Some sort of rebellion? Because if it is, I can relate."

Her eyes narrowed at him in warning. "Your father isn't in jail."

"No, but I spent a few nights there as a juvenile and I can see a cell in your future if you don't stop acting out."

She rolled her eyes.

"I'm trying to cut you some slack here," he said.

"Don't."

"Okay." He pulled out his ticket book and wrote her up for speeding. He handed the ticket across the table to her as Desiree's lunch arrived.

She stuffed the ticket into her purse without looking at it, picked up a piece of bacon that had fallen out of her BLT and took a bite, licking her lips as her gaze met his. "You want a bite?"

"No."

"Sure?" She cranked up the seduction, obviously in her comfort zone again.

He got to his feet. He'd hoped maybe he could talk some sense into her. Or at least reach out to her in a brotherly sort of way. He felt as if he owed her that for reasons he didn't want to touch.

As he left, he felt it again—something in the air. The way he could sense a storm coming. As if the atmosphere were electrically charged. He stopped to sniff the breeze, unable to shake the bad feeling he had. It was as if something was about to happen and nothing could stop it. Least of all Acting Deputy Jesse Tanner.

"Charity, punctual as always," Lydia Abernathy called from the back as Charity walked through the door of the Busy Bee antique shop a few minutes later.

Lydia smiled and waved from her wheelchair. She was a tiny woman, her hair a white downy halo around her head, her blue eyes bright. She looked older than Charity knew her to be. No doubt because of the accident that had severed her spinal cord and killed her beloved husband, Henry.

It had happened thirty years ago, before Charity was born, but she remembered Florie telling her that Wade had been driving the car. Henry had died instantly, Lydia had ended up in a wheelchair and Wade had gotten off without a scratch.

It was no secret that Wade felt responsible. He'd taken care of his sister for years, supporting her financially, opening the antique shop she'd always wanted and making sure she had live-in help.

They were close in spite of the past. Although Lydia, like most siblings, did take perverse pleasure in her brother's troubles. And Wade had his share right now.

"I heard about your upcoming nuptials," Lydia said as she moved her wheelchair over to the hot plate to collect the teapot. "I thought we'd celebrate with a cup of tea and a few of my sugar cookies."

"You know I can't resist your sugar cookies," Charity said with a groan. "The ones with the sprinkles on top?"

Lydia beamed. "Of course. Angus insists I do too much. He says he's taking over the baking."

Angus Smythe was Timber Falls' version of an English butler. Silent unless spoken to, always painfully polite, and very protective and attentive of Lydia. Plus, he was from England and came complete with the accent. He'd been a close friend of both Lydia and Henry. He was obviously devoted to her.

Charity dragged up a chair, glancing around the shop. The merchandise hardly ever changed. Lydia had collected pieces via the internet but had marked them up so much they weren't likely to sell. Charity suspected she just liked having pretty things around and wasn't in the antique business to make money. Fortunately, she didn't have to show a profit. She had her brother, Wade, when she needed money.

"So when is the wedding?" Lydia asked, handing her a cup of tea, a sugar cookie lounging on the saucer next to it.

Charity knew this wasn't why Lydia had asked to see her. "June. Everyone in town will be invited. I'm just starting the planning."

The older woman nodded. "Henry and I had a lovely wedding." Her eyes clouded over for a moment as if lost in memory. "Henry's buried back East, you know, in the family plot. I will join him when the time comes. I only stayed out here to be close to Wade." She grimaced. "Can you believe the mess he has himself in now? And all because he married beneath his class."

Lydia took a sip of her tea and settled the cup on the saucer. "I've never understood what he saw in that woman. I wish he'd had the sense to shoot her. That lie she told about him calling to say he was on his way to the house to kill her. What man would warn a stupid woman he was coming up to kill her? Although, Daisy could drive anyone to murder. Except *Wade*." She made it sound like a flaw in her brother's character.

Charity took a bite of her cookie. Lydia did make the most amazing sugar cookies. "What is the flavoring you put in these?" she asked, wondering if this was why Lydia had called her, to talk about Wade.

"It's my secret ingredient." Lydia took a sip of tea, then put down her cup, drawing herself up in the wheelchair. "I didn't call you over to talk about Wade or that woman he married. I need a favor."

Uh-oh.

Lydia leaned forward and whispered, "Have you seen that man Betty is with?"

"Bruno?" Everyone in town was talking about him. Drove an old trashed-out car and warmed a bar stool at the Duck-In bar when he wasn't hanging out at Betty's bumming free meals.

"Bruno. Is that his name? Well, I've noticed him walking by the shop and looking in as if he were casing the joint," Lydia said.

Casing the joint?

"What do you know about him?" she asked.

"Nothing." Charity was still trying to imagine Bruno "casing" the antique store. Sure, there were some valuable pieces and some small collectibles but she doubted Bruno would know the good stuff from the junk. And if he stole a pricey ornate oak buffet, how would he carry it? On his back? It certainly wouldn't fit in that old car of his.

"I want you to find out everything you can about him," Lydia said, glancing toward the front window.

Charity knew her shock must have shown. The Busy Bee was anything but busy this time of year and as far as Charity knew, Lydia never had more than a little cash in the till. Most people paid with credit cards or checks and that was when there was actually a customer. "I really don't—" Charity hedged.

"There he is," Lydia whispered.

Charity turned in time to see Bruno walk by. He was a large, not bad-looking man, with a thick head of shaggy blond hair. Bruno looked to be in his forties— a good ten years younger than Betty. Just the way she liked them.

"If you really think he's planning to rob you,

shouldn't you talk to Jesse?" Charity suggested. "He's filling in as deputy until Mitch is well enough to go back to work."

Lydia was shaking her head. "I would look like a silly old woman crying wolf. No, I need to know more about him before I say anything to anyone but you. You're the one with the talent for finding out everything about everyone."

Compliments worked every time. "Okay, I could do some checking on him," Charity said.

"Good," Lydia said, sounding relieved. "He…scares me."

"Angus would never let anything happen to you."

"Angus is a dear but he is no spring chicken," Lydia said.

Angus still looked plenty capable of protecting his mistress. He had always been a large, muscular man and he'd stayed in shape, which made him seem younger than his sixtysomething years.

"I also have my own pistol in my nightstand," Lydia added with a glint in her eyes. "A woman can't be too careful. Especially one with my…disabilities."

There was a sound behind them on the back stairs, a door opening, footfalls as someone came down the steps toward them. It had to be Angus. He never used the elevator Wade had put in for Lydia.

"Don't say anything about Bruno to Angus," Lydia whispered. "Or about my gun. I hate to worry the old dear."

Angus appeared from behind a cloth curtain. "You need anything from the store, Lydia?" he inquired in that wonderful English accent Charity adored.

"No, thank you, Angus."

"I'll only be a short while," he said and, nodding to Charity, left by the back door.

"He thinks I should sell the store, you know. Angus," she added as if Charity wasn't following. "He says I should travel while I can still enjoy it and that he would gladly take me around the world if I like. Did you know he's quite wealthy in his own right? But how can I leave Wade, especially now when he needs me?"

"He might be going to prison," Charity pointed out before she could catch herself.

"Yes," Lydia said. "I guess then there would be nothing but the store keeping me here."

"I should get going," Charity said, rising to her feet.

"Here, take a couple of cookies for later and maybe a few for Mitch?"

Charity could never turn down cookies. As she left, munching one of the cookies on her way to the newspaper office, she had an uneasy feeling about Lydia's fears over Bruno.

CHAPTER SEVEN

AFTER LEAVING DESIREE at Betty's, Jesse cruised around town, too restless to go back to the office. Timber Falls was dead. It had been weeks since there'd been a Bigfoot sighting and it was still the rainy season so there were only locals left in town and most of those had holed up to wait out spring.

Jesse always thought it was the isolation and the cabin fever—locked inside for months while it rained day in and day out—that caused the craziness in Timber Falls. It was one of the reasons he'd gone to Mexico.

But it was his family that had brought him home. He could put up with the rain, he told himself. In a few months tourists would descend on the town to escape the heat in the valleys and residents would take a large collective sigh as if saying, "Made it through another one."

He made a wider circle around the small town. He didn't kid himself. He was looking for Maggie and her fancy motorcycle.

Common sense told him she wouldn't be hanging around Timber Falls. Not with thousands of dollars in one of her saddlebags and an APB out on her. But what was she doing even passing through this time of year? If she was headed out of the country, she was taking

the long route. Timber Falls wasn't even off second-
ary roads.

But a biker *could* disappear in the woods around here
if she wanted to though. Or needed to.

What bothered him was the feeling that she hadn't
left. That coming to Timber Falls hadn't been just a flip
of the coin or a wrong turn.

IT DIDN'T TAKE Charity long to get the lowdown on Bruno
once she had his real name and even that was pretty
simple once she had the license plate number off his
old car.

His name was Jerome Lovelace. That explained why
he preferred Bruno.

For a moment she thought about asking Jesse to run
a check on Lovelace, but she knew he would tell Mitch
and she didn't want to worry Mitch. He hated it when
she got involved in anything even remotely dangerous.
Also she had her own sources.

She called her friend who worked at one of the Oregon law enforcement agencies and waited while Nancy
tapped the computer keys and chewed nervously at her
gum.

"Whoo-whee," Nancy whispered. "This boy's got a
rap sheet as long as my arm."

"What kind of offenses? Any burglary or robbery?"

"Looks mostly like driving while intoxicated, drunk
and disorderly, aggravated assault, domestic abuse,
driving without a valid license, driving without insur-
ance. He did some time for criminal mischief and for
fraud. Most are just misdemeanors. The guy's a loser."

"I gathered that just looking at him." Definitely
Betty's type.

"Oh, here's one. He got picked up for fencing stolen goods but got off," Nancy said. "Doesn't say what kind of goods."

"How about last known address?"

"A post office box in Seattle. You want it?"

"No." Seattle? So what had brought him to Timber Falls? Fencing stolen goods. Like antiques, she wondered. "Thanks. I owe you."

"So true."

Charity hung up and considered what she'd learned. Maybe Bruno wanted to advance his criminal career. Maybe he was contemplating burglary. But Charity didn't buy it.

She grabbed her purse and, leaving the newspaper office, started down the street toward the Busy Bee antique shop. As she neared the shop, she slowed. Wasn't that Bruno ahead of her?

She ducked into one of the store entrances as he started to look over his shoulder. She didn't think he'd seen her. She waited a minute, then peered around the corner of the building and down Main Street.

Bruno had just reached the Busy Bee. She scooted up the street, keeping to the edge of the buildings.

He slowed, looking into the large plate-glass windows at the front of the antique shop, then swung into the entryway as if also not wanting to be seen.

Charity's heart was in her throat. Was it possible Lydia was right? That Bruno really did plan to rob the place?

Bruno had disappeared from view. She ran up the street after him. Had he gone into the antique shop or was he just hidden in the recessed entrance?

Was it possible he'd spotted her, thought she was following him and was waiting for her?

She was almost to the setback entry of the shop. She glanced toward the window, pretending to study her reflection critically in the glass.

Bruno was inside the shop. He was admiring a purple vase, one Charity remembered as being marked four hundred dollars—certainly more than Bruno could afford, she would bet.

But it wasn't Lydia waiting on him. It was Angus. He was frowning, obviously suspicious of the man and maybe a little wary that Bruno might drop the expensive vase and have no way to pay for it.

As Charity walked on past the shop, she saw Angus snatch the vase from him and put it back. Angus looked up and saw her. With a small nod, he watched her pass. Bruno turned, too, frowning. A moment later Charity heard the shop doorbell tinkle behind her, heard the heavy footsteps and knew it was Bruno.

She pushed into the Spit Curl, pulled the door closed after her. She hadn't realized she was holding her breath until she saw Bruno's shadow fall across the front window, then retreat on down the street.

"You look like you've seen a ghost," Mary Jane Clark said from the beauty-shop chair. Mary Jane was getting a blond dye job to her dark roots.

As she watched Bruno saunter on up the street toward Betty's, Charity ignored Mary Jane just as she had throughout high school when Mary Jane had shown an interest in Mitch.

Bruno peered back just once and smiled as if he knew Charity was watching him. Clearly, he was enjoying her fear.

AFTER NOT FINDING a brightly colored motorcycle or the woman who'd been riding it, Jesse returned to his office, wondering if Detective Rupert Blackmore would be waiting for him. Or at least have called.

"She already made bail," Sissy said as Jesse walked into the office.

He didn't have to ask who she was. Daisy Dennison. He'd known she would be out before the fingerprint ink dried.

Sissy handed him another stack of messages. He flipped through them. None from Blackmore. He'd been so sure the cop would have all inquiries red-flagged. Maybe Blackmore really did just want to talk to Maggie about the murder. Maybe she wasn't a suspect.

But there were lots of messages from whiners about everything from a nasty smell coming from the neighbor's garbage cans to cars parked incorrectly along Main Street.

"Damn, don't these people have anything else to do?" he said as he headed for his office.

Sissy gave him her some-deputy-you-are look.

He sat down behind the desk and began making calls, pretending he was Mitch, pretending diplomacy was his middle name. Before he realized it, the afternoon had turned into evening. Sissy stuck her head in the door to say she was leaving and it was time to ante up for the next morning's doughnuts.

It wasn't until he'd gotten to the bottom of the pile of messages that he found Detective Rupert Blackmore's name and number where he'd scribbled it down earlier. He vaguely remembered doing it—just before he'd seen Desiree speed by.

If the cop was tagging inquiries, then he already

knew that Maggie had been in Timber Falls. If the detective was really concerned, he would have called.

So a phone call from Jesse wouldn't make any difference at this point since she was long gone, anyway.

But with one phone call, Jesse would know why the detective wanted to talk to Maggie. It would satisfy his curiosity. He started to pick up the phone. Hesitated. What was he afraid he was going to find out? It wasn't fear holding him back and he knew it. He knew he was crazy for not calling. Not to mention irresponsible. But his gut instincts were telling him to wait. And he'd always gone with his instincts. Right or wrong.

His stomach rumbled. He glanced at his watch. The detective wouldn't be in his office this late. Maybe in the morning. His stomach rumbled again. And Jesse had just enough time to get to Betty's before she closed. Idly, he wondered what Maggie Randolph was having for dinner tonight.

"WILL YOU BE all right alone for a little while?" Charity asked from the doorway.

"Call Florie again and you're dead," Mitch said from his recliner.

She smiled at him. "I was desperate."

"Uh-huh. You were paying me back for the times I insisted Florie stay with you." He motioned her closer, reached out and pulled her down to him. She was never more beautiful than when she was hot on a story. Unfortunately, he knew the look all too well. "Want to tell me about it?"

"Not yet." She smiled that secret little smile of hers, the one that gave him ulcers.

The only reason she wouldn't tell him would be if

she thought he would try to stop her because it was dangerous. Damn. He wished he *could* stop her. But he'd been here before and knew stopping Charity was like trying to rein in a speeding bullet. He reminded himself that this was his future, worrying about Charity. "Be *careful*."

She kissed him. "You know me."

He groaned but didn't let go of her, trailing kisses along her silken throat. At least this story had gotten her mind off the wedding. She'd been driving him crazy with discussions about orchids versus roses versus daisies, let alone all the choices for the reception.

If that wasn't bad enough, Florie had to start warning Charity about bad luck wedding superstitions. Charity pretended she wasn't superstitious. Uh-huh. But then later she'd asked him if he'd seen a blind man, a monk or a pregnant woman on his way to the Dennisons' the night he was shot.

All it seemed were bad luck before a proposal of marriage. But if he'd seen nanny goats, pigeons or wolves, then this would be a good omen that would bring good fortune to the marriage.

"I saw an entire flock of pigeons," he said, which made Charity laugh, but also look secretly relieved.

"Promise me that you'll call me at the paper if you need anything," she said now, her voice breaking a little as he nibbled at her ear.

"Promise."

She kissed him, a slow, sensuous kiss that made him desperately want to take her in his arms and make love to her. But even if he could with the cast and bandages, Charity was holding out for their wedding night.

He let go of her, not about to disappoint her now. She

would get the wedding she wanted. A white one. And everyone knew "married in white, she'd chosen right."

The moment she was gone, though, he called Jesse.

"I'd venture to guess she's chasing something to do with the Dennisons," Mitch told him. Charity had been chasing one story or another about them ever since she started the *Cascade Courier* right out of college. When news was slow there was always the town's only big mystery: the disappearance of Angela Dennison twenty-seven years before. It had become the stuff local legends are made of and Charity couldn't pass up a good mystery.

"Charity went to see Lydia Abernathy this afternoon," Mitch told his brother. Florie had slipped and told him. "And now she's headed for the newspaper office." With Lydia being Wade Dennison's sister he figured whatever reason she'd wanted to see Charity couldn't be good.

"Kinda late to be going to the newspaper. Damn, that woman is obstinate, isn't she," Jesse said, unable to hide the admiration in his voice. "Glad I'm not marrying her."

"Sure you are. Are you still in town?"

"I'm at Betty's." She was making him a sandwich to go. It had been the kind of day that made him anxious to get home and as far away from being a deputy as he could. Except he wouldn't sleep once he got home, anyway. "You want me to check on Charity? No problem."

"Thanks. I'd suggest taking Charity a piece of pie. Banana cream, if Betty still has some. That way Charity won't take your head off."

Jesse grinned to himself as he hung up. It was great seeing his brother in love—and admitting it. If Mitch

could fall so hard, wasn't there a chance for Jesse to
find true love?

Betty bagged up the sandwich, a slice of banana
cream and a slice of cherry for him.

As he drove down Main to the newspaper office,
Charity was just getting out of her VW. He pulled in
beside her and got out. "Here, let me get that for you,"
he said as she started to unlock the office. He smiled
and, holding the bag from Betty's in one hand, took
the keys from her.

"Mitch called you," she accused, not sounding
pleased about it.

Jesse tried to look innocent, gave up and said, "I have
pie. Banana cream."

She tried to hide a smile as he opened the door for
her and turned on the light. "You can tell Mitch—" She
stopped in midsentence, her eyes widening as she surveyed her office.

The newspaper was small, the office consisting of
only three desks, a light table, copy machine, darkroom
and a small press.

Everything looked fine to him. "What's wrong?"

Charity said nothing, just walked slowly into the
room and headed straight for one of the large filing
cabinets against the wall. The top drawer was open and
when he looked past her, he saw a newspaper clipping
lying on the floor between Charity and the darkroom.

He moved to her, touched her arm and motioned for
her to be quiet as he headed toward the darkroom. Using
his shirttail, he turned the knob. The door swung in.
He flicked on the light.

The metal grate that covered a large air vent in the
ceiling hung down exposing a gaping hole to the roof.

Dragging up a chair, Jesse peered into the ventilation system, careful not to touch anything. The opening was accessible from the roof and large enough for a small person to crawl through. He climbed down and checked the back door. It wasn't just unlocked. It wasn't even latched. He glanced down the alley. Empty.

"You always lock the back door?" he asked Charity.

She nodded. She hadn't moved, seemed to be frozen in her spot, eyes still wide. He figured she was reliving the last time someone had broken into the newspaper. That time she'd been in the darkroom and the burglar had grabbed her, bound her with duct tape and stuffed her in the storage closet. Obviously that incident had made a lasting impression on her.

"The door was definitely locked," she said in a whisper.

"Well, it looks like your intruder came through the air vent on the roof down into the darkroom and then made a hasty retreat out the back door. Could have been a kid—"

"No," she interrupted, shaking her head and seeming to pull herself together. "A kid wouldn't break in to steal a file of newspaper clippings. One of my files is missing."

He frowned. "How can you tell that?"

She didn't answer, just moved to the clipping on the floor and, using the pencil she'd picked up, she flipped the article over.

The headline read: Whatever Happened to Baby Angela?

Charity motioned toward the computer on the desk. Even from here he could see that the burglar had typed in the search keyword KIDNAPPING to access the file number.

"Someone is interested in the Angela Dennison case," she said.

"The file is missing?"

She nodded.

He swore under his breath. His bad feeling from earlier had settled deep in his gut.

"Interested enough to break in rather than wait until the office was open," Charity was saying. "Obviously, he doesn't want us to know who he is or why he's interested."

"Any idea who it could be?" he asked, hoping there was some weirdo in town who'd shown an interest in the case who was nuts enough to break in to read the file in private. No such luck.

She shook her head.

"Well, I think we scared whoever it was away, but there is no way you're staying here alone tonight to work."

Charity surprised him by not arguing. "It can wait until tomorrow."

Clearly she saw the potential for another story after this break-in. "You want to dust this clipping?" she asked.

He nodded and saw her glance at the sack from Betty's. "Just take the banana cream. The cherry pie and sandwich is mine."

She grinned at him as she drew out the carton with the slice of cream pie inside and took a whiff, closing her eyes for a moment, a smile on her lips.

"My brother is one lucky man."

She opened her eyes. "You know it."

Jesse walked her out to her car. "Straight home?"

"You're going to call Mitch the moment I pull away, aren't you?"

He smiled. "You know it." He watched her drive away, then took the investigation kit out of the back of the patrol car. He'd seen Mitch do this a few times and figured at this point there was no reason to call in the state crime lab boys. Not yet, anyway.

He got a half-dozen latents off the newspaper clipping and one good clear one from the back doorknob. He was hoping the burglar had taken off his gloves to peek at the articles. Maybe he hadn't planned to steal the file, didn't want to throw up a red flag when Charity found it missing.

So when he heard Jesse's and Charity's cars pull up out front after everything in town was closed and the sidewalks practically rolled up for the night, he'd just grabbed the file and run, dropping the one clipping and leaving a print on the back doorknob.

Of course, there was a good chance the prints would all turn out to be Charity's. Or Blaine's, the high-school kid who worked for her.

BACK AT HIS OFFICE, Jesse called Mitch. Charity had made it home safe and sound although Mitch was upset that someone had broken into the newspaper office, especially after the last time.

"Can you walk me through the process for sending fingerprints to the state lab?" Jesse asked his brother, taking a bite of his sandwich and booting up the computer.

Jesse did as he was instructed, figuring it would take a while to get an ID, if he got one at all tonight.

But to his surprise, the results came up immediately. He let out a curse and pushed the remaining sandwich aside.

"What?" Mitch said on the other end of the line.

"I didn't think they would come back so fast," Jesse told him. One print, the one from the back door, had come up with a match.

"That means there's an APB out on this person," Mitch said.

No kidding. The clean print on the back doorknob belonged to Margaret Jane Randolph of West Seattle.

"Tell me Charity hasn't gotten herself into trouble," Mitch said.

"Not to worry, little brother," Jesse said. No reason to tell him about Maggie just yet. "I'll call and see what's up and get back to you in the morning." He hung up before Mitch could argue.

Jesse stared at the number on the screen. Damn. Maggie wasn't on her way to Mexico. She was busy breaking into the newspaper to read the Angela Dennison file. For some reason this woman on the run from a murder investigation had stopped long enough to read a newspaper file on kidnapping.

Now what kind of sense did that make? None. And yet, it made perfect sense to him.

He opened the container with the cherry pie inside and took a few bites before he dialed the telephone number he'd scribbled down earlier. It was way too late but maybe big-city detectives worked late.

Maggie had broken into his soon-to-be sister-in-law's newspaper. It was high time he found out just what the hell was the story with his mystery biker.

He got Detective Rupert Blackmore's voice mail.

Blackmore had a deep, rough-sounding voice. An older cop, hardened from time and the streets, Jesse thought. He'd met a few of them. He hung up without leaving a message.

"Now why the hell did you do that?" he asked himself and swore.

He couldn't explain it. Just a gut feeling that he needed to talk to Maggie Randolph before he talked to the cop.

Disgusted with himself, he got up from the desk and went to the window. "Some deputy you are." He stared out at the dark night. It had started to rain again. Soon he would have webbed feet if he stayed in this town.

He'd have to find her. Find out what the hell she was doing in Timber Falls. What she was searching for. But he had a bad feeling he already knew, had known longer than he wanted to admit.

CHAPTER EIGHT

IN THE DARK tent, Maggie stared at the thick file. Her heart was still pounding. That had been a close call back at the newspaper. She'd never expected anyone to show up, not after hours and certainly not in a town that was dead by eight at night.

How long would it take the deputy to find out that she'd broken into the paper and taken the Angela Dennison file? How long before he notified Blackmore?

She should have left the file, but there wasn't time to cover her tracks, and she had to know what was in it. She'd only just started reading through the clippings, hiding in the darkroom with her flashlight, when she'd heard the cars pull up out front.

Would they have realized by now that she took the file? Maybe not. Maybe no one would know for a while. But if it came out, then Blackmore would not only know she was in town but that she'd stumbled onto the truth.

She shone the flashlight on the file, her fingers brushing the bulging worn folder. It seemed she had been the news for twenty-seven years.

After reading for a few minutes, there was no doubt in her mind that she was the baby who had been kidnapped twenty-seven years ago from her crib in a house a few miles from here. She was Angela Dennison, youngest daughter of Wade and Daisy Dennison, owners of Dennison Ducks, a plant where decoys were carved.

The file contained not only articles published by the *Cascade Courier,* but copies of ones from larger newspapers where the kidnapping had made front-page news when it happened years ago.

Angela Dennison was only a few weeks old when she was taken from her crib in the dark of night, never to be seen again. Not only was Angela the same age as Maggie, they shared the same birthday—March ninth.

And Maggie had been adopted not twenty-four hours after Angela Dennison's disappearance.

Many of the local stories had been written by Charity Jenkins for the *Cascade Courier.* She read through all the articles again. If she was right, she was the daughter of the most written about family in town.

Maggie put the articles back in the file and snapped off the light, plunging the tent in darkness. Her head ached and she felt sick to her stomach. Closing her eyes, she listened to the sound of the river and the wind in the trees…and the frantic beat of her heart.

It was all mind-blowing. According to the articles, the mystery had been solved a few months ago when the plant production manager had been killed after admitting to Charity Jenkins right before he died that he had taken the baby. But it was clear from the newspaper articles written after his death that he had not acted alone.

Apparently both parents, Daisy and Wade Dennison, had been suspects. Might still be suspects. She had studied the photo of Wade and Daisy Dennison for a long time. It was a black-and-white, grainy and not clear enough to see any resemblance.

Or maybe she just didn't want to see a resemblance. Didn't want to be part of this infamous family.

As she sat in the darkness, she tried to tell herself it could be worse. Wade Dennison was in jail for shooting the Timber Falls sheriff during a recent domestic dispute with his estranged wife, Daisy. How could it be worse than that?

Maggie felt hot tears on her cheeks. She hadn't let herself cry. Not at the pier when Norman had been killed. Not after, when she knew it was only a matter of time before Blackmore caught up with her.

She'd focused on only one thing: learning the truth. Once she knew, she'd thought that she would be safe.

But now she saw that that wasn't the case. She still had no idea why Blackmore wanted her dead. Her throat constricted as she fought back the sobs that made her chest ache. Scared and tired and sick over what she'd found, she curled around the pain as the sobs racked her body and tears burned down her cheeks.

She was Angela Dennison. Like it or not. And for some reason, her life was in danger because of it.

After a few minutes, she dried her tears and pulled herself together. Enough crying. She couldn't just hide out in this tent and feel sorry for herself.

If Blackmore had been behind the kidnapping, that would explain why he didn't want the truth coming out. So he must have had some connection to Timber Falls. All she had to do was find it.

The obvious place to start seemed to be her biological family. Wade Dennison was a powerful man in this town but he was in jail. Was it possible he had influence as far away as Seattle? Or was it his wife, Daisy, who might have known Blackmore?

Maggie turned on the flashlight long enough to hide the stolen file under her mat, then pocketing the light, she left the tent and headed for her bike. She had hours before daylight and a lot to do before then. It was only a matter of time before Blackmore found out she was in Timber Falls and came to finish what he'd started.

DETECTIVE RUPERT BLACKMORE was tired and cranky and his whole body ached after driving for hours. He still had miles to go to get to Timber Falls, Oregon. A waitress in an all-night truck stop refilled his coffee cup. He'd drunk too much coffee to try to stay awake and his stomach was killing him.

"Can I get you anything else?" she asked, drawing her order pad from her uniform pocket. She didn't look up as she tore off his bill and laid it on the table. She glanced at him then.

"No." He shook his head. "Thank you."

She gave him a smile, a granddaughterly smile. "Good luck. Hope you catch a bunch."

He watched her walk away. *Hope you catch a bunch.* Fish. She'd gotten the idea that he was going fishing no doubt from his hat with the lures on it and the old jacket and flannel shirt he was wearing. He smiled to himself.

Yesterday, he'd only gone home long enough to take a shower, change his clothing and collect several of the unregistered weapons he'd picked up over the years. At least the weapons weren't registered to him. They'd been ones he'd found at drug busts, ones tossed out of moving vehicles he'd chased down, ones he'd taken off dead gang members. Ones that could never be traced back to him.

At first he'd just collected them, like trophies of wild

game kills. At least he thought he had. But maybe he'd known all along that the day would come when he would need a gun.

Blackmail was an insidious thing. Even when you didn't hear from the blackmailer for years, you always knew the day would come when payment would be demanded. And unless you wanted your entire world to unravel like the yarn of a slashed sweater, then you paid—no matter the price.

He'd taken the pickup he used for his fishing trips. Thrown in his tent for good measure, along with his fishing jacket and hat. When he'd finally gotten everything loaded into the pickup and slipped behind the wheel, the fishing hat perched on his head, he'd glanced in the rearview mirror.

He'd been shocked at how much he'd aged. It was as if his hair and beard had turned completely gray overnight. When was the last time he'd looked into the mirror, really looked? Obviously not when he shaved in the morning.

He recalled old fishermen he'd met over the years, tottering along the edge of the water, squinting into the sun from a face wrinkled and weathered with age and water and wind, and realized he could have been one of them.

That's when it hit him. What the people of Timber Falls, Oregon, would see. An old fisherman. Not a cop.

Not unless they looked into his eyes. That was the only part of him that would give him away. The life-hardened ice-blue eyes that even he didn't like to look into.

He'd picked up a pair of sunglasses off the dash of

the truck, put them on and looked in the mirror again. He couldn't have picked a better disguise.

He left the waitress a good tip, paid his bill at the cash register and bought himself two of the best cigars the truck stop had to offer. As he headed for his pickup, he felt better than he had in days.

Maggie Randolph would never see him coming.

JESSE STARED AT the computer in the empty office. He knew he should go home and try to get some sleep. He could start looking for Maggie in the morning.

He leaned toward the computer, remembering what Sissy had shown him. Maggie Randolph had broken into the newspaper to research the Angela Dennison kidnapping case. While Charity's paper was too small to have an online morgue, a large paper in the Seattle area would, wouldn't it?

He went online, called up one of the two largest newspapers there, typed in the name Margaret Randolph and waited. Maybe there wouldn't be anything on her. Maybe she hadn't lived there long enough. Maybe—

A long list of articles appeared on the screen. He scanned down them surprised that most had run on the sports pages. He shook his head in wonder. It seemed Maggie liked to race motorcycles, participate in extreme skiing competitions and scuba dive in dangerous waters. How about that?

He started back up the list, spotted one marked Obit and clicked on it. Maggie's name was listed as the only surviving child of Paul Randolph who had been killed in a plane crash less than two months ago. He started to click off the obituary when he spotted another one farther down. He clicked on it. Again Maggie's name was listed as the only child. The obit was for Mildred Randolph, Maggie's mother. He skimmed it, noted that the mother had contracted polio as a child and had been in a wheelchair, and at the bottom saw something that made him catch his breath.

Memorials were to be made to an organization the Randolphs had started to assist older, disabled couples in adopting a child.

What were the odds that Maggie was adopted?

Jesse swore, more sure than ever he was on the right track. He moved the cursor back to the top of the list and clicked on the most recent article under Margaret Jane Randolph.

It was a story about a legal assistant named Norman Drake. His body had been fished out of the water near an abandoned pier on Puget Sound this morning. His death was being investigated as a homicide. Margaret Randolph was wanted for questioning in the man's murder along with that of Drake's boss, a local attorney named Clark Iverson who was murdered in his office last week. Iverson had been a longtime family friend and attorney for Randolph's father, the recently deceased Paul Randolph.

Jesse let out a low whistle. Maggie seemed to have left a trail of bodies behind her. And now she was in Timber Falls doing a little B and E to research an old kidnapping case?

Locking up the office, Jesse climbed on his bike. It was late but there was something that couldn't wait. He'd put it off for too many years already.

LEE TANNER CAME out onto his deck, squinting into the darkness, as Jesse shut off his motorcycle. "Son, I was hoping that was you."

Jesse saw with relief that his father was sober. It had been a long time now but he wondered if he would always feel that instant of fear just before the relief no matter how many years his father had been on the wagon. "I know it's late...."

Lee shook his head. "I'm glad you stopped by. I was just enjoying the night sky." The rain shower had passed, leaving the sky clear and full of stars.

Jesse joined him at the deck railing, trying to see his father the way Daisy Dennison must have almost thirty years ago. Lee still had a thick head of dark hair, but at fifty-five it was shot with silver. When Lee Tanner used to ride horses in the woods behind the house with Daisy his hair had been as black as Jesse's.

His father was still an attractive man, strong and lean, his dark eyes more solemn than Jesse remembered them, his demeanor more serene. Was that just from being sober? Or had his father found some kind of peace with the past?

Jesse was reminded that he'd thought the same thing of Daisy, that the years had mellowed her, as well.

"What's on your mind, son?" Lee asked, tilting his head back as he looked up at the glittering stars and sliver of silver moon overhead. A light breeze stirred the tops of the nearby pines, whispering softly to the night.

Jesse hesitated, afraid he was about to destroy any peace his father had found and send him back to the bottle. "The newspaper office was broken into tonight."

Lee looked over at him in surprise. This rainy season had been the worst. Murders and shootings and all interrelated in some way to the Dennisons.

"The burglar took Angela Dennison's kidnapping

file." Jesse saw his father tense. A deep silence stretched between them. "There's something I need to ask you."

"As a lawman or my son?" Lee inquired quietly.

"Both. I need to know if there is any chance Angela Dennison is your daughter."

Lee closed his eyes and sighed softly. "Why would you ask me that after all these years? What possible difference could it make now?"

"I think she's alive," Jesse said, the words tumbling out, words he hadn't dared even think let alone say until this moment. "I think she's in Timber Falls. And I think she's in bad trouble. I have to know the truth. It might be the only way I can help her."

His father's eyes came open slowly. He stared at his son, his whole body seeming to quake as he gripped the rail. "Angela alive?" Tears welled in his dark eyes, now no longer at peace. "Does Daisy know?"

"I don't even know for sure myself yet," Jesse said, but maybe part of him had known from the moment Maggie had lifted her head beside that rain-soaked highway last night and he'd felt as if he'd been hit between the eyes with a two-by-four. He hadn't wanted to see the resemblance. So like Desiree and yet so different.

"My God, if Angela really is alive..." Lee Tanner stumbled over to one of the deck chairs and lowered himself into it, looking suddenly older than his fifty-five years.

"I have to know, Dad."

His father was shaking his head in wonder, staring off into the darkness as if caught in the past again. "Everyone thought she was dead."

"Dad? Is there a chance that Angela is your daughter?"

Lee Tanner looked up. "It's been so long, Jesse. You

have to understand, we're different people than we were then. I know part of you believes the affair was why your mother left me—"

"I don't care about that. I *have* to know if Angela could be your daughter. My...half sister."

"Why would the truth ever have to come out? What difference—" Lee Tanner seemed to see the answer in Jesse's gaze. "Don't tell me that you're—"

"I've only laid eyes on her once," Jesse said quickly. "But if I'm right about her..." How could he explain to his father that he was instantly drawn to this woman, felt things he'd never felt? He couldn't explain it to himself. And his greatest fear was that this woman would always be forbidden to him.

"Oh, Jesse."

"I need to know the time frame."

His father seemed about to deny it, then said quietly, "I honestly don't know. But it's possible both girls could be mine."

Desiree, too. Hadn't Jesse always suspected as much? Wasn't that why he'd never taken her up on her many offers? Why he'd felt brotherly toward her?

Well, he didn't feel that way toward Maggie.

"Didn't you ever bother to ask Daisy?" he demanded.

His father looked up at him. "She went back to Wade for a while and swore that Desiree was his."

"And Angela?"

"We never spoke about Angela."

Jesse cursed under his breath. "When did Daisy break it off?"

His father seemed surprised by the question. "Daisy didn't. I did."

So that's how it had gone down. Mitch told him not

long ago that Daisy had said she loved their father. Did she still? "When was that?"

"Before I knew she was pregnant," he said and looked out across the dense forest that stretched in front of his place. "I couldn't keep having an affair, not while I was married to your mother. I knew it was wrong but Daisy and I— I suppose that's why Daisy never told me she was pregnant. I didn't talk to her again until—"

"Until my mother left," Jesse guessed. "Daisy must have called you to tell you that your wife had been up to the house demanding blackmail money."

Lee closed his eyes again in silent acknowledgment.

"That's when you changed your mind and gave her the money to leave," Jesse said, seeing now how it had happened. His mother had never loved his father. As far back as he could remember, Jesse had known she wanted to leave the three of them, had just waited for her husband to grant her a divorce—and pay her off.

His father said nothing. What could he say about a woman who was that desperate to abandon her two sons and husband and had been long before her husband had taken up with Daisy Dennison.

"Why did Daisy tell you about Mother going up there?" Wasn't it obvious? "She wanted you to face how badly my mother wanted to leave, didn't she?"

He opened his eyes. "Ruth was a good woman—"

"Don't even try to sell me on her, okay?"

Lee looked down at his boots. All these years he'd tried to spare Jesse and Mitch, pretending their mother had wanted them, just couldn't handle marriage to him, always blaming himself and making excuses for her.

"Did Daisy hope you two would resume your affair after that?" Jesse asked.

A few minutes stretched past. "Daisy wanted more than I could offer her then."

That surprised Jesse. Was it possible his dad had been serious about Daisy?

"Whatever Daisy was thinking, Angela's kidnapping changed everything for her," Lee Tanner continued, turning to look at Jesse. "If this woman really is Angela…"

Jesse nodded. "It could open up a can of worms that will make everything else pale by comparison."

They fell into a deep silence again.

Jesse reached into his jacket pocket and handed his father the DNA test. "I need this now."

He nodded, went into the house and returned a few minutes later. He handed his son the boxed-up test. It was hard to tell what his father was thinking, let alone feeling at that moment.

"If I'm right, a lot more than dirty laundry is going to come out," Jesse said. "There's been some deaths back in the city where she's been living."

His father's eyes widened. "You don't think she—"

"No. She isn't a killer." How did he know that? He just did. Just like he knew she was Angela Dennison. "I'm afraid she's in trouble." Hell, he *knew* she was in trouble—that saddlebag full of money, the APB out on her. He just didn't know how much.

He looked over at his father, saving the worst for last. "Dad, I need to know where my mother is."

Lee reared back as if he'd been punched. "Why would you—"

"Do you know where she is?" Jesse watched his father's face. "You do." Jesse groaned. "You've been sending her money all these years." He couldn't believe it.

"You're wrong. But I would have if she'd asked. She's your mother."

"She was *never* a mother to Mitch and me, and you know it."

"She brought you into this world," Lee said. "For that, I owe her. And so do you."

Jesse gritted his teeth. "Where is she?"

"You're asking as a deputy now, aren't you?"

"Yes. She could be a material witness in the kidnapping. She was at the Dennison house just before Angela disappeared and she was never questioned because she skipped town that same day." Jesse narrowed his eyes at his father. "Don't tell me you haven't wondered if she had something to do with Daisy Dennison's baby disappearing."

He expected his father to argue that Ruth Anne Tanner would never steal the woman's baby to get back at her because of the affair. He didn't. Couldn't. Even if Ruth hadn't given a damn about her husband, she had tried to blackmail Daisy. When Daisy threw her out without a cent, Ruth might have decided to get even and they both knew it.

"I don't know where she is," Lee said, his voice sounding hoarse. "My only connection to her is through my attorney and hers."

"Your attorney still Matthew Brooks?"

His father nodded with obvious reluctance. "Jesse, please don't go see her. No good can come of it."

"I don't doubt that," Jesse said, hearing the fear in his father's voice. Like Jesse, he must fear his former wife had kidnapped Angela and involved Bud Farnsworth out of vengeance.

Or maybe for money. It seemed Maggie had ended

up with wealthy adoptive parents. He could only guess how that had happened. "This has been a long time coming. I'm sure you know that."

Lee wagged his head. "I don't want to see you boys hurt."

"Then don't tell Mitch," Jesse said. "I'll protect my little brother for as long as I can. But if my mother took that baby…"

Lee looked away. "For Daisy's sake I pray Angela really is alive and that your mother had nothing to do with taking her."

Jesse studied his father, seeing something that he'd missed years ago. Lee's feelings for Daisy Dennison. How deep did they run? Jesse wasn't sure he wanted to know.

"You won't say anything to Mitch about this?" he asked his father.

Lee looked up in surprise. "And have Charity find out? It would be on the front page of her paper by tomorrow." He smiled as if admiring her tenacity, the same tenacity that had her now about to marry Mitch. "No matter what you find out, son, we're a family. We'll weather this storm just like we have all the others."

Jesse nodded, wishing he could believe that. "Tell your lawyer I'll be contacting him."

Lee sighed and looked out into the darkness. "I hope you know what you're doing."

As Jesse walked back to his bike, a few white clouds cruised by over the tops of the trees obscuring the stars and moon, darkening the night to as black as his mood. Maggie was out there somewhere. He could feel it. Fate had made their paths cross. But maybe not for the reason he'd originally thought. Or desperately wanted.

Either way, she needed him. And he doubted she realized it. He just hoped he could find her before it was too late.

As he reached to start the bike, he felt the damned cell phone vibrate in his pocket.

"Jesse!" Daisy Dennison cried the moment he answered the phone. "Someone has broken into Dennison Ducks. The thief is still there. The new production manager is on the other line calling from her cell phone outside the plant watching it happening right now. Someone's in Wade's office with a flashlight going through the files!"

"I'm on my way." Jesse snapped off the phone and headed the bike toward Dennison Ducks, already pretty sure he knew who the thief was and what she was looking for.

CHAPTER NINE

MAGGIE HAD JUST dropped through the air vent into the second-story office section of Dennison Ducks when she heard it. The soft scuff of a shoe on the concrete first floor below her.

She froze, listening. Had she only imagined it? She waited, heard nothing then snapped on the small flashlight and shone it around the office.

Quickly and quietly she moved past the secretary's desk to Wade Dennison's office. Her light caught on an eye gleaming from the corner. Her heart leaped to her throat, choking off her scream. She settled the flashlight beam on the eye, ready to run.

A large duck, its plastic eye sparkling, looked back at her. She realized the room was full of ducks. Every size, shape and color stared down at her from a shelf that ran the entire circumference of the room.

Hurriedly, she scanned the file cabinets, not sure exactly what she was looking for until she spotted the locked file drawer directly behind his desk. She moved soundlessly to the desk, picked up the letter opener and approached the file drawer.

The lock was old, the cabinet handle dusty, as if it hadn't been opened for a while. She pried with the letter opener until the lock broke and, holding the same flashlight in her teeth, quietly slid open the drawer.

That's when she heard the sound again. Someone moving through the plant below her. A stair creaked. Then another. Someone was coming up the steps to the office.

Deputy Jesse Tanner? Had someone spotted the light in the office and called the cops?

There was only one file in the drawer. The rest of the space was covered in dust. She grabbed the file, stuffed it into her jacket, turned off the flashlight and, not bothering to close the drawer, retraced her steps quietly across the room.

She could hear someone coming up the steps now, see the faint glow of a penlight. She reached out in the dark, located the desk and climbed up onto it. Any moment the person would enter the office.

She froze, immobilized with fear, as she caught a whiff of the same odor she'd smelled on the pier right before Blackmore had tried to kill her.

He was almost to the top of the stairs. Maggie pulled herself up into the vent and moved fast, no longer afraid of making noise. She could hear the thunder of running footsteps across the office, the rattle of the vent grate as it was banged aside.

In an instant she was on the roof and racing across to the pine tree she'd climbed for access. She scrambled down through the limbs, afraid someone would be waiting for her at the bottom.

But once on the ground, no one appeared out of the darkness.

She leaped onto her bike, started it quickly, taking off down the road at full speed. She hadn't gone far when she saw the headlight of the other bike. It came roaring up the hill, the headlight catching her broadside in its sights.

JESSE WAS ALMOST to the decoy plant when he spotted the single light coming out. A biker. Moving fast.

In his headlight he saw the gleam of the biker's helmet, recognized both it and the bike as she turned to look in his direction. First the newspaper and now Dennison Ducks.

She saw him, turned hard to the right, throwing up gravel as she took a shortcut across the ditch and flew up onto the dirt road headed away from town.

He went after her, telling himself she couldn't outrun him on this narrow rutted dirt road that wound through the mountains. She didn't know the road as well as he did. Nor could she take the familiar curves the way he could—and had on many occasions in his youth.

But then he'd forgotten that he wasn't dealing with just any woman. Maggie had been racing bikes since she was a girl. She stayed ahead of him no matter how hard he tried to catch her, hugging the corners, riding high on the road and staying in the lead.

Damn. He feared she would kill herself trying to get away from him, and yet he had to catch her. He couldn't let her get away from him. Not again.

They roared through the darkness, the dense forest rushing by, the road a winding ribbon of rutted dirt track.

He realized that the dirt road would soon connect to the main highway. The way she was riding and given the capabilities of her bike she'd outrun him once she hit pavement again.

He stayed right with her but just as he'd known once she roared up onto the highway she was gone, leaving his Harley in the dust.

He stopped, tore off his helmet and swore as the last red glow of her taillight faded in the distance. That woman could ride, but he'd known that about her.

He wondered, as he stared after her down the highway into the darkness, what else he would learn about Maggie Randolph before this was over—and that's what had him worried.

He shifted the cycle into gear and headed back toward Dennison Ducks. He still had to deal with Daisy before the night was over. But somewhere out there in the forest was a biker with a personal interest in Angela Dennison's kidnapping. A biker with a bunch of money in a saddlebag and a West Seattle homicide detective after her.

And he had no way to help her. Even a woman as capable as Maggie Randolph might be in more trouble than she could handle. He wondered when he'd see her again.

Not soon enough to suit him.

MAGGIE TOOK A series of back roads she'd memorized from the old logging road maps, putting as much distance as she could between her and the deputy. And the man who'd been in the decoy plant with her tonight.

Detective Blackmore wasn't just in Timber Falls. He'd been at Dennison Ducks. He'd been that close. Had he followed her to the decoy plant? Or had he just known that's where she would show up?

Her heart was still pounding. She'd smelled him. That same rank smell she'd caught on the pier just before he fired at her and she'd rolled off the pier with Norman's dead body and splashed down into the churning surf.

And right behind the killer had been Deputy Jesse Tanner. She'd known the moment she saw the single headlight who it was. She'd seen his bike in the garage, an old Harley. Had Detective Blackmore called him? Or had someone else?

She hadn't been sure she could outrun Jesse. It had been close until she reached the highway and opened her bike up.

Now she pulled over to the side of the logging road, shaken and weak from the fear. She shut off the engine to listen. The silence engulfed her like the darkness. She breathed in the night air and let it out slowly. She was safe. For the moment.

But now both Blackmore and the deputy knew she'd been at Dennison Ducks. Maybe even knew it had been her at the newspaper. Jesse Tanner was smart enough to put it together given her mode of entry into the buildings.

Detective Blackmore must have called the deputy to help him capture her under the pretense of taking her back to Seattle. And wouldn't Deputy Jesse Tanner have to give her over to Blackmore? Wasn't that the way the law worked?

Her heart rate began to slow. And she felt a stab of regret that Jesse hadn't caught her. That she hadn't *let* him catch her. By now she would know one way or the other if Blackmore had gotten to the deputy.

That kind of thinking could get her killed, she reminded herself.

So why did her instincts tell her Deputy Jesse Tanner could be trusted? And with more than her life. Or maybe she just wanted to believe that because she liked him. She smiled at that understatement.

JESSE FOUND DAISY'S new production manager waiting outside the back door at Dennison Ducks.

He parked his bike and walked toward the woman, surprised in more ways than one. He'd heard Daisy was taking over the running of the decoy factory now that Wade was in jail, but as far as he knew there'd been no announcement of a new production manager since Bud Farnsworth had been killed there in October.

Since Daisy had never shown any interest in Dennison Ducks—other than spending the income from it—Jesse, like the rest of the town, wasn't sure what to expect from her as far as management skills.

"You must be Deputy Tanner," the woman said, extending a hand. "Mrs. Dennison told me to wait for you here. I'm Frances Sanders, the new production manager."

Frances was tall and blond, in her late fifties with a kind face and a strong grip.

Jesse shook her hand, trying hard to hide his surprise since he knew damned well that Wade would never have hired a woman for the position.

"You expected a man," Frances said with a smile. "Don't let my gender fool you. I know what I'm doing. My father was a decoy carver. I grew up in the business."

"Didn't mean to infer otherwise," he said and returned her smile. "You're just a lot different from the last production manager."

"I should hope so from what I've heard about him,"

she said smoothly, then looked toward the plant. "I came by to pick up some reports and saw a flashlight beam bobbing around inside the main plant and called Mrs. Dennison at once. A few minutes later, I saw the second flashlight."

"Second flashlight?" he asked in surprise.

She nodded. "There was definitely two of them. One on the lower floor, the second upstairs in Mrs. Dennison's office."

Mrs. Dennison's office? Formerly Wade's office.

"I got a glimpse of both of them as they were fleeing. The one who took off over the roof was small and slim, a woman, I think. The other was definitely a man, larger."

Could he be wrong about Maggie? "They were *together?*"

She shook her head. "I got the impression the man was chasing the woman. She took off on a motorcycle, but you know that since I heard you go after her."

He smiled, impressed. "And the man?"

"Just caught a glimpse of him going through the trees." She pointed in the opposite direction. "Then I heard the sound of an engine. Truck, I'd say. Can't be sure, it was too far away."

He nodded. "Nice job. Have you been inside yet?"

"I waited for you. I didn't want to destroy any evidence."

"Let's take a look." And he stood back while she opened the door.

It didn't take him long to find where someone had broken in through a window at the back. Maggie had come in through an air vent via the roof, same as she had at the newspaper office. He'd known she hadn't come to steal decoys so finding what she'd been after was a no-brainer.

"Looks like the lock on the top drawer of the file cabinet has been broken," Frances noted.

The drawer was open, as if Maggie had been interrupted again. The drawer was also empty but he could see where possibly one file folder had been. The rest of the drawer was covered in fine dust. It seemed odd that Wade would keep this drawer locked and yet it had held so little. "Any idea what was kept in here?"

She shook her head. "Only Mrs. Dennison could tell you that."

Mrs. Dennison. He glanced around. Nothing else seemed to have been disturbed. What had Maggie been looking for? He could only guess. More information on Angela Dennison.

And what had the second intruder been after?

Maggie Randolph.

"Thanks for your help," he told Frances as she locked up after him. She was like a breath of fresh air compared to the last production manager. "Good luck with your new job."

Jesse had hoped he wouldn't have to see Daisy Dennison again. Twice in one day was way too much. But he climbed on his bike, deciding to get it over with tonight.

The Dennison mansion was a couple of miles from the decoy factory. As he turned onto the road that led to the house, he saw that all the lights were on, including the porch lamp. Daisy had obviously been expecting him. She answered the door herself after only one ring.

"Did you catch the thief?" She had a drink in her hand and she looked as if it wasn't her first.

"You mind if I come in?"

She looked contrite, stepped back and waved him inside. "What can I have Zinnia bring you to drink?"

"Nothing for me."

She seemed disappointed and he wondered if she got lonely in this big house with Desiree usually off getting into trouble. He wondered how Daisy would take the news if he was right about Maggie.

"As far as I can tell the only thing taken might have been a file from a locked cabinet in Wade's office," he told her.

Daisy looked down at her glass, then held it to her lips and took a drink.

"What was in that file?" he asked, seeing that she knew something about that locked filing cabinet drawer.

Turning her back on him, she walked into the living room. "Wade's...*personal* papers," she said over her shoulder.

Anger drove him deeper into the house. The place smelled of scotch and some too-sweet scented candle. He felt nauseous. "Let's not play games, okay? The newspaper was also broken into tonight. The burglar took only one thing. A file containing stories about Angela's kidnapping."

Daisy froze.

He could almost feel the tension emanating from her. "So I'll ask you again, what was in that file?"

When she spoke all the steel had gone out of her. "Why can't people just leave my family alone?"

He could think of several answers to that question, starting with the family's bad behavior, but he had a feeling the question was rhetorical. And he'd already shared his feelings with her earlier today. He doubted she'd put up with another lecture.

"Please," she said, turning to look at him. "Sit down." As if on cue, the German housekeeper appeared with a tall glass of lemonade he hadn't asked for and another drink for her mistress.

Jesse took the chair Daisy offered him and the lemonade. It was better than his. "Great lemonade," he said to Zinnia's retreating back. She gave no sign that she'd heard him.

"She doesn't speak much English," Daisy said.

He nodded, figuring Zinnia probably spoke more than Daisy realized. He wondered what it took to live in the same house with these people, let alone serve them the way Zinnia did. He shuddered to think.

"I'm not sure what was in the file," she said after a moment. "I know that he kept the correspondence with private investigators during the many years we searched for Angela. False leads, dead ends. I guess Wade didn't want me to see it. He had the only key and the cabinet was always locked."

"Whatever secrets were in there, they're going to come out," he warned. "If there is anything you want to tell me…"

Daisy put down her unfinished drink and didn't pick up the new one. Her eyes were shiny with booze and possibly regret as she looked up at him as if she'd been somewhere else. "The DNA tests were in there," she said, her voice barely a whisper.

"What DNA tests?"

"The one Wade took to prove that he was that woman's father. Hers was in there, too." Her voice was barely a whisper. The woman in question was the product of an affair Wade Dennison had had almost thirty years ago with the nanny.

So now Maggie had the DNA test results.

Daisy met his gaze. "You look more like your father than even Mitch does." She was crying as she started to reach for the intercom to buzz the housekeeper. "Zinnia will show you out."

"I can find my own way."

ONCE ON THE ROAD into town, Jesse opened up the bike and let it run. The night air was cold and damp. He watched the ribbon of dark road disappear under his front tire and felt that old pull.

But it wasn't as strong as it had once been. Instead, his mind quickly shifted to Maggie Randolph as he reached the edge of town—and how to find her.

The Duck-In bar was closing as he cruised through town on his way home. He was tired and was hoping for a few hours of sleep before he went looking for Maggie.

But as he passed the bar, he saw Desiree opening the passenger side of her red sports car. The top was up but he'd gotten a glimpse of the man behind the wheel.

He swore and flipped a U-turn in the middle of the street and went back.

Desiree turned at the sound of the bike, then smiled when she saw who it was and waited, holding the door open, not getting in just yet. Her gaze met his as if in defiance and she glanced toward the guy behind the wheel, no doubt wanting to make sure Jesse had seen who her date was. Bruno, the guy who'd been hanging out with Betty.

Jesse pulled alongside the car where Desiree was standing with the passenger door open. She seemed pleased that she'd gotten a reaction out of him. His contempt for her antics must have shown. Did his guilt show, as well? He couldn't help but think she was as confused as he was about their relationship and that of their parents.

"I was just at your house," he said. "Someone broke into Dennison Ducks. Your mother isn't doing too well."

The smile flickered and died. "Is Mom—"

"She's fine. Upset, obviously. Scared."

Desiree had paled. He could see that even under the glow of the Duck-In neon. She closed the passenger door and started around the car to the driver's side. She opened the door and motioned without a word for Bruno to get out.

"Hey, I thought we were going to *party?*" Bruno said.

"Out," she said. "Now."

He looked from her to Jesse, then slowly slid from the seat with obvious disappointment.

Desiree climbed in and, slamming the door, started the car.

"Don't speed," Jesse yelled over the powerful engine, his words lost as Desiree threw the car into Reverse and, tires squealing, headed home.

Jesse stared after her, figuring he'd at least saved her from Bruno, for tonight, anyway. He turned his gaze on the man. Bruno was still standing in the bar parking lot, his eyes hard with anger and booze. He was big, with wide shoulders and a blockhead on a thick corded neck.

From the looks of things, his nose had been broken more than once. Jesse suspected he was a bar brawler, someone who liked to fight and throw his weight around. He also had a good ten years on Jesse.

As Bruno advanced on him, Jesse stepped off the bike and pulled out his badge, shaking his head as he held it up. Jesse had done a little fighting himself in the old days.

But while the thought of kicking the crap out of Bruno had its appeal, he wasn't in the mood tonight.

"You don't want any of this," Jesse said.

Bruno stopped, seemed to give it some thought then turned and sauntered down the street toward the faint glow of neon at the opposite end of the street. Betty's Café.

Jesse pocketed his badge, swung his leg over the bike and started the engine. His body was wired, ready for a fight, and it took him a while to calm down.

He roared through town and out onto the open highway, letting the darkness engulf him, the air and the night soothing him a little. Still, part of him wanted to take the easy way out, just keep going and not look back. In the old days, Jesse would have been long gone. No goodbyes.

But that was the old Jesse. The Jesse who hadn't settled down, built his own cabin, met a woman who he couldn't quit thinking about, right or wrong.

He turned onto the jeep trail that led to his cabin and drove up through the trees and blackness. He parked his bike in the garage, closed the door and stood for a moment just looking at the cabin with a sense of pride—and awe. Home. He'd never needed it as much as he did tonight. He thought of Maggie standing here last night looking up at it.

Inside the cabin, he headed straight for his studio, shrugging out of his uniform and donning a pair of paint-covered cutoffs. He opened the windows to let in the night air, then turned toward his easel.

For a while, he just stared at the blank canvas, then picked up a brush and began to paint, trying not to think about anything. Especially his conversation with his father. Or the Dennisons. Or Bruno.

Mostly he wanted to forget just for a little while that he was now a cop. *The* cop in Timber Falls. Or that it was his job to find Maggie and arrest her.

After a moment, he lost himself in his work, in the feel of brush bristles in the paint, the paint on the canvas. The ability had been there for as long as he could remember, first drawing as a boy when he could make something appear on paper with just a pencil. Magic. That's how he thought of it. As if it came from somewhere else, certainly not from him.

A shape started to emerge on the canvas, almost startling him as he realized what he had painted. He stepped back and stared at the partial face and the expression he had captured. Maggie Randolph. Eyes the same rich brown as her hair. Smiling.

He tried to remember if he'd seen her smile like that in the short period of time he'd been around her. No. And yet he knew that when she really smiled she would look exactly like she did in the painting. The smile lighting her face from within. Radiant. Breathtaking.

He put down his brush. What the hell was he doing? This woman could be a murderer on top of everything else.

He glanced at his watch—almost 3:00 a.m. Too late or early for anything but sleep. Unless you were a man who couldn't sleep and you knew that somewhere close by there was a woman...

He quickly cleaned his brush, then went down to his bedroom. He put his uniform back on and strapped on the state-issued hip holster, before sliding the gun into place, not wanting to think about needing it. Worse, using it.

Then he headed for his truck. Maggie Randolph wasn't through with Timber Falls. He felt it in his gut. That meant she had to be hiding somewhere nearby. She'd had a tent and sleeping bag strapped on her bike. But neither had been there when he'd chased her earlier.

He considered the direction she'd taken when she'd hit the highway, just before he'd lost her. Away from where she was camped. He'd bet on that.

So he headed south, feeling as if he knew this woman. She hadn't been off his mind for twenty-four hours. He'd been tracking her, putting together tiny fact after tiny fact about her, discovering more and more that intrigued him. And worried him.

He knew how she would think because he would have thought the same way were he in trouble...and he'd certainly been there. He'd been face-to-face with the woman only a short time and yet he felt as if he had been waiting all his life for her.

Given who her father might be, that scared him more than he wanted to admit. Fate couldn't be that cruel.

The highway was empty, the night dark. This area of the country was littered with campgrounds, small intimate campgrounds that were completely deserted this time of year. Many of them closed. Because the forest was so dense, she would pick an empty campground to hide in.

The campsite would be as far from the road as possible. There were so many and with no one around, she would feel safe. No, not safe enough. She'd pick a campground that wasn't open thinking no one would look for her there.

Then she'd hide at the densest part of the rain forest. And like a nocturnal animal, she would sleep during the day and do whatever had brought her to Timber Falls under the cloak of darkness.

But after her exploits tonight, she would be holed up by now, trying to get some sleep. She would think she was still safe, that no one would come looking for her at this hour.

No one except a man who couldn't sleep. A man possessed.

CHAPTER TEN

IT WAS JUST breaking day by the time Jesse found her. He spotted a single tire track in a muddy spot at the edge of the pavement a quarter mile past the locked gate of a closed campground.

He kept going down the road without slowing, then parked the truck and walked back, hoping for the element of surprise.

Following the track, he wove his way through the dark woods, the sky above him a palette of pastels. As the bike track drew him deeper into the dark woods, he could hear the sound of the MacKenzie River, smell the water mingling with the scent of cedar.

This was the first morning in months that it hadn't rained—at least not yet. A sure sign that spring was coming.

The sky lightened over the tops of the trees as he walked. She'd hidden well. No one would look back in here for her. No one but Jesse Tanner who'd been raised here and knew all the good hiding places from back when he was running from the law instead of enforcing it.

As he moved cautiously through the empty campground, it dawned on him that she might not be alone. That maybe the production manager at the plant had been wrong and that Maggie *had* been with the man.

No, his gut instinct told him she was traveling solo. Whatever mission she was on, she was on it alone. She wouldn't have dragged anyone into this. The man Frances Sanders had seen had to have been chasing Maggie, just like it had seemed. Who, he wondered, was after her? And why?

Jesse was at the farthest point from the highway when he spotted the dark-colored tent through the trees. It blended in nicely with the terrain. He wondered if she'd planned it that way. He didn't see the bike anywhere around. Maybe she hadn't returned yet.

Cautiously he moved closer, the rush of the river next to the tent masking his footfalls.

Other than the river, the day seemed unusually quiet as if holding its breath—just as he was doing as he neared the tent.

It was a two-man tent. The flap on one end was open and he could see that the space inside was empty. That seemed odd. He felt a stab of worry cut through him. She wouldn't have left the closure unzipped unless—

He caught sight of her bike out of the corner of his eyes. It was partially hidden in the vegetation a half-dozen yards behind the tent near the river.

She was here. Somewhere. Had she seen him approach? Was she hiding? More like waiting to attack him when he got too close?

He moved cautiously toward the bike. If she was planning a quick escape, she wouldn't want to be far from her mode of transportation.

That's when he saw her. Just a flash of flesh through the trees. He swore under his breath as he saw that she was standing buck naked in a pool of river water, her back to him.

The water pooled around her waist as she sudsed her hair, working quickly in what had to be freezing cold water. Nothing could get him in the river this time of year, he thought with grudging admiration. She was tougher than he was.

He stepped closer, feeling the pull of her. She had taken over his life the past twenty-four hours. And now he had her in his sights.

Her back was lean and strong. Her shoulders in perfect proportion with her hips and height. Her skin seemed to glow in the first light of day, glistening from the droplets of water on her skin and soapsuds, only the hint of creamy white breasts at her sides, and he wished that he could paint her just like that. A water sprite at dawn.

He looked away, reminding himself that if he was right about this woman she was off-limits to him. He'd found her but she might always be as elusive to him as she'd been for the past twenty-four hours. The mere thought struck him like a blow.

That's when he spotted her clothing hanging from a tree limb at the edge of the river. He moved toward the clothing as she dipped below the surface of the water, coming up almost immediately.

Eyes closed, she flipped her long, dark hair back over her shoulder. It fell in a wet wave, plastering itself to her back. She let out a soft sound, shivered and hugged herself against the cold, one arm over her breasts as she turned, the other hand outstretched reaching for her clothes.

Her fingers touched the now empty limb, felt around then froze. Her eyes flew open.

MAGGIE SENSED HIS presence just an instant before she realized her clothing was gone from the tree. She blinked water from her eyes and saw him standing on the rocky shore just inches from her and he had her clothes.

She stifled a cry of surprise and alarm and hugged herself from the cold, hoping he didn't see how scared she was.

He held the clothes out to her and she realized he was trying not to look at her nakedness. He'd probably already seen everything there was to see but she was still surprised and touched by his chivalrous behavior.

She wondered how long he'd been standing there watching her. He was wearing his sheriff's deputy uniform, his expression solemn. There was no doubt he was here in an official capacity. Where was Blackmore? Waiting up on the road?

"Hello, Deputy Tanner." Her words sounded much calmer than she felt. Her mind was racing. He'd found her? How?

She studied Jesse Tanner's face feeling emotions that surprised—and worried—her. He was a deputy of the law. He would turn her over to Detective Blackmore. He would have to.

"You must be cold," he said, still holding her clothes out to her, keeping his eyes averted.

She *was* cold. Freezing. Her body felt numb from the waist down. She took a step toward him and her clothes, afraid she would stumble and seem even more vulnerable. Like being naked in the middle of the river with a cop holding her clothing wasn't vulnerable enough.

Looking away, he held out his free hand to her.

For a moment, she considered ignoring his offer of help. But she knew that would be foolish. Her body ached from the cold water and she had no chance of escape without her clothing.

She took his hand and let him steady her as she climbed over the rocks, all the time working on a plan of escape. All the time praying he hadn't already made some deal with Blackmore that involved the Seattle cop taking her back to the city.

"Nice little town you have here," she said.

He nodded, seeming a little amused, and without looking at her, handed her the bra, the white lacy one she'd been wearing the night she went to meet Norman at the pier. She put it on. Jesse seemed to be staring downstream as if completely unaware of and unaffected by her nudity.

She knew better than that but she liked that he tried damned hard to hide it.

He handed her the shirt.

She couldn't help thinking about his art, about him. He wasn't like Blackmore. A man she would bet would have leered before he drowned her in the river.

"You a local?" she asked, buttoning her shirt and trying to get some warmth back into her body. She would need to move fast when she got the chance.

"Born just down the road," he said. "I left for a while."

He handed her the matching white lace panties, seeming almost a little embarrassed. She balanced on a rock on one foot to pull them on. He held out an arm to steady her, eyes still averted. She accepted his help again, then held out her hand for her jeans.

He handed them to her and she pulled them on over the panties, buttoned and zipped them.

"Spent some time in Mexico," she said.

He smiled. "My paintings. You seem to know more about me than I know about you."

"Somehow I doubt that," she said. "What made you come back to Timber Falls?"

He shrugged. "I got homesick for something familiar and I missed my family."

"Yes." She certainly knew that feeling. She dropped her gaze, not wanting him to see the tears that suddenly burned her eyes.

"How's the ankle?" he asked.

"Better."

He nodded, turning to face her now that she was dressed.

She pointed to her boots a little farther from the river on the bank. Her socks were sticking out of the top of each boot. He moved out of her way to let her go to them.

If she could have felt her feet, she might have made a run for it. But she had no chance barefoot and she doubted she could outrun those long legs of his even with her boots on.

She sat down on a rock along the bank, feeling the sun rising behind her back, the day growing brighter.

He looked good in his uniform. But she hadn't missed the gun strapped to his hip. At least he hadn't drawn it, wasn't now pointing it at her. But, then, he might think he had nothing to fear from her.

Didn't he realize she would do whatever she had to if he tried to turn her over to Blackmore? Maybe not.

She slipped on her biking boots, then stood, hands on her hips, feeling warmer. She was still scared but at least dressed she might stand a fighting chance.

"I thought we should have a little talk," he said. "You had breakfast yet?"

"Breakfast?" Was he serious?

"I know a place that serves great pancakes."

She looked down the river for a moment, then at him. "I'd rather not go back into Timber Falls."

He smiled. "Not in the daylight, huh? I had a feeling you'd say that. I was thinking we'd avoid town and go to my place."

She eyed him and looked around, expecting Detective Blackmore to show up any minute. "You come out here alone?"

He nodded.

She studied him. "Why pancakes? Why not just run me in? Or shoot me right here? Better yet, you could have drowned me in the river when you had the chance and no one would be the wiser."

He seemed to flinch, those dark eyes widening in surprise. "I know you're running from something but what would make you think I would want to kill you?"

She shook her head. "Maybe because the last cop I trusted tried to?"

His eyes darkened. "Don't worry. I'm not much of a deputy. I've never killed anyone and I'm hoping I don't have to before this uniform comes off in a couple of months."

"That's supposed to make me feel better?"

He laughed. It was a great sound, deep and rich. It made a humming in her chest like an echo.

"Look," he said, "I suspect you're the kind of woman who seldom needs help, probably doesn't know how to ask for it even when you do. But I think right now you could use some breakfast—and maybe a good listener." He held up both hands as if in surrender. "I've been in trouble a few times myself. I know how hard it is to trust anyone. Especially a stranger. Especially someone in a uniform."

Except he didn't seem like a stranger. She'd felt safe with him. Her heart told her that if she couldn't trust this man, she couldn't trust anyone ever. Suddenly her chest gave as if she'd been holding her breath for days. She fought the tears that stung her eyes. "Pancakes?"

JESSE SMILED AND nodded, seeing her relax a little. "An old family recipe."

"Your mother's?"

He shook his head. Not likely. "My dad's. He used to get up every weekend and make pancakes for my brother and me." He smiled at the memory. "I think it was the only thing he knew how to cook at the time."

She returned his smile but he could still see the tension in her body like a coiled spring. He'd have to keep an eye on her. But the tentative smile had made him desperately want to see a real smile. A smile like he'd painted, a smile like he knew she would smile. Eventually. If he could get her to trust him.

A little voice at the back of his mind warned him he could be all wrong about her. He ignored it. He'd learned a long time ago to live with his heart not his head. It had gotten him into some tight spots that was for damned sure. But it was the way he'd lived his life and he wasn't about to change that just because he'd put on some uniform.

"You have what you took from the newspaper and Dennison Ducks?" He was still Timber Falls' only deputy and Charity would have his hide if he didn't get her

file back. Also, he was anxious to see what had been
in the locked file cabinet in Wade Dennison's office.

She nodded and he walked with her to the tent. Everything he'd felt the first time he'd laid eyes on her
was there and then some. The woman had some kind
of hold on him. He hated to think what that hold might
be—the one thing that would make her off-limits the
rest of his life.

Whatever emotions she evoked in him, that one simple possibility wasn't something he was likely to forget.

"If you don't mind," he said, ducking into the tent
with her. It was close quarters inside, but he had to make
sure she didn't have a weapon stashed under the sleeping mat. "Sorry," he said after he'd checked and found
nothing more lethal than a toothbrush.

She handed him two files both thick, one from the
Cascade Courier, the other from Wade's personal file
cabinet at Dennison Ducks. Wade's file had just what
Daisy said would be in it. All the reports from the investigators they'd hired to find Angela and the biggest
prize of all, the DNA test results on Wade and an illegitimate daughter he'd had by the family's former nanny.

"Charity will be glad to have these back," Jesse said
of the newspaper clippings.

"You know Charity Jenkins?"

He nodded, meeting her gaze. "She's my soon-to-be
sister-in-law. She's marrying my brother. The sheriff."

Maggie tensed. "Your brother's the *sheriff?*"

"Afraid so," he said with a smile that he hoped would
reassure her. "I try not to hold it against him."

"Tell me why I should trust you?" she asked, sounding scared again.

"Because I make great pancakes and I'd bet you

haven't had anything good to eat for a while," he said. "Also, you need my help."

"Do I?" She seemed amused by that. "I thought you just said you weren't much of a deputy."

He laughed. "You've got me there."

They stepped out of the tent. The sun peeked over the treetops, turning the forest to emerald.

"Mind if I ask what you're going to do with me after breakfast?"

Oh, he had all kinds of thoughts on that subject but none he could act on. "After breakfast you can tell me why you had to rob the newspaper and Dennison Ducks," he said.

She eyed him with obvious suspicion. "And then?"

"And then I do everything in my power to help you."

She met his gaze, then nodded slowly. "I believe you mean that."

"I do."

"I need you to promise me something," she said and bit down on her lower lip. She had to know he couldn't make her any promises. "Promise me you won't turn me over to Detective Blackmore," she said, her voice breaking.

She'd said the last cop she'd trusted had tried to kill her. Blackmore? Jesse was in no position to promise her that. Not only was he *the* law in Timber Falls, he could go to jail for aiding and abetting a criminal, if she turned out to be one.

He met her gaze and saw fear flashing like madness in her brown eyes. "I promise."

Her relief was so profound she seemed to sag under its weight.

He reached out and gripped her arm to steady her,

shocked by the touch of his skin to hers. He let go as if he'd been burned.

"We'll break your camp and I'll come back and take care of your bike," he said, hoping she hadn't noticed his reaction to her. "I'm going to have to insist that you come with me in the truck. Not that I don't trust you."

"Right," she said, but smiled at him. He saw that flicker in her gaze. She wanted to like him. The thought warmed him more than it should have.

BACK AT HIS CABIN, Jesse watched Maggie put away another stack of his pancakes. He'd taken back roads after hiding her bike and thought they would be safe. At least temporarily. He poured them both more orange juice.

"These are the best pancakes I've ever eaten," she said between bites.

"Either that or you just haven't eaten for a while," he said, smiling across the table at her.

She stabbed the last bite with her fork, soaked up the butter and syrup from her plate and popped it into her mouth. She looked up at him. Her eyes were several shades lighter than his own, hers rich with gold and ambers.

He stared into them realizing he hadn't quite captured her eyes in the painting he'd started of her.

"Thank you," she said.

"My pleasure. It gave me an excuse to make them."

"I'm not talking about the pancakes," she said quietly. "But the pancakes *are* amazing." Her smile brightened the entire room.

"Wait until you try my dad's," he said, basking in that smile and all the time hoping she'd be around long enough that she'd get the chance. "It's his recipe and he's had years of practice."

"Your mother didn't cook?"

He smiled at that. "She passed on when I was nine." *Passed on being a mother.*

"Oh, I'm so sorry." Her eyes turned to warm honey. "I lost my mother five years ago. I can't imagine losing her when I was nine. That must have been very difficult for you. Your dad lives close by?"

"Just down the road."

"I envy you." She ducked her head in what he figured was an attempt to hide the depth of her pain. "I lost my father two months ago."

The plane accident. "I'm sorry. You were close."

She looked up again, nodded and seemed to be swallowing back tears.

"Maggie, let me help you."

She got to her feet, scooping up her plate and silverware and taking them over to the sink. "The last man who tried to help me got killed." She rinsed her dish, then shut off the water and turned to look at him, leaning back against the sink as she did.

He stared at her for a long moment, then got up and went to the couch and sat. "I've always found it's easier to start at the beginning," he said. "I haven't read you your rights so anything you say can't be used against you in a court of law."

"If I tell you, I will be jeopardizing *your* life," she said, sitting down to face him from the opposite end of the couch.

"I'll take my chances," he said, turning toward her so he could watch her face. "Also, the job came with a gun." He saw that she got his humor. What more could a man ask for?

"Detective Rupert Blackmore is trying to kill me. I know that sounds crazy...."

"I've heard crazier stories."

She cocked her head at him. "Well, try this one on for size then. The reason he's trying to kill me is because I'm Angela Dennison."

He nodded.

"You don't believe me."

He wished he didn't. "Why don't you tell me why *you* think you're Angela."

Maggie took a breath and told him everything, starting with the fact that her parents had always told her she was adopted. She told him about the plane crash that killed her father, the conversation Norman Drake overheard just before her father's attorney, Clark Iverson, was murdered, the phone call from Norman demanding ten thousand dollars in return for proof that her father's plane crash wasn't an accident, her call to Detective Rupert Blackmore and finally what had happened the night at the pier.

"Whoever was behind my kidnapping has successfully kept it a secret for twenty-seven years," she told him. "They thought they were safe. If my father hadn't found out and decided I needed to know the truth..."

"Why do you think he did that?" Jesse asked.

She shook her head. "He hadn't been well since my mother died." Her voice trailed off. "I think he was worried that if I didn't know..."

"That once he was gone, the kidnapper might show up."

"My family is fairly wealthy," she said, as if it were some dirty, dark secret she wished she could keep.

Fairly wealthy. He smiled at her obvious understatement. "And you're the only child."

She nodded and met Jesse's gaze. "You knew this already," she whispered, her eyes widening with fear.

Jesse quickly said, "I knew some of it, but not all of it. I ran your bike plate. There's an APB out on you. You're wanted for questioning in both Clark Iverson's and Norman Drake's murders."

She let out a cry and was on her feet. "I didn't kill anyone."

"I believe you."

She stopped moving, stared down at him. "Detective Blackmore was at Dennison Ducks last night. He almost caught me." She moved to the window to look out, as if she half expected him to be coming up the road right now. "It's just a matter of time before he shows up on the pretext of taking me back for questioning. If you hand me over to him, I'll never make it back to Seattle alive."

"You're positive the man on the pier was Blackmore? You'd seen him before?" Jesse asked.

She nodded as she turned to look back him. "His photo was in the paper." Her gaze pleaded that he believe her. "He'd been given some award for bravery in the line of the duty. I know now that's why Norman didn't go to the police. He said he didn't recognize the voice of the man who killed Clark Iverson. I didn't believe him. Now I know why he lied."

"You think he recognized Blackmore?"

She nodded and sat down again on the end of the couch. "When I told Norman that I'd called the detective on the case, he went ballistic. Just seconds later Norman was shot and killed and…" Her voice trailed off. "Just before I rolled off the pier using Norman's body as a shield, I saw the killer. It was Blackmore."

Jesse didn't bother to ask why she hadn't gone straight to the police. Or the FBI. For the same reason Norman hadn't. She feared she wouldn't be believed and with good reason. What did Blackmore have to gain by killing her and the lawyer and his assistant while Maggie had just inherited a fortune?

Her story would spark an investigation. If this cop really was a killer, he was too smart to leave a trail. Instead, the heir who'd just inherited would be the number one suspect.

The plane crash would suddenly be suspect. The facts in Clark Iverson's death and Norman Drake's could be twisted just enough to make Maggie Randolph look like a greedy adopted only child who couldn't wait for her last parent to die to get the money. She had to get rid of her father's attorney because he'd become suspicious and Norman Drake had heard her kill him and was blackmailing her. That would explain the money in her saddlebag and the fact that Norman went swimming with the fishes.

Any other woman and Jesse might have believed it himself. But not Maggie.

"There is something I need to tell you," he said and he saw her tense. "I ran your prints after the newspaper break-in. I suspected Blackmore had inquiries about you tagged so he would know about them immediately. That could be how he found out where you were."

She shook her head and reached over to touch his hand.

He jumped at her touch, both startled and uncomfortable by it, and jerked his hand back.

If she noticed, she didn't say anything as she was quickly on her feet and pacing again. "He knew I would come to Timber Falls once he realized I was alive. I'm sure he realized that when Norman's body washed up and mine didn't. He will contact you for help." She looked at Jesse for his agreement.

Jesse shook his head. "If he was going to, I would have heard from him by now."

She took a shaky breath. "You think he plans to take care of me himself without involving you?"

"It certainly looks that way."

She shook her head. "I just don't understand what it is that he's afraid I'll find out. That I'm Angela Dennison? In that case, it's too late. Or that I'll find proof that he was behind my kidnapping?"

Maggie saw Jesse's worried expression.

"The actual kidnapper is dead," he said, obviously hoping to put an end to any thought she might have of looking for the kidnapper. "He confessed."

"I read about that in the newspaper articles. The former Dennison Ducks production manager might have stolen me from my crib, but according to the paper he did it on someone else's orders."

Jesse smiled. "I wouldn't believe everything you read in the newspaper. Especially in Charity's."

"Then you think the kidnapper has been caught?"

He rubbed a hand over his stubbled jaw. He hadn't shaved in at least forty-eight hours. "I didn't say that."

She smiled, relieved he didn't lie to her.

"I'd agree that Bud Farnsworth wasn't the mastermind behind it," he continued. "I think the first step is to prove that you are Angela Dennison. You already have Wade's DNA test results. I've checked and they

can be compared to your DNA to determine if you're
his daughter, but then you will still need Daisy Dennison's DNA to prove you are Angela."

She stared at him, surprised by something she'd
heard in his voice. "You really do believe I'm Angela."

He nodded slowly, as if he didn't want to believe it.

Maggie fought to hide her relief. Tears burned her
eyes. Dammit, she would not cry. She'd let herself cry
only that once in the tent; she wouldn't cry now.

But she hadn't realized how badly she wanted this
man to believe her. Needed him to. It validated the risks
she'd been taking and so much more. This man who'd
helped her that first night on the highway…there was
something about him that had kept him in her thoughts
ever since.

And that worried her. Just as this feeling she had
when she was around him that she was safe. He made
it hard to remember that there was a formidable killer
after her. She wasn't safe. Would never be safe until
Blackmore was behind bars.

And now she'd put Jesse's life in danger, as well.

JESSE SAW A determined look come into her brown eyes.

"I have to find the people responsible before they
find me," she said.

"Now wait a minute—"

"You were born here, right? You know these people.
I was kidnapped here." She was pacing again and talking fast. "How did Blackmore find me? Did he know
this production manager who supposedly took me out of
the house that night? And why kill me? It doesn't make
any sense to kill to cover up a twenty-seven-year-old
kidnapping. But I have to find out."

"Yeah, but hold on," he said, getting to his feet. "You start trying to get proof of who you are and asking a lot of questions and you'll bring the killer right down on you. You need to go somewhere safe and stay there until I find out who is behind this."

"No way." She was staring him down even though she had to look up to do it. He had her in height, girth and strength, and yet he could see that she would take him on in a heartbeat if that's what it took.

"If you're right, Blackmore has already killed three people and wounded you and he almost caught up to you last night," he said, trying to reason with her. "You can't take the chance that next time he won't miss."

"You're right," she said, throwing him off guard. "All I would be doing is waiting around for him to find me and kill me."

He told himself she'd given in too easily. There was a gleam in her brown eyes that he didn't like.

Before he could open his mouth, she said, "That's why I'm going to announce to the world that I'm Angela Dennison—and I know the perfect place to do it."

CHAPTER ELEVEN

"ROZALYN SAWYER'S PARTY?" Jesse exclaimed.

"I saw the ad in the newspaper. Everyone in town is invited. It's the perfect place to make my debut as Angela Dennison," Maggie said, leveling her gaze at him, daring him to try to stop her. "The Dennisons will be there, won't they?"

"The ones who aren't in jail."

"Let's start with them then," she said as if it were a done deal.

"You can't be serious. No way."

Her eyes were shiny and bright, her jaw set in stubborn determination. "I'm a target no matter what I do. But once I announce that I'm Angela Dennison at this party one of two things will happen. Blackmore will get out of Dodge, figuring it's over, there is nothing he can do now."

"Or he'll kill you because then he will know where you are and how to get to you."

She smiled and nodded. "Exactly."

"And you think this is a *good* plan?"

"Come on, you know I'm right."

"I know you're suicidal," he said.

"It will be like hiding in plain sight," she argued. "I will be a harder target to hit because everyone in town will be curious about me, right? They'll be watching me everywhere I go in a town this size. I'll be front-page news. Only someone really desperate will try to hurt me with all that heat on me." She smiled. "I'm right and you're starting to see it."

"Yep, it's definitely the fastest way to get yourself killed," he said, but he knew he didn't fool her. She had a good point and as much as he wished otherwise, he was starting to see some merit to her crazy scheme.

"Of course, I wouldn't want to spoil the party so I would do it at the end."

"How very thoughtful of you," Jesse said, hating that she was right. She was already in danger. Announcing who she was wouldn't add to that. Maybe it would even make her safer, although he wasn't counting on it.

"Under two conditions." He held up his hand before she could interrupt. "Keep in mind that I have every right to lock you up in jail if you don't agree."

She clamped her lips shut, eyes narrowed as he proceeded.

"First condition, you never leave my side the entire night," he said.

She rolled her eyes as if to say, "Don't push your luck."

"Second, do you know anything about firearms?"

"Let me see," she said, cocking her head to inspect the one he was wearing. "That would be a Glock nine-millimeter, ten-shot magazine, steel slide, double-action trigger, autoload."

"But can you shoot one with any accuracy?" he asked, only a little surprised at her knowledge of firearms.

She mugged a face at him. "I don't happen to have my marksmanship certificate with me but my father used to take me to the indoor firing range and I always hit what I aimed at." Her smiled faded. "I guess Dad thought it was a skill I might need one day."

So it would seem. "Shooting at a target is one thing, firing at a living, breathing person is a whole different ball game," Jesse said.

"You told me you never killed anyone," she reminded him.

He shook his head. "That doesn't mean I never *shot* anyone." He waved her next question off. "It was a long time ago. I was young and cocky and foolish."

She studied him openly as if she still found him to be at least two of those. But her look said she didn't find that to be a bad thing. "This will work," she said as if she thought he still needed convincing.

He smiled ruefully. "I wish I didn't agree with you but it sounds as if Blackmore is already in town. The best way to protect you is as Angela Dennison because you're right, everyone will be watching you. The news will spread like wildfire. And hopefully, it *will* make you a harder target to hit. That doesn't mean he won't try to kill you."

She nodded. "He's risking so much, I can't believe he's acting alone. Unless I can find a connection between him and the Dennisons or Timber Falls...."

He groaned. "Which, of course, you're not going to be doing."

She shot him a look. "I have to find out why I was kidnapped, who was behind it and why they want me dead. You aren't going to try to stop me, are you?"

"I could put you in jail for breaking into two businesses," he pointed out.

She smiled and shook her head. "Then I would be

easy pickings for Detective Blackmore. He would try to take me back to Seattle for questioning in Norman's and Clark's murder and I would never make it there alive."

Jesse quaked at the thought. "What makes you think he won't try that, anyway?"

"You'll stop him," she said and looked up at him.

At that moment, he would have wrestled Bigfoot for her. "You have a lot of confidence in me, more than is warranted, I fear."

"I know you're going to help me find whoever is after me." Before he could argue the point, she added, "And you need *my* help. I'm the only one who can identify Blackmore as the man on the pier who shot Norman and tried to kill me. But I need proof. Unless I can find the connection between Blackmore and my kidnapper…"

He cocked an eyebrow at her. "It's been twenty-seven years. What makes you think you'll find the real kidnapper after all this time? Even if he lived in Timber Falls back then, it doesn't mean he does now."

She smiled. "You don't believe that any more than I do. Blackmore wouldn't be trying to kill me if he thought I couldn't uncover something—and not just that I'm Angela Dennison. There has to be more."

"It's just crazy that anyone would try to cover up a kidnapping with multiple murders."

She nodded. "So the motivation isn't fear of prison for kidnapping charges. It's much more personal and complicated than that."

He stared at her. "What is worse than losing your freedom?"

She shook her head. "That's the way you and I think. Someone else might be just trying to save his skin."

"Like Blackmore."

She nodded. "Or keep their part in the kidnapping a secret because they regretted what they'd done so many years ago and now would lose their family, friends, social standing... I don't know. Different values for different folks, right?"

Yeah. But he had another theory. Some people cared only about themselves and did what made them feel good no matter how many people suffered because of it.

He realized he was thinking of his mother and when he looked up, Maggie was frowning at him.

"Did you get enough to eat?" he asked as he went back into the dining area to clear his dishes.

"Gobs," she said, following him. "I'm going to need something to wear to the party, a drop-dead dress—if you'll excuse the expression—one that won't show that I'm carrying a gun," she said, then seemed to realize that she'd never answered his question. "You asked me if I could pull the trigger if someone was intent on killing me. Someone who already killed my father, who for the record, was a very kind nice man. A killer who has already tried to kill me once?" She met his gaze. "In a heartbeat."

He saw that she believed it. He prayed if push came to shove, that she could do it to save herself. Because everything about her told him, that like her adoptive father, she was a very kind nice person. And the more he knew about her, the more interested he became in this woman.

He set to work washing the dishes in the sink to quell those feelings. She moved in beside him, opening one drawer and then another until she found a clean dish towel, completely ignoring his. "I can do these, really."

"If I couldn't shoot the person after me," she said

as if he hadn't spoken, "I wouldn't stay with you." She picked up one of the plates and began drying it carefully. "I know that I'm jeopardizing your life by being here." She put the plate in the cabinet and looked over at him. "You're risking your life because of me. I have to be able to do the same for you."

"That's the last thing I want."

"Too bad, because that's the way it is," she said, and stepped to him, standing on tiptoes. Her lips brushed across his cheek like a sweet whisper, sending sparks shooting along his nerve endings.

He flinched and stepped back.

"Sorry," she said, looking both surprised and confused.

"You shocked me, that's all. Static electricity, you know." He could see the lie reflected in her gaze.

She studied him. "You shock easily."

He laughed, feeling like a fool, and took the dishrag over to the table, putting distance between them, but still intensely aware of her. He could smell the scent of her on his skin, a faint tangerine fragrance that lingered like the memory of her touch.

No woman had ever affected him like this. He told himself it was because he couldn't have her. Might never be able to have her. But he knew it was a hell of a lot more than that or his heart wouldn't ache the way it did at the thought.

"Okay, what's going on?" she asked behind him. "I appreciate everything you've done for me, Jesse. But I feel like there is something else going on between us and I know you feel it, too."

He turned to find her framed in the sunlight spilling in from the window, her hair burnished mahogany, her eyes fired with gold, her hands firmly planted on her shapely hips.

"What is it you aren't telling me?"

Maggie knew she couldn't be wrong about the energy that sparked red-hot between them. "I know you're attracted to me. So what is it? You trust me, don't you? You don't think I killed Norman or—"

"No! I trust you," he said.

"Well, I know you're not…"

"Gay?" He laughed. "No."

She frowned. "Then, I must be wrong about you being attracted to me?"

He smiled ruefully and shook his head. "That's not it, believe me."

"Then what? Jesse, every time I get near you, you shy away as if you're afraid for me to touch you."

He met her gaze, his expression pained. "My father had an affair with Daisy Dennison twenty-eight years ago."

She stared at him at first uncomprehending. "You think I might be…" She laughed.

"Sorry, but I don't see the humor," he said.

"It's just that when I realized I was Angela Dennison and that Wade was in jail for shooting the sheriff, among other things, I wished anyone else in the world was my biological father."

"Be careful what you wish for, huh?"

She nodded. "That's why you want the DNA tests." She groaned inwardly. "What if we are half sister and brother?" The thought hurt. She couldn't believe her disappointment; it felt soul deep. Not that she hadn't always wished for a sibling but not Jesse. Not this man she'd wanted since the first time she'd seen him. She trusted him with her life but she wanted more. She wanted to know what it felt like to lie in his arms and—

Suddenly she felt like crying. She hadn't realized until that moment how much she'd been hoping that Jesse would make love to her before she had to announce to the world that she was Angela Dennison and wait for a killer to come after her.

"How quickly can we get these DNA tests?" she asked.

JESSE FELT THE cell phone vibrate. "Hold that thought." Once and for all, they would find out who had fathered Angela. They couldn't find out soon enough to suit him. He reached in his pocket, pulled out the phone and saw who was calling. "I still have forty-five minutes before I have to check in," he said to Sissy.

"Trust me, I wouldn't be calling you, but Daisy Dennison is demanding to talk to you and I mean now. You think *I've* got attitude?"

"I get the picture." He shot Maggie a look. "Put Daisy through."

"Have you heard the news?" Daisy barked.

"What news is that?" he asked warily.

"Wade made bail!"

Wade made bail? He looked over at Maggie again. Damn, this only made things more dangerous for Maggie until he could find out who was behind her kidnapping. If they were both right and she was Angela Dennison. "When did this happen?"

"Yesterday afternoon. No one notified me. He was released first thing this morning. That means he could be on his way to the house at this very minute," Daisy cried.

"You have a restraining order on him," Jesse pointed out.

"The same one he broke last time when he tried to kill me."

Jesse wanted to point out that his brother wouldn't have been shot and would still be sheriff and handling this if Daisy hadn't provided Wade with the gun. Better yet, if they hadn't been struggling over it. "I guess I could talk to Wade—"

Before he could explain that his hands were tied until Wade did something illegal, he heard a noise outside his front door. The soft scuff of footfalls on the steps. He tensed and motioned to Maggie to go upstairs and stay hidden and silent.

The knock at the door startled him. He hadn't heard a car engine. Whoever was at the door had walked up the mountain. His first thought was Detective Rupert Blackmore.

As Maggie disappeared up the stairs, he headed for the door, saying into the phone, "Mrs. Dennison, I'm going to have to call you back—" He opened the door. "Daisy."

She smiled, obviously satisfied that she had surprised him. "I'm glad you've dropped that ridiculous Mrs. Dennison stuff," she said, stuffing her cell phone into her purse as she pushed her way into the cabin. "I need to talk to you."

She wore an off-white linen suit. Her purse and shoes were white-and-brown and matched. Her hair was brushed back from her face and she looked younger.

For a woman who'd been a recluse for years, she certainly had become social since her husband had gone to jail.

Jesse closed the door and leaned against it, arms folded over his chest, watching her as she stopped in the middle of the room and looked around.

"You share your father's talents, I see," she said, turning to look back at him. His father had built the house Jesse and Mitch had lived in as boys.

"If this is about Wade making bail—"

She waved a hand through the air. "I've decided to hire a bodyguard since my gun was taken as evidence."

Jesse lifted a brow. A bodyguard? He guessed he should be glad she hadn't decided to purchase another weapon. "Do you really think that's necessary?"

"That isn't the reason I'm here," she said, ignoring the question. "Is there any news on the break-in at the decoy plant?"

He shook his head. "Nothing to report yet." He hoped Maggie stayed hidden until tonight. Once she made her big announcement all hell was bound to break loose. He wanted to be ready for it. As ready as possible.

He watched Daisy look around the cabin and realized all of this could have been handled on the phone. So why had she walked all this way and in those shoes?

She seemed to see something and headed for the stairs before he could push away from the door and stop her. "I heard you were painting again."

"Just a minute—"

She kept going up the wide wooden stairs toward the third-floor studio.

He went after her, glad to see his bedroom door was closed as he passed. "I don't really have anything you can see," he said as he took the stairs after her, unable to contain his anger. "It's all at the framer. But you're welcome to come to the show I'm having in June."

He stopped at the top of the stairs.

She stood in the middle of the room, her back to him. She didn't turn. Nor had she responded to his words. She seemed rooted to the spot, her body rigid.

As he moved toward her, he saw that she had one hand to her mouth. Her face was deathly pale and she was trembling.

He swore under his breath as he realized why she'd come up here. What she'd seen. The partially completed painting resting on his easel. He had captured only a likeness of Maggie, but enough that Daisy must have seen the resemblance to Desiree.

"Daisy—"

She turned. Her eyes welled with tears.

"Daisy?"

She bolted down the stairs. He heard the front door slam.

A minute later, Maggie appeared at the top of the stairs to the studio.

She looked past him at the painting of her, then moved toward it like a sleepwalker. She stared at it for a long moment, making him nervous.

He feared she didn't like it, didn't think it did her justice, that it might offend her.

"You have captured a part of me I've never seen before," she said quietly. She turned then to look at him. "She saw the painting, didn't she?"

He nodded.

And Maggie had seen *her,* he realized. "You think she knows it's me?"

"I think it spooked her."

Maggie nodded. "She was definitely upset."

He knew that, like him, Maggie was wondering if Daisy was upset because of the resemblance to Desiree or if she had recognized her other daughter, maybe had known where Maggie was this whole time, had followed her life because Daisy had been the one to get rid of her twenty-seven years ago—and was trying to again. Only this time permanently to protect herself. And she was using Detective Rupert Blackmore to do it.

"Are you all right?" he asked Maggie, fighting the urge to take her in his arms and comfort her.

"It's a shock to see her, in person. I thought I was ready to meet her, but I wasn't."

"You don't have to go through with this tonight."

She smiled at that. "We both know better than that. I can't spend the rest of my life looking over my shoulder. I heard you say Wade Dennison has been released on bail. He's still a suspect, too, isn't he?"

"My future sister-in-law thinks so," Jesse said.

"Charity? She must have good reason to believe that, being a journalist."

He smiled at that. "I think it's time you met her and my brother. We'll take along the DNA test results you got from Wade's office. We need to put as many pieces of the puzzle together as soon as we can."

"You know what the tests are going to tell us. That I'm Angela Dennison."

He nodded. "And who your father is. Or at least isn't."

CHAPTER TWELVE

MITCH COULDN'T BELIEVE it. Florie arrived with the news just after daybreak—long before the *Cascade Courier* hit the streets.

Wade Dennison had made bail.

Anyone who hadn't been planning to go to Rozalyn Sawyer's gala party that evening quickly changed their minds, according to Florie. Clearly, no one wanted to miss the fireworks when Wade showed up at the party later tonight—restraining order or no restraining order.

Mitch had to agree there was little doubt that Wade would show up. Wade Dennison *was* Timber Falls and Roz's party was the highlight of the year so far. Plus, if a man was prone to making scenes what better arena than a party with everyone in town in attendance?

"I got scooped," Charity bemoaned as she brought Mitch his breakfast tray. The phone had been ringing off the hook all morning as the news spread. "It's all over the county by now."

Mitch sat up a little straighter in his recliner. "I think you're missing what is really important here, Charity. Wade Dennison has no business being out on bail. He's dangerous."

"You don't think he'll come gunning for *you* again, do you?"

He smiled at the concern in her voice. "No," he said

with a laugh. "It isn't me I'm worried about. It's you. And Daisy."

Charity was already shaking her head. "Wade doesn't scare me and I don't believe for a minute that he tried to kill Daisy. If anything I think she might want *him* dead."

"Well, now that he's out on bail, she just might get her chance," Mitch said. He had a feeling this was going to be a long divorce.

And the worst part was, he was trapped in a cast. He'd never felt more useless in his life. He couldn't wait to get back to work. Jesse was capable enough but wasn't really trained for this type of trouble.

Mitch had thought about calling in a state officer, then rejected the idea. Jesse would see that as a lack of confidence in him and Mitch didn't want a rift between him and Jesse, not after all these years of being apart.

No, he just prayed that Wade didn't cause any trouble, but even as he thought it, he knew better. It was almost as if Wade had a black cloud hanging over his head, following him around.

If Wade had anything to do with baby Angela's disappearance twenty-seven years ago, then maybe this was his bad karma coming back to haunt him. Damn, Mitch realized he was starting to sound like Florie.

The phone rang. He reached over and answered it before Charity could do even that for him, then realized it would probably just be another call from gossip center.

"Little brother?" Jesse said.

Something in his tone warned Mitch. "What's wrong?"

"Is Charity there?" Jesse asked. "Can you get rid of her for a little while?"

Mitch could feel Charity watching him. He laughed

and smiled. "You scared me." He shook his head at Charity to indicate nothing was wrong, just his brother Jesse being Jesse. "What you need to do is buy yourself a good miter saw. You can use it to cut your own frames after you finish this project."

"She's standing right there," Jesse said on the other end of the line.

"Exactly. Maybe you don't want to cut your own frames now but when you're famous—"

"Would you mind if I went out for a while?" Charity whispered. "Sorry, but I need to stop by the paper."

"Just a minute, Jesse." He cupped the receiver. "Take your time, Jesse is coming over. He's trying to build—"

"You two have fun," Charity said, grabbing her purse. "Build whatever you like while I'm gone." And she was out the door.

Charity had heard plenty about the building of Jesse's cabin while it was going up. Fortunately, her eyes glazed over whenever the two of them talked about anything to do with hammers and nails now.

"She's gone," Mitch said into the phone the moment he heard the door close.

"We'll be right over." Jesse hung up.

Mitch stared at the phone in his hand. *We'll* be right over? And whatever it was, Jesse didn't want Charity to know about it. Another bad sign.

CHARITY COULDN'T BELIEVE her good luck. She'd been trying to come up with a good reason to leave the house all day. Mitch had been acting suspiciously, knowing she was on another story—and worried about her. She didn't want to worry him and she knew he would have a cow if he found out who she was going to meet.

Once in the car, she pulled out her cell phone and dialed the number from the email she'd received just that morning.

He answered on the first ring.

"It's Charity. I was hoping now is a good time—"

"You got the message? Good. Yes, come now. You do remember how to get here, I assume?" He hung up without waiting for an answer.

Charity took the back way, ditched her car in the woods and walked the last few blocks through the woods to the back of Madam Florie's. As she sneaked around the rear of the former motel, she hoped her psychic aunt was hard at work giving advice to some love-struck woman in Algona, Iowa, or a gambler in Elko, Nevada, and not peering out her window at bungalow uno: Aries.

Aries was one of twelve separate bungalows that had been motor court units, but were now furnished apartments. Florie lived in the main office building and did her psychic business from there.

At Charity's tap, Wade Dennison opened the door and quickly ushered her inside. The furnishings were sparse. A sunken couch with worn cushions, a thread-bare overstuffed chair and a cigarette-marred coffee table.

She could see through the doorway into both of the only other rooms. A small bath with a sink, toilet and shower stall. A bedroom with a bed and a beat-up chest of drawers. It could have been a rental in any town in the nation.

"It's not much," Wade said with obvious embarrass-ment. He'd fallen far from the mansion he'd built for Daisy. Charity knew it must irk him that he couldn't go near the place because of the restraining order Daisy had on him.

"Please sit down," he said.

She took the chair he offered. He perched on the arm of the couch. Jail seemed to have made him calmer. Or maybe he just wanted her to think that.

For just an instant, she considered what she'd done. Coming here. Worse, not telling anyone where she was. It hadn't been that long ago that Wade Dennison had threatened to kill her.

"You said you wanted to set the record straight," she said, pulling out her reporter's notebook and flipping it open to a clean page. She snapped her ballpoint pen and looked up expectantly.

If it was a trick to just get her here, she figured now was when he would make his move.

He didn't move. But he did hesitate, then he let out a long sigh and said, "I'm innocent. I didn't shoot the sheriff."

Another innocent man unjustly accused. "Your fingerprint was on the trigger," she pointed out, hoping this hadn't been a complete waste of time.

"But Daisy's finger was on top of mine," he said. "Daisy is trying to set me up. She's taken my freedom, my home, my business. Daisy called me and said she wanted to see me that night. She planned to kill me. I see that now." His voice broke. "Worse, I think she might have had our daughter kidnapped." He buried his face in his hands.

She wasn't buying it. "Why tell me this, Wade? You've never talked to me about anything."

He raised his head slowly. "I'm desperate."

"As flattering as that is…"

"Haven't you ever considered that I might be innocent?"

She thought that over for a moment. She'd definitely considered it. But right now he looked guilty as sin.

"Why would Daisy have her own child kidnapped?"

"I threatened to throw her out if the baby wasn't mine and take Desiree from her. I knew she had been having an affair—"

"With whom?"

He shook his head. "I didn't want to know. But a man can tell when his wife has been with someone else. I think she was in love with him and I think the baby was his. But I would never have harmed a hair on that baby's head. Never. And I wouldn't have really thrown her out or taken Desiree like I threatened. I think that's why she got rid of the baby, you know, because she was afraid I'd find out the truth and go through with my threat."

This was a theory she'd actually considered. It certainly explained those years Daisy was a recluse. Getting rid of one child to save another.

"The last time we talked you told me you were convinced Angela was your baby," Charity pointed out.

He shook his head. "I hoped she was. She could have been. There was this one night when Daisy and I…"

She got the picture. "Was Daisy thinking of leaving you for this other man?"

His expression told her she'd hit the bull's-eye!

"She wouldn't have done that. The only reason we're apart now is that she's mad at me after my illegitimate daughter showed up."

"Or is she mad because you offered your illegitimate daughter one million dollars to keep it quiet?"

"That wasn't it," Wade said, getting to his feet. "I

had an affair when Daisy was pregnant with Angela. That's what she's mad about."

Charity's brain was freewheeling. Was it possible Wade had engineered Angela's kidnapping because he thought it was the other man's baby and he knew Daisy wouldn't leave him with the baby gone?

It was a far-fetched theory, but it made as much sense as any of the others.

"Daisy seems happier now," she said. She left off, "Now that you aren't in her life."

Wade let out a laugh. "She has *everything* and if her lawyer has his way, she will leave me penniless if not in prison."

"You *shot* Mitch," she reminded him.

"It was an accident. That night was so crazy. I think that's when I realized what Daisy was up to. I know I was acting strangely."

"You almost *killed* Mitch."

He nodded, ducking his head. "I feel terrible about that. That's why I contacted you. I was hoping you'd do some of that snooping you do so well."

She took that as a compliment. "What am I snooping into? The shooting seems pretty cut-and-dried."

"Not that. Angela's kidnapping. Find out once and for all who took that baby and clear my name. I've had this hanging over my head for too many years. When the truth comes out…"

He believed he would be exonerated of everything and would be back in the mansion, back on top? Obviously so. Was it possible he really was innocent?

"You really think Daisy had something to do with it?" she asked.

"I think Daisy might be capable of anything, including getting rid of that baby so I would never find out it wasn't mine."

Charity closed her notebook. "Someone hired your production manager to take the baby out of the house. Did Daisy even know Bud Farnsworth?"

"Of course she knew Bud. But I think she told Bud to get rid of the baby and he gave it to someone else and really didn't know what happened to Angela after that," Wade said.

Charity remembered the night in the plant when Bud had tried to kill her over a blackmail letter that incriminated him in the kidnapping. Daisy had shown up, wounded Bud. What had she kept saying to him? "Where is Angela?" Could Wade be right about her?

"Bud couldn't have gotten into the house without some inside help," Wade said, his voice low. "Someone left the window in Angela's room unlocked."

Charity didn't have much to go on and Wade knew it. The case was ice-cold. Twenty-seven years. And it wasn't like she hadn't tried to solve it from the time she was a kid.

What intrigued her most was this mystery man Daisy had the affair with. Charity had heard rumors for years. But was this a man Daisy had actually fallen for? Someone she would have left Wade for? Now that was interesting.

THE RESEMBLANCE WAS unmistakable, Maggie thought as she and Jesse entered the back door of the house and she saw the man sitting in the recliner. The same deep dimples, dark hair and eyes, and easy smile.

"Meet my little brother, Sheriff Mitch Tanner," Jesse said. "Mitch? Say hello to Angela Dennison."

Mitch's mouth was agape as he stared up at her.

Maggie smiled tentatively.

"How... Where..." He shot a look at Jesse. *"Angela?"*

"Looks like a slam dunk but we still need the results from the DNA tests," Jesse said. "We just couriered a batch to the lab in Portland. Albert said he should be able to get us the results in twelve hours. Midnight tonight."

Mitch looked from his brother to Maggie again. "I'm sorry to stare but..."

"It's all right. I know I look a lot like Desiree." She saw a look pass between the brothers and groaned. "You aren't telling me that Desiree might also be your half sister?"

"It's possible," Jesse admitted.

"You told her?" Mitch asked his brother in surprise.

Jesse nodded and shrugged. "Kinda had to."

"Oh," Mitch said, studying him. "It's like that, is it?"

Jesse grinned bashfully.

Mitch shook his head. "Other than looks?"

"It all adds up—dates, background, recent events," Jesse said.

"I *am* Angela Dennison. I would stake my life on it. Actually, I am."

Mitch frowned.

"Someone's trying to kill her," Jesse said. "A Seattle cop."

Mitch groaned and leaned back, closing his eyes. "What the hell is it with this rainy season?"

"There's more," Jesse said.

Mitch opened his eyes and narrowed them at Jesse. "How did I know there would be?"

"The cop is in town. He's killed three other people and tried to kill her, as well."

"You haven't gone to the Feds?" Mitch demanded.

"It would be her word against his and he just happens to be an old cop with a lot of commendations, his most recent from the mayor."

Mitch swore under his breath. "A Seattle cop? How does he fit into all this?"

"That's what we're going to find out," Maggie said, making Jesse smile at her determination.

"We don't think he acted alone in the kidnapping. We need to find out how he ties in," Jesse said. He quickly filled his brother in on everything. When he finished, Mitch was looking at Maggie with open admiration. Jesse couldn't help but smile since he had to admit his choices in women in the past had left something to be desired.

"So," Maggie said when he'd finished, "we realized the best approach would be for me to announce who I am at the party tonight and see how it shakes down from there."

"Rozalyn Sawyer's party?" Mitch cried, echoing his brother's earlier surprise. "*We* decided? Are you nuts?"

Jesse shrugged. "I felt the same way when Maggie first came up with the idea."

"Maggie?" Mitch asked.

"I was raised as Maggie Randolph," she said. "I'm going to need a dress for tonight. Can your fiancée help me with that?"

"*Charity?*" Mitch looked to his brother. "You aren't suggesting—"

They heard Charity's car pull up out front.

"She's going to hear about it tonight, anyway," Jesse pointed out.

Mitch was holding his head as if it ached. "Do either of you have a clue what you're about to do?"

Jesse smiled. "*I* have an inkling. Maggie's in for a surprise."

Charity came through the door just then. Maggie hadn't been sure what to expect given the way the men were acting.

A beautiful woman about her own age with a long mass of reddish-blond curly hair swept in. She had bright blue eyes and instantly Maggie felt drawn to her.

"You must be Charity Jenkins," Maggie said, going to greet her. "I've read a great many of your newspaper articles. You write very well."

Charity looked both surprised and confused and decidedly curious. As Mitch had done, Charity stared at her as if she thought she should know her.

"I'm Angela Dennison and I need your help," Maggie said.

"Charity speechless. It's a wonder to behold," Jesse said as he took his future sister-in-law's hand and led her to the couch across from Mitch and started to fill her in, as well.

Charity, if anything, was a quick study. "You're the one who stole my file."

Maggie nodded. "Sorry. Jesse has it. I kept all the stories in proper order."

Charity smiled at that and looked to Jesse. "Is she really—"

"We'll have the DNA test results by tonight," Jesse said. "Maggie wants to make her announcement at the party."

Charity looked at Maggie. "You're using yourself as bait?" she asked, cutting right to the chase.

"Something like that. I'm going to need a dress," Maggie said. "One that I can hide a small handgun in. Can you help me?"

Charity had been watching Jesse and Maggie while they'd told their story. Now she looked at Mitch and smiled that sly matchmaking smile of hers.

Mitch groaned, knowing it was impossible to stop Charity without telling her that Maggie might be his half sister—and Jesse's. That was one can of worms that would be opened soon enough.

Charity stood. "Come on. You're about my size. Let's see what we can find in my closet. I live next door. So you and Jesse just met?"

As they went out the door, Mitch shook his head. "Dad know about this?"

"Yep. He already gave me his DNA test."

Mitch looked up at him in surprise. "Then it's possible…"

Jesse nodded solemnly. "I'm afraid so."

"This is a damned dangerous plan."

Jesse couldn't agree more. "That's why I want you there, carrying. I might need all the help I can get. I don't expect the kidnapper to make a move at the party—"

"You're hoping for some reaction, though, aren't you?" Mitch said. "How are you planning to protect her after the party? Especially if this Seattle cop is determined to get to her?"

Jesse took a breath and let it out slowly. "For starters, not let her out of my sight."

Mitch just looked at him.

"What?"

"You've got it bad for this woman."

"Bro, I can't explain it. That's why I have to get those DNA test results and get my head around however they come out."

"Charity's going to flip when she finds out that I've been keeping this secret for all these years," Mitch said.

Jesse smiled at his brother. "I think she'll still marry you. Anyway, June is a long way off. She might not even still be mad at you by then."

"Where are we going?" Maggie asked as they left Mitch's and took back roads as they had earlier. She had pulled her hair up into a ponytail and was wearing a baseball cap that Charity had lent her.

"My dad's house. His name is Lee Tanner. He's a good guy. You'll like him."

Her look said she'd make up her own mind about that.

He liked that about her. He liked a lot of things about her. He just wished he knew for sure who her father was if she really was Angela Dennison. Until he did, he'd have to keep her at arm's length. And that was the last thing he wanted to do.

CHAPTER THIRTEEN

RUPERT BLACKMORE HAD brought a tent but the rain changed his mind about camping. He checked into the only motel in town, the Ho Hum. He used cash, but he wasn't worried about being recognized—not with his old pickup, fishing hat and gear.

He liked to think that the only person who knew him in this town was Margaret Randolph and he was looking for her—not the other way around.

Of course, he couldn't be sure her kidnapper didn't also know him—just not in this disguise. Nor was the kidnapper expecting him to turn up in Timber Falls, right?

He was pleasantly surprised how small the town was. Finding her should be easy—if she was still around. He figured after him almost catching her last night at Dennison Ducks she would have split. Since she hadn't already gone to his superiors or the Feds, he figured she wouldn't. This could be the end of it. No one in this town would ever have to know of her existence.

He spent the day fishing, keeping his eye out for her, but deciding to take advantage of where he was. Hell, he might as well consider this a little vacation. Admittedly, he was relieved he wasn't going to have to kill her.

She was rich. She'd return to Seattle. She'd keep her

mouth shut. He'd retire and move to Arizona. None of this would ever have to come out.

He'd convinced himself that everything was going to work out as he drove through town, stopping at the gas station. A teenager came out to pump his gas.

Rupert got out of the truck and walked back to the restroom on the side of the building. When he came back out after using the facilities, he saw that the kid was washing his windows so he wandered into the office.

It was one of those old gas stations with nothing more than a counter and a pop machine in the office, an attached single-bay garage and two pumps.

As he was leaving, he picked up a newspaper, leaving thirty-five cents on the counter.

He walked back out to his pickup, paid cash for the gas and sat for a moment as the kid went back inside, paying no attention to him.

His hands shook as he read the story about Daisy Dennison of the famed Dennison Ducks decoys. He remembered the bumper sticker he'd seen on the guy's pickup that night, the night a man he'd never seen before met him in a deserted warehouse parking lot and handed over a wriggling baby wrapped in a tiny quilt with little yellow ducks on it.

He'd put the bundle on the passenger seat, looking up as the pickup and driver took off into the night. That's when he'd seen the sticker and the muddy Oregon plates. He couldn't make out the plate number. Even then had he planned to find out where the baby was from? Probably. After all, he was being blackmailed and now he had a clue who his blackmailer was. A Dennison Ducks bumper sticker on the back of the retreating pickup. Timber Falls, Oregon. Home of the famous decoys.

He pulled away from the service station, reminding himself that he'd been a good cop. Before and even after that one fateful night.

He'd been young, a little too cocky, a little too convinced that he wasn't just going to save the world, he was going to be one of those cops who got commendations all the time on television and in the newspapers.

And he had, despite what happened that night thirty years ago. It was a convenience-store robbery and he and his partner were just around the block. They came screaming up in the patrol car just as the perpetrator took off down the dark alley.

Rupert had been the first one out of the car. He ran down the alley. It was so dark. He'd yelled for the perp to stop, heard him climbing a chain-link fence at the end of the alley and in what little light there was, fired.

The pressure had been on him to succeed. He'd found out that Teresa had another guy interested in her; he wanted to look good and prove to her she was marrying the right guy.

He had wanted the bust. Needed it.

But when he neared the fence and the downed body lying in the pool of blood, he saw that it wasn't the perp at all but a kid of not more than nine, shot once in the back of the head.

He'd been so upset, he'd dropped his gun. It had gone off and shot him in the leg. A freak accident. Unlike killing a nine-year-old boy in an alley. He must have been in shock after that, sick to his stomach, throwing up, barely conscious when his partner found him.

By that time, his weapon was missing. Later he

would realize that someone had come in behind him and picked it up carefully from the ground. An opportunist who saw that the gun with his fingerprints on it could be valuable in the future.

His partner, a guy named Wayne Dixon, came upon the scene, saw Rupert on his knees, wounded, bloody and missing his gun and thought that the perp had overpowered him, taken his gun and shot him and the kid.

Rupert had been in no condition to tell him he was wrong. Later... Well, later, he'd let the lie stand. Telling the truth wouldn't bring the kid back and would only hurt his career and his chances with Teresa.

She'd come to see him at the hospital. He'd proposed on the spot and she'd accepted.

He put the rest behind him, thinking it was over.

Over until the night he got the call to meet the man in the warehouse parking lot. To get rid of a baby. And the blackmailer would get rid of the gun. He would never be contacted again, he'd been promised by the distorted voice on the phone.

So he'd met the man at the warehouse parking lot, taken the baby. But then the baby quilt had moved and a small cry emitted from deep inside. That had been his mistake, opening the quilt and looking down into that little face. It had taken his breath away.

If there had been any way, he would have taken her home to Teresa. But he and Teresa had only been married a few years and he hadn't known then that they would never have a child of their own. Plus how would he have explained the baby to her? He didn't want her to know about the mistake he'd already made in his life. He would have done anything to keep her from knowing. He still would.

He'd bundled the baby back up and driven away from that warehouse parking lot, heading for Puget Sound, thinking he would get rid of the baby and maybe the blackmailer would never contact him again. That was the deal, wasn't it? And everyone knew blackmailers kept their word.

Right.

But that didn't mean he didn't abhor being blackmailed. He guessed that was partly why he balked at the order and instead of getting rid of the baby in Puget Sound, he sold her to the Randolphs' attorney, Clark Iverson. The other reason was the money. He bought Teresa a house. He made some rich couple parents. For twenty-seven years everyone had been happy with the outcome.

And then the adoptive father got sick, stumbled on the truth and decided his daughter needed to know so she could be united with her biological parents.

And Rupert Blackmore, once a good cop, became a killer again.

Not that he ever forgot about the bumper sticker on that pickup. Or the blackmailer. He'd done a little investigative work and found out who the baby was and that she'd been kidnapped. And then he'd let it go, thinking he had a place to start looking for the blackmailer if he ever heard from him again.

A few months ago he'd read about Bud Farnsworth being killed and that he had been the alleged kidnapper. Rupert had recognized the guy in the newspaper article. He was the man who'd brought him the baby. But it had been clear that night that this Farnsworth guy was working for someone else—someone he feared.

Now Rupert Blackmore wondered if Margaret Randolph had seen this story. Would she be so stupid as to knock on the Dennison family door and tell them who she thought she was? Tell them about what had happened at the pier?

No one would be that stupid, especially given the mess the Dennison family was in right now.

He tossed the newspaper on the floor and drove down Main Street toward his motel. Maybe he'd stay around another day. Just to make sure Margaret wasn't still around.

He drove past the sheriff's department. It was little more than a narrow building that shared half the space with city hall. From what he'd heard, the town sheriff had been shot and his brother was acting deputy. The brother had little to no experience, so he wasn't too worried about either of them.

At the edge of town, he pulled into the only café. If Margaret had been stupid enough to go to the Dennisons' this morning then it would be all over town by now and he'd been in enough dinky towns to know where to find the gossip in this one.

Still wearing his sunglasses, he parked and went inside Betty's, making a point of sitting by the window in the sunlight.

A fiftysomething bottle blonde came out from behind the counter with a menu and a glass of ice water. She set both down in front of him.

"Still got cherry, butterscotch and chocolate pie," she said. "Homemade."

Rupert looked up at her after a cursory glance at the menu. "I'll take a cheeseburger loaded, fries, a chocolate milkshake and a piece of the cherry pie," he said.

She smiled. She wasn't bad-looking, but hey, he was no Prince Charming. And her name tag read Betty.

"Bigfoot hunting or fishing?" she asked, clearly taking him for a nonlocal.

"I've never heard of Bigfoot fishing," he said flirting with her a little. What the hell? He figured it couldn't hurt. "How exactly is that done?"

She brightened to his smile. "Everythin' bites if you got's the right bait," she said, murdering the expression.

He laughed. "I don't care if they bite. I just like fishing."

"That's good because this isn't the best time of year for fishing around here," she said, eyeing him.

"But it's quiet and the river isn't crowded."

"Can't argue that," she said, and went to place his order.

She came back to the counter where she had a cup of coffee she'd been drinking before he came in.

"I've never been up here before," he said to her and turned to look out at the deserted street. "Is it always this quiet?"

She shook her head. "Everyone's getting ready for the party tonight."

"Party?"

"Sawyers. The daughter, Rozalyn, returned to town and she's throwing a party. Just redid this old Victorian on the edge of the town. You might have seen it on your way in?"

He shook his head.

"It's kinda back off the road. Great old house." She sipped her coffee. "You staying at the Ho Hum?"

He nodded.

"You'll probably hear the party, then," she said with a laugh. "I hope you aren't a light sleeper."

He shook his head. "I sleep like the dead."

A bell dinged and she went to get his meal. As she slid the food across the table to him, several more customers came in. They looked like regulars. They glanced at him, took him for what he appeared to be, and sat down.

Outside, low dark clouds scudded past. It looked as if it was going to rain any minute.

He ate, listening to Betty talking to the other customers. A no-big-news day. Good. Except for this party tonight. Sounded like the entire town would be there.

He ate his burger and fries and watched the street. No fancy motorcycle went past. No word circulating of a young woman in town looking for her past.

Yep, she'd fled town. He finished off his milkshake, cleaned his plate and started on the pie.

But, he wondered, what would she do next? What could she do? She had no proof. It would be his word against hers. If she couldn't go to the cops and she couldn't run, wouldn't she have to return to Seattle? The woman was rich. Her father had left her dozens of businesses around the world. She would have to return to Seattle eventually.

Sure he'd put an APB out on her, but that was just for questioning in the murders. It was possible he could reach some sort of deal with her. Once she understood that she was only alive because he'd spared her.

Maybe he wouldn't have to kill her. He liked the idea more than he wanted to admit.

And then he would just fade away into the background. Arizona. It was far enough away that she'd feel safe.

He was feeling good by the time he left a big tip for Betty and headed for his motel room. Maybe he'd take a nap and come back later for the dinner special: pork chops and dressing, applesauce, green beans, mashed potatoes and pork gravy.

The kidnapper would never know that he hadn't held up his end of the bargain.

LEE TANNER CAME out onto the deck as Jesse drove the pickup into the yard and shut off the motor. Lee's gaze went to the young woman who climbed out. He looked as if he'd been cold-cocked with a sledgehammer.

She had that effect on people. Maybe especially on Lee Tanner given how much the woman looked like Desiree.

"Maggie, meet my father, Lee Tanner," Jesse said as they climbed the steps to the house.

Lee extended a hand. Maggie took it. "You're Angela," he said. It wasn't a question but she nodded, anyway. "I just finished lunch but I could—"

"We've eaten," Jesse said, cutting his father off. Charity had cooked up lunch, all the time talking fifty miles an hour with Maggie. Hadn't he known they would hit it off?

"Were you planning on going to Roz Sawyer's party tonight?" Jesse asked him.

Lee shook his head. "Why?"

"I thought maybe I could change your mind," he said. "Maggie's going to announce who she really is tonight at midnight."

Lee lifted a brow.

Jesse grinned wryly. "Yeah, by then we'll actually know who her father is. We'll still need Daisy's DNA test results to prove without a doubt that she's Angela but I don't expect any surprises there."

"What can I do?" his father asked.

"You still have a gun?" His father nodded. "I'd like you to come to the party and have it, just in case."

"This have to do with those murders back in Seattle?" Lee asked.

"Yeah. There's a cop after her. He's already killed three others." Jesse pulled out the faxed copy of the photo of Detective Rupert Blackmore and the mayor. "He's the one on the right. It isn't a great photo."

"I'd recognize him if I saw him but you're not expecting him at the party, are you?" his father asked.

Jesse shook his head.

"We don't think Blackmore is behind the kidnapping," Maggie said, speaking up. "We think it was someone local."

Jesse met his dad's gaze. "Someone inside the house left the baby's window unlocked."

"It wasn't Daisy," Lee said. "It wasn't her."

Jesse nodded, although not sure of that and wondering why his father was so adamant. "Well, there were other people in the house that day." His mother for one. He hadn't told Maggie about that yet.

"I'll be at the party," his dad said. "Just let me know if there is anything else I can do."

"Thanks." Jesse grinned at his old man. "I knew I could count on you." He turned to Maggie. "She's also quite capable of taking care of herself."

Maggie smiled at that.

Jesse shook his dad's hand and watched while Maggie hugged him. He could see the conflicting emotions in his dad's face. Clearly, Lee Tanner wouldn't have minded if Maggie turned out to be his daughter.

Jesse hoped his dad would have to settle for daughter-in-law, but then again, that was way down the road and he wasn't sure it was the road Maggie wanted to take. There were fireworks between them and some bond neither of them understood. Until the possibility of shared blood was established or eliminated...

He wouldn't let himself think about it. There were too many hurdles yet to leap. Keeping Maggie alive. Finding out the truth about her biological father. Finding the kidnapper.

Maggie was right about that. She wouldn't be safe until they did.

He watched her walk over to a wall filled with photographs his father had taken of him and Mitch from the time they were babies. She ran her finger over a black-and-white of him.

Jesse felt his father's gaze on him, a look of worry in his expression. His dad knew him too well, knew how much this woman meant to him...how much was at stake tonight.

CHAPTER FOURTEEN

JESSE HEARD A sound, looked up and saw Maggie at the top of the stairs. His heart leaped to his throat. He had never seen anything so breathtaking. So beautiful.

Maggie wore a bright red dress that accentuated every one of her assets. Her dark hair was down and floating over her bare, lightly freckled shoulders.

"You are amazing," he said, his voice breaking.

Her dark eyes glowed as she started down the steps, the dress a whisper against her skin.

"You're just saying that because you know I'm carrying a weapon under this dress," she said, obviously trying to lighten the mood and maybe feeling a little embarrassed by the fact that he couldn't take his eyes off her.

She had a weapon hidden under that dress all right and it wasn't a gun. It was enough to knock him to his knees just thinking about it.

"You can't tell where, right?" she asked, looking worried.

He shook his head. "I would never know you were armed."

She smiled, pleased.

She wouldn't be using the weapon unless he had failed and the target was closing in. He had no intention of letting that happen. His hope was that Maggie wasn't going to have a need for the gun. Not tonight. Not ever.

She moved toward him like a dream.

He stood transfixed. "You look stunning," he whispered.

She smiled as she took the last few steps down the stairs to him.

He caught a hint of perfume, something exotic that fit her perfectly. Charity's doing.

She touched a hand to his cheek, her brown eyes dark as she looked up at him. Her lush lips were painted a pale inviting pink. They parted in a sigh and he felt his heart do a flip inside his chest, all the air rushed from his lungs and it was all he could do not to take her in his arms and kiss her.

MAGGIE FELT TONGUE-TIED as she looked at Jesse in the tuxedo. Had a man ever been so handsome? And yet it was his dark eyes that captivated her as she moved toward him as if her body had a mind of its own.

She ached to touch him, to feel his arms wrapped around her, to lose herself in his embrace.

Just one kiss. She would have given anything for just one kiss. Tonight she would know if her feelings for him would always be forbidden or if she could have her heart's desire. Just the thought made her forget that there was at least one killer after her, and maybe more after her announcement tonight.

She stepped to him, so close she caught his male scent mixing with the soapy clean smell of him. No aftershave. Just a maleness that made her knees weak. If she even thought of Jesse's lips on hers, Jesse's arms wrapped around her...

"You are extraordinary in that tux," she said, her voice breaking. Everything about him made her blood fire and her skin warm.

When he looked at her with his dark eyes, her heart hammered with a need like none she'd ever known.

"You know how I feel about you—"

He touched his finger to her lips and shook his head. "I know."

She swallowed back the tears that threatened. She wanted him, needed him. She'd known few men intimately. Most had not interested her enough that she wanted to go beyond a few dates.

Jesse had captivated her that first night. His art alone had seduced her. But it was when she'd watched him from the screened-in room, watched him run his hand over her bike that she'd realized she yearned to feel the warmth of his palm on her bare skin, his gentle fingers, the whisper of his skin pressed against hers.

He removed his finger from her lips, his gaze like a caress.

"Jesse," she said on a breath, as if that one word swelled with the emotions she felt for him.

He seemed to tense as if he knew what she wanted, what she needed, and he felt the heat of this banked fire between them and knew that if they fanned even the slightest ember it would flare and burn blindingly bright, sweeping them up in a maelstrom of passion that neither could nor would resist.

He didn't move. Didn't reach for her. But she could see it was as hard on him as it was her.

"Ready?" he asked, his voice low.

She nodded, unable to speak. She had to be strong

tonight, whatever happened with the DNA test results. Whatever happened after her announcement.

"A hug for luck?" she asked softly.

HE'D BEEN AFRAID to touch her, afraid he would be lost. But he opened his arms, knowing that tonight could change everything between them, and she stepped into them and rested her head against his chest, her arms looping around his waist. He closed his arms around her, hugging her tightly as he closed his eyes at the wondrous feel of her. They stayed that way for a long moment, holding each other.

Then she stepped back and he reluctantly let go of her. She smiled up at him. "Showtime?"

He nodded and glanced at the clock. Almost eleven-thirty. She would make her announcement at the stroke of midnight—the same time Albert had promised to call with the DNA test results. Another thirty minutes.

The cell phone vibrated in the pocket of his tux. He pulled it out.

"How you holding up?" Mitch asked.

"Okay. What's the news there?"

"Roz just announced her engagement to Ford Lancaster," he said. "Charity's crying tears of happiness. Roz also did as you requested, announced that she had a special surprise at the stroke of midnight."

"Good. We're on our way."

"Be careful."

"Always." He disconnected and looked at Maggie. "Ready to rock and roll? The stage is set. You're the star performer come midnight."

She nodded. "I have my fingers crossed."

He nodded, knowing she was referring to the DNA test results. "Me, too."

The party was in full swing as they sneaked in the back way. Charity opened the door for them. "Everyone is here," she reported. "Daisy showed up with a bodyguard and you'll never guess who—Bruno. Betty's here, too. Talk about a strange trio."

"What about Wade?" Jesse asked.

"Haven't seen him yet. Roz has a couple of guys outside watching for him. If he shows up, they will detain him until midnight." She glanced at Maggie. "Wow, that dress looks sensational on you." Then she looked back at Jesse and grinned.

"Go on back to the party," he told Charity, not appreciating her matchmaking right now. "We'll be upstairs."

She took off and Jesse watched after her for a moment, hoping the fact that she hadn't spotted any unfamiliar faces was good news.

They took the back stairs, climbing up to the third floor. Music and a cacophony of voices rose from the lower floor of the large old Victorian.

Jesse glanced at his watch. "Five minutes and counting."

Maggie nodded. She didn't look nervous or worried now. He watched her check her gun, then shoot him a grin. He couldn't help but admire her determination. He would give anything to have this night over.

Sneaking out to the stairs, he peeked over the railing and spotted Mitch in a corner in his wheelchair.

Daisy Dennison was indeed in attendance with Bruno and Betty close by. Desiree was flirting with several local guys who hung out at the Duck-In.

Lydia was in a more modern wheelchair than Mitch's,

sitting demurely in a corner with Angus looming over her, seeing to her every need.

Roz and her fiancé, Ford Lancaster, were at the center of the room accepting congratulations. Roz's father, Liam, was talking to some woman—

With a start, Jesse saw that it was Charity's aunt Florie. She looked so different. Her hair was a warm brown color instead of fire-engine red and it was cut into a cap of short curls rather than being wrapped around her head like a turban. And her eyes didn't have that thick turquoise eye shadow over them, either. Nor was she wearing some blindingly bright caftan. She wore a simple blue dress and she had obviously totally captivated Liam Sawyer. He seemed to be hanging on her every word.

As Jesse's gaze scanned the rest of the crowd, he spotted his father. Daisy looked beautiful. He saw that reflected in his father's gaze and felt a sharp jab at heart level. Oh God, his father still felt something for the woman. Th,e realization shocked him.

He turned to look at Daisy. Her eyes were locked with Lee Tanner's across the room. Was this the first time they'd seen each other in all these years?

It was clear that whatever had been between them hadn't completely died.

Just then, the large old grandfather clock began to chime the midnight hour.

"It's time," Maggie said next to him.

He glanced at his watch and nodded. They took the back stairs down to the second floor, then Jesse moved out to the top of the stairs.

The music was louder down here, the chattering crowd a dull roar. Jesse caught Charity's eye. She said something to the leader of the band and the music stopped instantly.

As the grandfather clock finished chiming midnight, Roz called for everyone's attention. The crowd quieted and followed Roz's gaze upward to the stairs.

A hush fell over the huge room below as Jesse held up his hands for quiet.

"There is someone here tonight—" Jesse was interrupted by a disturbance at the front door. Wade Dennison came bursting in, his face flushed. "You're just in time," Jesse said, and Maggie joined him at the railing.

A murmur rippled through the crowd.

Maggie smiled down on everyone. "I apologize for interrupting the party. Rozalyn was kind enough to let me make my announcement here tonight with all of you together."

She glanced toward Daisy, who was looking up at her in shock. Wade just looked confused.

"My name is Angela Dennison," she announced.

The murmur rose to a roar. And at the middle of it, Daisy let out a cry. Jesse saw her expression. Shock. Then horror. Just before she fainted.

Jesse motioned for silence as the crowd moved back to give Daisy air and Desiree rushed to her mother. Lee had gone to her, as well, and was demanding someone get him a cold washcloth.

"What the hell kind of stunt are you trying to pull, Tanner?" Wade demanded. "That woman is not..." His voice broke. He stared at Maggie, then seemed to shrink back from her as if no longer sure of anything.

"I'm here tonight because whoever is responsible for my kidnapping is now trying to kill me," Maggie said.

Lydia was fanning herself, Angus leaning over her.

Another roar from the crowd. Jesse touched Maggie's arm. He wanted to get her out of here. She'd done what she came to do. Now he just wanted her far away from here and safe.

"I intend to get to the truth. To find out who kidnapped me, who wants me dead now."

The crowd was in an uproar. "Is it really her?" Betty was asking no one in particular. It was as if Angela's ghost had appeared and everyone seemed shaken and excited.

Jesse glanced at his watch. Albert still hadn't called with the DNA test results. But it was time to clear everyone out and get Maggie out of here. He motioned to Charity and she touched Roz's arm.

"Party's over!" Roz announced and she and Ford began ushering the guests out. "Thank you all for coming."

Betty offered to keep the café open late for anyone who wanted coffee.

Daisy had come around. Lee and Bruno helped her up into a chair. She sat looking up at Maggie as if she'd just seen an angel. Jesse knew the feeling.

Desiree stared up at her sister for a moment, then turned on her heel and left, no doubt headed for the bar. Jesse hoped she would be all right. He knew this had to be a shock for her and Desiree had had too many surprises in her life lately.

Lydia was still fanning herself in the corner. Angus was frowning in Jesse's direction, obviously upset that Lydia was distraught. Wade had slumped into a chair on the opposite side of the room from Daisy, his head in his hands.

Liam had offered to take Florie home and as Roz

and Ford closed the door on the last of the other guests, Jesse's cell phone vibrated.

"We'll be in the kitchen helping the staff clean up," Roz said as she and Ford left them alone.

"Yes, Albert," Jesse said into the phone as he ushered Maggie into the first room off the stairs. "We're ready for the test results." He met Maggie's gaze, his heart in his throat.

"Okay, here's what we've got. Two matches each, but the two groups don't match."

"In English," Jesse snapped.

"Quite simply, your test and your father's match. Miss Randolph's test and Mr. Dennison's match." Wade was Maggie's father!

"Albert, I could kiss you." Jesse let out a long breath. Maggie's eyes were on him. He let out a howl and, dropping the cell phone, picked her up and spun her around. As he brought her down, he dropped his mouth to hers and kissed her.

Her arms came around his neck and she pulled him closer, her lips parting, her breath mingling with his. Her mouth was pure sugar, her body soft and rounded and pressed to his. He never wanted to let her go.

Jesse slowly raised his lips from Maggie's, grinned down at her, their eyes meeting, a silent understanding passing between them.

"I guess it's time to make our second announcement," he said.

Maggie's eyes were shiny bright. She smiled ruefully, as if like him, she couldn't wait to get away from here and finally be alone with each other.

They descended the stairs finding everyone pretty

much where they'd left them. Daisy got to her feet and walked toward Maggie. Jesse tensed.

"You're the woman in the painting," she whispered.

Maggie nodded.

"How long have you known she was alive?" Daisy asked Jesse.

"Until a few minutes ago, I couldn't be absolutely sure she was Angela Dennison," he said. "The DNA sample Wade supplied in the death of his illegitimate daughter matches hers."

Wade had come over to them, as well. He stood looking poleaxed. He didn't notice Lee Tanner slump down onto the couch, his face filled with anguish and relief as he buried his face in his hands.

"I—" Tears welled in Wade's eyes. He stepped to Maggie and gave her an awkward hug. "We'll find out who's trying to hurt you, who kidnapped you. We'll find him."

"We have to go now," Jesse said, looking over at his brother. Mitch nodded.

"I'll talk to you soon," Wade said, touching his daughter's hair, dropping his hand to hers. Jesse saw her squeeze his hand.

"We'll talk," she said and looked to her mother as Wade left.

"I don't know what to say to you," Daisy said, still looking stunned. "It's just such a shock."

Maggie nodded.

Lydia wheeled up. "Come see me, child," she said, taking Maggie's hand. "I'm your aunt Lydia. I own the Busy Bee antique shop in town. Promise you'll come see me?"

Maggie nodded and smiled down at her aunt as Lydia and Angus left. "I promise. As soon as I can."

"We have to go," Jesse repeated, and took Maggie's hand. He was worried that the longer they stayed, the more chance of an ambush as they left.

Mitch was already wheeling himself toward the back door, Charity at his side when she motioned that she needed to talk to Jesse a minute.

"You might want to keep an eye on Bruno," Charity said confidentially. "I did a little checking on him for a friend. His real name is Jerome Lovelace and he has quite a rap sheet."

"For a friend?"

Charity groaned. "For Lydia, all right? She got this idea that Bruno might be thinking of robbing the antique store."

Both Jesse and Mitch rolled their eyes at that, just as Charity no doubt figured they would.

"Don't make me sorry I told you," Charity warned.

Jesse laughed. "I appreciate the heads-up, Charity." The news didn't really surprise him. He watched his brother and Charity leave. When he glanced back, Bruno was by the front door, eyes hooded. Jesse hadn't heard him say a word all night. But Jesse could feel his eyes on them as they left. Mean eyes.

RUPERT BLACKMORE TRIED to calm down. He'd been sitting in Betty's Café, having a cup of decaf when the door burst open and the café suddenly filled to overflowing with people—and the news.

Angela Dennison had announced she was alive at the party tonight.

Rupert could barely hear the clamor of voices over

the rush of his pulse. Blindly, he dropped money on the counter and, sliding off the stool, stumbled out the door. He doubted anyone noticed him or the way he clutched his chest as he leaned against the side of his pickup.

If he was right, if the kidnapper still lived here in this town, then he knew that Rupert hadn't lived up to his end of the bargain.

What would he do? Turn in the service revolver with Rupert's fingerprints on it? Rupert could see the headlines now. His reputation would be destroyed, he might lose his pension and Teresa. Tears blurred his vision.

He'd have to tell Teresa himself. He didn't want her reading about it in the paper. What choice did he have? None.

It was too late to kill Margaret Randolph. The cat was out of the bag, so to speak. But she'd announced at the party that she was looking for the kidnapper and wouldn't rest until she found him. Worse, she'd taken up with the deputy sheriff.

Rupert was sure he'd covered his tracks well on the recent murders. It was time to go back to Seattle. Retire. Move to Arizona. Maybe if he changed his name...

He managed to get the pickup door open and pulled himself onto the seat, closing the door behind him. He'd left the key in the ignition, not worried about anyone in this town stealing his old pickup.

He started to reach for the key, leaning over the steering wheel as he did. That's when he saw the note. It was taped to the radio. It had his name on it.

He gripped the steering wheel. His heart was pounding so hard he thought it would burst from his chest as he looked out to see if anyone was watching him. No one he could see in the darkness.

Hands shaking, he pulled the note from the front of the radio. The tape gave. It was one small sheet of white paper folded in half, his name neatly printed on the front. Detective Rupert Blackmore.

He opened it and let out a cry as he read the words. *I have your wife. Finish the job. No loose ends.* The paper fluttered from his fingers and he grabbed his cell phone from his jacket pocket, his fingers shaking so hard it took him three tries to key in his mother-in-law's number. It was late. Teresa would be in bed asleep. So would his mother-in-law, Marlene. He'd wake them both and feel foolish.

The phone rang and rang.

He felt his heart drop to the soles of his flat feet.

CHAPTER FIFTEEN

MAGGIE WATCHED THE dark forest blur by the cab of the pickup, so many emotions racing through her she felt numb. Jesse hadn't said anything since they'd left Roz Sawyer's house.

She watched him look in the rearview mirror for the hundredth time and realized he was worried that Blackmore or the kidnapper might be following them.

She hadn't realized how much had been riding on tonight. The announcement and her biological parents' reaction hadn't surprised her. Her sister Desiree's had. It must have been such a shock to them all. At least her aunt Lydia had welcomed her and that warmed Maggie.

She glanced in her side mirror as Jesse turned onto the road to his cabin. As far as she could tell no one was following them.

Leaning back into the seat, she closed her eyes, remembering the look on Jesse's face when they'd gotten the DNA test results. She smiled to herself, opened her eyes and looked over at him.

He hadn't touched her since they'd climbed into the pickup. Nor had he said a word. His big hands gripped the wheel as he drove, his eyes on the road or the rearview mirror.

Now that there was nothing keeping them apart had he changed his mind?

He pulled up the pickup in front of the cabin, cut the engine and sat for a moment just staring out at the darkness.

She ached to touch him, to feel his mouth on hers, to lose herself in his arms. Silence and darkness settled over them. He seemed to be waiting for something.

A faint light blinked once, then twice from out in the darkness beyond the cabin.

Jesse seemed to relax and she remembered overhearing Lee Tanner's promise to check out the cabin before they returned. Obviously the flashing light signaled everything was okay and that state troopers were in position. Without looking at her, he opened his door and trotted around to hers, taking her hand but not looking at her as he quickly drew her up the steps all the time watching behind them.

JESSE REMEMBERED CHARITY'S words just before they left Roz Sawyer's house. Charity had been waiting outside and pulled him aside.

"Do you have any idea who she is?" she'd asked, following his gaze to Maggie as she got into his old pickup.

"She's Angela Dennison."

"She's Margaret Randolph and Margaret Randolph is now head of a huge business conglomerate. She's been running it for months, ever since her father's health began to fail."

How did Charity find out the things she did? He hadn't asked Maggie about any of that. It hadn't mattered. But now he realized what she was saying. Maggie had a company to run in Seattle. What were the chances she would ever want to stay in Timber Falls?

Charity had leaned in to whisper, "She's not just amazingly smart, she's incredibly rich."

What could a woman like Maggie see in a man like him? Especially long-term.

Now, as he led Maggie up the steps to his cabin, he feared Charity was right. As long as they'd thought they might be blood-related, they had kept their distance. Now that there was nothing to keep them apart, Maggie might be having second thoughts.

THE MOMENT THE door closed, Jesse let out a sigh and turned to look at her. What had Charity said to him as they were leaving the Sawyers? Something that had upset him.

"Jesse, if you've changed your mind—"

He grabbed a handful of her dress and dragged her to him, his big hands cupping her face as he brought his lips down to hers.

"Oh, God, I've wanted to do that from the moment we left the party," he said against her mouth.

Her eyes filled as she looked up at him, her lips curving into a relieved smile. "I thought you might be having second thoughts."

He met her gaze and shook his head. "You?"

She smiled up at him and, circling his neck with her arms, pulled him down for a kiss.

When she drew back to look at him, he hugged her tightly to him, his breath against her hair. "Maggie." He said her name as if he couldn't believe this was real.

Then he covered her mouth again, his tongue teasing hers, exploring her mouth, her lips as he swept her up in his arms and carried her up the stairs.

A cry of pure joy welled in her chest. She could feel his heart pounding, in perfect sync with hers.

As the kiss ended, she touched his face, cupping his jaw, and looked up into his eyes. They'd reached his bedroom. He stood her on her feet, his gaze never leaving hers. His eyes were dark with desire and she felt a shaft of heat shoot through her. "Oh, Jesse."

JESSE JUST STOOD looking at her in that bright red dress. He'd never seen anything more beautiful. He'd never wanted a woman more in his life. What had he done to get this lucky?

He tried not to think about the future. Thought of nothing but Maggie and this moment he'd prayed for, the moment he could hold her, kiss her, make love to her.

Love.

He slipped one bright red strap from her freckled shoulder. She didn't move, her gaze locked with his as he slipped the other strap down. Her breasts swelled beneath the silken fabric as she took a ragged breath.

"I have wanted to make love to you since the first night I saw you," he said, his voice sounding hoarse.

She smiled. "I watched you from the window with my bike. Do you have any idea what you do to me?"

He shook his head. He only knew that this woman had come into his life and it hadn't been the same since. He'd been restless that night, the first time he'd seen her, but that feeling was gone with her here. He couldn't bear to think what it would be like without her though.

He pushed the thought from his mind. Hadn't he always lived life minute to minute? This wasn't a time to be thinking about forever. Not now. Maybe not ever.

"All you have to do is look at me, Jesse, and I melt inside," she whispered, and brushed her lips over his, sending a quiver of desire spiking through him. "I have never felt more safe, more secure, than in your arms."

He started to tell her that she wasn't safe. Not by a long shot, but she hushed him with a finger to his lips.

"You make me feel things I have never felt before," she said, looking deep into his eyes. She slowly began to unbutton his shirt, her fingers brushing lightly over his bare skin as she shoved aside the material and flattened her palms to his chest. A fire swept through him, his blood ablaze for her.

Reaching with both arms around her, he unzipped the dress. It fell to the floor in a whisper. She wore a tiny pair of lace panties, black and in stark contrast to her pale freckled skin. The bra was also black, and her nipples were hard as pebbles against the lace inserts. He groaned at the mere sight. Between her breasts rested a small-caliber pistol.

He removed the weapon, putting it down gingerly on the dresser. He brushed his thumb over one nipple as he did. He heard her soft moan. It fueled the fire in him.

He swept her up and carried her to the bed where he laid her gently down, sliding her panties over her slim hips as he did. He tossed them aside and crawled up onto the bed next to her, slipping the bra straps down and unfastening the front hook.

The bra fell away to expose her full rounded breasts. His mouth dropped greedily to each distended tip, the nipple hard against his tongue. He felt her hands work-

ing at the tuxedo pants. The real world dissolved in
the distance as in minutes they were naked, wrapped
in each other's arms, their bodies one. Alone, safe, together. Nothing else mattered.

RUPERT BLACKMORE REALIZED he was getting too old for
this. The climb up the side of the hill had left him weak
and breathless. He leaned against the trunk of a large
cedar and tried to catch his breath.

He stood listening to the pounding of his heart and
the night. A breeze moaned softly in the dense pine
boughs overhead and he thought he could hear a stream
nearby.

He tried not to think about Teresa, what she'd been
told, where she was, what had happened to her. He tried
not to let the fear or the anger make him stupid, force
him to make a mistake.

He'd already run across one state trooper. The blow
hadn't killed the man. Just bought Rupert time. He wondered how many more were in the woods around Jesse
Tanner's cabin. How many more he'd have to take down
before he finally reached Margaret Randolph.

This felt wrong. All wrong.

He told himself it was because he didn't want to kill
the young woman. But he would. He had to if he hoped
to see his beloved Teresa again.

He fought back the grief and regret that threatened to
completely overwhelm him and concentrated on the terrain in front of him. His eyes had adjusted to the darkness. He moved quietly through the woods, figuring he
should be coming up on another state cop pretty soon.

He hadn't gone far when he stopped to listen. A chill

rattled up his spine. He'd survived this long as a cop on instinct and right now his instincts were telling him to get the hell off this mountain, to get the hell out of this state. To run.

But he knew he couldn't run far enough. And if he ever wanted to see Teresa again...

He heard the crack of a twig behind him. That's when he knew why this had felt all wrong. He'd been set up.

MAGGIE LAY STARING up at the wooden plank ceiling smiling to herself, her body warm, sated. She'd known he would be a wonderful lover. Just the thought made her quiver inside. No man had ever made her heart beat with such fierceness or her body respond with such joy.

But it had been more than physical. She had known that if they were allowed to come together it would be amazing. She still felt awestruck by the feelings he had evoked in her. She loved him. She felt like she had from that first night when he'd come to help her on the highway.

She listened to Jesse's rhythmic breathing next to her, his thigh against hers, his body still hot from their lovemaking, the scent of him still filling her senses.

Sleep beckoned but she fought it. Being here with Jesse felt so right but she knew it could be taken away from both of them in an instant. For a while she had forgotten about Blackmore. About her kidnapping.

She couldn't give in to this feeling of happiness. Not knowing that the killer hadn't given up. Blackmore would be coming for her. And he might not be coming alone.

Blackmore. There had to be a Timber Falls–Seattle

connection. One that she'd missed in the research she'd done. Jesse had picked up the sheriff's department file on her kidnapping earlier and they'd pored over it before the party, but they hadn't found any link.

Where did Blackmore fit in? There had to be some connection.

She slipped from the bed.

"Are you all right?" Jesse said, instantly feeling the loss of her.

She smiled back at him. "I'm just going to check something. I'll be back."

She padded barefoot out of the room, grabbing his robe as she headed down the stairs to where he'd put all the information he'd collected. Printouts of stories about Blackmore, the official file on the kidnapping, everything gathered about the original suspects.

She looked through the sheriff's department file again first. Wade's and Daisy's accounts contradicted one another's. Was there something there?

She opened the file Jesse had put together for her on Blackmore. Within a few minutes, she felt Jesse come up behind her.

"Blackmore?" he said, reading over her shoulder. He dragged up a chair next to her.

"Look at this," she said, pointing to a photograph taken at one of Blackmore's many award ceremonies where he had been honored for his bravery, his heroism, his excellence as a police officer.

In this particular photograph, Rupert Blackmore was only in his late twenties. He was surprisingly handsome and almost bashful as he took the commendation from the then mayor of Seattle.

"Do you see it?" she asked.

Jesse leaned down to kiss her neck. He took a deep breath, breathing in her scent. Putting his arms around her, he buried his face in her hair. He wished she would come back to bed.

"Look at this," she said.

He pulled back and looked down at the photograph she was pointing at. It was a copy, black-and-white, and the resolution was bad. But he saw that she was pointing at the cutline under the photo, not the men in the snapshot.

He read the cutline hurrying over the list of names. Then reread them, leaning in a little. One name jolted him from any thought of sleep.

Blackmore, Hathway, Curtis, Johnson, Abernathy, Cox, Frank, Peterson. "Abernathy?" H.T. Abernathy. One of the cops receiving a commendation for assisting in some case.

"There must be a million Abernathys, right?" she asked. "What are the chances he could be related to Lydia?"

Jesse got up and went to find the cell phone. He dialed his brother's number. "I need to talk to Charity," he said when Mitch answered.

"Jesse? Do you have any idea what time it is?"

"Two-twenty-nine in the morning," he said. He could hear his brother call to Charity in the next bedroom.

"Do you ever sleep?" Mitch grumbled.

"Not much."

"It's Jesse," Mitch said. "He wants to talk to you."

"Yes?" Charity said, sounding sleepy as she picked up the extension.

"What was Lydia's husband's name?" Jesse asked her.

"What are you doing playing Timber Falls Trivial Pursuit?" Mitch asked.

"Yeah, strip Timber Falls Trivial Pursuit," Jesse said. "I'm losing so help me out, okay."

Charity groaned. "Don't talk about strip anything, okay? I want a white wedding."

"I admire that about you," he said.

"Yeah," she said. "Henry."

Henry. H.T. "Henry Abernathy?" Jesse repeated, hoping she didn't hear his excitement. "You know what his middle name was?"

"Are you kidding?"

"Okay, what did he do for a living? He owned an antique shop or something, right?"

"Jesse, are you drunk?" Mitch asked on the extension.

"No antiques," Charity said drowsily, as if she'd lain back down. "He didn't have anything to do with antiques that I know of. I think that was just something Lydia came up with after he was killed. He was a cop."

Jesse met Maggie's gaze. All the breath had rushed out of him. "Where was that?" he managed to say, afraid Charity had fallen back to sleep she was so slow to answer.

"Bellingham, Washington. Good night, Jesse." She hung up.

"Is everything all right up there?" Mitch asked, sounding concerned.

"Fine. Thanks." He hung up.

"What?" Maggie said on a breath as he put the cell phone on the table by the door.

"Henry Abernathy was a cop in Bellingham, Washington."

"That's not far from Seattle," she said. "It says here they were working on a mutual case. That means they could have known each other."

He nodded, frowning. "But Lydia's husband died before you were born. Even if he knew Blackmore, it doesn't make any sense where you come into this."

"Unless Aunt Lydia also knows Blackmore." She was shaking her head, not wanting to believe it. That little old white-haired lady? She couldn't see her with a man like Blackmore.

"Did anyone mention how she ended up in a wheelchair?" he asked Maggie. When she shook her head, he told her how Wade had been driving the car. The night of the accident that killed Lydia's husband and put her in a wheelchair.

Maggie closed her eyes. "You think she would try to get back at him by stealing one of his children?"

"It sounds crazy to me but some people…"

She opened her eyes and looked at him. "If her husband knew Blackmore, it's the only link we have so far. She must know him. It's too much of a coincidence."

He nodded in agreement, obviously not wanting to believe it any more than she did. "I think we'd better pay Aunt Lydia a visit come morning."

Maggie rose from the table and went to him, putting her arms around him, just wanting to curl up next to him in the big bed for the rest of the night.

He stroked his hand over her hair and looked into her eyes, clearly thinking something along those lines.

That's when they heard the first gunshot.

CHAPTER SIXTEEN

JESSE RUSHED UP the stairs with Maggie at his heels. He dressed quickly and grabbed his gun.

"Stay here." And he was gone out the door. She heard him lock it behind him.

Maggie dressed in jeans, a sweater and boots. She retrieved the small handgun Jesse had given her.

Where was Jesse?

She went to the screened-in deck and stood in the darkness looking down into the jungle of trees and ferns and vines. She couldn't see him. Beyond the screens, a breeze whispered in the pine boughs. Dawn softened the darkness to the east over the treetops. But it was still pitch black in the woods surrounding the cabin.

The moment she heard the two quick soft pops, she recognized them from the night at the pier. Someone shooting with a silencer. Jesse's gun didn't have one so he hadn't fired.

She turned and ran down the stairs, slowing down only long enough to open the front door and ease herself out onto the steps. She waited for her eyes to adjust to the darkness, then with the weapon in both hands, headed toward the place where she'd heard the shots.

She hadn't gone far when she saw the body. Jesse? Oh, God, not Jesse.

Breath left her as she started to rush forward.

"Maggie." She swung around, ready to fire. She pulled up short when she saw that it was Jesse.

She fell into his arms, surprising herself by crying. "Oh, thank God, I thought…"

"It's okay, baby," he whispered against her hair as he held her to him.

"Who is it?" she asked, glancing at the body on the ground.

"Bruno. His real name is Jerome Lovelace." Charity had investigated him for some story she was doing.

"The guy who was Daisy's bodyguard at the party," she said. "Is he…?"

Jesse nodded. "Dead, yes. Shot twice, both bull's-eyes."

She glanced up at him. "Blackmore."

"Whoever shot Bruno shot to kill."

She looked into the trees. Still hours before dawn. "What about that earlier shot?"

"Looks like it came from Bruno's gun."

She glanced at the weapon lying on the ground next to Bruno.

"It's been fired once."

She heard a noise and turned, bringing her weapon up.

"Easy," Jesse said. "It's just the state cops. They were protecting the perimeter hoping to catch whoever fell into the net."

The state officer looked chagrined since the killer had slipped the net. "All our officers are fine. We had one down. Hit from behind. Possible concussion. One of the men caught a glimpse of the shooter as he escaped off the mountain. Big man. Older. Possibly wounded. Limping. He got away."

Blackmore.

Back at the cabin, Jesse checked to make sure they were alone while the state boys took care of Bruno.

"Why would Blackmore kill Daisy's bodyguard?" Maggie asked.

Jesse shook his head. Nothing made any sense. He picked up the cell phone and called Mitch.

"This better not be trivia again," his little brother warned him. "It isn't even light out yet."

Jesse heard a soft click on the line as Charity picked up the extension. "Bruno, aka Jerome Lovelace, is dead. Two slugs. Killer used a silencer. Bruno might have wounded the shooter, but he got away."

Mitch swore.

"Either Bruno came up there to kill Maggie and someone whacked him before he could," Mitch said. "Or—"

"Or he was here to kill someone else and got himself whacked," Jesse said.

"Did I mention where Bruno was originally from?" Charity asked, making it known she was on the line. "His last known address was a post office box in Seattle, but I found an old car registration in his glove box—"

Jesse heard Mitch swearing in the background.

"And he used to live in Plentygrove not far from where Daisy was originally from," Charity finished.

"Thanks, Charity. Talk to you later, bro." Jesse hung up and looked at Maggie. Plentygrove? "We need to take a little trip."

"Are we going to talk to Lydia?" she asked.

"There's something else I need to do first." He'd

only put it off because he became involved with Maggie. "We're going to pay my mother a visit."

Maggie frowned. "But I thought your mother was dead?"

"She left my dad when Mitch was six and I was nine. She's been dead to me ever since."

Maggie raised a brow. "And you suddenly have an urge to go see her?"

"She was at the Dennison house on the day of the kidnapping," he said. "And it seems my mother lives in the same town that Bruno hailed from. Maybe it's a coincidence but I have to wonder what brought him to Timber Falls. Certainly not the weather."

ALL THE WAY off the mountain, Rupert Blackmore could think of only one thing. Murdering the person who'd set him up. The person who had his wife. The person who'd been responsible for Angela Dennison's kidnapping. The person who'd blackmailed him.

He'd listened to enough gossip at the café to know who the obvious players were. But he'd found in his career that sometimes a man had to look behind the obvious.

He drove back into town, went to his motel room and took a shower, bandaging the flesh wound to his leg. He knew better than to run where Bruno had shot him. The state cops would have the roads out of here blocked. And he wasn't ready to leave, anyway.

He called one of his snitches.

"Do you have any idea what time it is, man?"

"Just listen." He opened the wallet he'd taken off the man who'd been sent to kill him. An amateur. "Find out everything you can for me about a man named Jerome

Lovelace, and I need it yesterday." He gave him his cell phone number, hung up and began to go through Jerome's wallet.

RUTH ANNE TANNER had remarried a guy named Art Fellers and lived in an older part of Plentygrove. That had been all the information his father's lawyer had been able to get on her but it was enough to provide Jesse with an address.

It turned out to be a one-story ranch built in the 1950s, but well kept up. It was late morning when he and Maggie walked up the sidewalk to the front door. The lawn had been cut recently and someone had planted geraniums in matching pots on each side of the door.

He rang the bell and waited. Inside the house he could hear music. He was trying to place the song rather than think about his mother when the door opened.

Jesse had thought she'd look older, be gray, maybe even fat. He definitely didn't expect her to be pretty anymore. But the woman who answered the door had a cap of dark hair that was only flecked with gray and she was slim, athletic-looking. She wore a cap-sleeved T-shirt that matched her Capri pants and white sandals. Her face was unlined; the only wrinkles were around her eyes as she squinted into the sun peeking through the clouds to see them.

"Yes?"

This woman didn't look almost sixty. She was pretty and, he realized, she looked happy.

Bitterness tore at his insides. "Hello, Mother."

Her eyes widened and she gripped the door, leaning into it as if she needed the support. She blinked either because of the glare or because she was trying to place him and didn't know which son he was.

"Jesse, but I can understand how you might have forgotten."

Her gaze shifted to Maggie and she seemed to regain her earlier composure. "Please, come in." She moved back and as much as he didn't want to, he stepped into her house after Maggie.

The house was clean and cool inside, the furnishings nice but not expensive.

"Jesse." Her eyes welled and she looked away as she wiped the tears at her cheeks. "Would you like something to drink?"

"Nothing—"

"I'd take something cold if you have it," Maggie said and followed Ruth Anne into the kitchen. "I'm… Maggie."

Jesse followed, just wanting to get this over with.

The kitchen was clean and cute. There was a photo on the fridge of a bald man with his arm around Ruth Anne at some party.

Obviously she'd left Timber Falls and made a new life for herself. He'd always imagined her alone, bitter, hateful, spending his father's money on booze or drugs.

Maggie touched his arm and he took the glass of iced tea she offered him.

"Please, sit down," his mother said, motioning to the breakfast nook.

"This isn't a social call," Jesse said more sharply than he'd meant to. He took a sip of the drink, his throat dry, his nerves raw.

"Do you mind if I take a look at your garden?" Maggie asked and didn't wait for an answer as she opened

the patio door and stepped out, closing the door behind her.

Jesse waited for his mother to say something. Like
she was sorry. Right. Could he ever forgive her? No.
How was Mitch? What did she care? He thought she'd
at least ask about his life.

She didn't. She sat down at the table, folded her
hands in front of her and seemed to be waiting.

He wanted to yell at her. To tell her how badly she'd
hurt him, his brother, his father. To ask why. To make
her feel guilty.

But instead, he heard himself ask, "Did you have
anything to do with Angela Dennison's kidnapping?"

She leaned back in her chair, her eyes clouding over
as if the name forced her to return to a place she'd
left far behind, something seeing him obviously hadn't
done. "She was never found?" She sounded surprised
by that.

He realized he had her eyes and felt an ache in his
chest.

Tears welled again in her eyes and her lower lip trembled. "I can't explain the woman I was when I—" She
made a swipe at her tears, as one coursed down her
cheek, and shook her head. "I didn't take the baby. I
never even saw her. As I was leaving I passed the nanny.
She had come down the stairs. She had a cold," his
mother said, as if just remembering that detail.

All that had been in the sheriff's report. "Did you
see anyone else in the house other than Daisy and the
nanny?"

She shook her head. "Wade came home. I passed
him on the road. His sister was with him in the car."

"Lydia?" he asked in surprise. That hadn't been in the file.

"Why are you asking these questions now after all these years?"

He looked past her to Maggie standing by a row of huge sunflowers. "That woman out there is Angela Dennison. Whoever kidnapped her is determined to kill her."

Ruth Anne winced and looked through the patio doors at Maggie. "She is beautiful. She looks like Daisy." She slowly shifted her gaze to Jesse. "And her father?"

"Wade," he said.

She nodded. "Good. I'm sure you're relieved since you're obviously in love with her."

Jesse got to his feet, angry that she could know anything about him. "Do you know a man named Jerome Lovelace? He goes by Bruno."

She shook her head, seeming distracted. "Your father... I always hoped he and Daisy would get together," she said as she stood.

He stared at her. Was she serious?

Maggie came back in and he ushered her toward the front door.

His mother didn't try to keep him any longer. Didn't ask about his life or Mitch's or their father's.

"Goodbye, Jesse," Ruth Anne said at the door. She smiled and nodded as if pleased by him.

He didn't say goodbye, just stepped out the door, but he couldn't help himself. He turned to look back at the last moment before the door closed. That's when he saw it behind his mother. One of his paintings on the wall in her living room.

The door closed and she was gone again.

"Are you all right?" Maggie asked, and took his hand.

He nodded, surprised that he was. "She seems happy. She was so miserable with us."

"People change. She wasn't even yet your age when she left, right?"

He nodded, surprised that he could no longer feel hate for the woman he'd just seen. "She made a lasting impression on Mitch and me. I didn't think Mitch would ever ask Charity to marry him he was so scared of marriage. I'm thirty-five and I've never been serious about anyone before."

She looked away. "I used to wonder what normal families were like."

He laughed. "Me, too. Think there are any?"

"She had your painting on the wall," Maggie said, and looked over at him. "She hasn't forgotten you or your brother. She just couldn't handle things at that time of her own life."

He nodded. "I guess I wanted her to say she was sorry."

"Would the words really have made that much difference?"

He shook his head. "She did tell me something about the afternoon of the kidnapping. She said she passed Wade coming home when she left. Lydia was with him."

"Her name keeps coming up," Maggie said.

"It's just strange that it never came up in the sheriff's report that Lydia had been out there that night," Jesse noted. "How did she get home? Did Wade drive her or did Angus pick her up?"

"You think Lydia might know something?"

"It's worth asking her." Jesse realized Lydia could provide an alibi for his mother. If Ruth was telling the truth, then Lydia had seen her leave *before* the baby disappeared.

And what if Lydia had looked in on Angela that evening? She might have been the last person to see Angela before she was kidnapped.

"Let's not forget the possible connection between her now deceased husband and Blackmore," Maggie said.

Jesse shook his head. He hadn't forgotten. So far, it was the only tie-in they had between Blackmore and Timber Falls.

CHAPTER SEVENTEEN

RUPERT BLACKMORE FOUND only one thing of interest in Jerome "Bruno" Lovelace's wallet.

A business card. It was worn and soiled as if it had been pulled out a lot and there was writing on the back, hard to read notes.

He looked at the front of the card. The Busy Bee, Antiques and Collectibles. Proprietor Lydia Dennison Abernathy.

His cell rang. Teresa. But it wasn't Teresa, just as he knew it wouldn't be. His source had come up with information on Jerome Lovelace, a small-time offender from Seattle via Plentygrove.

There was only one offense that Rupert found interesting. The fencing of stolen property. The property in question had been antiques.

He'd learned a long time ago that cases had threads, threads that directed you where to go.

He studied the card, following the thread, following his gut instincts.

Abernathy? He rooted around in the drawer of the motel's bedside table for the phonebook. It was so small and thin he'd missed it at first.

Abernathy. Why did that name sound so familiar?

IT WAS DARK by the time they returned to Timber Falls. Jesse called Mitch as soon as he was close enough to town to get a signal on the cell phone.

He told Mitch what Maggie had discovered about Henry Abernathy and a possible connection to Blackmore.

He didn't mention that he'd seen their mother. "I also stumbled across a note that revealed Wade brought his sister home the night Angela was kidnapped. Maggie and I are headed there. We're almost to Timber Falls."

"Lydia was at the house that night?" Mitch said. "Why didn't she say anything years ago?"

Good question.

"Jesse, be careful."

Jesse had just clicked off the phone when he heard a loud pop an instant before the front tire blew.

"Get down!" he yelled at Maggie as he wrestled the steering wheel, fighting to keep the pickup on the road.

He shoved Maggie down as the windshield shattered with the impact of a second shot. The other front tire blew an instant later.

The pickup careened down into the ditch, still moving too fast. Jesse saw the tree coming up and tried to brace himself in that instant before the pickup crashed into it and the lights went out.

"JESSE!" MAGGIE CRIED, sitting up.

He was slumped over the steering wheel. She could see blood on his forehead.

"Jesse!" Still stunned from the impact, Maggie touched his shoulder, shook him gently. He didn't respond. She fought to get her seat belt unhooked. Jesse

needed her. Her mind raced. She had to get him help.
Get help. Someone had shot at them. Someone—

Her door burst open. Rough hands grabbed her and
dragged her out of the pickup. She screamed and fought.
A strong hand clamped a cloth down over her mouth.
Something nasty-smelling on the cloth. She tried not
to breathe, wriggling and fighting to free herself from
the unyielding arms that held her.

She took a breath. It was the last thing she remembered.

JESSE WOKE TO the smell of smoke. His first thought was
Maggie. The house was on fire. Get Maggie out.

Only he wasn't in the house. He sat up, blinked at
the wetness in his right eye. He lifted his hand to his
forehead. It came away wet and sticky. Blood?

He glanced around, confused. He was bleeding and
his head was killing him. He was in the pickup, behind
the wheel and yet he could smell smoke, feel the heat
of the blaze.

"Maggie?" The pickup was empty, the passenger-side
door closed. Maggie was gone. Gone for help? Where—

He heard the clank of a door sliding closed and
looked out through the thickening smoke, through the
spiderweb around the bullet hole in the windshield and
saw the blue van, glimpsed the familiar logo on the side.

Panic and pain rocketed him forward. It all came
back in a flash. The sound of a shot seconds after the
front tire blew. The windshield shattering. Another shot,
another tire. Then the ditch. The tree coming up fast.
Then blackness.

He seemed to be moving in slow motion. He unbuckled his seat belt and tried to open his door. Jammed.

He scrambled across the seat to the passenger-side door and tried to open it, then saw that someone had jammed a tree limb against it. Had jammed both doors, he realized, trapping him inside.

Flames crackled, smoke roiling upward, making it hard to see. *Maggie.* Whoever was driving that van had Maggie. He felt it at gut level, heart level.

He managed to get his gun out of the holster, steady it with both hands as he saw a figure shrouded in smoke come around the back of the van toward him.

He raised a foot, kicked out the already shattered windshield and fired. The figure veered back behind the van, disappearing.

A whoosh and flames flared in front of him.

Jesse began to wriggle through the hole where the windshield had been. He heard an engine rev. The van tires squealed on the pavement.

Sprawled on the hood of the pickup, he raised the gun again but knew he couldn't fire for fear that he might hit Maggie.

Flames leaped all around him, the smoke so thick the van seemed to dissolve in it as the vehicle roared away.

Get out of the pickup. Now!

He slid off the hood, hitting the ground at a run. Blood ran down into his eyes. His head felt as if it would burst.

Behind him he heard another whoosh. The explosion, as the gas tank blew on the pickup, knocked him to the ground, knocked the air out of him.

He rolled over to look back at the pickup. It was a ball of flames. Past it, he saw the gas can at the edge of the woods, saw where the gasoline had been poured around

the pickup and set on fire. The killer had planned for
him to die in the pickup, burn to death.

What did the killer have planned for Maggie?

The thought terrified him. He had to get to her first.

He had the cell phone out of his pocket. He wiped a
sleeve across his eyes and punched Redial. Mitch answered on the first ring.

RUPERT BLACKMORE LEFT his pickup at the motel and
walked downtown. He took the dark side streets, staying to the shadows.

He was a block and a half away from the Busy Bee
when he heard the sound of an engine. He stepped into
a doorway, flattening himself to the dark entry.

As the vehicle passed, he saw that it was a van,
dark in color with something printed on the side. All
he caught was the word *antiques*.

The van slowed a good block before the shop, pulled
in front of an underground garage. The driver got out
and disappeared inside the building.

Rupert waited only a moment, then moved toward
the van.

MAGGIE WOKE TO darkness and the smell of old wood.
She tried to move. Couldn't. Not even a finger. She was
lying on her back on something hard and she could tell
that there was something around her, close, something
solid, as if she were in a box.

The thought filled her with terror. She fought not to
breathe too fast for fear she would use up all the oxygen
inside the space, but she knew she was failing.

She couldn't move her head, but cut her eyes to each

side, saw little fissures of light leaking in at the edges
of her vision.

She realized she could hear. She opened her mouth
and tried to call for help. No sound came out.

Was she paralyzed? The pickup. She remembered
crashing into the tree. Jesse?

Her pinky finger brushed against something rough.
Wood. She heard a sound. Footsteps. A metal door
rolled slowly open next to her. Light. Through the crack
at each side of her vision, she caught the flicker of a
flashlight beam.

Her body was lead. Only her little finger moved.
She tried to scratch the side of her prison but it made
only a faint noise.

She heard the groan of springs, felt herself tilt a little
as someone stepped next to her. She was in a vehicle of
some sort. The realization surprised her. Also scared
her. Was she going to be transported somewhere?

She heard the soft scrape of something being moved
next to the box she was in, felt the vehicle rock again,
then smelled it.

Her heart stopped in her chest and if she could have,
she would have cried out. Stale cigar smoke.

CHARITY WAITED TO put down the phone after Mitch
so he wouldn't know she'd been on the line and heard
everything. She'd been working in the spare bedroom
on this week's edition but now she went into the living room where Mitch was on the phone to his father.

"Honey, I'm going to take a shower," she whispered,
pretending she had no idea what was going on.

He smiled and waved to her in acknowledgment. She

headed for the large bathroom he'd added at the back of the house. The one right next to the back door.

It was crazy. But then she'd done worse for a story. She turned on the shower, then slipped out the back door. She couldn't very well take her VW. Mitch would hear her start the engine.

So she walked the three blocks to the Busy Bee. The light was on in the back. She knocked and waited, her hands in her pocket. One gripping her loaded Derringer. The other clutching the small can of pepper spray.

She hoped Jesse was wrong and that Lydia could explain—

The door opened. Charity hadn't even seen Lydia come out of the elevator at the back. Maybe she'd been in the shop. Sitting in the dark?

A chill rippled over her as Lydia opened the door.

"Charity! I was just thinking about you," Lydia said. "Come in. Come in."

Charity stepped inside the darkened shop, thinking this was probably the worst idea she'd ever had.

RUPERT SHONE HIS penlight into the back of the van. It held a half-dozen pieces of furniture, an armoire, a cedar chest, a vanity, a chest of drawers and the most unusual piece of all, an old Chinese coffin by the door.

He thought he heard a scratching sound like mice. He froze. God, he hated mice. When he was a boy a mouse had run up his pant leg. The memory even after all these years made him break out in a sweat.

He started to back out, slowly, staying low, keeping the penlight on the floor, just in case one of the mice came after him.

He was just about to step off onto the loading ramp next to the side door of the van when he heard it.

Breathing. It was coming from the coffin.

MAGGIE WAITED FOR him to open the box and kill her. Instead, she heard him let out a curse, heard the rustle of fabric, then heard him standing over her.

The lid groaned and something metallic rattled. A padlock. The box was padlocked shut. Her heart raced as she listened to him try to open it. Didn't he have the key?

The padlock rattled again. Then silence.

Her left hand began to tingle as feeling came back into it. She could move her little finger of that hand now and several more fingers on her right hand but she couldn't lift her arm.

He must have given her a drug of some sort that paralyzed her body but not her mind.

Oh, God, what had he done to Jesse?

Feeling was coming back into her body. She just had to remain calm. Time. She would be able to move if he gave her a little more time.

He was still standing over her. She could hear him breathing.

Then she heard another sound. This one in the distance. Footsteps. Someone was coming! Jesse?

Closer, a metal door slid quietly shut, then movement near her, the sound of furniture being moved, then stillness.

The footsteps beyond her prison were coming closer. A car door opening. The vehicle rocked and seat springs groaned. A door slammed closed. An instant later, the engine started and she was moving again.

"WHERE'S ANGUS?" Charity asked as she stepped inside the Busy Bee and the door closed behind her. "I didn't see the van."

"It's his day off," Lydia said. "He went to a movie in Eugene, but he didn't take the van. It should be parked in the garage. Why don't you keep me company until he returns. I just put on a pot of tea and I have cookies. I thought you might be stopping by."

Charity followed Lydia to the elevator, telling herself that Jesse had been mistaken about the van he'd seen. Or someone had stolen it. Or—or it wasn't really in the garage and Lydia was lying.

The elevator opened on the second floor directly into Lydia's beautifully furnished apartment.

Like a sleepwalker, Charity followed the older woman as she zipped in the wheelchair through the living room to the kitchen and large dining room.

The teapot was whistling as they entered the warm kitchen. A plate of cookies had been put out. Lydia proceeded to pour them both a cup of tea.

Charity watched her closely, afraid she might put something in her tea. But Lydia made the tea just as she always had and smiled as she handed Charity a cup.

Charity took the seat at the table Lydia indicated and set down her tea.

"Here dear, have a cookie. I know you can't resist my cookies."

JESSE SAW LIGHTS coming up the highway, recognized his father's pickup and rushed up the road to meet him.

"My God, son," Lee said, as Jesse climbed in.

"The Busy Bee," Jesse said. "Take me to the Busy Bee. Hurry."

His father spun the pickup around in the highway and took off toward town. Jesse filled him in.

"Mitch said Lydia should be alone at the apartment. It's Angus's day off. He always goes into Eugene on his day off," Lee told him.

"In the van?"

Lee shook his head. "Usually that BMW Lydia bought him."

"Then who has the van?"

Lee shook his head. "They probably leave the keys in it. You know how people are in Timber Falls."

He knew.

"What do you want me to do?" Lee asked.

"Drop me off. I'll take the back. You watch the front. Don't come in unless you hear gunfire."

Lee nodded as he neared Timber Falls. "I love you, son," he said as he slowed and Jesse jumped out, running down the street to the back of the Busy Bee.

Jesse was almost there when he saw the van up the street. The taillights flashed. It was leaving!

The van started to back up. But then as if the driver had spotted Jesse, the van pulled forward.

Jesse started to grab for the cell phone in his pocket to call his dad when he saw where the van was going.

RUPERT COULDN'T SEE the driver. He'd hidden behind a large piece of the furniture that blocked him from the driver's view, as well.

He thought the driver would leave town. Maybe take Margaret Randolph somewhere out in the woods to kill her. But he heard a large garage door clank open and when the van moved, it didn't move far. The garage door clanked down and Rupert realized the driver had pulled into the underground garage. That was odd.

The engine shut off.

Rupert held his breath as he slipped the gun from his pocket to his palm. He was wedged behind the armoire. While he hadn't been able to see the driver, he could see the antique coffin and he could hear breathing still coming from inside. Just like the scratching noise he'd heard.

He waited.

The side door of the van slid open. He felt the van rock as someone stepped in. A man. Large from the way he rocked the vehicle.

He felt rather than saw the man bend over the coffin and work a key into the padlock.

Rupert waited for the *click* of the padlock opening. Waited for the man to slip the padlock from the hasp.

Click. Click.

Silence. He heard the man rise slowly, warily, and knew he'd either been spotted or sensed. Either way, he had to move. And quickly.

MAGGIE LISTENED AS someone bent over the box she was in. The padlock rattled. She could hear him breathing. Jesse!

No, not Jesse, she realized with a sinking heart as she heard the person insert a key into the padlock. It was whoever had put her in here.

She prepared herself for when the lid opened, willing her arms to work enough that she could fight him off. But first she would lie perfectly still. Let him think the drug was still working. That she was no danger to him.

The lock clicked open. Her heart leaped to her throat. Light. Air. Out of this horrible box.

That's when she heard the first gunshot. A boom that echoed like a cannon blast in the small space almost deafening her.

With all her might, she shoved at the lid of the box, flinging it open.

Another gunshot. Something large fell, rocking the vehicle. She heard a curse and a groan. Then the lid of the box was slammed shut again as something heavy fell against it.

RUPERT HAD STEPPED out from behind the armoire and seen the man turn. Something metallic flickered in the man's hand.

Rupert had been struck by the fact that he'd never seen the man before. Somehow he'd expected his blackmailer to be someone he knew.

That instant of surprise was his first mistake. Not pulling the trigger more quickly was his second.

The knife blade glimmered in the dull light. Long and slim. As it shot through the air and buried itself to the hilt in his chest.

Rupert had gotten off two shots.

And then as he fell forward, he saw Teresa in his mind coming toward him, toward the aquamarine pool next to their RV. She had a cocktail in both hands and she was smiling.

"Everything is going to be all right now that you've retired," he heard her say. "Didn't I tell you you would love Arizona?"

THE BUILDING WAS an old warehouse with a loading dock and underground garage. Jesse thought it was empty, abandoned. All the windows were covered with weathered sheets of plywood crudely painted with No Trespassing.

But as Jesse pried a piece of plywood from one of the windows, he saw that someone had been using the place and for some time.

The first floor was filled with antiques. Good stuff. Tons of it. He slipped in, dropping to the floor and moving as quietly as possible through the pieces to the stairs that led to the parking garage.

That's when he heard the shots.

CHARITY TOOK ONE of the cookies, but didn't take a bite. "Lydia, I know you were at the house the night Angela was kidnapped."

Lydia looked up in surprise. "Who told you that?"

"It doesn't matter. It's true. A while back you told me the nanny overheard Wade and Daisy arguing. But it was you. What about the baby? Did you go up to her room?"

Lydia looked down into her cup. "It was a horrible row just like I told you. Wade and Daisy thought I'd left, thought Angus had already picked me up. I knew Daisy had been having an affair. I didn't want my real niece growing up with some bastard's child." She met Charity's gaze.

"What did you do, Lydia?" Charity whispered, her hand dropping to the pepper spray in her pocket.

"You haven't eaten your cookie, dear. Angus made them especially for you." Lydia's hands had been on her lap. Now she produced a gun from under the knitted throw draped over her lap. "I've always told people how you can't resist my cookies. You wouldn't want to make a liar out of me, would you?"

AT THE SOUND of the gunshots, Jesse rushed down the stairs into the underground garage. The blue van was parked just inside, the side door open.

At first all he saw inside were more antiques. There had to be a small fortune in antiques in this warehouse. What the hell?

Then he saw Blackmore lying at the back of the van, his chest a red bloom of blood, his eyes wide and dead.

An armoire had been knocked over. Jesse straightened it to get to Blackmore, pushing it off the coffin. To his amazement and horror, the lid of an antique Chinese coffin began to rise and there was Maggie.

"Jesse," she whispered, the word barely audible.

He shoved back the lid of the coffin. Her movements were jerky and she couldn't seem to use her legs. Oh, God. He swept her up out of the coffin and carried her around to open the door and placed her in the front seat of the van.

"Baby, are you all right?" he cried.

Maggie nodded, her head jerky, her body awkward, at odds with itself. "Drugged. Wearing off," she whispered. Her voice was hoarse, her throat hurt. She managed a smile and she thought he would break down and cry as he rocked her in his arms. She looked over his shoulder, suddenly afraid. "Where—"

"Blackmore's dead in the back of the van." He pulled away to look at her. "How did you—"

She was shaking her head. Or at least she thought she was. "Not Blackmore. Someone else."

He tensed. "Who?"

She shook her head and then her eyes widened in alarm as she caught the glitter of steel. "Knife!"

Jesse spun around, using the van door as a shield. The knife hit the door and clattered to the concrete floor.

He had his weapon drawn again but he could see nothing in the dark corners of the garage. He glanced up, saw the large overhead light. If he could get to the switch.

"Can you lock your door?" he asked Maggie without turning around. He heard the soft snick of the lock as his answer.

He reached over and slid the van door closed and locked it.

He used his boot toe to move the knife closer, but he didn't dare bend down to pick it up. He kicked it back under the van and, locking and slamming the van door he'd used as a shield, moved fast toward the garage door.

In the blind darkness, he raked a hand down one side of the wall. No switch. Rushing to the other side, he did the same.

He heard the noise behind him. Shoe soles on concrete, then cloth on concrete. The killer was under the van, going for the knife.

Jesse found the light switch. Jerked it down, knowing as he did that he would provide the killer with the perfect target. As the overhead light flooded the garage with a dingy gold glow, he leaped to the side, crouching at the end of a tool bench.

Where was the killer?

MAGGIE COULD FEEL life coming back into her body, but she was still so weak.

She watched, feeling helpless, a horrible feeling for a woman who'd never needed help before. She thought of her mother. In a wheelchair all of those years and yet not helpless. Strong. Courageous.

Tears wet her eyes. She watched Jesse disappear into the darkness at the edge of the lit garage.

Where was the man with the knife? The man who had killed Blackmore?

She glanced over and saw the keys dangling from the ignition. Moving awkwardly, she slid over behind the wheel. She started the van.

Suddenly a face appeared at her side window, startling her. She let out a shriek. Angus tried the door, swore when he found it locked.

She threw the van into Reverse, swinging it around. Angus leaped out of the way. She saw Jesse come out of the dark, the gun in his hand. But Angus was facing her. She caught his expression.

She shifted the van into First and gunned the engine as she let her foot up off the clutch.

Angus had the knife in his hand and was turning when she hit him. He went down, disappearing under the hood of the van. But the knife was already in the air. It whizzed past Jesse's head missing him only by a breath.

Then Jesse was at her door. She opened it and he took her in his arms and he rocked her, his breath damp against her neck.

"EAT YOUR COOKIE," Lydia said calmly. "Angus put a special ingredient in it, just for you."

Charity stared down at the cookie in her hand, then at the gun Lydia had pointed at her.

"I wouldn't eat that cookie if I were you," said a voice behind Charity.

Relief washed over her at the sound of Lee Tanner's voice. He moved into her view. He held a gun in his hand and it was pointed at Lydia.

"I'll shoot Charity," Lydia said, not seeming all that surprised to see him.

"It's over, Lydia. Angus is dead."

Her gaze shifted to him, tears suddenly welling in her eyes. "Angus?"

In that instant, he stepped to her and jerked the gun from her hand. She didn't fight him.

Charity dropped the cookie in her hand, swearing off sugar cookies for the rest of her life.

"Not Angus. I can't lose another man I love," Lydia said. "He's such a good man. Just like my Henry. You know Henry was a cop."

"Yes, Lydia, I know," Lee said.

"It's all Wade's fault," Lydia said. "Angus never forgave him for putting me in this chair and killing our Henry. Then when Wade married that tramp and we thought she'd had another man's baby...."

"Daisy isn't a tramp," he said.

She looked up at him. "It was you, wasn't it?"

Charity looked at her soon-to-be father-in-law.

"You were the one Daisy was in love with," Lydia said and let out a soft laugh. "Why didn't I see it before?"

EPILOGUE

JESSE STOOD IN the art gallery, the bright sun shining in through the windows.

Spring had finally come to Timber Falls. Mitch had mended and taken over as sheriff again. Jesse had turned in his uniform and his gun and had gone back to painting.

But he didn't kid himself. Everything had changed. Maggie had come into his life. He'd almost lost her. And then, she'd left again.

He hadn't seen her in several months now. She'd had to return to Seattle. Her father's businesses needed tending, she had a house to see to and was needed to testify in the murders of her father, Clark Iverson and Norman Drake.

"Don't worry," Charity had told him. "She'll be back for my wedding. Maggie wouldn't miss my wedding."

Jesse wasn't so sure about that. He hadn't been able to reach her for the past few weeks. Her assistant at company headquarters said she was out of the country and wasn't sure when she'd be back.

The last time they'd talked he'd felt frustrated. He needed to hold her, to talk to her in person, so he hadn't had much to say. Now he regretted it, wished he'd told her how he felt. Even long distance.

"Son," Lee Tanner said, coming up to rest a hand on

his shoulder. "Your art show is a tremendous success. You should be proud."

His first big show. He couldn't believe that most of the paintings were already marked Sold. "Thanks."

Lee studied his son. "Have you heard from Maggie?"

He shook his head. "She has a lot on her plate right now." The truth was, there really wasn't any reason for her to return to Timber Falls and Jesse knew it.

Timber Falls had quieted down. There hadn't been a Bigfoot sighting in months. Nor a murder. Angus Smythe was dead. Lydia Abernathy behind bars awaiting trial for kidnapping, blackmail and multiple murders.

Before his death, Detective Rupert Blackmore had left a detailed account in his motel room at the Ho Hum of what had happened thirty years ago in a dark alley and the blackmail that had resulted in it.

It seemed Maggie owed her life to him. Not once, but twice.

Blackmore had saved her that night in the garage. His wife, Teresa, and her mother were found unharmed. They'd been detained by a policeman back in Iowa where Blackmore's mother-in-law lived, and held overnight in a jail cell. It wasn't until the next morning that the policeman had realized he'd been sent a false arrest warrant for the two.

Charity had been so sure that Bud Farnsworth was trying to tell Wade who'd hired him to kidnap Angela just before Bud died. If that was the case, then Bud had been trying to tell Wade that it had been Lydia, Wade's own sister.

Over the weeks since, the story had been hashed out

at Betty's Café for hours on end. Rumors had been running rampant, as was Timber Falls' style.

Most everyone in town believed that Lydia had become embittered after the accident and was set on getting even with her brother and that's why she'd kidnapped Angela. Others believed Lydia did it to spare her brother the embarrassment when it came out that the baby wasn't his.

Whatever had motivated Lydia, Wade had hired her the best lawyer his money could buy. But, then, he didn't have much money. Daisy was going through with the divorce. It was rumored there was a new man in her life. In fact, several people had seen her with Lee Tanner.

The general consensus was that it was nice that the two had found each other, especially after what they'd both been through.

The antiques Angus had stored in the warehouse turned out to all be stolen. It seemed Angus had been working with a man named Jerome "Bruno" Lovelace for years. Lydia was right about one thing, Angus was quite wealthy in his own right. And he'd left it all to his favorite step-niece, Desiree. She had gone away to college but she'd called Jesse before she left.

"You are the one person in town who will appreciate this," she said. "I took a DNA test. I guess I've always known but I wanted to be sure, you know, after everything that happened. You and I…"

"You're my sister," he said.

She laughed lightly. "You knew, too."

"I figured. You were too wild, too much like me," Jesse said.

"I guess we'll all have to get together one of these days, you, me and Maggie," Desiree said.

Jesse knew Maggie would like that. "Let's do that."

"I guess you know about our parents," she'd said before she'd hung up. "I'm okay with it. Wade, well, he's talking about leaving town. I think it's the best thing. Mom's taken over the decoy plant. Who knew she had it in her?"

Lee Tanner turned now as Daisy came into the art gallery. Jesse couldn't believe the change in his father. His step was lighter. He was definitely happier.

It was good to see Liam Sawyer with Florie, too. Roz and her fiancé, Ford Lancaster, had also stopped by and bought one of the paintings.

As Jesse looked around the gallery, he was glad to see how many of the locals had turned out. Timber Falls was an okay town. He would hate to have to leave it. That, he realized, would be up to Maggie. If she still wanted him.

He noticed that only one of his paintings hadn't sold. It was one he'd done of a Mexican cantina. In it a young woman was dancing and the men at the bar were watching her. He noticed that someone had put a Hold sticker on it.

And then he turned. How had he known it was her? Maybe the way the air seemed to contract. Or his heart kicked up a beat. But there she was standing in the doorway. Maggie. And he knew then who'd had the painting put on hold.

She moved to him, hesitant at first. She must have seen his expression because she broke into a smile and ran the last few steps, throwing herself into his arms.

"I thought I would never get home," she said.

"Home?" he echoed, holding her close.

She pulled back and looked up at him. "I'm never leaving you again, Jesse Tanner. Never."

He heard his brother's voice behind him. "Ask her to marry you, fool."

Jesse laughed and looked down into Maggie's brown eyes, losing himself in them. He'd wanted her from that first night, had been waiting for years for her to come into his life. He couldn't believe how kind fate had been to him. Florie said it was written in the stars.

He figured heaven did have something to do with it.

"I'd planned on something a little more romantic..." he said, then cleared his throat. "Will you marry me, Maggie Randolph?"

"Tell her you love her, fool," Mitch whispered behind him.

"We could have a double wedding," Charity said.

"Shush," Lee Tanner told them both. "He's doing just fine."

Maggie laughed, glanced around the room at all the people waiting to hear her answer, then she smiled up at Jesse. "I love you, too, Jesse Tanner. Marry you? Absolutely."

* * * * *

HARLEQUIN®

INTRIGUE

Use this coupon to save

$1.00

on the purchase of any
Harlequin® Intrigue® book.

Available wherever books are sold, including
most bookstores, supermarkets, drugstores
and discount stores.

- ✂

Save $1.00

on the purchase of any Harlequin® Intrigue® book.

Coupon expires August 27, 2014. Redeemable at participating retail outlets
in the U.S. and Canada only. Limit one coupon per customer.

52611445

5 65373 00076 2   (8100)0 11916

BJDINC0614COUP

REQUEST YOUR FREE BOOKS!

2 FREE NOVELS
FROM THE SUSPENSE COLLECTION
PLUS 2 FREE GIFTS!

YES! Please send me 2 FREE novels from the Suspense Collection and my 2 FREE gifts (gifts are worth about $10). After receiving them, if I don't wish to receive any more books, I can return the shipping statement marked "cancel." If I don't cancel, I will receive 4 brand-new novels every month and be billed just $6.24 per book in the U.S. or $6.74 per book in Canada. That's a savings of at least 22% off the cover price. It's quite a bargain! Shipping and handling is just 50¢ per book in the U.S. and 75¢ per book in Canada.* I understand that accepting the 2 free books and gifts places me under no obligation to buy anything. I can always return a shipment and cancel at any time. Even if I never buy another book, the two free books and gifts are mine to keep forever.

191/391 MDN F4XN

Name _____ (PLEASE PRINT) _____

Address _____ Apt. # _____

City _____ State/Prov. _____ Zip/Postal Code _____

Signature (if under 18, a parent or guardian must sign)

Mail to the Harlequin® Reader Service:
IN U.S.A.: P.O. Box 1867, Buffalo, NY 14240-1867
IN CANADA: P.O. Box 609, Fort Erie, Ontario L2A 5X3

Want to try two free books from another line?
Call 1-800-873-8635 or visit www.ReaderService.com.

* Terms and prices subject to change without notice. Prices do not include applicable taxes. Sales tax applicable in N.Y. Canadian residents will be charged applicable taxes. Offer not valid in Quebec. This offer is limited to one order per household. Not valid for current subscribers to the Suspense Collection or the Romance/Suspense Collection. All orders subject to credit approval. Credit or debit balances in a customer's account(s) may be offset by any other outstanding balance owed by or to the customer. Please allow 4 to 6 weeks for delivery. Offer available while quantities last.

Your Privacy—The Harlequin® Reader Service is committed to protecting your privacy. Our Privacy Policy is available online at www.ReaderService.com or upon request from the Harlequin Reader Service.

We make a portion of our mailing list available to reputable third parties that offer products we believe may interest you. If you prefer that we not exchange your name with third parties, or if you wish to clarify or modify your communication preferences, please visit us at www.ReaderService.com/consumerchoice or write to us at Harlequin Reader Service Preference Service, P.O. Box 9062, Buffalo, NY 14269. Include your complete name and address.

SUS13R

SPECIAL EXCERPT FROM

H HARLEQUIN®

I N T R I G U E®

Read on for a sneak peek of
WEDDING AT CARDWELL RANCH
by New York Times *bestselling author*

B.J. Daniels
Part of the CARDWELL COUSINS series.

In Montana for his brother's nuptials,
Jackson Cardwell isn't looking to be anybody's hero.
But the Texas single father knows a beautiful lady in
distress when he meets her.

"I'm afraid to ask what you just said to your horse," Jackson joked as he moved closer. Her horse had wandered over to some tall grass away from the others.

"Just thanking him for not bucking me off," she admitted shyly.

"Probably a good idea, but your horse is a she. A mare."

"Oh, hopefully she wasn't insulted." Allie actually smiled. The afternoon sun lit her face along with the smile.

He felt his heart do a loop-de-loop. He tried to rein it back in as he looked into her eyes. That tantalizing green was deep and dark, inviting, and yet he knew a man could drown in those eyes.

Suddenly, Allie's horse shied. In the next second it took off as if it had been shot from a cannon. To her credit, she hadn't let go of her reins, but she grabbed the saddle horn and let out a cry as the mare raced out of the meadow headed for the road.

Jackson spurred his horse and raced after her. He could hear the startled cries of the others behind him. He'd been riding since he was a boy, so he knew how to handle his horse. But Allie, he could see, was having trouble staying in the saddle with her horse at a full gallop.

He pushed his horse harder and managed to catch her, riding alongside until he could reach over and grab her reins. The horses lunged along for a moment. Next to him Allie started to fall. He grabbed for her, pulling her from her saddle and into his arms as he released her reins and brought his own horse up short.

Allie slid down his horse to the ground. He dismounted and dropped beside her. "Are you all right?"

"I think so. What happened?"

He didn't know. One minute her horse was munching on grass, the next it had taken off like a shot.

Allie had no idea why the horse had reacted like that. She hated that she was the one who'd upset everyone.

"Are you sure you didn't spur your horse?" Natalie asked, still upset.

"She isn't wearing spurs," Ford pointed out.

"Maybe a bee stung your horse," Natalie suggested.

Dana felt bad. "I wanted your first horseback-riding experience to be a pleasant one," she lamented.

"It was. It is," Allie reassured her, although in truth, she wasn't looking forward to getting back on the horse. But she knew she had to for Natalie's sake. The kids had been scared enough as it was.

Dana had spread out the lunch on a large blanket with the kids all helping when Jackson rode up, trailing her horse. The mare looked calm now, but Allie wasn't sure she would ever trust it again.

Jackson met her gaze as he dismounted. Dana was already on her feet, heading for him. Allie left the kids to join them.

"What is it?" Dana asked, keeping her voice down.

Jackson looked to Allie as if he didn't want to say in front of her.

"Did I do something to the horse to make her do that?" she asked, fearing that she had.

His expression softened as he shook his head. "You didn't do *anything*." He looked at Dana. "Someone shot the mare."

Someone is hell-bent on making Allie Taylor think she's losing her mind. Jackson's determined to unmask the perp. Can he guard the widowed wedding planner and her little girl from a killer with a chilling agenda?

Find out what happens next in
WEDDING AT CARDWELL RANCH
by New York Times *bestselling author B.J. Daniels,*
available July 2014, only from Harlequin® Intrigue®.